"Wonderful. Like an unexpected encounter with a good friend, Alex MacLennan's **THE ZOOKEEPER** leaves you glowing with its empathy and insight. One of the most gentle and remarkable novels I've read in a long while."

—Jay Quinn, author of *The Good Neighbor*

"In this shrewd and finely-tuned novel, Alex MacLennan explores the uncomfortable choices we make when we trade solitude for companionship, the freedom of wilderness for the comfort of civilization. MacLennan never lets us forget that we are, all of us, animals."

—Carolyn Parkhurst, author of *Dogs of Babel* and *Lost and Found*

"Alex MacLennan would make a very fine Zookeeper himself. He takes good care of his menagerie of characters, nurtures and protects and understands them. The result is a thoughtful and sensitively conceived first novel that beautifully opposes its human and animal protagonists. **THE ZOOKEEPER** marks MacLennan as a writer to watch."

—Louis Bayard, author of *The Pale Blue Eye*

"A sad, wistful look at contemporary urban gay life, **THE ZOOKEEPER** shows us the parallels between the animals in a Zoo and a young Zookeeper's search for his own living arrangement. The result is funny, heartfelt and true to life. This story of the search for a nest box of one's own is the work of a writer for whom the observation of daily life, with its small victories and despairs, and the form of the novel, seem as natural as breathing."

—Andrew Holleran, author of *The Beauty of Men*

"Alex MacLennan's **THE ZOOKEEPER** is a wonderful debut—at once warm and intelligent, funny and affecting—about home and homelessness, and the ways in which we must free ourselves in order to go in search of the habitat of our true selves."

—Richard McCann, author of *Mother of Sorrows*

THE
ZOOKEEPER

THE
ZOOKEEPER

ALEX MACLENNAN

alyson books
NEW YORK

© 2006 by Alex MacLennan. All rights reserved.

Manufactured in the United States of America.

This trade paperback original is published by Alyson Books,

P.O. Box 1253, Old Chelsea Station, New York, New York 10113-1251.

Distribution in the United Kingdom by Turnaround Publisher Services Ltd.,

Unit 3, Olympia Trading Estate, Coburg Road, Wood Green,

London N22 6TZ England.

First edition
May 2006

06 07 08 09 10 **a** 10 9 8 7 6 5 4 3 2 1

ISBN 1-55583-936-3
ISBN-13 978-1-55583-936-9

Library of Congress Cataloging-in-Publication Data has been applied for.

Author photo by William Waybourn.

Front cover image by csaimages.com.

Book design by Victor Mingovits.

To Mom and Dad

and Brad Koerner, who read it in three days

PROLOGUE

The cardboard PUPPIES FOR SALE sign shimmers into view on the scraggly green side of the road. James focuses on it, looking through the heat for the break in the fence, the turnoff onto the dusty dirt-track driveway that leads to the old farmhouse. The idea that he will take the puppy home that afternoon runs through him like a live wire. His hand coasts over the steering wheel as he thinks of Sam's reaction, even Anne's and Karen's, when he arrives home with their wet-nosed new family member. It will be just what they need, he thinks. A confirmation that he—that all of them—will always be the same.

Or maybe, he thinks as another fly buzzes in, I'll wait to pick up the puppy until I've talked about it with Anne. Let her have her say, what with the other news and all. Maybe I'll head by the grocery and buy some flowers for Anne instead, and tea cookies or chocolate cupcakes for dessert. Cinnamon rolls, he thinks, throwing an arm over the back of the seat and swinging the car into a wide, gravel-spitting turn.

His head explodes with the flat blaring of a horn as the grille of an eighteen-wheeler barrels into the corner of his eye.

ONE

WITH NO one in the darkened hallway to hear him, Sam explained to the monkeys that it was one whole year now that he'd been alone.

"Not alone, alone," he enunciated carefully, as he noted the timing, coloration, and consistency of the speckle of vomit he had just finished cleaning off the floor. Sam was meticulous about his work, utterly focused. He was supposed to meet a new man later that night.

The flickering light of the darkened hallway made a rumpled pattern across Sam's face, and the stale smell of hay filled his nose. He spoke slowly, carefully, directing his gaze as if to a circle of kindergartners, to each small face in turn. He knew the monkeys couldn't really understand him, but, somehow, he also believed that they could. The various clicks, shufflings, skitterings, and squeaks of small animals at dusk surrounded him like a cocoon. Sweat trickled down his neck. It was, as always, stiflingly warm.

"Good alone," he reassured his charges, pleased with the correction. Laurel had only mentioned "someone new" would be at their table that night: a friend of a friend, a local newscaster, someone Sam would like. He didn't want to be anxious about it and couldn't afford to be agitated around his monkeys. "Happy alone," he murmured as soothingly as he could. From the quizzical looks on their faces, it seemed the monkeys weren't convinced.

Sam hosed out the last of the green trash cans in the concrete corridor behind the animals' cages, leaning into the wires that separated him from the animals and dropping his voice to a whisper. A juvenile—the one who had thrown up twenty minutes before—poked with tiny, marvelously wrinkled fingers at Sam's cheek. "It's fine, though," he promised again, as their faces continued to tick in the half light. "It's actually kind of a relief."

Sam turned back to the wet floor and wall, breathing in steamed air that smelled like a combination of gentle bleach and monkey chow. He loved that he could, at least temporarily, hold the François' leaf monkeys' elusive attention. The small, hyper animals, all silky black with bright eyes and shocked-looking tufts of white fur, were different from Sam's howlers, and it was nice to end the day with his more active charges once in a while. He let a burst of hot water escape his thumb at the end of the hose. My howlers, he thought with a twinge of guilt. He was running late and wouldn't check in with them again. I don't spend enough time with them, he thought. Even if I am almost their only booster at the Zoo.

The Zoo's black howler monkeys weren't crowd-pleasers, but Sam loved their soft, solid appearance, the economy of their movement, and their simple social rules. Mother, father, one child at a time; their black or tan fur, the easy yawns that betrayed sharp canine teeth, their slow, sleepy movements through each day. Specifically, Sam loved their calls. A male howler monkey's whoop, shocking and reverberant, still forced a chill down his spine. It was one of the loudest sounds in the animal kingdom, loud as an elephant's trumpet or a lion's roar, and Sam often came in early to hear the male's call set off a chain reaction of cackling night herons, chattering grackles, and hooting siamangs.

He returned his attention, and a bleach-dipped towel, to a stubborn stain on the wall as the monkeys, antic and comical, bounded around their brightly lit cage above him. Other animals—a fennec fox, three species of tamarins, a warren of naked mole rats—peered out at Sam or ignored him from their own cages along the hall. Their energy enlivened the corridor's warm, artificial dusk and made Sam appreciate his role in it all, keeping things running behind the scenes. He rubbed his thumb against the window wire, and a female grabbed at it, stroking the smooth whorls of skin. He'd lost the thumbnail months ago while impatiently hammering two logs together, and the skin remained sensitive enough that he sometimes felt it could predict the rain. He let the old François' leaf monkey claw at it, testing it and probing it with her tiny nails and sending tiny shocks sparking all the way up his arm. He was a little bit sad and surprisingly grateful for the touch.

Cool concrete at his shoulder, Sam checked off the items on his life's list: a good apartment, a mostly good job, Laurel and the gang at the restaurant, time with his nephew Jamie that he cherished and mostly didn't resent. Still, he admitted, resting his forehead on the wire of the monkeys' cage, an insistent discomfort nagged at him, like the stained walls he could never get completely clean. Another female, missing two fingers on her right hand, played idly with his wiry, prematurely graying hair.

Sam stood back from the cage's interior window and closed the heavy metal door, blocking all but a tiny window of the monkeys' nest box from his view. They were in and fed for the night, comfortably hunched over their raisins and chopped carrots in the straw. He wished he could climb in with them, just settle into the warm straw and plentiful food, and be picked over by loving fingers, surrounded by breathing bodies, for the night.

As a new keeper, Sam had been much more interested in the animals' public enclosures: the swings and water fixtures and choices about what enrichments meant the most for scientific and aesthetic success. Over the years he had come to prefer the smaller, enclosed cages where the more social animals clumped for the night, and where the cats and bears and elephants backed into safe, defensible corners to sleep. He loved those tiny cages and had, at times, envied his animals their place in them. Lately, though, Sam sometimes felt that his animals were being cheated in there, distracted by food and warmth from the reality of unchanging, unyielding walls. And yet—the monkeys had huddled into a shifting but orderly line and were preening each other for nits—there was something sweet there. He promised himself he would make time the following weekend to scrub away the brown stains from the walls.

A failing safety light flickered against the concrete walls and startled Sam alert. Five-thirty. His meeting was in half an hour, and he was going to be late. And then that stupid "date." A clicking anger took off in the back of his brain as he stopped to wipe up a last slick of vomit. He had to take care of his animals, but this meeting was important, too.

The presentation—despite a flurry of last-minute updates and the addition of information from his observations of the Zoo's three underserved howlers over the past year—was essentially the same as what Sam had proposed a year before, and again the year before that. He wanted to establish a larger colony of, and expanded habitat for, the howler monkeys, and had rushed an updated proposal together when Gwen told him the new director wanted "creative ideas" and to see "what the actual keepers had to say." Sam had hope. The new director had come up through the ranks at San Diego and was an animal person—a former primatologist and vet—and seemed to have a better understanding of the animals' needs than his business-minded predecessor had. Sam needed this project. He deserved it. The door swung shut behind him with a bang.

Sam glanced at his watch again and tripped himself into a jog toward the top of the Zoo, unbuttoning the top of his uniform as he ran. Already, he could feel the sweat on his chest, smell the ripe scents of a hard day's work. As he ran, the paths at the Zoo—twisting from the main entrance on Connecticut Avenue down to the rushing river at the bottom of Rock Creek Park—opened before him. The visitors were mostly gone for the day, and Sam could smell spring in the air. Newly green trees hovered over the discarded wrappers that littered his path, and he stopped to pick them up. He passed mangy bison, dust-covered rhinos, and dull, spotted giraffes eating from high baskets of straw.

Despite the stress that pulsed consistently in his brain, Sam ran carefully; a cold rain had fallen that afternoon, and the fallen pink petals of magnolia blossoms were already turning to a slick brown mud beneath his feet. He bent over his knees to catch his breath, legs tingling and cheeks hot, and saw Jack Kinsley already limping his way toward the exit with a cigarette in hand. Squinting into the late afternoon light, all Sam could see were Jack's silhouette, white hair, and the glowing end of a cigarette winking like a firefly where the rest of his face should have been. Jack waved, a quick chop of his hand through the air, and Sam waved back as he headed into the keeper's office, his breath accelerating when he hit the door.

"Hey," Gwen called as Sam burst in, the long, flat syllables of her Australian accent giving her every remark a kind of imperious laziness that drove Sam mad. "I'll see you in ten minutes in Baskin's office. Don't be late, or all of our preparation won't do any good."

"Our preparation?" Sam muttered as he passed her, head down. The sound of bird calls disappeared behind the heavy metal door. Gwen Daniels was Sam's boss, still new to her job after years as an assistant at a private facility in Minnesota. She wasn't very good and looked more like an aerobics instructor than a Zookeeper. Sam joked with the other keepers—a generally heavy, disgruntled bunch—that she must spend hours each morning applying makeup to achieve her "natural" look.

"Don't waste time shaving either," she told him. "It's informal, and being on time is more important than being neat."

Sam checked his face and was surprised by how bristly it was. Shit. He'd wanted to look especially professional. And handsome for later, just in case. "I'm always on time," he muttered, rubbing the steel gray stubble on his cheek. He had wanted to shave before the meeting, always felt uncomfortably *animal* after a long day of sweat and stubbly growth. "You're the one who's always late," he whispered into his hand.

"What?" Gwen asked brightly, as she backed with a shrugging thumbs-up out the door.

"I'll be there!"

QUICKLY, SAM checked his messages, fuming through the empty, whirring clicks of the answering machine. He hated taking the time to check, but things sometimes happened, and he needed to be available if anyone needed help. Luckily, the messages were innocuous: Laurel's restaurant was being reviewed, and she wanted to celebrate, and his sister Karen's message simply said, "Give me a call." The coast was clear.

He spun into the locker room, pushing his mind back to his presentation and snagging on Gwen's false-sounding offer of help. He knew that, despite his doubts about her, he couldn't afford to ignore the offer. Closing the door behind him, Sam flipped off his shoes and struggled out of his uniform, grabbing a towel to tie around his waist. He sucked in his gut, nodded to the few other keepers who were still finishing up, and stepped down into the green-tiled shower room.

Hurriedly, Sam scrubbed under his arms and over his chest, momentarily soothed by the fresh-smelling soap. He was glad that, after years of shoveling and lifting and cleaning every day, his arms looked big and strong. I could pass for a lumberjack, he smiled, embarrassed by the thought. Maybe this thing tonight will work out. Deep in his chest, he could feel how good it would be to have someone to shower with again but pushed the thought away, rubbing his head harshly and letting the hot water cup and drop in sheets to the floor. By the time Sam turned off the water and stepped back into the locker room, he was totally alone. He dried off, rubbing the thin towel over his springy hair.

Twelve minutes later, Sam stepped through high glass doors into the Zoo's administrative offices. He checked his hair in a mirror and dropped to one knee to retie a shoe. Sam had brought in a freshly ironed blue oxford, striped green tie, and pleated pants that his mother had bought him two years ago. He didn't want to look either too good or not good enough. At the Zoo, casual was about as dressy as people got. The director's assistant waved Sam into the executive office, and he waited outside the office's polished wooden door.

Through the wood, the droning voices of Gwen, the director, and the curator buzzed just below Sam's ability to sort them out. Their voices swelled and failed, and Gwen pulled open the door with a great, glazed smile on her face. Sam had four copies of his newest research and the article he wanted to submit to *Science* cupped in his sweat-slicked palm.

"Come in, Sam. We've just been discussing your proposal," Gwen started, warning Sam about something with her eyes. "David and John are looking forward to your take on why this howler colony could really help the Zoo," she announced cheerfully, speaking loudly so her bosses could hear and focusing her eyes squarely on the metal name tag on Sam's chest. He realized, instantly, that they had already decided to reject his proposal. He felt himself beginning to sweat and, taking a deep breath, stepped firmly through the door. Silently, he passed out his existing research, the painstaking budget proposals for a month-long research trip to Brazil, and the informal polling that suggested a larger howler community could draw visitors to the Zoo. He laid out his points carefully. Sweat dripped down his sides. His supervisors nodded politely, and glanced briefly at Sam's detailed sketch of the soaring mesh pavilion he had designed. He could hear the papers shuffling on the desk.

After finishing his presentation, Sam held his hands determinedly in his pockets, making small, awkward tents with his clenched fists. The director cleared his throat: "Sam, thank you for this. I know John was very impressed, as am I. You've done some nice work updating this from what I hear." He went on, stuffing the room so full of careful words and smiles Sam thought he might choke, and finally said no. Gwen and John made small, sad faces at Sam, and then Gwen leaned forward, glancing to the others for approval, and began to speak.

"Sam," she said, reaching a smooth hand toward his, "I know this is a disappointment. But we do have another challenge we'd like you to take on."

TWENTY MINUTES later Sam stood in the cool air, shaking his head to rattle all the new thoughts into place. Gwen's hand was on his shoulder, and she was looking up at him, telegraphed empathy in her eyes. "I know you're disappointed, Sam, but, really, think about Jack. You know he's been having serious problems completing his duties lately, and I think he could use some help. He is almost seventy, you know. His leg's not getting any better. We've actually offered to retire him twice."

So the rumors about Jack were true, Sam thought, and his nose wrinkled as if he'd smelled a bad smell. Spring seemed lost to the evening's cold wind. Gwen rushed ahead.

"I know you're very loyal to him, Sam." She paused again, looking down at the hands she had wrapped around Sam's arm. He was glad he had on a thick coat. "I recommended you for this because I know you'd want to help him." She smiled. "We're only asking you to shadow him for a while."

Sam stared up Connecticut Avenue for his bus while Gwen repeated the offer he had just heard inside. He didn't want to look at her; was suddenly, actively, grateful for his height. At six feet, two inches, it was so easy to look down on people without getting caught in the act.

"Now, we're going to introduce a cross-training program for all the keepers at the Zoo, sort of a disaster-preparedness training, which is good and necessary, of course. But I'm telling you that we're also using it as a chance to, well, to shore up some of the weaker keepers. Tommy's with Angela at the Elephant House. Kate's teaming up with Gerald in the Aviary." She waved her hands. "Basically, we're aiming to establish some more obvious leaders among the staff." She paused while Sam recalculated his ranking, position, and potential at the Zoo. "Now, I know that you're primates and he's cats, but I also know that Jack was good to you when you first started here, helped you feel at ease. You've told me as much. I'd really like you to put in some time with him now, see if we can't help him get back on track again." She waited a second in the wind from the street. "Sam? Can I buy you a beer so we can talk?"

He declined, careful to sound appreciative but managing to avoid looking her in the eye. He kept his eyes focused on the low buildings and sunset across the street. The meeting had felt like a betrayal of some kind, a confirmation that something bigger wasn't working. He loosened his stupid tie; wished he didn't have to go anywhere but home; wished he didn't have to be smart, or handsome, or anything for the new man waiting at Terra downtown. He shook and stretched his hands. Still, the idea of helping Jack did sound good. He had felt distant from the other keepers and isolated by his focus on his monkeys and research, and he needed something to pull him back more fully into the life of the Zoo.

Traffic whipped the air into gritty swirls that stung his eyes, and a rush of damp air reeked of swamp. He removed his arm from Gwen's manicured grip and said good night, promising to think seriously about the idea. Despite himself, he thanked her for her help and was rewarded with a grateful smile. Maybe his blind nondate would be all right. He adjusted his backpack, made sure that his research was neatly stored away, and climbed onto the bus toward home.

TWO

LIGHT CHATTER spilled from Terra's front door, seeming to push out against the chilly night. Sam watched the people moving around, or at their tables, with a bouquet of yellow roses in his hand. He wished for a moment that he could just stand alone in the cool air outside and watch it all happening through the dark, wood-paneled glass, that he didn't have the pressure on this night of meeting someone new. Everything will be fine, he told himself. Of all the places in the world, Terra was the one place he could simply sit and talk and fit in.

Through the window, he could see the restaurant starting to fill up; about a quarter of the small, paper-covered tables were full. Laurel's gorgeous, black-haired manager, Miguel, was gliding between empty tables and the door, making each guest feel individually welcome with a hand placed on their shoulder or arm. The entire room seemed to radiate comfort; heavily framed black-and-white photographs of flowers and Laurel's family jeweled the warm, putty-colored walls. Sam hung back, for just another moment, to watch.

Laurel had opened Terra almost a year before, on an alley east of Dupont Circle that was famous for crushing the life out of restaurants and small, hopeful stores. Sam called it the Galapagos Strip. He worried about Laurel, knew how hard she pushed herself, how tired she sometimes got; she had so much wrapped up in the place. Still, looking into the rustling dining room, he felt for the first time that day totally at ease. She really had created something magical. Fresh produce and locally raised, organic meats. Baby spinach with tiny spiced crab cakes, a robust ham and goat cheese strata, the intimate, casual dining room. A truly neighborhood feel.

He caught sight of Laurel where she leaned against the entry to the kitchen. Light played in her dark hair, and her eyes rested on what Sam knew was her favorite photograph: Laurel and her dad at her graduation from culinary school, two years before he had died and left her the money to open Terra and make her dream come true. Sam's eyes stung. When Laurel glanced up, the warm weight of twenty years of friendship— of rough-kneed playground confessions, tortured long-distance phone calls, and drunken hysterias in tapestry-draped dorms—shot across the room and through the windows onto his face. He wanted to catch that warmth, like a tossed ball on a backyard summer night, and send it back to her twofold, threefold, a thousand times over. If he could, he would have powered Laurel and Terra, his family, the Zoo, all their lives with his own energy. He wanted to, but the stamina required to juggle and amplify so many people's needs and happiness and lives exhausted him sometimes.

He shrugged, squared his shoulders, and walked in, unconsciously taking notes. His funny neighbor Nick sat alone at a table pushed up against the wall, intently reading a well-worn book; a young straight couple from his building peered into the kitchen; a group of gay men bustled past him on their way out; and, as always, Laurel's big table of friends and strangers centered the room, bright in the reflected light of candles and the sconces on the walls. Through the back wall, which had a large pass-through window looking onto the kitchen, Sam could see Arturo and Mathilde moving with purposeful grace in their white jackets. He loved Laurel's cooks; with their dark, soft skin and heavy bodies, they looked like grandparents who, while wanting Sam to stop this foolishness with the *chicos* and find a proper *mujer* of his own, loved him anyway. Suddenly, the restaurant felt full.

His cheeks flushed as he waved the flowers in Laurel's direction. She came over when Sam caught her eye.

"Congratulations!" He meant to shout it. But his voice suckered him, a deflating balloon, as he pushed the flowers into her hands. He hated his voice sometimes. It was as if it knew before he did that it might embarrass him, that there might be too many people around who could hear.

"Thank you, sweetie."

Laurel, wearing a light gray shirt with a loose scooped neck, held the flowers against her chest and moved closer to pat Sam's arm. She let her eyes—a meadow of haphazard, gold-flecked blue—rest on his collarbone. "The flowers are gorgeous. Thanks. How are you?"

"Good. Nervous, I guess. How are you?" he whispered in response. "Hey—what about this new guy of yours—Andy, right? He here?"

Laurel's free hand waved the question away, then moved to her neck. She shook her head ruefully and stroked the thick strand of pearls she always wore.

"You're done with him already, aren't you?" he laughed, and she nodded and buried her nose in his chest. They had an ancient friendship: she cooked, he ate; she lived, he coordinated people's lives. Taking the flowers back from her, he scanned the room again; Miguel was approaching, hands out for the flowers, moving quickly. Sam handed them off, watching the slight waves of Miguel's back muscles catch the light.

"I'm fine, honey. Andy was, you know . . . ? I'm just so busy. Besides," she looked over the rustling space, "for tonight, I really just wanted my absolute nearest and dearest around." She started to rub her hands together, a sure sign that she was ready to get back to work. The restaurant was filling in as they talked. "Wait— How are you really?" she asked quickly, remembering. "How did the meeting go?"

"Argh," he growled for her, clenching his hands into claws and rolling his eyes. "Not great, of course. I swear, Laurel, I'm so sick of it sometimes. It's like," he searched for the words and failed, "I don't know. Not good. Sometimes I just want to quit everything, just walk out the door and try veterinary school again, or move to the rainforest or something. I just want to get out." Laurel seemed distracted, and Sam knew that she was busy and he shouldn't be dampening her big night.

She put her hands back on his chest.

"Well," she turned her hands against his shirt, "I think you should really do it this time." She looked directly into his eyes. "It's never going to be the right time. You'll never get all of your ducks into their perfectly aligned rows. You've never—" She stopped herself. "We're both old enough to know that doesn't exist." As she was speaking, she raised a hand to coddle his cheek, a gesture that mollified and annoyed Sam at the same time.

He opened his mouth and shut it, feeling a little bit slapped. She was right, but he didn't want her to be. And she also didn't have the obligations he did. I'm the one who had to put other people first when my plans were being made, he wanted to remind her. Unlike some of us, I didn't get a hundred thousand dollars to make *my* dream come true. He caught himself, took a deep breath through his nose. It was Laurel's night, and he wanted her to have it. The smells of cinnamon and sautéing garlic tousled in the air, and they looked at each other for a moment, uncomfortable with not knowing what to say.

"I'm sorry," Laurel started, and as Sam was opening his mouth to cut in, Miguel stepped in and saved them. Reaching out two tan arms and taking them both by the shoulder, he interjected, "Sam's fine. Laurel's fine. Stop worrying about each other for one second and enjoy the night." He clapped his hands at their small protests and pushed Sam toward the table and Laurel back toward her kitchen. "You are both fine. Stop mothering. Just have fun!" He winked at Laurel and swept to the front door to greet another trio of guests, calling out over his shoulder that Sam was to take the middle seat. Sam walked over to his friends, grimly determined to welcome whatever was to come.

At the long, wooden table, Molly, in her new cats-eye glasses, sat with an arm over the back of Kara's chair. Kara, from long experience with her lover, had pulled her sandy brown hair from under Molly's arm so that it flowed like a waterfall over Molly's elbow. As they did every Tuesday, they'd left their adopted daughter, Mae-Lin, at home with Molly's mom. Gary and Celeste were poking through a basket of bread, bickering, and Celeste shoved Gary playfully, flashing her new engagement ring. Three new people—friends of Miguel's, this man he was supposed to meet—filled in the end of the table. As Sam approached, the entire table collapsed with laughter, and he could tell that the man in the seat next to the empty one had a strong, beautiful voice. He paused, nervous that the laughter was somehow at his expense.

Then time slowed, and Sam began recording every instant as if he might be called on to file a very important report. To his right, Sam saw the edge of a collar making a shaded angle against a sinewy, unfamiliar neck. He noted blond stubble glinting on an undiscovered chin. He sat down, careful not to stumble or jerk his chair. Their elbows brushed. They smiled, and the man shifted, barely, toward Sam in his seat. Sam's entire body was trembling; he felt like he was naked, dancing, flying, resting in a warm and shallow sea. The man chopped a hand through the air to punctuate a joke, and Sam watched a smooth, muscled forearm slide from beneath a starched blue shirt. The scent of pale oranges ached in Sam's nose.

He watched the man's hands, graceful and aggressive, and felt his stomach leap. Sam thought he had seen him before; blue-gray eyes danced in the lights above the table, and his hair blended beautifully between blond and sandy brown. He had probably once broken his nose. His eyes matched his shirt perfectly, and Sam imagined the feel of that thin cloth stretched across broad shoulders. Sam wanted to put his arm across the back of the man's chair, but at the last moment dropped his other arm around Celeste's shoulder instead. He gave her a quick kiss on the cheek and centered himself, wholly and desperately, on the menu.

"I'm Dean," the man spoke into Sam's ear, saving him the first move. He spoke his name quickly—a glittering knife; a bandage off a cut. While they shook hands, Dean's eyes darted down and he bit his bottom lip; he seemed to be asking a kind of secret question about Sam's thumb and its missing nail.

"Long story," Sam offered, shrugging and looking down at his own hands. They looked like chimp hands, big and rough, with thickly overgrown nails. He hated the nails on the larger chimps and apes. They were so thick and broken and used. They made him think of the animals scraping and clawing to get away. Miguel took their orders, smirking.

Sam requested his favorite goat cheese tart in a daze. A live wire ran through his whole body; his leg was shaking, and he realized that he'd begun to sweat.

Leaning in, Dean whispered conspiratorially into Sam's ear, "You know, Miguel told me there was someone here he wanted me to meet. He didn't warn me about that nail, though. You have to be the Zookeeper." He smiled again. Sam felt Dean's warm breath startle the hair on his ear, felt Dean's smile, smiled back. He was conscious of every cell.

"*The* Zookeeper? Well, I mean, I'm not the only, there's more than—" he began in a fast jumble. Stopping himself sternly, he completed his sentence. "Yes, I'm the Zookeeper. But there's actually, I mean, obviously, there's more than just me."

He wanted to smack himself but took a sip of wine instead. Dean laughed, so Sam added, "Actually, we have a really good team at the Zoo. There are a lot of us who work really hard." Dean nodded encouragingly, and Sam took a second sip of wine. "And you're the—" Sam began, but was interrupted by a loud toast to Laurel and to Terra, which brought a happy sting of tears to his eyes. He felt a pang of guilt but couldn't turn fast enough back to Dean. "You're the TV guy, right? Channel 8?"

"Meteorologist. Weatherman. Five o'clock news." Dean said it with a hearty, false delight, shrugging his shoulders but keeping his eyes on Sam. "I'm angling for a move into features, though, so wish me luck. You've never seen the show?"

Sam winced. "I work weird hours—you know, the whole Zookeeper thing—so I've never actually seen you before. But . . ."

"It's OK." Dean saved him again. "My actual air time is still pretty sporadic. I've been focusing more on—"

Sam's mind wandered briefly, grateful that he was meeting Dean at Terra—Laurel's and, by extension, his own personal space. He'd been there since the beginning, staring at the littered floor and trying to catch her vision, teaming for half the painting, unpacking crates of utensils and dishware, and measuring carefully before hanging Laurel's photos on the wall. Sam was aware of his arm through his shirt, glad once again for the physicality of his work at the Zoo.

"Umm, excuse me, Sam?" Molly asked with an ironic quiver at the edge of her voice. "Miguel somehow forgot to introduce us all. Who's your new friend?"

Sam almost knocked over his wineglass. He had completely ignored his friends and the dinner and was putting everything into this stranger he'd never met.

"Molly, this is Dean. Dean, Molly." Sam hated his red cheeks, his own circulatory system for betraying him again. "I'm sorry. I thought you'd already met." He hoped he sounded convincing. "Dean, this is Kara, Molly's partner, on the right."

Dean smiled and leaned across Sam to shake the women's hands, commenting on Molly's earrings and making a joke about Kara's bright yellow drink. In turn, he introduced Sam to his companions—a couple who were also friends of Miguel—as well. He turned back to Molly. "So, how do you know Laurel? I love little 'stories' like this. How did this place come about?"

Sam leaned back, watching the conversation circle, happily dumbstruck by the night. He didn't want to say too much, was so grateful that Molly and Dean were playing the table so well, was suddenly terrified that he was speaking too quickly, that he was talking too much or not enough, that his hand gestures looked too feminine for this new, strangely perfect man. He breathed more easily when he saw a single drop of sweat trace a path down Dean's temple just behind his eye.

As he finished his dinner, Sam asked, again, if Dean had plans with his friends for later that night. He downed a huge gulp of wine to cover his nerves. It was his second glass, and the confusion in his stomach was battling it out with an aggressive energy that made him feel delirious and bold. He swallowed again, willing Dean to watch his neck move, wanting Dean to want to taste him. He wanted Dean's Adam's apple as well, wanted to drizzle it with honey and gnaw on it as if he were a bear. He was full, but his mouth was watering anyway. Dean nodded. "Too bad. It's beautiful out. I was thinking of walking through the Circle on my way home."

He felt ridiculous for saying it. A lump had formed in Sam's throat halfway through the statement, and he had swallowed awkwardly on the word "Circle," making it gurgle and jump. "I guess I've had a few drinks," he told the tablecloth. "I'd like to, I mean do you want to, or, I thought we might—"

"We should definitely," Dean cut in, "leave. Together. Let's walk."

They dropped their napkins into the savory demolition piles of their plates, pushed back their heavy wooden chairs. Sam scratched his fingers between two chairs and put one knuckle to his lips, feeling flayed skin and tasting salt from a tiny spot of blood. While Dean watched, Sam tested it a few times with his tongue. "Get your coat," Sam instructed, sounding tough even as he wished he could run into the bathroom and hide. He took a breath. "I'll be right there."

Dean turned toward the door, and Sam walked back to the kitchen to say good night. He leaned into the pass-through window, his elbows resting on the wide, heavily painted shelf. Laurel and Miguel were caramelizing two shallow ramekins of crème brulé in their hands, a blue flame torching the air by Laurel's eyes. It smelled like sugar and cinnamon. Sam leaned farther over the counter, dipping halfway into their warm, private world.

"I'm leaving, guys. Just charge my card for my share." He raised a hand to appear nonchalant.

"You're leaving?" Miguel demanded. "Just you. You alone. No one else?"

"We're leaving, thank you very much." Sam turned and pointed at Laurel, holding her eyes to let her know he was taking her dare. "I don't take risks, huh?" He tried to ask it with a jaunty humor. "We'll see, right?"

She grinned wide, showing white teeth.

"I'll talk to you tomorrow, sweetie," he added and then nodded in Miguel's direction. "Tell him he can hear about it on the news."

Sam thanked Miguel for the matchmaking before finding Dean where he stood, tall and handsome, by the door. He was intently focused on the buttons of his light, shiny jacket, meticulously brushing away specks of something that only he could see. Busily patting at his pockets, he didn't look up until Sam sidled into his airspace and tapped him on the arm.

Outside, the air fertile with the wet earth smells of spring, Sam and Dean walked slowly together in the softening night. Sam's earlier aggressiveness abandoned him, leaving him expansively hollow inside. Their hands repeatedly brushed against each other's as they walked. Dean kissed Sam's bristly cheek on the wide steps of his building and moved them into a shadowy alcove before kissing him again. The wet from their mouths made maps of warm oceans around their lips. Dean asked Sam if he could take him on a date, and Sam could feel his lips as he said, "Yes." He watched Dean's fingers punch his number into his cell phone.

"So," Sam continued, hoping it didn't sound like a whine, "how long do I have to wait before seeing you again?"

Dean's eyes skirted the steps before he looked at Sam again with a bright smile. He took Sam's hands and swung them in the air between them, making the distance between their bodies easy and light. "I'm actually going up to New York for a few days this week." His eyes lit like fireworks with the words. "My agent finally got me a few meetings with network people up there. I'm sure it's nothing." He paused, seeming to rein himself in. "It never seems to be anything these days, but I leave tomorrow morning." He smiled again. "The friends I'm meeting tonight are actually sending me off." He lifted their hands together to look at his watch. "And I'm actually late." He gave Sam another quick kiss. "I'll be back late on Thursday. What about Friday night for our first date?"

"Friday night," Sam nodded, outwardly calm. "Hey! When can I watch you on TV?"

"I'm kind of a spot filler right now," Dean apologized. But he shrugged and laughed, clearly glad Sam had asked. "I'll call you sometime when I'm about to go on air." His eyes moved up the street. "I really need to run. Tonight is supposed to be this big good-luck thing," he offered, grinning and raising his sharpened hand to his forehead in a military salute. "I'll call you Friday morning. I'm really glad we met." He sprinted off and then looked back and waved. Sam lingered on his stoop in the cool air and went in.

———

SAM'S APARTMENT was nestled halfway down a one-block, one-way street where a patchwork of neatly gentrified condos jostled with exhausted-looking, redbrick buildings whose yellowing glass aged the windows and doors. The door swung inward with a bright jangle of the silver bells he had studiously "forgotten" to take down since Christmas, and he kicked off his heavy boots, glad for the feeling of his feet on the cool floor. Locking both the knob and deadbolt behind him and humming something that included the word "Dean," Sam entered the large, open angle of the room that served as foyer, dining, and living area, dropped his bag on the side table, and shrugged off his coat. The light from a street lamp just outside caressed the uneven, dark wood floors like a sunset pulling its way across the sand of an eastern beach. Sam put his shoes in the closet of his small bedroom, closed the heavy drapes and turned on the lights. Feeling rich, he smiled at the photos of family and friends that formed a protective grid over his bed.

In the kitchen, three messages blinked red on the answering machine. He switched on the living room light and pressed Play. The calls were Gwen, cheerily informing Sam that she had rearranged his schedule so he could start shadowing Jack the next morning; Karen, asking if he would take Jamie for the weekend and emphasizing that he needed to call her right back; and Dean. Dean. Calling from his cell phone as he watched Sam walk in his apartment door.

"Sam. I'm looking forward to this weekend. Take good care of your animals. I'll be jealous of them all week long. Bye." Sam bounced around his kitchen like a spastic lemur, clutching the phone to his chest. He wanted to call Laurel and shout. He grabbed the phone and his bag and, carefully removing the howler proposal, placed it on the desk in the "second bedroom"—a walk-in closet that served as his office and held ten years' worth of papers, winter coats, a small desk and computer, and his bike. The room deflated him a little bit. It held too much; too many items that were never used and would never, realistically, be looked at again. The smell of cedar—a gift from Karen—reminded him that she had said to call "no matter how late." He straightened the scientific journals, Howler Advisory Committee administration files, and unread sections from the Sunday *Washington Post* on the desk and added his latest rejected proposal to the pile. The room was tiny, and normally he loved it. He needed to call Karen. The small room suddenly felt just small.

She answered on the first ring and launched immediately into a fast-paced declaration that Jamie didn't know what was good for him and was claiming that he wanted to stay in public school. The shorthand was understood: Sam and Karen were members of a tight-knit pack; two siblings with only one parent; teammates forged in years of fighting over the bathroom, entertaining each other on boring after-school afternoons and the harried, tightly scheduled teamwork of the first years after Jamie was born. Karen was without question the alpha dog. He felt a sharp flash of the familiar resentment that she always assumed he would just be there.

Karen wanted Jamie to have the best: early admission to an unconventional private high school that, according to its literature, seemed to teach everything in small seminars, encourage Jewish principles and practice, hold all classes under gently flowering trees, and send every student to the Ivy League. After she had married David Goldberg, an aggressive, outdoorsy lawyer from her firm, and realized that she would finally be able to give Jamie the kind of education he deserved, she had moved the family into the right neighborhood and spent the last two years befriending the neighborhood moms who sat on the school's PTA. Sam had been brought into Jamie's application process a year before; during a preliminary interview, they had discovered that Jamie's having a gay uncle made the family seem more diverse.

Sam shared Karen's need to protect Jamie and offer him every chance. When, at eight years old, Jamie had fallen in love with karate, Sam had rearranged his schedule at the Zoo to take him to two classes a week while Karen worked.

"Karen," he countered, trying to be gentle. "I'm tired. Just tell me what you need."

"Just talk to him, would you?" she sighed, knowing Sam was hooked. "You know this would be good for him. He's so smart and sweet and good and, well, he reminds me of you right now, he just seems sort of aimless and—"

"Aimless?" Sam interrupted sharply. He wanted to think about this new man, this excited bubbling in his chest, not listen to his sister insult his life. Karen, immersed in her shiny new life, sometimes acted as if Sam were at a dead end, as if he'd never had drive and direction beyond feeding animals and shoveling shit. As if he hadn't been admitted to the preveterinary program at UC Davis but stayed in Maryland to help her and their mother take care of Jamie instead. "Look, Karen," Sam had detoured from his route to the fridge and ice cream and had dropped to one knee on the linoleum kitchen floor. He was picking at a dried drop of paint and trying vainly to push it back into its spot on the wall. His thumb tingled. "I really don't want to hear about how I'm not inspiring enough for—"

"Sammy," she cut in, applying her big sister's authority with a sweetness that always disconnected his anger from its source, "I didn't mean it like that. I just mean that he has potential." Sam felt as if she was pouring him a glass of Kool-Aid after tripping him to the ground, proffering sweetness after making him cry. "You do great things. You care for rare animals; you teach little kids about the world. You know we love having a Zookeeper in the family." She laughed. "It makes great dinner party talk."

Sam brushed his hand across the kitchen floor, wishing the Zoo felt as interesting as everyone told him it was. He needed to mop, he noticed, rubbing the paint chip absently in his palm as she talked. The place was always a mess.

"Anyway," Karen continued, "you know how much Jamie looks up to you. You could really help him make the right choice."

And that was it for Sam. "Help him make the right choice." Karen had punctured his annoyance, and equilibrium was restored. Sitting on the cold tile floor, Sam agreed to talk to Jamie and asked her to send any new information she might have on the school. He inched his way off the phone with his sister, promising to think about it and to call her with some ideas. He agreed to take Jamie the following weekend and scraped the wasted paint into the sink.

Dean seemed to have evaporated in the aftermath of Karen's call, and the light in Sam's apartment seemed dim. He treated himself to a scoop of ice cream, focusing on thoughts of Dean's mouth, and dropped onto the living room couch. He had repainted all of the walls of his apartment over the past year, covered them in a warm white that almost erased the previous versions of plum, or blue, or aggressive mandarin yellow that his ex, the lawyer, had convinced him to choose. He had decided not to do second coats; the white over earlier colors was soft and gave the apartment an unusual, patterned look. The living room was now a slightly mottled sky blue, and a huge painting of a lily's white and yellow throat hung on the wall. The couch was comfortable enough, but he wished he was outside, and he leaned back to peer briefly out the window at the spring flowers pooled in lamplight at the curb. The sky was black and starless, strung across with antennas and clipped by the roofs across the street. I want flower boxes, he thought, and, as he did each spring, briefly envied the suburban yards and gardens that surrounded his mother's and his sister's homes.

Sam made himself a cup of thin, warm tea and, wiping a film of dust from the leaves of the spider plant in the bathroom, made his way to bed. He piled the extra pillows in a long, human shape and curled himself around them, hugging two and clutching two between his knees. Pretty soon there might be someone here with me, he thought, and smiled, then turned out the light.

THREE

FROM HER perch at the pass-through kitchen window, Laurel watched Sam leave. She passed a warm, damp cloth from hand to hand, and listened to her restaurant breathe. This was the best time for her; Terra's small rush was broken, no one was waiting for service, hoisting their paper menus, asking questions, ordering wine. She could lean back and have a sharp cup of coffee and watch her customers eat and drink and laugh and slowly fade away again into the night. She loved that moment of magic: add the right touch to each part, mix them all together, and watch something new emerge. For some reason, she thought of her mom.

She could hear the diminishing clatter of the kitchen, and she kept part of her mind centered there. They'd gone through a lot of grouper; she'd have to call in another order before shutting down. The rest of her energy she focused on the front of the house and the restaurant's ebbing tide. In a few minutes she would join her friends, once a few more customers had left, once she'd pulled the thick paper, marbled with wine and crumbs, from another table. In a few minutes. For now, she remembered Sam laughing, and blushing, and looking happier and lighter than he had in months.

———

THE NEXT afternoon, with less than two hours before Terra would open for dinner, Laurel's phone rang. She was in the kitchen helping Arturo with the prep work, and she dried her hands in anticipation of a reservation or more news about her review. She sensed it, reaching for the phone. She had put in the work, mortgaged her father's inheritance, assembled the right group of partners, played the right game. Maybe, finally, the reward that sat like a fat answer to that equation had come. A reservation for eight. Someone famous. Another critic, wanting to get in on the buzz. It all seemed so delicious, spinning in her head, as she chimed "Terra!" into the phone. She heard her sister's voice, instead, deeply under control over the line.

"What's wrong?" Laurel asked quickly, sandwiching the phone between shoulder and ear and rolling a lemon to free the juice. Waiting for Emily to continue, she deftly sliced it in two. Emily loved delivering family gossip and bad news, and always seemed to choose inopportune moments to do it. Expecting the latest tidbit about their oldest sister Charlotte, Laurel told Emily to "talk fast," squeezed the lemon over a baking dish of dried cranberries, and dropped her hands into the dishwater in the sink.

"Mom has Alzheimer's, Laurel," her sister said slowly and without any of her normal flourishes. Her voice made Laurel feel like a child again, or very hard of hearing, or slow. Emily was married, a mother to three small girls, and her voice was all gravity and concern. It said that Emily was poised and ready to take back all the weight of the news she was dropping on Laurel in case the baby sister buckled under the weight. Laurel knew it was *designed* to sound that way. Her first thought was, "Fuck you."

Laurel knew Emily wouldn't really take on Mom's sickness; she just needed everyone to think she would. Mom's sickness. Laurel's mind spun and reeled; she hadn't even taken it in. Alzheimer's. Mom's sickness. She took a long shuddering breath, moved over to where Arturo was chopping a mound of onions, and consciously inhaled the sharp clean smell. At least it would explain the stinging in the corners of her eyes.

"Well?" Emily pushed into the silence. "Laurel?"

"God, Emily, how do they know?" Laurel began pacing and put her damp hand to her forehead. The skin felt bumpy and pimpled to her touch. "What happened? When did all this happen? What does this mean?"

Emily told her, in an excited, conspirator's voice, of the increasing indignities of the past three months—three months in which Laurel hadn't been told much at all. Just after Christmas, she explained, she had noticed their mother misplacing little things like her keys or the grocery list and forgetting events: bridge with her ladies, a dinner at Emily's house with the kids, book club. Not surprisingly, when Emily confronted her, she'd ignored that there was any problem at all. Laurel suddenly remembered the confused names and memories of their past few talks. Noticed suddenly, like cloudy moments puncturing the skies of warm sunny days, the questions that her mother had stopped asking, the details she never needed anymore. Mom had forgotten to call her for the last two weeks, a Saturday morning fixture since Laurel had moved to D.C., and Laurel had refused to call her mother out of spite.

"But Alzheimer's, Emily? Isn't she still kind of young for that? Are they sure?"

"They're sure. You know how I've been going to the doctor with her lately? It was mostly just 'she's getting older' type stuff for a while, just all these weird, individual, little things." She took a deep breath. "Anyway, now we've seen a ton of doctors, and I just got home from the specialist who confirmed it. I just took Mom home. Of course, she's completely denying anything's wrong," Emily huffed into the phone. "I would've talked to you about it before, but, you know, you've been so busy with the restaurant and Mom didn't want to bother you—really she doesn't want to deal with it at all—and, well, even today she was saying she's always thought Dr. Weyerhauser was a crank." They both laughed. "You know her. Anyway, we really didn't know it was anything until now, Sis. The doctor just told us the news."

Listening to Emily and then not listening anymore, Laurel felt overwhelmed by a great rush of dirty water, as if she were a sink backing up with soggy, unwanted food. She started toward the bathroom and then saw Miguel stepping through the door with a bouquet of fresh pink and yellow tulips that wavered through the water standing in her eyes. She stopped still, covering the receiver of the phone with her hand. Miguel was in front of her. Arturo was standing behind her, stuttering questions in his painfully slow English. She remembered that the restaurant was opening in an hour. And Emily, saying their mother was sick, was going crazy, was going to die someday, was on the phone.

She pushed Arturo toward the industrial refrigerator and mouthed "Tuna." Waved to Miguel and gave him a thumbs-up for the flowers, tried to incorporate a smile.

"Laurel?" Her sister's voice, like a tinny transmission from Mars, was repeating her name in her ear.

"I've got to go, Emily. The restaurant opens in an hour. I'll call you back tonight." She returned to the sink and ran blisteringly hot water into the dishes, reinflating the bubbles from before.

"Laurel. The restaurant? I just told you that Mom has Alz—"

She couldn't hear it again. She wanted a cigarette as strongly as she knew she was supposed to have quit. "I know. I have to go. I'll call you first thing tomorrow." She hung up, glad to have bought herself some time. She sank her hands, wrists, and elbows back into the water that was so warm.

FOUR

SAM WOKE early for his first morning with Jack, the memory of Dean fizzing in his mind. His lungs felt eager for the fresh morning air. He was at the gym by 5 a.m., and though it had been a few years since he seriously worked out, he managed twenty minutes on the treadmill before dropping down to read the paper on a stationary bike. He showered and changed in a furtive corner at the gym, having forgotten how daunting the showers and locker rooms in his neighborhood could be.

He arrived at the gates before six, earlier than the Primate Team meeting, earlier even than the commissary and vets turned on their lights. Night lighting was still on, filtering through the cool air until it was gradually replaced by the sun. The howlers were quiet, and Sam walked slowly into the Zoo, relishing the rustling peace. He walked past the sloping grass where red and gray kangaroos would be lounging in a few hours, past the giraffe, elephant, and rhino enclosures, imagining the animals inside, snuffling and leaning against each other as they slept. Since he was so early, he walked down beyond the lions and tigers, watching for any that might still be out prowling the pale light, their eyes lit like internal lamps, their grunts and growls sounding closer in the dark. His howler male boomed, and Sam hooted to the black swinging siamangs on his way back up the hill, rocking his head as they started their rhythmic, repeated calls. Look up into the budding trees, Sam knew they would be moving the golden lion tamarins into their outdoor forest in another month, and his mind raced with spreadsheets and logistics and the thought of their skittering freedom among the shadows and yellow-green leaves. He tried to count the days. He clocked in at the office and forced himself to bypass his monkeys as he headed to his first day in Lion Island down the hill.

He wanted to check things out before starting his own string of cages and chores, knowing that if he got distracted by his own work, he'd never get to Lion Island at all. Walking slowly down the wide paved path, Sam felt a tremor in his step, a combination of the morning's exercise and his nervousness at taking on this new task. He wasn't sure about Gwen's motives, but he appreciated the directive to look out for both Jack and the animals in his care. And he owed it to Jack to make this work. Jack had been an unofficial mentor for Sam in his first years, a lifetime Zookeeper who took him in, protected him from politics and prejudices, and taught him the best ways to be accepted by the old guard at the Zoo.

He thought back to his first, nervous day, armed only with his education and the degree he hoped would give him an edge. By lunch he was physically exhausted, scared, and nauseous, and knew he had come fully unprepared. A circle of keepers had pushed toward Sam at the lunchroom's long table, laughing and pointing their scarred, stubby fingers and poking his chest. He hadn't understood the jokes, had bloomed with cold, sick sweat, and had choked down his sandwich only because not to eat would have looked even worse. Looking back, Sam knew it had just been the traditional ribbing given to every new keeper, a rite of passage of sorts, but back then he'd felt like the new kid in school, a new animal being tested by a long-established group.

Jack Kinsley had saved Sam that day, throwing an arm around Sam's shoulders and assuring him that all "newbies" were treated the same way. "Being a Zookeeper," he told Sam in quick, choppy sentences, wasn't about "theories and observations and stuff like that." It was something "you can only learn from shoveling shit and riding animals' backs. Takes a while to learn that, Sam, but you'll do fine."

Tony, in the Elephant House, had almost been killed by an Asian cow nine years before Sam arrived, and his place in the hierarchy was forever assured; surviving a dangerous encounter with an animal remained, for most Zookeepers, a point of pride.

It was a full year before some of the older keepers really accepted Sam: being gay and awkward, and rushing home every night to take care of his sister's little boy certainly hadn't helped. Jack was the one who told him that they used Tony's story to scare all the new keepers when they started. Jack had seen something in Sam and saved him. Seven years later, Sam was an old hand, breaking the newbies in. He shook his head. He couldn't believe how young he had been then and how old he sometimes felt now.

When he stepped through the smudged glass doors of Lion Island, past the constant black fluttering of the bats and into the underground bunker that was the keeper's workspace, there was a faint smell of whiskey, covered heavily with the bleach they washed the floors with every night. Jack shuffled in the corner with his back to the door. He was rearranging some papers on his desk, keeping shadows over his barnacled red nose and sunglasses over his eyes. His thin gray hair—though it was matted down now on one side, as if from sleeping—whisked back into two points as if he had just come off the range. Jack was garrulous in an old-fashioned, manly way, always chuckling and offering big smiles and slaps on the back. He was a legend at the Zoo, a man who had cared for and raised and wrestled lions, tigers, jaguars—all the big cats—and a senior statesman always speaking up for the little guys at the Zoo. But Jack was almost seventy, and what respect he still commanded was beginning to slip away. Sam was surprised to see him there.

Sam called out, and Jack turned, a little unsteadily, and smiled. His eyes were watery and red, heavy-lidded, but sparkling bright. Yellowed teeth barely showed beneath a wet smile. "Sammy! I hear they've got me training you again, kid!" He spread his arms wide and took a few steps forward. He didn't look very good, his stomach straining over and hiding his belt, the uniform of his shirt missing a button.

As Jack gave him a quick, wide-armed hug, the gorillas appeared in Sam's mind. He hated seeing any of the great apes brought into their inside enclosures, hated knowing that they would be locked inside for any extended period of time. Like the tigers without their miles-wide natural territories, there was no way the gorillas were better off reined in; Sam checked on them only in their spacious wedge of topographically diverse, creatively overbuilt, and deliberately overgrown yard. Jack looked, and felt, like one of those gorillas that morning. He shuffled his papers with hands like great black paws, searching out popcorn among meager drifts of straw. When he turned back around, Sam could see his own reflection in Jack's eyes and seized, instead, upon an image of Dean. He didn't know him very well yet, but he felt rescued anyway. Dean felt like the key to so much for Sam, like hope, and happiness, and some kind of guarantee. The thought of Dean alleviated some tightness in Sam's chest. He felt like the gorillas, set free.

"Anyway," Jack continued, "the girls were restless last night." He waggled his fingers like a magician. "I came in early to make sure they were OK." He turned his back to Sam again. "Are you with me all day?"

"A little later, I think. I've got a sick juvenile that I need to check in with, but I wanted to drop in and say 'Hi.'" He began running through the day's schedule in his head. "After that, I'm all yours. How about 9:30 or so?"

Jack nodded and waved over his shoulder, and Sam stepped back out into the dawning light. After a quick visit with all his animals, he directed two younger keepers in their prelunch tasks and headed back to Lion Island for the rest of the morning. Jack had settled at his desk in a pool of warm light, smiling broadly, with two mugs of coffee steaming at his side. He had obviously brushed back his hair, and Sam smelled the effects of Jack's hair products and a vigorous gargle with Listerine. It punctured and highlighted the close, meaty smell.

Jack stroked the wooden arm of his chair continuously. "Let's get started then, buddy," he laughed, clapping his hands together and rubbing them hard. "I like to start with a cup of black coffee," he began, narrating his remarkably uncluttered day as they walked slowly around the interior of the warm, concrete room beneath Lion Island, the cages that ringed the space, empty except for one older tigress sleeping down at the end. According to Jack, she hated the cold and never went out before the sun was fully up. As they walked the perimeter of the cement cages, he showed Sam the iron traps where he pushed the huge chunks of horsemeat to the cats, and the large closet, stinking of bleach and blood, where he kept the hoses and meat cart and mops. He finished his tour back at his little desk with the binders, where he recorded each cat's eating and sleeping habits, along with any physical or behavioral change.

Jack had shown Sam those awkward, black, three-ring binders once before, on a day when Sam was the one who needed reassurance, and Sam had loved them ever since. Today he showed Sam again, with reverence, moving one finger down columns of animal records going back years, licking his lower lip occasionally as he pointed out his neatly labeled and painstakingly recorded notes. His spelling was full of errors. His grammar was a mess. But his notes were terribly neat and compact and small, and his observations of the cats were full of love. The books got darker and more confusing over the years; whenever a cat would die—"King" in 1968, "Claw" in 1974, and "Caroline" and "Shia" in 1982—Jack would continue marking a simple black column below their names for years. Sam rested his hand on the first of the weathered books. Even now, with everything backed up and collated by computers, Sam did all his initial research and recording by hand, filling huge binders with notes. He knew it was sentimental, but the weight of the heavy books reminded him of the value of each animal's life. All Sam's animals had their own books too.

Sam and Jack spent most of the day together. At lunchtime, Jack offered Sam a thin baloney sandwich wrapped in wax paper. Jack's tottering, blonde-wigged wife, Maggie, packed him a full metal lunch box every day of the week, and she had prepared an extra sandwich for Sam on his first day. Jack stroked that lunch box so lovingly that Sam's own single heart felt torn.

By 2:30, Jack had finished his work for the day, and he hung around with the other older keepers until he had to prepare for the night feeding at 5. Sam was amazed by how much Jack had actually accomplished in such a short amount of time, and by how few of the safety precautions and modern observation techniques Jack used—or ongoing research he actually bothered to do. Walking back to his own string of animals, he thought of the many checks and balances in place for the primates, the dual levels of recording for research data, the long-term and strategic plans painstakingly designed for each genus, each species, each individual animal. The meetings he sat through for hours each week. Jack was really from another world, shuffling about in his subterranean lair, sneaking whiskey, surviving alone, and becoming more isolated every year. Day one, Sam thought, as he headed home. Here we go.

FIVE

IT WAS a long five days. So when Dean's message confirmed their date, Sam felt some knot deep inside him relax. "Friday, 7:30," his confident, clipped voice promised, "and I'm taking you to the best restaurant in town." Sam didn't even know which restaurant that was, or what he should wear, but he decided to trust that Dean would make everything work. On his lunch break Sam had managed to dart out and have his hair cut, leaning back for a shampoo and imagining Dean's long fingers running through his hair. Sam had been ready an hour early, had wiped down all the counters and changed his shirt three times.

Scurrying from room to room with a dust cloth, Sam righted a few books on their shelves and arranged the bills and letters in their hanging baskets on the kitchen wall. He wished he had left early, had grabbed some fancy cheese or crackers, had bought a new shirt to wear. Sam checked himself in the mirror a thousand times and chopped into his thick hair with gel, making it stand up in unexpected, attractive chunks. At the last minute, he removed the toilet paper from a cut on his chin and decided that he looked pretty good. Laurel was right. Dean was getting a catch too. Twisting and turning, he told his reflection a few more times that he was handsome. A suggestion of the dark hair on his chest showed at his collar, and it helped him feel brave.

He made a final check of the apartment. Thankfully, the cleaning lady had come that week, so a basic once-over was all it had needed that afternoon. Sam hated cleaning at home; he figured he already did enough mopping and scrubbing at the Zoo. Still, he had spent half an hour that afternoon on his knees, working out some anxiety by scrubbing the toilet and tub.

In the living room, he poked a finger into a spider plant's broad pot, wishing, as always, for more green space, more garden, a little plot of lawn. Sometimes, the squirrels and pigeons and sparrows outside his third-story window weren't enough.

Sam was wiping down the kitchen counter again when the phone rang, and he buzzed Dean up from the street. He leaned into the cool refuge of the refrigerator and pulled out a pre-opened bottle of wine. Sam loved his refrigerator and stood for a moment breathing in the clean smell of baking soda. A light rap on the door interrupted him, and he called out for Dean to hold on while he finished pouring two glasses of wine. Wiping fresh sweat off his forehead, Sam counted to five, avoided his image in the mirror by the door, and welcomed Dean with a glass so that their hands would have something to do.

"Hi." Warm butter. Dean's voice resonated deep inside Sam's chest.

"Hi."

They both looked at the floor. Sam couldn't look directly at Dean, couldn't dare take in his whole face at once, the smooth skin and wide jaw, the dancing eyes and unbelievable grin. Dean offered flowers in a trade for the wine. They were perfect bright purple irises with deep-yellow throats, Crayola daisies, and freesia like white pea pods on slim green stems. Dean leaned in and gave Sam a soft kiss on the cheek. Sam stood there, dumbstruck by his luck.

Backing into the kitchen, Sam heard Dean chuckle and the sound of his shoes on the hardwood floor. The door clicked shut as Sam opened a cabinet and pulled out a tall vase. Suddenly Sam felt fingers, then a hand, resting on the high middle of his back. He froze, waiting to breathe, and then turned until Dean's hand settled onto his chest. The words "Nice apartment" slid from Dean's lips, and then they kissed, linked by the wine and flowers in their hands. A moment later, Sam stepped away, busying himself by filling the vase at the sink. He fumbled the faucet; he couldn't feel his hands.

"You shaved," Dean commented, touching a hand to his own cheek. "What happened to all that sexy stubble? I'm on a date with a Zookeeper,

34

right? I was looking forward to getting all scuffed up."

Sam laughed since he didn't know what to say, and they drank their cold wine as they leaned against opposite counters. Sam could feel the exact space of the room, the negative space between two objects in a drawing, and gulped the last of his wine so he could disrupt the gulf before it became too real. It was all too terrifying.

"We should go," Dean cut in, tapping his watch face twice.

His sleek, silver car waited pristine in a circle of lamplight, and Sam was afraid that he would stain it indelibly with the smell of chimps and sour straw, cotton candy, and tourists from the Midwest. He smiled at Dean and got in. Sliding into the smooth seat, he felt the leather mold to him. He felt like a monkey in a spaceship. Leaning over him, Dean shut the door with a mild, pneumatic click.

Dean drove tightly, smoothly, except for a constant fiddling with the radio and his keys, and announced they were stopping by his condo—a renovated warehouse—so he could grab his forgotten coat. They smiled at each other from opposite sides of the industrial elevator that whisked them to the top floor.

"Wow." Sam was awed and confused by Dean's apartment. It looked like it should be in a magazine about New York lofts. One huge room ran away from Sam's eyes as he stood at the door. Dark, concrete floors spread from under pale, shaggy rugs, a wealth of space interrupted only by artistically placed, hulking furniture that seemed designed to adorn the huge, night-blackened windows and subtle, abstract hanging art. "It looks like something from New York," Sam joked as Dean walked him through the apartment with his arms spread like a television host. "I know," Dean responded gleefully as he scooped up his phone. "*Architectural Digest*, August 1998! I asked the designer to give me the exact apartment, except I had to keep a few pieces." Here he ran his hand down a mottled armoire "that I've had since I was a kid." While Dean was upstairs grabbing his jacket, Sam quickly toured the apartment, trying to look casual as he assessed and catalogued the photos and books, picture frames, candles, the pool of smooth black stones filling a silver tray. He wanted to glean clues from this moment in Dean's apartment, wanted to decipher what each and every artifact could mean.

Downtown, standing beside his car, Dean looked like a prince of tall gray buildings and flashing lights, and Sam, riding that energy, tried to step out of the car like a star. He followed Dean into the soaring, white arches of the restaurant—another spaceship, Sam thought—filled with tall, handsome people who might have been genetically engineered. For a moment he wished they were someplace quieter but quickly lost himself in the view as the hostess led them up a curving, open flight of stairs and onto a balcony overlooking the kitchen and diners below. The restaurant was crowded and buzzing with attractive, thin people in various shades of black. Sam felt out of place with his scuffed shoes but loved every moment of it; his usual role reversed. Tonight, the kids and parents couldn't gawk at him as they walked by, shouting questions as he hosed down the fake rock and dead wood of an animal's cage. Tonight, Sam was the tourist, the onlooker, the scientist making observations on the denizens of another world.

The hostess directed them to a high, burgundy-leather booth that rose to meet the ceiling, and Dean pointed to the seat where Sam should sit. He had given Sam the view, and his smile, when he thanked the hostess for the table, was proud. "Like it?" he asked, sliding in next to Sam. At Sam's happy nod, Dean touched his hand. Sam's skin felt drizzled with the sparks of electricity that Dean was sending off.

A bottle of wine arrived. Dean swiped his finger down the side of the silver wine sleeve, covered in jeweled drops of condensed water, and put the finger in his mouth. Sam imagined Dean's lips folding around his finger, thought of feeling Dean's warm insides. Waving the waiter away, Dean poured two glasses of wine and, smiling, asked Sam again what he thought.

"It's great. I don't know; it's so—"

Dean's phone rang. He mouthed "Sorry" and put a finger in the air to halt Sam's thought, his eyes already sliding to his hand and the person on the other end of the phone. Sam fought down annoyance and disappointment, then fought down the splotchy red blush that he felt heating his cheeks. Dean does have a lot going on, he told himself. He's got people relying on him; they might need him to deliver the news. The wine lingering on his tongue tasted sour.

"I'm really sorry," Dean apologized, after hanging up. He grabbed Sam's hand. "I always forget to, I mean, I really meant to turn it off." He made an elaborate show of turning off his phone. His hair fell over his forehead, and his face hung over his menu. Sam wanted to help.

"So, was it an important call?"

"Yeah," Dean brightened. "No." He took his silverware in his hands and began moving the knife and fork in a nervous dance. "It's just my job, this work, this. . . . I mean, I love it, I really do. I'm just always on. You know, of course I know that my phone should be off for a night like this, but . . . " he smiled, and Sam felt the wine's lightness fly into his scalp, "I forget; it's like, what if it's New York? Or some amazing breakthrough story? I have to be available, you know? I'm trying to get out of weather. So the phone thing, I guess it's just what I do."

He took a crusty roll from the wire basket that had been silently placed on their table and tapped his fork against the roll. "It's the greatest job. A total dream come true."

Sam nodded, his menu folded under his hands, wondering why his own job didn't feel that way anymore and waiting for Dean to say more. "It's just that sometimes, I swear, I think I'll never make it to the next level. Anchor. Or one of the networks, or my own show, or. . . . " He tossed the uneaten role back into its cloth-lined basket, making Sam painfully aware of the buttered chunk he had just popped in his mouth.

"But didn't you just start this job a few months ago?" Sam asked, pushing his bread plate a few inches back.

Dean smiled and nodded, fast and tight.

"Right." Dean clicked the fork and knife together twice. "But what about that bald thumb of yours? Is it extra sensitive to touch?"

Sam chewed his bread.

"OK, OK. Enough!" Dean laughed. "I talk all day," he resumed, smoothing the tablecloth on either side of his plate. "I want to hear all about your work." The words sounded to Sam like a promise, confirmation that this was a new kind of man—one who asked questions, who was interested, who wanted to understand. "And your family . . . you mentioned a sister, right? Start talking. I want to hear it all."

When the waiter returned, they paused to order their dinners and were soon talking happily again.

After the meal they walked down the long staircase together. The evening swirled around Sam like golden wine. He was singing "My television news reporter date" under his breath, timing the words to each step. Sam was full and happy, and a little bit drunk. Dean had ordered a second bottle of wine with the meal and two fat glasses of Port after dinner, and the manager had sent over a tiny assortment of scalloped cookies and champagne. Sam hated the port but swallowed it down. He figured he needed to be better at trying new things. They were laughing their way down the stairs, Sam's feet feeling very solid on the marble, when he heard Dean's name shouted out from below. Looking down, he saw a sharply gorgeous woman with dark red hair waving one long, sleeveless arm. She smiled a beaming, feral smile—"Dean! Get down here, you!"—and pushed her way through the crowd at the bar to await the two men, like a toe-tapping queen, at the bottom of the stairs.

"Gina!" Dean shouted. He grabbed Sam's hand and pulled him down the stairs. I'm in for it, Sam thought, dizzy. This man is my bookend. He's going to make me fall in love.

When Dean introduced them, Gina placed a hand on Sam's chest and said, "Aren't you just the biggest, most handsome thing?" and leaned in to kiss him on the cheek. The sharp green drink in her hand puckered on her breath. She pulled them into the crowd around the bar and announced, "Everyone! You all know Dean, and his friend Sam here practically runs the Zoo!" Her arms were draped like an eagle's wings around their shoulders, and Sam felt mercifully sheltered as they entered the gauntlet of shaking hands.

Dean disappeared into the crowd as Gina pulled Sam, with constant, whispering asides and introductions, into her group. Trailing in her wake, Sam let himself be led, enjoying the inclusion in the popular club, slightly nervous that Dean was no longer at his side. Finally,

Gina deposited Sam on the edge of a stool with a woman in a miniskirt who pretended to smile. She was slightly drunk and swayed into him, clawing him with shiny fingernails that could easily have killed a mouse. "Watch out for that one," she muttered, slightly vacant, nodding her head petulantly at Gina's bobbing hair.

"What?" Sam asked her, assuming he'd misunderstood. She pushed herself up and away and, shorter than he had thought, was lost immediately in the crowd. Alone, Sam was relieved to sit back and observe. He wondered at how many colors there were: skin, shirt, jacket, hat. His nervousness faded as he catalogued repetitive hand movements, obvious sexual displays, and classic avoidance behavior. The sound of Dean's laughter broke over him, and Sam focused on his date, feeling a little bit jealous at how well Dean fit in with this smart, funny crowd. Terra was never this crowded, and the people there, to Sam's thinking, all seemed more at ease. He wished he was back there, that they were back at Terra together, safe and quiet, holding each other's hands.

Dean's breath filled his ear. "Ten minutes," he promised and touched Sam's hair with his lips. As he moved away again, he turned to catch Sam's eye, shrugging and smiling a tiny smile. Suddenly the spotlights above the bar descended upon Sam.

———————

SAM AND Dean did not have sex that first night. But Dean "dropped by" on Sunday afternoon, and in ten minutes they were naked, grappling on the couch, Sam's bed, the floor. That first hot afternoon, the light came through Sam's windows in lazy shafts, and Sam explored Dean's hard, lightly tan body. He traced the fine, translucent hair of Dean's arms and the smooth planes of his chest. Ravenous, he tasted the delicious line of sunny golden hair circling Dean's belly button like water running into a drain, and then followed it down to the darker, denser hair of his groin. Sam was shocked by the hungry way Dean's teeth and fingers dug into his mouth and flesh. The way Dean took Sam's mouth, fingers, armpits, dick, shoulders, toes, thumb into his mouth, tasting and testing and moistening it all. They came, and when Dean darted up to shower and catch a planned movie with a friend, Sam fell into a blind, black, comforted sleep.

He woke amazed. And, over the next weeks began to catalogue everything about Dean. Schedules and movements, eating habits and facial expressions, especially mating habits and sexual styles. He was amazed that Dean wanted him to be the top, grabbing Sam's heavy waist and pulling into him with an intensity Sam tried, anxiously, to match. Sam loved and feared the grit and yearning in Dean's voice when it came to sex. Being wanted was incredible. Being wanted in such a primal way felt somehow dangerous—like they were falling together, delirious and unhinged, into a deep, black pit. Sam loved sex with Dean, but what he cherished was what came after. He listened as Dean's voice deepened and dropped, watched his eyelids flutter like hummingbirds' wings as he began to fall asleep. Noticed that Dean's hands, normally so manic, stilled when they had finished and wrapped tightly around Sam's back.

Sam enlisted Laurel for her comments but got mostly quiet smiles in return. Like every animal Sam had studied, Dean consistently defied expectations. He would never eat fat, ordering grilled salmon and broccolini steamed without oil, and avoiding the rolls of bread that Sam loved. Then he would push Sam into an ice cream shop and order triple scoops of chocolate for them both, lapping at his own while watching Sam eat. On the nights Dean stayed over, Sam would stay up late, moving around the quiet apartment and returning to the bedroom every few minutes just to watch Dean breathe. They both woke easily and early, and Dean was always leaping for the door, the gym, or home to change before Sam had finished brewing his coffee or the birds had started to sing. On those rare mornings, however, when neither had to work, Dean would sometimes refuse to rise. He would hold Sam's hand and then his body down, pulling Sam into him until they were both so sweaty that it would require a playful scramble to the shower together before they headed out into the day.

In the small of his back, Dean had a perfect pool of light brown hair. Sometimes, lying with his cheek resting on Dean's solid butt, Sam could ripple the hairs with his breath, stroking them like hundreds of tiny brown minnows. He loved when that tiny whorl was slick and wet, either from sweat or the attention of his mouth and tongue. Sam, attempting to control his descent through cataloguing and observation, was drowning in a flood of images. He decided he was absolutely happy to drown.

DEEP WITHIN that first, kaleidoscopic month with Dean, Sam volunteered a day off to assist Jack and the other big-cat keepers in preparing an empty enclosure at the Lion House for the arrival of a male Sumatran tiger. It was a warm May afternoon, and the first tendrils of thick summer heat were in the air. Sam had just finished a final check of the enclosure's grassy tiers, coating heavy rubber balls with animal fat and tying chunks of horsemeat to low stumps and overhanging walls to make the animal stretch. The thick smells in the heat made Sam woozy; he felt a miniature version of the forecasted thunderstorm building behind his eyes. Pinching his nose, he hurried to the heavy gray door, thrilled for the chance to take part in the day.

Sam had done his homework: he knew how rare Sumatrans were and that their chances for survival were being bulldozed along with their habitats in the wild. He had offered Jack numerous suggestions culled from the Sumatran Work Group's literature and scientific journals; Jack had dismissed him with: "Thanks, kid. I know how to breed my cats." Sam knew how lucky he was to be a member of this team; it was only his recent, mostly lopsided partnership with Jack that let him take part. I still deserve the howler exhibit, he thought as he banged to be let back inside, but felt a little ungrateful for the thought. A dark, uneven scent-mark stain, which had resisted relentless scrubbing, blotted the concrete beside the door.

The tiger, named Borneo by a well-intentioned but geographically misguided donor, had been in a small quarantine pen at the hospital for almost a month, and everyone was anxious to get him into the spacious enclosure that would be his new home. For weeks, Sam and Jack had been spending their lunches peering in at Borneo through a tiny window crisscrossed with powerful, almost invisible mesh. He was beautiful, pale for a tiger, his shiny, red-gold coat glistening. His markings were gracefully delineated like strokes from a Japanese brush.

Borneo was also entirely new to the captive gene pool and had been selected as a mate for Sheba, the Zoo's previously unbred female. Sam was beginning to love Lion Island, and he felt like a parent today, hoping that Sheba and Borneo would be a good match. The cats were so different from the small, self-sufficient monkeys in their cacophonous family groups, the stoic howlers, or the ponderous grace of the Zoo's mountain gorilla clan. These were tigers. Even Sheba, raised in Jack's own hands, was terrifying when she showed her huge, yellow-dagger teeth.

The storm hit as Sam stepped inside. Jack was a mess, his fluttering, pudgy hands and protruding belly leading him in nervous circles around Lion Island's internal work area, and Sam put a hand on his shoulder and smiled. The weather outside was primeval; golden pollen and sharp grass cuttings whipped into tiny tornados across the dark sky. Leaves turned their dusty bellies upward. Water, deliciously warm and wet, spun in the air. The sky threatened lightning, so despite the tension of the introduction, the cats were brought inside one by one. Ultimately, all three lions and six tigers were steadily prowling the perimeters of their cages. That constant, bored pacing was normally hard for Sam to watch—especially for wide-roaming animals like the big cats—but this day the animals were fierce and active and agitated. They smelled an intruder in their territory and were snarling and growling and scent-marking the bars of their cages without pause. Sheba was particularly wild, wrinkling her snout and baring her fangs in the direction of Borneo's cage.

It was a good sign. Sam stood a few feet back from the meeting point of their cages and rocked on his heels, crossing and uncrossing his arms. He flexed his hands to relieve them of sweat. Gwen and Dr. Baskin whispered to each other behind their hands, while Jack blew nervously on his. Animal introductions were always nerve-wracking. Sam had been a keeper long enough to know that almost any animal will eventually habituate to its neighbors and surroundings, but a good introduction could make the work of the keepers a thousand times easier. The vets would inseminate Sheba with Borneo's sperm if it was necessary, but operations could be traumatic for the animals, and impregnation was far more likely if the animals did it on their own. He thought of Dean again and was suddenly very warm.

Borneo paced the dimensions of his 11-foot-by-16-foot cage, leaping effortlessly to the straw-covered ledge, snuffing at the closed gate to the outdoors, and disappearing into the matted darkness of his simulated stone cave. He seemed to be ignoring Sheba, who continuously sniffed at the adjoining bars and let a low moaning growl escape her mouth. The noise felt like longing, and Sam felt a bubble of excitement rise in his throat. He wished Dean was there and then thought how much better it would be to tell him about it later, maybe fiercely, in bed. Sam imagined grappling Dean from behind, of licking and biting Dean's neck. His mouth watered, and he closed his eyes.

He opened them to a deeper hush from the crowd. Even the normally jaded keepers were silent, watching something as close to sacred as many of them knew. Borneo was crouched powerfully on the floor of his cage, literally shaking with contained energy. His face and thick fur pressed against the bars that separated him from Sheba, and he was licking her muzzle through the bars. *Licking* her. It was as if they had recognized each other instantly. She kept half-turning to offer her hindquarters to him, then returning to rub her forehead and cheeks—a territorial marking and sign of affection—against the bars between them and whatever part of Borneo she could touch.

As Jack ushered everyone out of the room, wanting to "give them some privacy to say hello," Sam felt himself start to laugh, or maybe he felt himself start to cry. Love was such a weird, world-shattering thing. Even a tiger would say it feels good.

Sister and Brother

"It hurts," she cries through sensitive teeth, stretching the word into a moan and biting it off at the end. Karen had looked forward to it, to giving birth, to the end of being pregnant, anyway. Instead, it feels like hell. She had thought it would mean the end of the ugliness, the fat, the swollen feet. Instead, it is a constant, endless, impossibly swelling pressure on her insides, her stomach, the taut skin below her belly, deep inside. Karen feels like everything she is, and was, is roiling around inside her along with this alien beast that is stretching her open, that is trying to push itself out of her and turn her inside out. She is lying on her side, one white leg crossed under the other, her feet in a knot of damp, green sheets. The metal railings on her bed feel electric. She wants to put her tongue on them and lick.

Relief, tiny and insufficient as it is, comes first from the drugs and then her mother's hands. They are soft and wet like the scratchy blue cloth she pulls across Karen's forehead, mixing cool water with hot sweat. She is murmuring small comforting words. "Baby girl you're beautiful you're doing fine I love you you're having a beautiful baby boy I'm so proud of you . . ." pours from her mother's soft pink mouth, mixing with the soothing water in her hands. Her mother's hands are all Karen can feel in the whole world beyond the bright white pain and fear.

She had been golden nine months before, a sun-blind vacation in Florida for seniors too cool to bother with the traditional spring break craze. She had danced, bronzed and invincible in her blue-and-yellow bikini, with an artful blaze of pale pink skin showing where the yellow strap had fallen onto her arm. Biting into plump limes, licking salt off sandy, corded necks, head rolling with alcohol. And then waking up, lips and eyelids swollen, skin tight, feeling hollowed and filled with brackish seawater at the same time. She had woken up staring into the huge shoulders and stiff, gelled hair of a boy with a Calvin and Hobbes tattoo and his sun visor still on. A boy whose waist, even before she got pregnant, was thinner than hers.

This feels like payback for all the years of drinking and boys and ignoring her mother and Sam. Like she has tried to run too far and is now being pulled back and tied down with a huge, lumpen ball of flesh that she can never untie and never let go. Revenge for being so stupid, she thinks, grinding her teeth even more. She is trapped now, pushing pushing pushing pushing against herself, feeling herself rip and tear, and all in penance for one stupid night, the last five stupid, drunken years. The pain tears through her eyes, and for a second everything goes away.

When it is over, when the pain has finally crested and subsided into a dull throb, Karen suddenly has a baby. Of my own, she thinks, and decides, right then, with his small, oddly heavy, unnervingly red and hot head resting open-mouthed on the paper smock that covers her chest, that he will have everything he needs in life and that her mistakes won't cause him harm. Karen might have lost her own Daddy, but her boy will never miss out on anything that any parent can give. She doesn't know how to help him, though, and his tiny weight suddenly presses impossibly down on her chest.

When she looks up, her mother is still stroking her forehead, and Sam has been let into the room—she had never even gotten the boy from Florida's last name—and she moves her hands over her baby's head in a tiny mirror of her mother's on her own.

"I'm going to take good care of him, Mom," she promises, the words welling through the wet fibers of her expanding chest. "I'm going to do better from now on." Her breath is confusing to her, and she takes a moment to listen to it, whistling in odd, thin gasps through her mother's assurances. "Mom?" Karen asks, shielding her eyes from the flickering, fluorescent light, "I'm going to name him James, I think. I'm going to make Daddy proud."

Into the wide silence Sam asks, "Can I hold him?" and the words burst like pent birds and fly crazily around the room.

In those first, impossible hours after Karen and Baby Jamie come home, her mother and brother hold her up every single day. She lives at home, with Mom downstairs and Sam's bedroom just a few doors away, and they keep her from falling; they are the crutches under her arms. Karen has an automatic babysitting pool that protects her from the loneliness and fear she would have faced alone. She cries uniformly for the first few weeks, and yells and screams, but mostly she and Sam spend long afternoons recovering, as they call it, on the back porch in the sun. He makes tuna sandwiches with potato chips crushed in. She hates breastfeeding, tries to give James tiny pieces of the wet meat. Karen still won't go to the neighborhood pool, but her skin begins to look smooth again, she can feel herself getting tan. She does hundreds and hundreds of sit-ups. Her friends call; there are parties. She is remembering to feel her age.

It is late on a weekday afternoon. Karen is on the lounge chair, and Sam is squatting in a blue plastic wading pool with James when they hear their mother enter through the garage, earlier than usual, and begin moving things around and setting things in place.

She turns the dishwasher on, and Karen and Sam look at each other over Jamie's head. Jamie looks into the water, unconcerned.

"Karen, can you come into the kitchen for a minute," Mom calls from the dark interior of the kitchen.

Karen looks at Sam again, a cold rose blooming deep inside her chest. He mouths "go" and turns his face back down to his nephew's tiny head. He cups water in his hands and splashes water on the baby's tiny, doughboy chest. As she enters the air-conditioned kitchen, the skin on Karen's arms pimples into goose bumps. Her feet are cold and sweaty on the tile floor. She pulls a T-shirt off her chair and sits to face her mother at the table. Mom stops wiping the table with a sponge, sits down, and looks Karen in the eye.

"Karen," she begins, looking into her iced tea, "I've been thinking about things, and I've decided that we need to make some changes around here." She reaches out and touches Karen's cheek, and Karen suddenly knows that everything is going to be all right. She had cried to her mother two nights ago that her psychology degree was now useless, that her life was over, that everything had fallen apart. And within two days, Mom had come up with a plan. Karen sits up in the chair that has been hers as long as she can remember and listens for her mother to tell her how everything will be all right.

A few weeks later, Karen is alone in the house, feeling rich with freedom but alone with all the time and space. Sam is volunteering at a Dolphin Research Center in the Florida Keys, and Mom has Jamie at the pool. Karen sometimes feels guilty that her son became "Jamie" so quickly. That "James" had quickly become too big for her sweet, baby boy. It will do for now, she decides. She is trying to be firmer in her convictions. He can be James when he grows up and has a family of his own.

Mom has asked Karen to clean Sam's room, since Sam is taking the basement to give Jamie a room of his own. Sam had moved his furniture before he left, and made them promise not to touch anything while he was gone, but Mom has changed the plan and asked Karen to get everything moved downstairs that weekend so they can paint the room before Sam goes off to school. Even though Sam is just going to Maryland now and will still live at home, Mom seems to want to make it a big deal for him; the whole house has a guilty, apologetic feel. Before Jamie, Sam had been planning to go away to California to one of the best pre veterinary schools in the country, but that seemed impossible to all of them, now. Mom said they were going to decorate and set up his room for him while he was away. She has even bought him a new computer, and they will have everything set up when he comes home.

Sam had complained about the move downstairs, but Karen knows he must secretly want the freedom of the sliding glass door that opens onto the weed-cracked driveway at the side of their house. The new arrangement also lets Karen move Jamie into his own room, upstairs near her, but out of her own bedroom. Mom had brokered the deal as if negotiating between two departments at her job.

As Karen begins pushing through Sam's things, she focuses on what a beautiful room she will make for Jamie. She turns on the radio. She loves reorganizing rooms. She will paint the room sky-blue so he will always feel the whole world is easily within his reach.

Digging through a pile of books and notebooks from Sam's senior year, Karen unearths a small metal box—a lockbox—with a plastic button and a keyhole keeping it shut. She sits down, wondering why Sam would have a locked box, and where the key might be. Unfolding her legs, she hops up and carries it into her room. Sam will be gone for almost a month, and she tells herself that she is just setting it aside before moving it downstairs with the rest of his things. She gathers an armful of books and tromps down the two flights of stairs to the basement.

Hands on hips, Karen decides that Sam has done very little to set up his room. It looks un-committed-to and incomplete. She realizes, standing in the dark, wood-paneled room, that she has no idea who her little brother is. Pushing the books into a pile on his unmade mattress, she runs upstairs, takes a knife and some pliers from the utility box, and hurries up to her room. It takes her five minutes to break open the lock, and when she tips open the surprisingly light lid, she loses, for a moment, the ability to breathe. A thunderstorm of revulsion, arousal, pity, and fear rockets through her chest. She sits on her bed with the cold metal box warming on her knees, and wishes, illogically, that Jamie and her mother, that Sam in particular, would leave her in the freshly vacuumed house and never come home again.

The box has books in it, gay books, and magazines covered with photos of naked, hard men. Men alone, with muscular chests and spread legs, men squeezing their own dicks, or pouring soapy water over themselves, or spreading their butts apart and staring—invitingly—over their shoulders. Turning the pages, she reads highlighted, bold sentences like "my mouth watered with anticipation as his powerful tool swung before my eyes . . . " Her own mouth fills with saliva that is either from the tan skin of the men or the memory of the last man she was with. She isn't sure if she is excited or if she is going to be sick.

More pages, different magazines. Men alone. Men together, veined hands on veined . . . Oh, my God, she thinks. Only once the words have lost any meaning does the meaning of the pictures fully sink in. Sam. Oh my God. You're gay. A fat laugh bursts from between her fingers, and her eyes well over with tears. It is impossible, but it also, amazingly, makes perfect sense. Karen shifts in her seat until she is sitting with her back straight and knees together. All these years of no girlfriends, she thinks. All the times I had to cut off assholes with their snide comments at school. Poor Sammy. She sits for a minute and thinks.

Carefully, thoughtfully, she replaces each magazine and book in its exact place, protecting her brother's privacy and her own. She decides, as she carries the box downstairs and places it at the bottom of Sam's new closet, buried under Sam's more public books, that she will not mention her discovery to anyone. By the time her mother and son come home from the pool, Sam's new basement room is entirely arranged, and his old room is perfectly empty, scoured clean. If Sam notices anything upon his return, he never says a word.

SIX

"GOD, IT'S hot."

The sun was crisping the skin of Sam's arms. To his right, Dean sat thoughtlessly shirtless, a thick droplet of sweat clinging to his nipple. Sam had just applied suntan lotion to Dean's back but kept his own shirt on; the contrast of his red arms and neck against his pasty, hairy chest (his "Zookeeper's tan," Laurel always laughed) was too dispiriting in the face of Dean's smooth perfection. Laurel, on the other side of Dean, had made a tent of her tank top and her knees. The three of them were on Sam's concrete stoop, watching neighbors and strangers pick through a miniature city of picture frames and plants, pots and pans, out-of-style clothes, and other assorted stuff. Sam hated giving things away, but a charity yard sale, and a long morning with Laurel and Dean, made it seem worthwhile. The smells of banana oil, heated plants and soil, and too many people wavered disconcertingly in the air. Laurel and Dean were talking and laughing, and Sam was beginning to feel left out.

Annoyance, like an insect buzzing his ear and nose, undermined his satisfaction with the morning. He was busy, he was surrounded by friends and neighbors, he was doing something for the community. A neighbor in a blue cap walked by, and Sam gave a quick salute. Laurel and Dean didn't notice. They were too busy giggling about something behind their hands. Don't replace me with each other, he wanted to tell them. And don't expect me to sustain *your* relationship now too. He looked away from them and wiped some gritty pebbles from under his sandals, picked at a piece of flesh on his toe. This is stupid, he thought, his head thick with pollen. He swatted at nothing in the air for something to do.

49

The whole block was swarming with lazy Saturday strollers cupping frozen lattés and bottled water in their hands. Sam's neighbor Nick had coordinated a block party and yard sale as a fund-raiser for his school, and enlisted Sam as the coordinator for his building. Being needed, the sweet frustration of additional responsibilities, had given the morning and the weeks leading up to it an energized, productive air. He was on break, having already checked one too many times to ensure that every individual salesperson had thick black pens and multicolored sticky dots. Dean had just called him a mother hen.

Or guardian angel, he thought, looking at Nick's fussy organizing a few doors down. A small, white-and-gray cat darted across the street and appeared in front of them from the shadows under a parked car. Sam and Laurel called out "Hi" at the same time, and Dean put his arms around them both.

Sam took a long drink of iced tea. It was truly amazing, this thing with Dean, even if it sometimes felt too powerful: the disorienting shine of Dean's intense perfection, the whirlpool of Sam's own feelings for Dean. Just last night, Dean had announced that he'd negotiated a trial upgrade to features reporter, the next key step on the career path he had long desired. "No more weather," he'd crowed as he arrived at Sam's apartment bearing a chilled bottle of champagne and quickly turning the air conditioner down. Sam, proud and expectant, had pushed aside his sticky labels and signs, given Dean a long hug and many kisses, and thrown together an easy pasta dinner for them both while Dean began brainstorming some features to pitch about the Zoo.

And then this morning, in Sam's cool bedroom, sex that had left handprints on the walls. He could still smell the fresh steam from the shower they had shared.

Now, Dean and Laurel were laughing and nudging each other, and Sam was a little bit annoyed. Ostensibly, their job was to watch for anyone interested in Sam's motley collection of IKEA bowls and unread books and make any necessary sales, but so far, Dean seemed far more focused on explaining "the dangers lurking in your grocery-store aisles," in a booming, horror-movie voice. Check that, Sam thought, noticing

Dean's sharp glance out into the crowd. He took another drink of tea and tried to ignore Dean's obvious appreciation of two shirtless men examining an old desk in front of the town house next door.

The men, heads down and glistening in the sun, had meandered into the spill of Sam's items for sale. When Laurel pointed them out to Sam, he shifted closer to Dean instead of getting up. The taller of the two looked up from under his cropped black hair and caught Dean's eye. Sam stiffened and dropped his arm over Dean's shoulders, as he called out in his friendliest voice. "Take a look around, guys. Let me know if I can help you. Everything here's mine."

Dean bounded up and away from him and toward where the man was standing, leaving a cooling patch of shadow under Sam's arm.

"Mike!" he shouted, stepping around a pile of Sam's worn-out throw pillows. He pulled the man's tan shoulders forward so they could kiss. "How are you? When did you get back from L.A.?" Mike was easily forty-five-years old, with tan skin stretched tautly over perfectly sculpted muscles. He was wearing trendy orange shorts with too many pockets and a tiny white tank top stuffed into the back waistband. A sliver of pale skin edged the shorts at his waist, nearly as white as his smile.

Laurel scooted quickly into the space Dean had vacated and put her arm through Sam's. She whispered "something wicked" into his ear, but he ignored her; his absolute focus was on Dean and the man on the street. She'd added outdoor tables near Terra's front door, she said, and he tried to envision it. Dean's hand ran down the man's arm. That first review, she continued, hadn't helped as much as she'd hoped. "Uh huh." He could feel her rubbing his back.

"You've got nothing to worry about," she whispered hard into his ear. "His eyebrows are obviously waxed."

"Sam!" Dean called up, waving Sam down. "Laurel, come meet Mike and Kenneth, you guys! They just got into town." Laurel waved and smiled and stayed put. Sam trotted down. "Nice to meet you," he said, shaking hands with them both. "Hi, Ken." He could tell Kenneth was the type who wanted his full name used and shortened it casually out of spite.

He heard Dean quietly telling Mike that he and Sam had been dating a little while now and that he wasn't really in a place to be set up. Sam flushed cold, then hot, but he kept smiling and making small talk. Kenneth seemed to know mostly about restaurants and bars, and raved about a party in the Hollywood Hills where Elton John had shaken his hand. He was "in the industry," he explained, and when Sam pressed, admitted a little defensively that he was an assistant at a video production house. "Well, that's good too," Sam offered, looking forward to running back to Laurel and laughing it off. They were in town for a fund-raiser, Sam overheard. Mike was telling Dean that it was too bad he couldn't make the party tonight. It was going to be fabulous.

Turning to look at Laurel over his shoulder, Sam could see her talking to a woman in a purple head scarf, pushing some picture frames into her hands. He knew he should have felt good. Dean had said no to a setup; he had told his handsome Los Angeles friend that Sam was his boyfriend. He felt strangely sick, though. He knew he wasn't ugly, knew Dean was crazy for him, knew he was a catch. But he'd still been discounted immediately by Dean's friends. As the conversations faded and the two tapered backs walked away, glinting in the sun, Sam was left standing, briefly, alone. Dean came and put his arm around him.

"They are such great guys," he enthused, grinning and kissing Sam on the cheek, "don't you think?"

A WEEK later, Sam sat with his howlers, who hung motionless in the sun. The black-furred male blended into the shade, and the buff-colored female and juvenile were slung on their perches, their shaggy hair as still as late summer hay. The only movement was that of an occasional fly buzzing the animals and the faint, wavering heat distortion in the air. Sam was observing, attempting to take behavioral notes from his perch on the warm wooden bench that sat across from the monkeys' ironbound outdoor space. He was also killing time. Although he relished the extra time to spend with his animals, a disappointment in their utter lethargy rolled through him every few minutes like a wave. He wanted the animals to match his energy: Dean was coming to see him at the Zoo for the first time, and a sweet anxiety was roiling inside.

Guilt also played a part. Sam had been scheduled to rush out to Bethesda for dinner at Karen's and to see the plans for their new kitchen, but when Laurel had called, asking him to meet her later that night, he had happily cancelled on his family. He'd left a quick message midday when he knew no one would be home, and called Dean to arrange a last-minute tour. Looking up at the monkeys again, Sam realized that he was holding something back from his family for once. Let them wonder about me for a few days, he shrugged. I've certainly spent enough of my life doing it for them. The female raised her right arm and scratched at her side. Sam noted the movement and promised himself he would call his sister and offer to take Jamie for another weekend as soon as he got home.

When Sam had called to invite him, Dean had cheered and needled him at once. "You're actually going to let me see your precious, private Zoo?" And sweetly, "Of course, Sam, I'd love to."

Sam wanted to kiss the phone. He also thought he'd invited Dean to the Zoo before but couldn't be sure. He decided he didn't care.

"I can't be there before about 6:30, though," Dean continued. "Is that too late? What time do you have to meet Laurel for this talk?"

Sam had promised him that 6:30 was fine, that Laurel would be at the restaurant until at least 10 p.m. He was spending more and more time with Jack at Lion Island, and it felt good to check back in with his own work for a while, even if his plans for the howlers remained stalled. "Lazies . . ." he muttered, as the male's tail twitched at a fly. His watch beeped and Sam jumped. Late again. He rushed to Connecticut Avenue to wait.

After climbing into the air-conditioned car and receiving a sweet kiss on the cheek, Sam directed Dean to the staff parking lot at the bottom of the Zoo. They chose a distant space under a tree, where they kissed greedily for a few minutes before getting out of the car. "Yum," Dean growled as he wiped his mouth with the back of his hand. "Man, you taste good. I'm so glad you didn't take a shower first. You're lucky we already have plans, or I'd be licking you up and down right now."

Sam laughed, gave Dean a quick, dry, kiss, and led him by the hand into the Zoo, bouncing ahead and pulling him up the hill. He was imagining a long walk under the trees as the breeze cooled them, of introducing Dean to the few keepers still finishing up. "What do you want to see first?"

"You!" Dean laughed. "Can you show me the shower?" He grabbed Sam's hips.

"No, seriously," Sam laughed, flicking Dean's hands away. He wanted the day to be sweet. "What do you want to see?"

"Your monkeys," Dean offered, changing course. "Lion Island. The howlers, the tamarins. Everything."

He rested a hand on Sam's back, in the spot between his shoulders that seemed designed for it, and Sam left it there. He looked at the slanting sunlight burnishing Dean's hair and face and wanted to touch the impossibly small, white hairs that fringed his cheeks. They walked around the Zoo's gentle twilight for over an hour, talking about nothing and holding hands.

SEVEN

LAUREL TOLD Sam about her mother on the low stone arc of steps that winged the fountain on 22nd Street. He watched her trail a hand in the running water as they sat still in the dark but warm evening air. Laurel was quiet, so Sam talked. He detailed his walk with Dean: Dean's requesting that Sam not shower for their next date and that Dean's admitting as they walked through the smells of animals, cotton candy, and summer-tired trees, to wanting Sam to talk dirty to him in bed.

"Which is great." He almost hiccupped the words, and Laurel's eyes widened and zeroed in on his own. "I mean, it's like, I actually feel sexy with him, and even if . . . " His words disappeared into the sound of water, into his nervous grin. He didn't say that he loved being the object of such fascination. It felt too dangerous, too personal, even for them. Laurel leaned forward, forgetting the pebbles she had gathered in her palm.

"So anyway, I think I like it," he asked, the pitch of his voice rising with uncertainty. He presented his melting ice cream cone as a failed explanation of what he was trying to say. "But it's really weird. I mean . . . awkward, but he gets so excited by it, so I guess—"

"My Mom has Alzheimer's." She swatted his uncertainty like a fly.

"Oh my God, Laurel," he said, reaching out a hand and covering her knee. He thought of stern, tall Mrs. Hoffman, lean and direct in her soft button-downs and jeans. Of the weekends she'd cooked him eggs Benedict, with homemade hollandaise sauce, as a special treat. Mrs. Hoffman. He could hear her low, clipped voice and laughter. Laurel was going to be an orphan before he was. He didn't know what to say but scooted closer so that their bodies could connect. "How is she? I'm so sorry. Are they sure?"

"They're sure." The words, like her eyes, dropped like a stone into the water, and in its ripples she told him everything, that she'd only been home twice since finding out, that her mother—apart from a new instinct for hoarding sugar packets *and* sugar-free gum—seemed fine, that her insides felt torn in two. She took his hand. "I haven't told anyone else."

Sam watched her warily, from ten-year-old eyes. It was as if he receded away from the news and into himself, getting smaller within his skin. Green ice cream melted into the napkin covering his hand. "Laurel . . . " He'd known her since they were nine years old; he took her hand and stroked it, useless as a child.

She told him that it wasn't advanced and that Emily was checking in on her every day. She told him she wasn't worried, and the tightness that had gathered on his forehead began to ease. He knew what she was doing; she would keep talking until she had pushed through any possible questions he might have, until any objections to her immediate plans would be overruled. She peppered the heaviness of the news with laughs about a nerdy fruit purveyor who was begging her for a date, about Molly and Kara's quest for the "perfect" preschool for Mae-Lin; she promised him she would tell Molly and Kara soon, some night at their own dining room table, surrounded by plants and 1930s prints, after Mae-Lin had gone to bed. She would handle it, and he would help her. There was nothing for Sam to do but agree.

As they sat and talked, and then sat in silence, night stole in and obscured the quivering leaves.

A FEW nights later, Sam got more unwelcome news.

He was sitting in a smoke-filled corner booth of an Irish bar in Cleveland Park, surrounded by the regular mix of younger, mid-level keepers who had gathered for drinks and nachos and pre–Labor Day weekend complaints. It promised to be a warm, sunny holiday weekend, and they were loudly commiserating about the crowds. Sam had been nursing his beer, watching everyone do a round of frothy shots, when Kieran pushed himself to a standing position and loudly shushed the crowd. "Everyone!" he announced, making a leaning semicircle so he could look everyone at the table in the eye. "Everyone, I have something to say." He was grinning, and a few flecks of yellow cheese dotted his chin. Sam's mind flashed on standing up, grabbing Kieran, and pulling his tight, wiry body against him. He wanted to taste the salty cheese mixed with Kieran's mouth.

Someone shouted, "Talk!"

Kieran announced that he had met with Sandy, the hoof stock curator, that morning, and that he was going to be the lead keeper on a new exhibit. He swept his arms to describe the American Savannah that was going to showcase prairie dogs, native grasses and plants, and the two bison that had been moldering in the old mountain-goat exhibit for years. The director, he had been promised, was committed to making lower-cost, highly educational projects like this work, and Kieran was going to take the lead.

Sam sat very still, ignoring the fizzling mustache of beer on his face, and concentrated on keeping his features arranged in a smile. Kieran was twenty-four. He was suddenly ugly, and Sam considered, momentarily, the consequences of tossing his drink at the man swaying above him across the booth.

"That's great, Kieran," he ventured, listening for the sound of it. "You really deserve this. I know you've been putting in a lot of work." The other keepers followed Sam's lead, as he numbly raised his beer for a toast. Opportunities like Kieran's were too rare. The beer bubbles continued to pop on Sam's chin until Carol, normally disgruntled and muttering up at the Bird House, wiped them away. "I'm sorry, Sam," she whispered, squeezing his arm as Kieran continued to sway.

The next day at noon, he took his bag lunch to a sunny bench behind the administration building, where he could be left alone to think in peace. Eating his soggy tuna sandwich, Sam looked over his notes from a few months ago. All his plans for the howlers, useless. And "grasslands" getting a major exhibit within a year. Suddenly his sandwich tasted bad, and he put it aside. He wanted to avoid Gwen forever, to walk away from it all.

"What do you think I should do?" he asked two free-ranging tamarins who'd found their way to the heavy branches above Sam's retreat. He'd get back to it. He'd get his howler article published and use that as leverage for next year.

That night, telling his mother about Laurel's mom on the phone, Sam realized that he wasn't anywhere near as upset as he felt he should be. He was sorry that Laurel's mom had Alzheimer's; he wanted to help her through this time. He even missed Mrs. Hoffman in the way that your hand remembers the soft, feathery feel of a child's head after they have wandered away to play. He was deeply worried about Laurel, but he was fine. He hadn't gotten his howler exhibit, but he was fine. Jamie and Karen were fighting, but he was fine. I have Dean now, he realized, sitting at his window watching the sun fade over the redbrick buildings across the street. The leafy tops of the trees on his street looked soft and golden in the light.

EIGHT

JACK LICKED the sweet remnants of a glazed donut off his fingers as he entered the room to the sound of Sam's curses resounding off the walls. In the warm office, at the end of its narrow hall, the dented wheelbarrow was on its side, a puddle of fluid pooling below. Sam was squatting in a pile of heavy slabs of marbled red meat, fumbling with the slick chunks and muttering under his breath. He had knocked over the wheelbarrow in a rush to get things done, to get back to his howlers, to get the tamarins back in their depressing cages after a summer of freedom, to return to his own tiny kingdom where all the paths were matted down into dead-grass ruts.

"Sam?" Jack asked tentatively, peering into the office like an animal nervously scouting out an unfamiliar space. In response to a rudely grunted reply, he waded into the meat spill and, placing his hands on Sam's shoulders, gently pushed him up and backward into a rough, green, plastic chair. "What's going on?" His eyes were bleary as always, but they were so kind and clearly concerned. "Hey, what's the story, buddy?" he asked again, cuffing Sam gently on the neck.

Sam smiled weakly, glad that Jack was there, slightly nauseated from the rich smell in the hot room. "I'm fine."

Jack ignored him, clambering down to one knee and righting a hunk of meat.

"It's just that, I'm so tired of doing whatever they tell me, you know?" Sam whined, knowing how annoying he must sound. Jack looked back at him with confusion. "Gwen and Dr. Baskin and everyone. I just, I *know* how good the howler project would be for the Zoo—I've even got some

59

new ideas on making it multispecies and more interactive—but they just won't hear it. Dean was saying again last night what a great opportunity it would be for me. It's just a little on my nerves." Sam's hands rested in his lap like dogs that wanted their bellies rubbed, fingers waving like legs in the air. He kept his eyes down. "Gwen's always hinting that *something* great is coming down the pike, but . . . I don't know." Sam looked up with a nervous smile, raising and dropping his hands back to his knees. "I'm sorry I knocked over the wheelbarrow. I was so frustrated this morning. Dean says I need to stop being so nice."

Jack's eyes were sparkling with the moisture that always stood in them, and his face cracked into a huge smile. "God, boy, but you're young," he laughed, kneeling in the diminishing pile of meat. The pants of his green uniform were slowly staining an ugly brown-red. While Sam was talking, he had righted the wheelbarrow and gotten the majority of the meat back into it. His fingers, palms, and wrists had drying patterns of blood on them as well. Leaning back on his ankles, he took a deep breath and cocked his head to one side.

"You remember when that poor crazy lady climbed into Simba's enclosure in 1995?" Sam nodded, thinking back to the awful storm of media attention that had almost overwhelmed the Zoo. Jack had been at the center of it all—the Zoo's "Lion Man," its lead cat keeper, and one of the lonely voices advocating for the animals in everything that happened after that night.

"I remember coming in early that morning," he began, "because I just had a...feeling that something was wrong." Jack pulled up a chair for himself, sitting with his knees almost touching Sam's. He rubbed his face, and Sam wished Jack would have washed his hands first. "I had received a call from the local community liaison. People were complaining because the roaring from the cats was so much louder than normal. I hate calls like that." He looked at Sam who smiled back. "You understand."

"Anyway, when I got in that morning, Simba was just, well, he was all lit up inside. Tearing around the yard like a wildcat—heh—like when he was a cub, and I couldn't get him into his interior cage for anything. Couldn't get out into his yard, either," Jack continued, and Sam wanted to correct him, make him call it an enclosure, but Jack flashed him a look to pipe down. "So when I finally got out there and found, well, when I found what was left of that poor lady—under the African olives, you know—I almost didn't know what to do." Sam leaned forward, fighting the urge to lick his lips. The story was legendary—the lady who climbed over the concrete barricade and dropped into the lions' enclosure in the middle of the night. Her note had said something about communicating with aliens. Sam and his friends had dissected the articles and begged the cat keepers for the real scoop. They staunchly defended the lions, who had done simply what lions have to do. Even Sam's mother had agreed it couldn't be considered the animals' fault. "So I fed Simba and the other cats and called it in like I would any emergency. I should've known it wouldn't die there."

"You know the rest. The Zoo went crazy; the news went crazy. The director at the time took me out of the picture, wouldn't let me talk to the press." He chuckled. "I guess they thought I agreed with Simba instead of the people calling for him to be put down. I think they needed a better"—here he flexed his fingers into quotation marks—"'public face' for the Zoo." He shrugged, shook his head.

"It didn't matter that Simba is a lion, kept in a cage his whole life, suddenly presented with the kind of prey his entire evolutionary history had programmed him to attack. Didn't matter that *he* hadn't escaped but that *she* had climbed in there on her own. Didn't matter that . . . ." He faded out, sounding a little bit angry but mostly tired. "I almost got fired for that one."

I wish I could get fired, Sam wanted to say.

"He was just being what he is, Sam. He couldn't help it. And most days, I really think he's fine. He eats his meat, his pills, the occasional squirrel or rat. He has his hot sunny yard in the summer and his private cave whenever he wants it. Cats sleep twenty hours a day anyway, Sam. You know all this." Turning to his locker, he pulled a small, silver flask from his jacket pocket and blatantly took a drink.

"Now, do I wish he had more room? That they all did? Hell, yes. Cats are roamers too. But, you know, Sam, he's fine living here. They all are. Give him prey, and he'll go after it, and thank God for that. We are what we. You'll get your howlers or you won't. Big deal. You're still one of the best keepers I've ever worked with. It's who you are. Accept it."

It's what *you* are, a part of Sam wanted to say, although a part of him felt relief and wanted to thank Jack for letting him just be. Except that he *did* want to do more. The problem was, he simply didn't know who he was supposed to be, and the mire of his obligations sometimes left him feeling stuck and blind.

Sam started to respond, but Jack shook his head, standing up to replace the flask and then measuring pills out into his hand. He was silent for a second while he made small incisions in a few of the steaks and began stuffing the pills into the meat.

"Do you know how much trouble I got into over that? For defending an animal's right to be an animal? For suggesting that he hadn't done anything wrong?" His hands shook as he worked pill after pill into the thick, smooth flesh. Calming down, he added, "I mean, she was the crazy one, right?" He looked up to Sam. "Hell, they'd have loved it if I'd quit."

Again, Sam tried to protest, but Jack went on.

"But listen, Sam, I love my cats and taking care of them, and I knew that Simba needed me more than ever. Life is crazy. Some people climb their whole life, always looking for the next mountain, always thinking the next thing will make them happy. Some people sit still because they can't see the mountains at all, just the dark shadows. That woman? Well, I don't know what exactly she saw, but I think she found it by climbing over that ledge. We all just have to find our place. Don't assume that a few setbacks mean that your place isn't here."

Sam remained silent as Jack pushed the wheelbarrow out of the office, looking back over his shoulder at Sam sitting alone in his chair.

"One last thing, Sammy—who cares if they're going to give you some new title or bigwig job. You've already got the best job in the world." He made a clicking noise twice with his tongue and walked out. Sam sat in the overheated room for a few minutes, muttering about "his place" and "natural instincts." He hadn't wanted to be lectured that morning, even if what Jack said was true. Sam felt a little bit guilty as he gathered his things and walked away from Lion Island into the high, thin sun. He was supposed to shadow Jack for half of the day. They both understood that he wasn't in the mood.

NINE

SAM PICKED up Jamie at the Bethesda Metro station at dusk the next Friday night, the first hint of winter creeping into the air. Sam had been feeling guilty lately, spending so much time with Dean and at the Zoo, that when Karen had called asking him to take Jamie while she and David shared a last-minute weekend away, he hadn't been able to refuse.

As soon as her green SUV swung into the passenger drop-off lane, Jamie slung himself out and onto the pavement, backpack weighing his lanky body down, baseball cap pulled low. Karen's hands followed him across the empty space of her car, alternately shoving at Jamie with her fingers and attempting to grab him back for further hugs. Her eyes shone with bright tears as she waved and pulled away, thanking Sam, admonishing Jamie to be good, promising to miss him and see him on Sunday afternoon. Jamie gave her a half wave, sulked in response to Sam's prodding and jokes, and sat mostly silent on the train.

After exiting the Metro at Union Station, they quickly passed the newsstand and bathrooms and turned into the crowded, underground food hall. Sam preferred the restaurants, upstairs, that ringed the vaulted, gold honeycomb of the great hall and missed the thought of their reflections in the dark marble floor. But Jamie loved the mobbed food court adjacent to the movie theater, so Sam maneuvered them past the rush of late commuters on their way to the Metro or an outbound train.

Sam loved Friday nights with Jamie—filling him with junk food and then weighing him down with popcorn, candy, and a soda so large he normally peed three times before the movie let out—things Karen would never let her prized possession do. As much as Sam hated the theater at Union Station—it was like a dirty, overcrowded cage—Sam knew that Jamie loved watching the hordes of teenagers, and Sam loved letting Jamie have his way. Something in him enjoyed the annoyance: an impressive foregoing, a penance for something he couldn't name.

"So, what's it gonna be tonight? Pizza? Burgers? Sushi?" Sam prodded as they passed bright, empty-faced clerks at one register after another. From beneath his low-pulled navy baseball cap, Jamie's answers were an unintelligible monotone. He dropped behind Sam, tucked his arms into his body, and stuffed his hands into his pockets where they looked like little fists. Sam pulled them into the shelter of a marble pillar and took his nephew's elbows in his hands, stooping to catch Jamie's eyes beneath the brim of his hat.

"Jamie? What's going on? I'm sorry we're rushing, but the movie is in half an hour, and we need to get something to eat. Aren't you hungry?"

Jamie's eyes were unnervingly wide and almost teary, and he was trying desperately not to meet Sam's gaze.

"Jamie? What's wrong? What's going on?"

Jamie shook his head again and took a huge, gulping breath that moved like a wave from his chest into his neck and mouth. A chicken in a rainstorm, Sam thought, and remembered an Easter Sunday once, nearly thirty years ago, when he had run from the heaven-green fields of children and families and hidden eggs, unable to find a single friend in the whole crowd, and cried the whole way home in his mother's car. Jamie looked like he might explode. Sam shepherded him upstairs and hailed a cab.

Jamie remained silent for most of the ride home. His sneakers, which used to bob and dangle from the seat, rested on the ridged plastic floor. Sam made the cab driver turn off an angry, conservative diatribe on the radio, and Jamie managed a smile in return. They could give each other this quiet, Sam thought, leaning back into his seat, and deciding to trust that Jamie would tell him what was wrong when he could. Cool wind lightened the close, backseat air.

As he paid for the cab, Jamie waited by his side. Sam punched Jamie lightly in the shoulder as they opened his building's door.

Jamie went straight to the TV, and Sam went to the kitchen, dialing the pizza place while flipping contentedly through his mail. Opening mail always calmed him. The simple process of it—open, file, discard—felt orderly and productive. Making the world make sense again. It often put his mind to rest.

Wincing at the newest issue of *Science* magazine and thinking briefly of the howler article he still needed to rewrite, he tossed flyers for Chinese restaurants and pizza delivery joints into the trash and set aside a few bills. He gave his order to a surly girl on the phone and promised Jamie that dinner would be ready in half an hour, grabbing up the magazine to read for a few minutes before pouring them drinks. A large manila envelope, covered with numerous stamps and dark red instructions, dislodged itself from the back of the magazine and fell to the floor.

He picked it up, running his hand along the tile and realizing he'd have to mop after Jamie left. The return address—*Dr. James Anderson, TCR Station, Brazil*—made him flush. The envelope itself was like nothing Sam had ever received and made him think of the ominous packages in an old movie about archaeologists and hidden, ancient cults. He glanced into the living room and, seeing Jamie entirely focused on the TV, ripped open the envelope. He wiped a bead of sweat from his forehead as an excited pulse began beating in his neck. The envelope contained a few, neatly written sheets, a heavily stapled article, and an already posted return envelope attached. The letter read

Dear Dr. Metcalfe—

My name is James Anderson, and as you may know, I direct the primate studies at National Geographic's Tropical Canopy Research Station here in Brazil. A colleague recently forwarded your draft article on howler communication to me, and I was very impressed with your findings, particularly given the limited number of animals you are able to observe.

Sam opened the kitchen window and took a heaving gulp of cool air. Someone recognized his work *and* thought he was a doctor. It might be a good night after all.

You may be familiar with my work with the howlers and tamarin species here. As you can guess, the observations I'm getting on social interactions are truly exciting. Many of the theories you propose complement certain elements of my own research, and I think you could bring an invaluable perspective to our work here.

Please consider the proposal outlined on the following pages. I will be in Rio for a few days next month to do some business and will have a better opportunity to make some calls. Our mating season begins—

"UNCLE SAM!" Jamie yelled, and Sam's head jerked up from his childhood dream-come-true. He dropped the envelope and jogged the few steps into the living room. "What's the last word of 'Auld Lang Syne,'" Jamie asked, and Sam dropped onto the couch with him, snaking an arm around his small shoulders. For a moment, he simply loved his life. Brazil could wait; it was time to call out answers to the game show on TV.

After Jamie grumbled and scuffed his way to bed, Sam cleaned up dinner and stood for a moment listening to his nephew breathe. He tried calling Dean, then unplugged the phone since Jamie was sleeping in the living room, and went to bed.

He woke up early the next morning and checked his voicemail to see if Dean had called. No. He listened to, and saved, Karen's recorded "Bon Voyage." He ate two slices of cold pizza with congealed cheese and then, feeling guilty, ran out to get bagels for Jamie. The letter from Dr. Anderson, hidden on the counter under the pizza box, had disappeared from his mind.

They spent the day visiting Laurel, doing errands, and wandering around town. They saw the movie they had planned to see Friday night, Dean having left an apologetic message while they were at the mall. Their night was pretty quiet. Jamie didn't mention his bad mood, and Sam didn't bring it up.

SUNDAY MORNING dawned bright and clear, and Jamie surprised Sam by suggesting a day at the Zoo. It was barely 8 a.m., but a cool breeze was already vibrant through the windows, and Jamie's eyes were bright. He had missed the monkeys, he said. Sam just nodded while he munched his toast, holding in a face-stretching grin, and headed back to the kitchen and the paper. He had to keep swallowing orange juice to counter the sweet lump that was rising in his throat. While Jamie showered, he left a message alerting the day's keepers that he and his nephew would be poking around.

An hour later, in the slowly warming sun, they walked around the Zoo. It was early enough that the walkways were mostly empty; artists, mostly older and seated, lazily sketched the slow-moving animals, while graduate students made meticulous, detailed notes. They checked in on Sam's howlers ("boring," Jamie declared) on a few of the smaller animals, still in their interior enclosures, and then moved downhill before beginning the long, uphill walk back to the street. Jamie laughed at a tiger swatting at an invisible something in the air. The day was remembering summer, and the smell of yesterday's ice cream was rising off their path. Jamie was quietly swinging a fallen branch and murmuring comfortably to himself.

"So do you want to talk about Friday night?" Sam asked as he pointed out a timber-wolf pup peering over the back of a log. Distraction tactics. "Look up there."

Jamie didn't respond immediately, and Sam simply continued to walk by his side. Pointing out the empty beaver dam, he purposefully bumped Jamie's elbow. Occasionally, he caught himself palming Jamie's cap. For a moment he lost himself in the peaceful, rustling quiet of the leafy green pathway. He did, truly, love his Zoo.

Leaning their elbows on the aluminum railing over the sea lion exhibit, Jamie swung himself over and hung like wet laundry from his waist. Despite knowing it was against the rules, Sam let his nephew hang.

"Has Mom talked to you about Roosevelt yet?"

Sam stiffened. Karen had prepped him for this, her voice tight with determination. And she had extracted a promise that he would *do the right thing* by telling Jamie to go. He hated being told what position to take, but, in this, at least, he thought he agreed with her. Clearly, however, Jamie had his own ideas. He was definitely his mother's son.

"She's mentioned it. . . . Yes." Sam responded, lightly rapping his knuckles on the ridges of vertebrae climbing Jamie's curved back. "I thought it wasn't for another year, though. Is that what this is all about?"

Jamie remained prone, hanging over the edge of the pool. He took a deep breath.

"It's just that, Mom's so mean, and she's so, so mad at me all the time, and I just, I don't know if I want to go to Roosevelt, you know? None of my friends are going there. Well, Bobby Morris is, but I don't even really like him, and he sucks at soccer, and if I go to Washington then I know I can get on the JV team, and David and Vu will too and I just—Mom just doesn't get it. She's so mean."

He took another gulping, upside-down breath. Sam waited him out.

"All she cares about are her stupid friends and the stupid PTA, and she doesn't even care what I want. She says she won't make me do it if I don't want to, but she's giving me a total guilt trip. She's totally making me go." He twisted sideways and wiped a tiny drop of spit from his chin. "She totally yelled at me in the car on Friday on the way to meet you," he continued, "and she's got Dad totally doing whatever she says." He angled his head up so that he could look Sam in the eyes.

Sam wanted to jerk him up off the railing, shake some sense into him about how lucky he was. *Two* parents who loved him and the chance— the gift he was being given—to leave the obvious path and see what else the world might have in store. He also wanted to hang over the railing himself and whine. He rubbed Jamie's back instead. "Don't say 'mean,' Jamie. Tough, yes. Mean," he finished, "no."

"But I don't have to go, do I, Uncle Sam? You didn't go to any fancy school, did you?" Jamie was spent. As if all the words in the world had poured out of him like a waterfall, as if he was hanging upside down so that he could pour all these thoughts into the perfectly blue pool below. A single sea lion swam in numbingly repetitive loops.

"Jamie." Sam reached down and grabbed his sides, feeling ribs slide under the skin. He pulled his nephew upright and got them walking again.

"Jamie, your mom isn't. . . . She's just . . . she wants what's best for you, that's all."

Jamie glared from under the blue lid of his cap.

"For a minute let's just forget what your mom wants and talk about you. Why don't you want to go to Roosevelt, and why *do* you want to go there, too?"

They fell into a slow walk up the winding and shaded path. Jamie trudged beside Sam, kicking fallen leaves and pebbles out of his way. Sam let him be silent, wishing he knew what to say. He wished Dean were there, or Laurel, or anyone who could buffer the intensity of the conversation. Anything to keep the conversation light. He wished he was in Brazil, with Dr. Whatever-his-name-was, doing research that was straightforward and productive and made sense. And then he was immensely grateful that Jamie actually wanted his advice.

As they passed into a quiet stretch of wood, Sam was surprised by a new kiosk that fronted a large span of tall, undisturbed trees. They were walking past the golden lion tamarins' outdoor staging area, and Sam stopped them to read. He was distracted, suddenly, and proud. He had written the new language for the kiosk with the education department but hadn't expected to see it so soon. Things generally moved slowly at the Zoo, and the tamarins wouldn't move outside again until the spring.

"Look," he pointed the kiosk out to Jamie. Under his breath, he began to read:

Zoos began captive-breeding golden lion tamarins almost ten years ago as part of an international program trying to rescue them from extinction. Golden lion tamarins are tiny, birdlike monkeys, with hugely expressive hands and eyes. They are very social, very fierce, and very fast.

Jamie's eyes roamed the dark brown display. In addition to the text and small photographs of male, female, and juvenile specimens, the surface included two maps of South America, each with tiny red dots that showed the tamarins' historical and current habitat. It was sad how much space they had lost. Jamie was tracing the smaller collection of dots with his finger. Sam thought he heard him say, "Cool."

Golden lion tamarins have black eyes and jutting jaws and orange-gold "manes" that give them their name. Hunted almost to extinction in their native habitat, the remaining wild population was captured and divided up among a number of Zoos and research centers around the world.

"See?" Sam liked seeing his words presented so solidly. He wanted Jamie's attention again. Jamie's head turned up, and Sam could see his eyes, interested, from under his cap. He pointed out the tamarins' nest box—a vertical Igloo cooler with a small hole cut into the cover—and took up the narrative himself.

"Anyway, a group of Zoos created a breeding program to ensure the genetic health of the species in the Zoos. You know this, right?" Jamie nodded, giving Sam permission to go on. "Well, we went a step further here, allowing our tamarins, during the summer, to live out here in the trees basically free. Remember when we saw them that day over by the Ape House?"

"Uh huh," Jamie responded, screwing his face up. "It's cool, Uncle Sam." Jamie was a good kid. "If I was them though, I think I'd run away." He kicked at a rock, and it skidded off the path into the trees.

Shit. Sam almost tripped. Karen was a worrier; he'd assumed things with Jamie weren't really all that bad.

"Well," he started cautiously, feeling his way. The cool sunlight was too bright, and the path seemed strewn with fallen branches. "The tamarins don't . . . seem to need to run away. I mean, we take really good care of them here. They have space to roam, yes, but as long as their nest boxes are warm and their feeding trays are full . . . " His voice trailed off. What was he trying to say?

"You know, Jamie, the Zoo's already released over 100 tamarins successfully back into the jungle. They have a good life here, and then they get to go free. I get to be a part of that. Getting chances like that doesn't come without hard work."

Jamie sighed. His shoulders shrugged in obvious anticipation of another lesson Sam was about to send his way.

"Listen to me. Sometimes it's hard to make animals like the tamarins embrace freedom. Some get eaten by eagles or other predators. Some just can't handle the stress of constant hunting and hiding after having had everything provided by the Zoo. Overall, though, Jamie, when you give an animal its freedom, it thrives."

Sam stopped, momentarily confused. He felt off-track. Was he telling Jamie the right things? Telling him to defy his mom, or helping him choose Roosevelt on his own? He wondered for a second if he should be listening more closely to his own advice. "It's just harder for some animals to adjust."

"I wish *this* family believed in freedom," Jamie snorted in response. "Look at Mom; look at you. You've told me this same story about the tamarins at least a thousand times. You've been a Zookeeper your whole life," he continued. They were passing the Native American Heritage Garden; the leaves of the plants looked like slicing blades.

"And it's not that being a Zookeeper isn't cool; it's just that I want to actually do something with my life, you know? Let *me* decide about Roosevelt, be a scientist, don't be a scientist, be a soccer player. I don't care! But Mom won't let me decide for myself. I want to be a doctor or something, Uncle Sam. She always tells me not to make the mistakes you guys did."

Sam saw red. My only mistake, he wanted to snap back, was giving up my dreams to take care of you. An elephant's weight of guilt landed immediately on his chest. He gave Jamie a quick, sideways hug.

"*Don't* you ever wish you could really do something, Uncle Sam? What do you think I should do?"

"Just go to Roosevelt, Jamie," Sam snapped and walked away from his nephew for a minute, having done what his family demanded and already planning to treat Jamie to an ice cream cone in exchange.

———————

THE SKY was gray, the air was getting cold, and Dean was in New York. Dean was in New York, and Sam was sitting on his stoop in the sweet dark night of fall, wishing he weren't alone.

Sunday afternoon, returning from the Zoo with a rejuvenated Jamie, Sam had replayed Dean's apologetic message while the dishwasher chugged in the background. Dean wouldn't be able to meet Jamie this time; he was sorry. He'd gotten a last-minute call from his agent, he explained. A meeting too good to pass up. Sam hung up. Karen picked Jamie up a few minutes later, and Sam was left in his apartment alone.

He grabbed the mail, his cordless phone, and a bottle of warm red wine and went out to sit for a while on his front steps. He tried Dean once but got an immediate my-phone-is-turned-off voicemail, and poured himself some wine. He sat quietly drinking, absently batting the letter from Dr. Anderson against his knee and letting the drink's warmth combat the quickly chilling concrete under him. An empty glass sat next to him, catching on its rim a final glimmer of afternoon light. Sam had brought the extra glass as insurance against looking lonely. He was deciding, at that moment, that the extra glass actually made him look not only lonely, but insecure as well.

He was worried that he'd given Jamie the wrong advice. Specifically, that he had given the advice Karen wanted him to give rather than what he truly believed. He so often just acquiesced; it was like a valve in the back of his brain interpreted every situation through Karen's needs, Laurel's, his mother's, even Dean's, he supposed, and then just routed Sam's true reaction to somewhere he could no longer find. He had once been told by a massage therapist that he "collected" stress on his back, and Sam thought it might be the accrued weight of his own, subverted voice.

He shook his head and drained the last of the wine. A tremor of worry ran through him; with this trip to New York, was Dean taking some kind of unacknowledged break? Inside, he tried Dean again, and Dean answered on the first ring.

"Oh my God, Sam, that's amazing," he crowed when Sam told him about Brazil. "You are considering this seriously, right? I mean, the chance to go study your howlers in the wild? It's such a great opportunity, honey." He took a breath. "I would never want to hold you back."

Sam felt the break before Dean's last sentence, like the sharp crack of a tree branch that has just died overhead. He was afraid to look above his head for fear of the falling limb.

Sam knew he was being ridiculous. He wanted to hold onto Dean, to climb into his strength and nestle between his arms, but he feared the branches would give way beneath him. Dean's voice sounded thin, like that cracking branch, like the first night of fall without the comforting blanket of air conditioning and insect sounds. Sam knew he should be thankful for the support. What he really wanted was to be grabbed onto and needed and held.

"You really think so?" Sam managed to ask. The realization that loving someone this much was utterly impossible whipped across his forehead so strongly he was amazed that it didn't leave a mark. An image of his father shot past his eyes: in their driveway, attempting to get Sam to play catch, becoming disappointed, and then not attempting anymore. An image of his mother, telling the lump in Sam's chest and throat that his father was never coming home.

And Dean, responding to something, immediately offered a soft assurance in Sam's ear. He promised Sam that he would miss him *terribly* if he left and invited him to dinner with his college roommate for later that week. Something to look forward to. Something to make the moment pass.

After they hung up, Sam sent a brief, noncommittal email to Brazil, pleading a busy time at work and promising to follow up after the New Year. Duty met, he put the terrifying, inviting letter in the back of his howler file. It was easier to keep things the way they were. He hadn't even looked at the howler proposal in months.

TEN

LAUREL WAS saying horrible things about her mother into the phone. She was, as she felt like she always was, sitting at her small office desk, fighting to make any one thing about Terra go right. The construction project that blocked Terra from the view of Dupont Circle's crowds was being extended for another month. The environmentalist-approved salmon she was serving as her special wouldn't arrive before the weekend, and she was going to have to get her fish off a local purveyor again, at almost the menu price. And she would have to do it without two of her kitchen staff who had called in sick with the flu.

Underneath it all, she wanted to kill herself for how little time she'd actually made for her Mom.

As she explained all this to Charlotte, imagining her in her clean, well-funded lab at Stanford, Laurel wanted to let the pieces of her body fly apart and shatter, wanted to collapse to the floor and just lie there, waiting for anyone to come and pick her up.

"Laurel, it's just that I simply can't get out there," Charlotte explained patiently and with the soft, gently superior tone that had infuriated Laurel for as long as she could remember. It was like Charlotte channeling Mom channeling a damn Breck girl or something. "My research is at a crucial stage, and Erik needs my support while he prepares for his opening. . . ." She could hear Charlotte's mouth forming a capital "O."

Laurel dispersed again, into thoughts of the upcoming Friday night and the wild storm of trying to keep her kitchen afloat while Miguel had to manage the whole floor. The lighthouse beacon of Sam's offer to help shined briefly against the darkness, but was lost as Mathilde dropped a metal bowl of sticky brown marinade with a shattering clatter on the floor. Laurel felt her shoulders jump and twist painfully. Her neck ached; she rubbed her forehead strongly enough to strip off skin.

"Laurel?" It was Charlotte's voice, pulling her back. "Laurel? I said, you're just going to have to find a way to do more."

"More, Charlotte?" Laurel shot back. "As opposed to the *nothing* you're doing? Is that right? Just abandon the restaurant and go? My God, as if Mom being sick wasn't enough of a burden. . . . " She laughed, worrying the pearls at her throat. "You just have no idea, do you? It's always been up to me to make everything—"

"You know I can't talk to you when you're like this, Laurel," Charlotte returned, calm as a desert oasis, and just as deceptively smooth. Laurel hung up the phone.

She fought her way through a three-hour dinner and sent her staff home, telling them that they would be closed on Saturday and Sunday for a family emergency. She printed a small, neat sign on the printer below her desk and hung it in the perfect center of her glass door. There were only a few reservations to cancel anyway. That night, climbing heavily into bed, she refused to cry, tightening her chest against a bursting that she was suddenly convinced, once started, would never stop. She didn't wake up until noon.

Thirty-six hours later, after a furious round-trip drive to Pennsylvania to visit her perfectly fine-seeming and uncommunicative mother, Laurel was finally back at home. Everything at Terra was as set as could be hoped for Tuesday. Fuck the lost weekend, she told herself. She would go in early tomorrow, come up with a brilliant new plan. She could reschedule things, again. Juggle responsibilities. Maybe she could drive to Pennsylvania for a long afternoon and morning, every other week?

For now, she was going to relax. Laurel stood in her apartment's tiny golden kitchen, mixing dough with her hands, kneading and pulling it, trusting her own muscles and the rising heat of the bread. It felt as if her own brain, her own mind, were also being massaged as well, by gentle invisible hands that mimicked her own. "Mom wasn't that bad," she told herself. Standing there with her feet planted wide, arms and shoulders working, she edged herself toward a kind of peace. She finished kneading, wiped her hands on the towel tucked into the waist of her khaki pants, and grabbed an old wooden spoon to push the bread into the heavy loaf pan.

It was an old family joke: Laurel had started baking as the only way to keep her fingers warm. As a teenager she had constantly moped around the old, high-ceilinged house with her hands hidden inside her sweater sleeves, cupping her elbows like a cheerless pretzel. For years she had loudly declaimed the family's puritan use of the heater, removing her fingers from their warm sleeves only long enough to tap loudly on the thermostat and call out "Sixty-five degrees!" to anyone who might hear. Eventually, when she started baking, her hands stopped getting cold.

THE NEXT day, Laurel treated herself to a long-anticipated matinee in Cleveland Park. She strode through the blustery wind, shoved between both sunshine and clouds, and watched children in expensive jackets trail mothers in long, shapely coats. They were the mothers, like Emily, who did not work and who walked their young children in strollers and oversized rubber boots. Who hand-sewed bumblebee outfits for Halloween. Laurel took a deep breath, resenting them a bit. She felt like she was jealous of everything these days.

And yet she wanted none of it. Frigid tunnels of wind had smacked tears from her eyes as she hurried through the bright afternoon, clutching her coat against the wind. She didn't want to follow the hedonistic trail of restaurant smells, didn't want to explore the dining rooms and kitchens of every place she saw. Instead, she imagined herself leaning against the stiff smooth back of her velvet seat, the warm breathing dark of the Uptown Theater. She wanted candy and popcorn. She wanted the sweet release of a Coke. She wanted, fundamentally, for her mother to be healthy, for her restaurant to run itself, and for everyone, just once, to simply leave her the hell alone.

She smiled up at the theater's towering front. She loved the Uptown, the last of D.C.'s true movie palaces, the kind of place she'd gone, in Philadelphia, as a kid. The popcorn was always a little bit stale, as if they just kept whatever they made the night before, but Laurel loved it. Loved the vaguely sour smell of the air, the scuffed seats, the permanent semidarkness. She felt anonymous, privy to a secret escape that no one else could share. In the past, Laurel had tried to bring people into her Monday movie-going ceremony, but no one quite understood. Her afternoons at the movies were the closest thing she had to church.

Still, images of her mother's imagined dissolution swirled at her, and she angrily pushed them away. Glad for the cold metal handle of the huge, shining, glass doors, Laurel stepped into the theater and inhaled the warm, sweaty smell. Her other option had been to cut off all her hair. She couldn't really go home every week—could honestly hardly manage the one time a month she was already—barely—managing. Couldn't overwhelm her harried days anymore. She had the restaurant, the remnants of a life. Mathilde needed an immigration lawyer. Her liquor license was under review.

Inside the theater, Laurel took a deep breath of the past seventy-five years. She purchased her ticket, confirming that she only needed one, then stood briefly, looking down at the permanent paths worn into the diamond pattern on the purple and blue carpet. It felt like an ancient temple painted in ornate patterns and designed for women wearing hats and gloves. It had seen better days, but Laurel loved it just as it was. Her mom had seemed so normal last week. Popcorn, Red Vines, and a Coke in hand, she walked alone through the theater doors.

The vaulted room enveloped her, a welcoming darkness in defiance of the sharp brightness outside. She didn't have to walk too far into the happy, eternal dusk of the theatre before finding her favorite seat waiting for her. It was as soft as the butter on her popcorn, deep crimson velvet, comfortably frayed. She briefly congratulated herself; a weekday matinee was perfect: It was like a secret whisper that no one else she knew was able to hear.

Laurel took her seat, two-thirds of the way back, on the far left of the center aisle, equidistant from the two other moviegoers in the room.

She deposited her jacket and purse on two seats to her right, grabbed a mouthful of popcorn and settled in. The movie wouldn't start for another half hour, and she sank into her enfolding throne like a princess or a movie star wrapped in anonymity more precious than gold.

Only a sprinkling of additional people entered, and most were alone. Her skin itched when a college-age couple sat near her and picked their way through an inane conversation about her friend who liked his friend who was dating someone else. She was annoyed at the noise their talking made, annoyed that they didn't respect the sanctity of the space. Then she realized: she hadn't been on a date in months, hadn't even flirted with anyone since Andy, and she hadn't even had time to miss it. Or had she? How twisted and shrunken inside had she become?

Taking a Red Vine and more popcorn in her mouth, she smiled straight into the face of being alone. Everything, even dealing with Mom, was so much easier when she had room to breathe. She sighed, smelling salt and butter on her breath. The concessions began their giddy, sales-oriented song and dance.

Two hours later, as the credits rolled by, Laurel sat alone in the still-dark theater. The movie hadn't even been sad, but the beauty of its crashing colors and pure invention made her swell near to bursting inside. Alone, as the movie's credits rolled, Laurel was making a horrible, embarrassing noise. She had gone to the movies to cry.

ELEVEN

THE THICK warmth under Lion Island was oppressive, and the cats' fur looked dull in the uniform light. Jack was shoving hunks of raw meat through the rusted metal hinges of the food trap as the cats snarled and bared their teeth to his careless hands. He was looking back over his shoulder, a Zoo-banned cigarette between his teeth, talking to Sam through coughs and curls of smoke. He looked more tired than ever. The smell of alcohol punctured the normal smells of smoke and mouthwash, so Sam was watching Jack with a closer eye than normal.

"So, the doctors say she's doing OK, right?" Sam asked, hoping that Jack's appearance wasn't a mirror of the status of Millie's health. Jack had just admitted, leaning his elbows on his dark little desk while they shared lunch, that Millie's cancer, which had been in remission, was giving her problems again. He had held up his thin sandwich with shaky hands as he attempted an implausible laugh. Millie was Jack's whole life, and she was probably going to die. She wouldn't be making him bag lunches for long.

"Doctors!" He snorted and wiped the wet from below his eyes. "I haven't trusted a doctor since I was twelve years old! Millie's doctor says she needs rest, and more tests." He squeezed out the last rhyme in his best mincing whine, dancing his fingers over his sandwich before breathing in deeply and taking another bite. It was the same thin ham sandwich Millie had been making him for well over forty years. "So we'll get more tests," he shrugged, "and our daughter's going to send us some money for a cleaning lady for a while." He took another swig from his shiny plaid Thermos, pushed himself off from his elbows, and started talking to Sam about the cats again. Jack wasn't one to accept charity lightly. Sam knew things must be bad.

Sam and Jack were old buddies now, with an easy routine to their days. Sam officially spent three half-days a week working with him at Lion Island, making sure records were kept and safety precautions taken, and filing carefully worded reports twice a month. In addition, they had lunch together two or three times a week, and Sam often dropped by just to talk. Sam felt good with Jack, warmed his hands at the heat radiating from Jack's potbelly and red nose, and worked hard not to attach it to feelings about the father he didn't have. It felt ungrateful, sometimes, the comfort and easy dependence Sam felt with Jack's straightforward, male support. Sam rarely acknowledged missing his father at all. I was so young, he always said. I never really knew things any other way. And yet he loved just sitting with a man like Jack, and wondering, sometimes, what growing up with his own father would have involved.

Jack was also a safe haven for Sam's unhappiness at the Zoo. Despite putting off Dr. Anderson's offer in Brazil, Sam knew things at the Zoo hadn't changed, and he was wondering, when not distracted by loving Dean and mentally levitating his family, how long the Zoo would be a viable home. He found himself barking at the younger keepers he supervised, and had been caught by other keepers rolling his eyes behind Gwen's back. He checked the American Zoo and Aquarium Association's website for nearby job openings every week. Jack, bubbling like a bitter coffee with his own grievances against the changes at the Zoo, was good company. Their friendship also cemented Sam's inclusion in the Zoo's "old school," a connection that years of working side by side with the older keepers hadn't quite made firm. Somehow, his relationship with Jack proved that Sam could spray shit and handle animals with the best of them.

Sam was glad for the change. He knew that his relationship with his primates had settled into a routine of modulated predictability, and the shock of the cats' huge indifference was appealing at times, as was their fierce, yellow-toothed wrath. Gorillas, he could see, were slow and graceful with their keepers, even if it made him vaguely uneasy to work with them. The smaller monkeys—tamarins, spiders, even some of the more social lemurs—were like a room full of kindergarteners after a sugary snack, and Sam could laugh with them for hours as they followed both their own inner messages and their keepers' every move. His howlers, though. Their slow ease, the hidden power of their voices and calls. They always seemed so . . . satisfied. Fruit or chow, shade or sun. The way they lived almost entirely alone. He loved them too much, he knew. Maybe that was the problem. Gwen kept saying that, where Sam's howlers were concerned, he never suggested anything new.

But Lion Island was entirely different. The cats' stealthy awareness was calm and electrifying at the same time. They required a wholly different energy, and it felt good to flex new muscles for a while. Since Sam's only true responsibility with the cats was to keep an eye on Jack, his time there, despite increasingly troubling mistakes on Jack's part, was usually whiskey-smooth.

After feeding all the cats and locking them into their indoor cages, Sam and Jack walked slowly together onto Lion Island's broad grassy terraces. They walked in the crunching grass, clambered over low, concrete retaining walls, and scouted for fecal matter to bag. Sam was very aware of animal scat at the moment. He had recently intercepted an email from a graduate student at UC Davis who was trying to collect fresh lowland gorilla feces as often as possible. A partnership with FedEx allowed Sam to send her the gorilla's collected poop overnight for analysis. Gwen had initially resisted due to the tiny additional cost but, realizing how disaffected Sam was, had relented. She was finally realizing how removed Sam was, and saw some expensively mailed feces as a small price to pay. Monkeys and big cats and now nutritional science too. As a small gesture, it had worked.

Walking in the dry grass, they were a silent pair. Jack wandered the tiered enclosure aimlessly, stopping to stroke a rough set of scratches in the bark of a tree or bending over to look at something in the grass. Sam heard him muttering from time to time. Whenever he turned a concerned, helpful look in Jack's direction, Jack would scowl and look away. Their movements were interrupted by a small crowd that began to gather along the high concrete wall above the exhibit, and a volley of bright questions suddenly rained down. "What are you doing in the tiger's cage?" "Hey, Mr. Tiger Man!" "Where are the animals?" "Why are you moving their toys?"

Burying a huge chunk of cat chow under a bush and moving "toys" like logs and heavy plastic balls to precarious spots where the slightest attention would send them tumbling, Sam smiled quickly up at the group, squinting into the thin sun, and then looked back away. Jack was the star here on Lion Island, and Sam wanted to let him shine.

But Jack wasn't answering, and as the calls became more insistent, Sam stopped what he was doing and faced the crowd. "What are your questions?" he asked, shading his eyes with a hand and mustering the broadest smile he could. "First of all, we don't like to call them cages. And Jack is really busy now. I'm helping him out today. What do you want to know?"

Sam basked in the sunlight of their attention. He realized that he loved answering their questions and putting on this little educational show. Standing tall, he crossed his arms behind his back and answered every question that came his way.

"Are you a vegetarian?"

"No, but a lot of animals are."

"Do they have names?"

"They do. This is Sheba's enclosure. But," he held up a finger, "it's very important not to think of these animals as pets. They are wild. You'll notice that Jack and I are out here, and the tiger *isn't*. So, even though we give them names, it's really just for us."

"Do the animals get lonely?"

"Well," he paused, having struggled with this question many times. The low yellow sun was shining sharp and bright in his eyes. "The lions live together, in groups, like in the wild. And tigers definitely don't get lonely. See, most of the big cats are solitary animals—they like to live alone. So, actually, making them share a home with other cats would be meaner. Same with reptiles and lots of animals. The social animals like monkeys," he resisted the urge to explain that he *normally* worked with the primates and the distinctions between different types, "are kept together. You've seen the family of gorillas at the Great Ape House, right?" A random bobbing of heads confirmed they had. "We keep the social animals together, so, no, I don't think our animals are lonely at all."

Sam was glad to have gotten away with the answer. And that they hadn't asked if the animals got bored. Those were hard questions for a Zookeeper. He'd made his peace, and knew that the animals received great care, taught important lessons, and lived safer, healthier lives than if they had remained in the world's dwindling, terrifying wild. But if the question had been, "Do Zookeepers feel trapped by their lives?" Sam knew he'd have had to say yes.

LATER, JACK thanked Sam with a rough slap on the back and a backward glance. He was rushing home to see Millie, who had called mid-afternoon and asked him to come home. With blooms of fear in his eyes, Jack said Millie's voice sounded "wavery," and he fumbled more than once as he grabbed his coat. Sam offered to close down Lion Island that afternoon, and the light had already started to fail when he finished the day's notes. Sam was impatient, hurrying through some final, meddlesome tidying in Jack's office before running over to check his own animals at the end of the day. He and Dean had a date, and he refused to leave even one minute late.

About to step out, Sam heard a step and looked up to see Gwen's flushed face and green uniform blocking the light. "Bravo, Sam," she said loudly, clapping her hands three quick times for emphasis. "I hear you made quite the spokesperson out there this afternoon. I thought you didn't like being on display like that? You seemed to have a lot of good information to share." There was a mix of goodwill, humor, and calculation in her voice that confused Sam, so he didn't respond right away. He leaned back in Jack's chair and waited for her to go on. "You really are good with the cats, Sam," she continued. "And Jack really does seem to need the help. What's going on with him?"

Sam closed up the office and walked out with Gwen into the chilly night, turning uphill toward the Small Mammal House and the end of their day. She questioned him gently, cautiously probing Sam's impressions of the last few months. Despite her height, Sam noticed, she always matched his stride with ease.

As they entered the warm building, Gwen bumped Sam's side.

"Checking on the howlers?" she asked with a wink. "Let's walk through together. I've got a jackrabbit mare with a bit of a limp, and I'd love your 'nonofficial' advice." Sam laughed, glad that he and Gwen at least had this. Despite his complaints about her lack of support for his howler ideas, he knew how much she loved the animals and respected her for it. Even without beers and nachos for lubrication, they could always talk about this.

Gwen peppered their walk through the quiet, shuffling interior of the Small Mammal House with questions about Sam's work, his life, and his impressions of a new primate keeper she had just hired. Sam talked about his howler research for a few minutes but trailed off quickly, realizing just how much more of his energy was going to his time at the Lion House with Jack. They stepped outside, stopping in front of the howlers' outdoor enclosure and watching empty wooden swings being nudged by the wind. A temporary sign, nothing more than laminated paper on hooks, explained that when the weather changed, the Zoo's howler monkeys, like most tropical animals, retreated to their nest boxes earlier and earlier in the day. Sam had helped the Education Department write and design the sign, and he stood with Gwen, quietly, before it. It was badly frayed. As he was resolving to put in more time with his howler research, Gwen interrupted his thoughts.

"Sam. We all love Jack. He's an institution here at the Zoo, you know that. And I know you're dedicated to your primate work, so I," she faltered here, momentarily, and Sam felt a smolder of frustration kindle inside. She rallied, replacing the apology in her voice with steel. "Well. Here's the thing. As you know, I'm not going to be able to get your expanded howler exhibit into this year's budget, and probably not next year either. The director is really pushing for a few big, visible projects, and we've been awarded the right to expand our breeding program for big cats—Sheba's pregnancy has caught some important eyes—and, well, we're also just starting to plan something tropical that will really put us on the map."

"And I know your howler research is valuable and important, and we will continue to fight for it," she enunciated every word, "but the reality is that this Zoo is going in a bigger, showier direction. This is Washington, D.C., for God's sake, and the new director needs to show how good we are." She paused here and put a hand on Sam's arm as they went back into the building. "And as for your howler proposal, I hate to say this, but you really haven't shown us anything new. Three howlers or twenty, to the public it's still just antisocial monkeys sitting on sticks."

She unlocked the door to the keeper's corridor and pushed her way in ahead of Sam. They waved to a few departing keepers and moved to where they could watch Sam's howlers cuddled together in their toasty cage. "Sam. We want you here at the Zoo. I will do whatever is in my power to let you do anything you want. Putting tamarins in the Great Ape House was wonderful, and I want you to keep coming up with ideas. We really do hear them." She kicked a booted toe against Sam's foot. "I really do. But for now, what I think is best for you is to keep spending time with Jack and the cats and supervising the younger keepers on your primates. I think I can guarantee that the rewards will be great."

She wouldn't say anything more specific than that, and Sam left that night confused, excited, and very wary about what it all might mean. Stepping into the eternal rush of Connecticut Avenue, his thoughts turned away from Jack and Gwen and cats and monkeys and toward his own night, his new lover, and home.

"IT SOUNDS like she wants to push Jack out," Laurel called over a huge pot of bubbling risotto. She had recently changed over to a winter menu of heavy soups and thick, warm side dishes and was turning her arm in slow revolutions over a massive, heavily scratched metal pot. Sam had rushed to Terra straight from work, anxious to check in on Laurel before meeting Dean for dinner downtown.

"Push him out?" Sam parroted, confused by Laurel's idea. "But Jack's been there forever. I mean, he practically built Lion Island himself."

Laurel tossed a look at Sam that suggested he was either a saint or an idiot savant. Her free hand tucked some loose hair behind her ear and then reached over to touch his cheek. He noticed that her hair didn't have its usual shine. "Sweetie, listen to yourself," she began. "You know that the Zoo is about the future right now, about what's going to be popular and important to the public next year, in five years, ten years down the line. Look at you—they hired you because you were not only a keeper but a researcher—you yourself have said that Jack is a thing of the past." She grimaced. "I'm sure they want him to leave." She paused for a moment and frowned into the pot. "Grind some pepper into this for me, would you?"

"Fair enough." Sam leaned past her and gave the grinder two quick turns. The steam felt good on his skin. "Now," he turned to face her, blocking the easy distraction of the pot. "How's your mom? What's going on?"

Laurel handed Sam a long spoon and indicated that he should stir. "Listen. My sister called today, and it sounds like Mom's getting worse." She leaned back against the counter and rolled her palms over her face, forehead, and hair. Sam stopped himself from dipping a finger into the risotto and looked at her. She looked doughy and unformed, like she was fading, like what happens to certain animals at the Zoo. They aren't ill, or dying, but they are no longer truly there. No longer inhabiting their shapes the way they used to. Laurel looked like she had lost track of the bright, sharp edges of the world.

"I mean, she's fine," Laurel announced, tossing her head back and turning her gaze a full rotation around the kitchen, reorganizing as she went. "She's just forgetting more. Emily went to visit her and spent twenty minutes unloading mints and candies from her underwear drawer."

She said it quietly, without the laugh Sam would have expected, and as she said it, stepped back to the risotto and took the tall wooden spoon out of Sam's hands. "They're doing more tests this week, but we don't know anything for sure. I just wanted you to know. I'll probably go home again next week to see everyone."

Sam needed to fix this. He had the next weekend off, for a conference on nutrition and primate reproduction he'd signed up for months ago. He'd cancel it. Laurel mattered more.

"I'll come with you," he offered, putting a hand on her arm. "I'm coming with you. You shouldn't have to do this alone."

She turned on him, twisting the spoon through the rice. "Oh, come on, Sam, don't do this. I love you, but I don't need you trying to take care of me now, too." She looked back into the pot. "You've used your family as an excuse not to live your own life for too long; I'm not going to be another one. I'm fine. I don't *need* any help right now, and I'm not going to let you ignore your own stuff on my behalf." She shook the spoon at him, smiling so that her canines showed. "I watched you do it in college for Jamie and Karen. You still do it. Go to your conference. Go have sex with Dean. You're not skipping anything for me."

Sam stepped away from her and leaned against the cold, solid, refrigerator door. "Excuse me? Laurel—I help them, I . . . it's not a burden. And I can skip the conference this weekend; it's no problem. I don't mind. Your mom's sick, and you're hurting. I want to—"

"I *know* you don't mind doing it Sam. That's your problem. You never *mind* anything. And it's always the perfect excuse not to risk doing whatever it is *you* might *actually* want to do." She stuck the spoon in her mouth and sucked it clean. Lighter than before, she tapped him twice on his chest with the handle. "You've been telling me about this thing for weeks. This session. That speaker. Just let yourself have it for once, okay? I promise I'll be fine." She stopped, looking almost giddy, as if the steam from the rice was a drug.

"God," Sam said into her satisfaction. "Fine. You win. Though, I'm not sure what all that was. . . . " He waved his hand to indicate the whole of the last few minutes. "And I'm happy, Laurel. I really, *really* am." He stepped toward her and took her free hand. "But, seriously, you need the support. I'm coming with you."

She stepped away from him, grabbed some thyme. "Thanks, honey. But you're not coming with me. Now get out of here and have a good time with Dean."

Mother and Son

Anne Metcalfe is always exhausted; on Friday nights she depends on an enthusiastic welcome from her son. When she walks through the garage door, despite the relief of air conditioning against her skin, she is disappointed when he doesn't jump up to greet her. It has been a horrific day at the office and a deadening commute home. In the car, windshield wipers ineffective against a spitting rain, she had envisioned another weekend of fighting with Karen, sharing errands and yard work with Sammy, and falling asleep and waking up alone. His lack of enthusiasm is almost more than she can bear.

Sammy is Anne's bright spot; she looks for him through the doorway like a beacon in a storm. He is where he always is, in the same spot on the brown carpet of the family room, one hand digging into Buffet's fur, nestled among his books and animals and staring at the TV.

A shrug of her purse and work papers means she needs a hug, and he comes to her dutifully, leans into her quickly, and asks how soon they can go. "Soon," she promises, "I just need to . . ."

She disengages herself and goes upstairs to pull off her pinching shoes.

In her bedroom, Anne sits heavily on the deserted plane of the bed. She has too much work to do: bills to pay, the office's annual report, and enough energy spent worrying about her kids for two parents, not one. She doesn't want to worry. Sam has very few friends, and she knows it, but he seems so content with his scrambling pets and music videos and those nature shows on TV. He doesn't seem to want any friends, and she can't really blame him. She'd been much the same as a girl. And it doesn't seem so unusual for a fourteen-year-old boy to spend Friday nights doing errands with his Mom.

When she makes it downstairs to the kitchen, Sammy is breathing heavily from his sudden rush to wash his face, crate the dog, and turn off the TV. He's so skinny, she thinks, missing her chubby little boy, and bites her cheek when she recognizes the thought. He's so tall now. The night feels unusual, and Sammy's heavy impatience is odd. She wonders if he is annoyed with her, with how much time she took. She assures herself that he's just in a rush.

Anne's older child, Karen, has transformed into a popular sixteen-year-old and is free from family obligations on Friday nights. She is always gone before Anne gets home, and her absence has become something of a relief. Sammy is so much easier. He makes more sense than her emotional, overheated girl. As she rearranges her purse and conducts a last-minute check in the fridge, however, Sam starts drumming his fingers on the counter, accompanied by a loud, impatient sigh. It is a habit he acquired from his father, the finger-drumming, and it nauseates her to see it. She swallows the painful memory it evokes and tousles his hair despite a grimace that confuses her and makes her flush. Friday night, she reassures herself, is a treat for Sam. It means a new fish for his aquarium, a new science fiction novel or comic books, dinner at McDonald's, and ice cream for dessert. It makes sense, his exasperation. He is understandably eager to go.

As they step outside, the shouts of kick ball and Marco Polo ring dully through the warm, chirping air, and the thought of summer nights and fireflies makes her think of James. It cuts the air out of her lungs. She pushes the thought down again, knowing it is the wrong thing to do. She is in denial, her therapist would say, but she needs for the past to stay away. She needs for it to be gone. And, since Sam always seems uninterested in talking about friends and his school life anyway—he shrugs and says "I dunno" and pours his hamster like a slinky between his palms—Anne goes right along. Unreadable is better than unbearable, she decides. She lets him choose the radio station in the car.

When she pulls into a spot at the grocery, Sam says he'll wait in the car. His eyes skitter to the window, avoiding her own, and she is shocked by how grown-up he looks—how much he looks like James. The baby fat is dropping off so quickly that she has the urge to grab his cheeks and hold the sweetness there.

The car smells like salt and french fries from their dinner. Anne is wearing jeans and the "Queen of the House" sweatshirt that Sam and Karen gave her at Christmas. She is in her blissfully comfortable white sneakers. They have already been to the comic shop and McDonald's, and the singing pleasure of their evening has pushed her exhaustion far to the back of her mind. The grocery will be less fun without Sam, but it is fine. She will know he's in the car.

"Sure, honey, you know you don't have to come in with me if you don't want to. Just lock the doors when I get out." I always say that, she thinks, and is about to add, "But I always say that," when Sam sighs and says, "You always say that, Mom. Lock the door, lock the door. Of course I'll lock the door. You know, we are in the suburbs, Mom. Nothing's going to happen."

She wants, for a flashing second, to tell him to shut up. She rolls her eyes and sticks out her tongue instead.

"Yes, Mr. Grown-up, I'll leave you alone," she says and, despite herself, digs at him with a tight edge to her smile, "with your comic books to sit in the car." Laughing to show she is joking, she starts to shut her door. "Do lock it though," she adds. "I'll be back in half an hour."

Anne loves the grocery on Friday night. It's like a farmhouse in the countryside, the way that as the evening blacks itself out against the night, the supermarket blazes brighter, more welcoming, more warm. The parking lot, at dusk, becomes an island of comforting motion filled with smiles and friendly faces. The night's black sky and distant stars seem banished in deference to the bright community of lights. Even the group of stores reassures her—supermarket, beauty salon, movie theater, pet shop, a Chinese restaurant and Baskin Robbins huddled protectively around a bank. They are wonderfully familiar, a map she could draw—blindfolded—on the back of her hand.

The Olde Pet Shoppe, she thinks, and stops. It is such a relief, she knows, that Sam is old enough to go to the pet store by himself and that, more often than not, he isn't all that anxious to go. It had always felt a little bit dirty there, dank and subterranean among the narrow aisles and high canyons of aquariums and cages filled with snakes and scuttling noises. It had always seemed too small and ugly and claustrophobic. It smelled. In Pennsylvania, it had been James' job to take his Sammy-boy there.

The pneumatic doors whoosh open, and the newly renovated supermarket opens itself to Anne, enveloping her in its cleanly sweet, plastic smell. Anne squares her shoulders against the onslaught of memory and reclaims her grip on the padded red handle of the shopping cart. Under the smooth wheels, the floors sparkle with light. She arranges her face into a productive smile and moves into the generous greens and yellows of the produce section. She feels safe here; the shiny abundance and reliable order of the grocery always calm her down. It lets her, for a moment, believe that life is simple and easy again, that she is simply a mom out shopping on a Friday night.

Each neat row of cereal boxes says that her husband isn't dead, that he is waiting for her and the kids at home. Each sealed jar of sweetened applesauce assures her that Karen will make it safely home. The pain of James' death still comes, duller now at least, at every unexpected time. Knocking on a cantaloupe and almost tasting its sweet summery flesh, she breathes and brightens again. I have shopping to do, she thinks, and ice cream with Sammy at the end. The thought of her son waiting in the car catches in her throat. She will treat him to anything he wants.

When she emerges from the white artificial light of the supermarket thirty-one closely marked minutes later, she feels relieved and accomplished, as if her world has been reassembled and put right. She begins to look forward to the weekend after all. At the edge of the curb, an older man with a battered green car argues with a young, blonde girl who is trying to help him lift his bags. The girl is Karen's age but doesn't have Karen's nice complexion. Anne berths her cart far from their altercation and, perching against the metal railings on the curb, takes one large paper bag on her hip and walks to the car, waving for Sam. She offers an apologetic smile to the girl who is now wiping her hands on her gray-and-red smock. When the man catches her smiling, she smiles and shrugs her shoulders at him too.

She reaches the car and knocks on the driver's-side window; Sam's head jerks up with a scowl. After leaning over to unlock her door, he carefully sleeves his comics back into their bag, and slams out of the car.

"Sam?" She asks his back.

Without responding, he jogs up to the store, grabs the three remaining bags in his fists and hauls them back by the time she has wrenched the trunk open and maneuvered her one bag in. "How did you get all those bags here so fast?" she asks, feeling discomfortingly fat, and old, and slow. She is struck by his empty grunt of an answer. He's so strong, she thinks, carrying all those bags. And he gets mad just like Jim. The weight returns to her chest. "Sam, is something wrong?"

"Can we just go get some ice cream now?" he breathes out furiously through his nose.

What is going on with him, she wonders? She wants him to stay just as he is, or was, just for a little while. Anne loves their nights. She worries, sometimes, that she gets too much out of them, that they are filling an empty space inside her, but they had always seemed so good for Sam too. He doesn't feel he has to come with me, does he? No.

She closes her car door and turns on the ignition. Sam is hunched over the slick of comic books in his lap. Twisting against the seat belt to look at him, she holds his eye and asks in a serious voice, "Samuel Metcalfe, is something wrong tonight? You're acting very angry. Are you sure you don't want us to just go home?" And then she sits, and waits, and watches Sam's face move over itself in enough directions that she wants to reach her hand across the distance and soothe his skin. "Sammy . . ."

"Mom, God! Can't I just want to read my comics? Let's get ice cream and go home. It's not like either of us has anything else to do tonight," he spits, the last few words hidden deeply under his frown.

But Sam does have other things to do tonight. His new friend Eric has invited him to the movies and a party with a group of older, cooler, football-team friends. They are all juniors or seniors, and while Sam's skin prickles and tightens every second he's with Eric, he doesn't feel comfortable going out with all the guys who had laughed at him in the hallways only days before Eric took him under his wing.

Eric and Sam had been assigned seats together in algebra, even though Eric was two years older than Sam. Their teacher, Mr. Arnold, called them a motley crew and went on to explain he expected order in his classroom, like the numbers and equations he was going to teach. Sam sweated a lot when Eric talked to him, and tried not to look at him too often, and he prayed all the time that no one could tell.

After a few weeks of laughing and doodling and flirting with the girls around them, the boys had started to consider themselves friends. Eric invited Sam to sit at his table at lunch, and Sam, trying desperately to appear nonchalant, declined. Eric's shrugged "whatever" crushed a little piece of Sam's chest, and they both turned back to the green blackboard and Mr. Arnold's chalk-covered shirt. Sam had no plans for lunch, other than the normal group of unpopular kids who sat long-legged in the hall outside the language rooms and ate bag lunches while joking about what they'd seen on TV. Sam knew his way among his friends there. Eric's crowd of muscular boys with narrow waists was too terrifying to approach without a plan. What would he say, smaller and less popular than the blue-and-gold–wearing athletes? Who would he talk to? Wouldn't they make fun of him? What if they could tell?

But they were still math buddies, and Eric continued to joke and suggest that they hang out. He started giving Sam a ride home on Tuesdays when there was no football practice, and they would do their math exercises at Burger King or in the food court at the mall. Sam loved riding next to Eric, doing math with Eric, doing anything at all with Eric. He tried hard not to notice the muscles and short blond hairs on Eric's legs when he came over, straight from practice, wearing shorts. Instead, he focused on Eric's stories about the team's game against Sherwood or Rockville and tailored his own conversation to things that Eric might want to hear. He learned, barely, to talk football. Here, just maybe, was Sam's true, forever, best friend.

So when Eric invited Sam to join his "buddies" for a movie and a party that Friday night, he had seriously thought about going. Some of the guys had started talking to him in the hallways between classes, and once he had even joined them at lunch, sitting with his elbows tucked into his ribs and sweat running down his sides from his underarms. Eric put him next to the curly-haired captain of the football team, and he stared up from his seat with reverence; they were monuments surrounding him, icons built into the side of a mountain he could never hope to scale. He wasn't scared of the movie anymore, but the party made him nervous. What if he wasn't having fun, or if other kids made fun of him? Enough people already whispered rumors behind his back. Thank God his Dad was dead so he had an excuse for being so weird. He imagined a pulsing, swirling party where the pretty girls and cool guys were all laughing with wide mouths at jokes he wouldn't understand. He imagined them laughing at him.

That Thursday at dinner, when Sam's mom asked if she could count on "her man" for their Friday night date, he had frozen for a second before mumbling, "Sure, Mom," and continuing to pick his way through the green beans on his plate. She knew he hated green beans, and he knew she wouldn't let him go to the TV until they were finished. Karen announced that she was going out with Mike Laverty (another football player, a senior) on Friday night, and Sam stumbled through thoughts of Eric, his mother, and the imagined party, while Anne and Karen cautiously negotiated whether Mike was a nice boy and what time she would have to be home.

All this fights its way through Sam's head while he sits in the Safeway parking lot with his mother, wishing he could be with Eric, not understanding why he is so furious about it all. It is a brawl between discordant body parts and his brain. Anne, for her part, simply looks away from Sammy's small outburst, releases the brake and, waving to a neighbor with her twin five-year-olds skipping in tow, pulls out of their space and into the lot's wide aisles. The car feels to Anne like it is moving sluggishly through a thick liquid, and Sam kicks rhythmically against the underside of the dashboard with his too-big, man-sized feet.

Anne pulls into a space near Baskin Robbins, puts the car in park and jerks the brake back on. "Well, I'm going in for ice cream," she tries to say with a cheerful bounce, but her nervousness and confusion have broken through. She looks at Sam's angry face and feels her own crumple in response. James is gone. Karen is flying out into the night like

95

an angry bird. And now her Sammy-boy is disappearing into his own skin and leaving her too. Sometimes she feels like she can barely breathe.

It's all too heavy, she thinks, rummaging uselessly through her purse for her wallet. She can't find her wallet. Her eyes water up, and Sammy suddenly looks scared.

"Well?" she asks, beginning to cry and laugh at the same time. It feels as if she is gargling emptiness. "I'm going to go get some ice cream. What else am I supposed to do?" Clear tears fill her lower eyelids and begin dropping onto her shirt.

And Sam can't look at her; Sam doesn't know what to do. "Sorry, Mom," he mumbles as he stares into her purse and pulls out her wallet. "I guess I'm just in a bad mood." Smiling hopefully, he places the wallet in her hand, asks her to split a sundae, and suggests that they get out of the car.

TWELVE

IN THOSE first long months of their romance, Sam consumed every moment with Dean ravenously, too thrilled with pure sensation to be afraid of falling in love. He felt like his mouth was watering all the time. Sam taped Dean's broadcasts so that they could dissect and evaluate (and rave about) them together at the end of the day, cooked elaborate meals and raved about Dean's trendy restaurants, and worried endlessly about every moment of disconnect or change in Dean's tone. Rolling mounds of monkey chow in a rusted wheelbarrow, Sam would hear a bird chirp and remember the pitch of Dean's laugh. He tried to imagine when, during his day, Dean might think of him.

A few weeks after Gwen had begun suggesting a new kind of role for Sam at the Zoo, Dean stopped by one evening after work. Sam was in pajama bottoms and a T-shirt when Dean came through his door, kissed him quickly, and pushed Sam down onto the couch.

"Guess what?" he started, pacing in front of the television, his hands fluttering like butterflies. He circled the coffee table and stretched forward to take Sam's hand. "Well? Guess what?" He was shaking with excitement and staring straight into Sam's blank, wide-open eyes. "New York called!" He crowed. "A producer in New York wants to talk to me! To me! I have an interview next week!"

Sam's mind blanked, then raced from his own neglected article to the wilted promise of his invitation to Brazil, which suddenly felt like his only hope for happiness in the world. What is it I want to escape from, he wondered, trying to ignore the question and jumping up to give Dean a kiss. New York? He needed to disengage. Quickly, he moved into the kitchen, fumbling in the cupboards, pulling out glasses and wine.

"What happened?" he managed. "You haven't mentioned New York in a while." Uncorking a green bottle, he filled his mouth with pungent, cold wine. He hoped his voice sounded light.

"I know," Dean's voice returned from the other room. "I think I've been trying not to think about it."

Sam poured Dean a glass, took another slug, and poured more wine for himself.

"After my meetings up there, you remember right when we first met, I didn't hear anything for such a long time, and my agent just kept saying we'd have to wait and see. I hadn't forgotten about it or anything, but you *can be* pretty distracting, you know. . . . "

Sam heard the last few words as he felt Dean's arms slide around his waist. Warm lips brushed his neck. Sam turned and offered him the wine, shocked and excited that Dean had already pulled off his shirt. He lightly pressed a cold glass against Dean's nipple and watched it contract. Laughing, Dean filled his mouth with the cool wine and kissed Sam deeply. Wine ran down their chins. "New York!" he cried to the ceiling. "Who knows? You've always said you wanted to see the Bronx Zoo. Maybe you'll even get to work there some day!" Dean tipped a little more wine on his chest, and Sam, distracted and wanting to feel drunk, bent down to lap the wine off his smooth, warm skin. Dean pushed Sam's head farther down, and he heard, echoing above his head, "New York!"

ON THE night of the Zoo's annual Winter Ball, a grandly soaring tent covered the Tortoise Lawn below the Great Ape House, its white spires creating a festival air. Thousands of blinking holiday lights glittered against the cold blue-black sky, and two interns, dressed up in fuzzy penguin costumes, parted a clear, heavy tarp to let the guests in. Inside, forty tables of ten, covered in white tablecloths and silver glitter, shone under candles, tall blue flower arrangements, and lights. A small orchestra in white jackets, their golden instruments flashing in the light, played easy, low music punctuated with occasional high notes. Dean, somewhere offstage, was the evening's emcee.

Sam was terribly bored. He was seated with a table of executives from a Japanese electronics corporation who had provided a majority of the funding for the Zoo's recent bid to acquire a new pair of giant pandas. Though Sam hadn't worked with the Zoo's earlier pair of pandas directly, he knew not only the animal "basics" but which fork to use for salad and the basics of making the donors feel good. His mom said that Sam was only shy and awkward inside his head.

Lisa, the panda's lead keeper, wasn't at the party that night. She identified more with animals than people and had moved over to the Great Ape House, where she spent the majority of her free time grooming her charges through heavy iron bars or sending off thick, emotional applications to work with the Jane Goodall Institute in Africa. Sam had been assigned to shepherd short, meticulously groomed Thomas Witherspoon, whose flushed, balding head and ruddy cheeks made it clear he had already had too much gin. Mr. Witherspoon, as Sam was determined to call him, directed local marketing programs for his chain of superstores and signed the all-important checks. The director of development had very frankly told Sam that he and Mr. Witherspoon *would* be a good match.

He was saved by Jack and Millie, who, as they strolled by shaking hands with older board members and some of the more eccentric donors, took possession of two empty seats at the table behind Sam. They spent most of the evening tapping him on the shoulder with comments on the outfits, the decorations, and the food. Witherspoon's smile never faltered, and he slipped his card to Sam before leaving early to escort some of the Japanese executives home. He breathed an invitation for "a nightcap" into Sam's ear. His voice was slurred with the bright, berry-tinted smell of gin, and Sam gripped his hand briefly and pushed him on his way. He was focused on Dean, gorgeous in his tuxedo, conducting the silent auction onstage.

By evening's end, over $250,000 had been raised, and Dean had pulled Sam behind a wall of tall, blue velvet curtains for a kiss.

"How'd I do?" He asked, rubbing his hands together in the cold of their tiny artificial alley against the tent's outer wall. He was flushed with excitement from the auction and proud of himself for how much money he'd managed to flirt, cajole, and guilt out of the crowd. He'd even, in a masterstroke of feigned enthusiasm, auctioned himself off to a tall, round woman in a long silver dress and more diamonds than Sam could understand, adding $2,700 to the auction's total. It was only for lunch and a tour of the studio, but Sam was a little jealous and, he had to admit, a little bit proud.

"You were amazing, honey." He gave him a fast, aggressive kiss, staking his territory despite Dean's caution about being out at the event. "I think Millie's in love with you! Everyone here is!" He punched Dean broadly on the shoulder and laughed, suddenly nervous at the mention of the word they'd carefully avoided so far. Don't say "love," he reminded himself. And less wine, he thought, wrinkling his nose.

Dean put his hands on Sam's arms, rubbing his sleeves; the fabric of his shirt was smooth against his skin. He looked Sam straight in the eyes. "Sam." It sounded as solid as a boulder in a river. It was so strong that Sam looked away.

"Sam." Dean repeated. "Sam. I love you too."

"I—"

"Now, let's get out of here, so we can—"

Jack bungled through the curtain with Millie trailing behind. He spread his arms and grabbed them both by the back of the neck. "Mr. Dean!" He shouted, prompting anxious shushing from the three people close enough to hear. Sam wanted to push Jack backward, to shove him out of the close, sacred space he had just discovered with Dean. The director was making his final, fund-raising appeal. "My boy Sam here promised we'd all go out for a drink, and my beautiful lady and I are ready to go." He looked Dean up and down and clapped him on the back. "You up for it, buddy? You think you can keep up?"

"I think I'll do all right," Dean responded, slowly. He looked to Sam with the question in his eyes: Do we give in, or do we claim the night for ourselves? At Sam's apologetic shrug, Dean turned and led the group back into the main tent. Disappointment ruled his voice. "Let's go."

Walking out of the tented pavilion, they passed through a crystal netting of white, blue, and golden lights that gave way to the sparkling, deep blue sky overhead. A valet brought Dean's car. He drove them all downtown, telling anecdotes about his show while Millie cooed and gently stroked her leather seat. Sam held Dean's hand, pulsing it regularly to tell him he appreciated his flexibility, that he loved him too, that they would have each other, *just* each other, soon enough. Jack napped in the back. At Kramerbooks they hunched over comically towering glasses of liquored coffee and laughed about the lousy service and bright Hawaiian shirts that defied the dark, cold night. Through the glass awning above them, dancing pinpricks of light resolved themselves into snow.

Dean loved him. It was all Sam could think about as the verbal games spun around the table. He loves me, he repeated, tasting the words like chocolate or honey. He loves me. Dean had said it first. And now, here they were, a happy, successful couple, sharing a night with the closest thing Sam had to a dad. He felt a warm light bloom inside of him and held his breath when he felt the happy sting in his eyes. He didn't cry, he knew, though maybe, with this man, he might start to learn how. They drove Jack and Millie home, laughing all the way. Standing on their tiny lawn with Dean waiting in the car, Sam kissed Millie good-bye and accepted her demand that he visit them on Christmas. It felt like a family. He'd have to tell his Mom.

Back in the warm cocoon of the car, Dean was chuckling to himself.

"What's so funny?" Sam asked, wanting to burrow deep inside Dean's thoughts.

"Nothing," he replied, taking Sam's hand like a bear cub's paw and padding it between his own.

"No, what?" Sam continued, leaning in and smiling up at Dean from where he nuzzled into his neck. He breathed in the smell of Dean's slight sweat and paler cologne. Oranges in November. He could breathe his Dean for days.

"It's just, I have to laugh at them a little bit," he explained.

Sam looked up at him. "Who?"

"Jack and Millie," Dean began, becoming more animated as he mimicked Millie's wide-eyed stare and bobbling head in his backseat. He started laughing about her awe at his leather interior, their level of amazement at the "unusual" menu items, their lack of vision and knowledge of world events. "Did you see the look on her face when I mentioned the elections? It's like she thinks the world takes place entirely between her kitchen and Jack's little office at the Zoo." When he finished speaking, he chuckled for another minute, leaning against the window. His forehead left a soft, round print on the glass.

"Are you drunk?" Sam wanted it to sound mean.

"Huh? No. Was I— I'm sorry, Sam." He turned toward Sam and put a hand on his leg. "Was that mean of me?" He ran a hand through his hair. "I guess, maybe I'm jealous?"

Sam waited for more.

"I don't know, this just felt like a big night for us, and then to have to spend the whole evening *entertaining* them, when I could've been alone with just you. . . ."

Sam's mind tore through the reasons that Dean's statements weren't as dismissive as they sounded. Dean toyed with his keys, and the car's heater ticked incessantly; finally Sam punched it off. "Cute," he focused on the word. Dean said they were cute. And he just said he was angry because he wanted to be alone with me. Sam was torn. He needed to believe that Dean liked Jack and Millie, that he enjoyed them and their straightforward view of the world. Still, some lizard instinct in Sam was rising up, resisting the easy explanations, wanting to make a point. Fearing that anger, Sam cast about for something to focus on; he looked at Dean's still-beautiful face, out the window at the cold night, at his own hand in Dean's hand, for another way to see.

"But you like them, don't you?"

"Like them? Of course I like them. I mean, let's not go out with them every night, but— It's like visiting your grandparents or something: There's a lot to learn, but, small doses, you know? And I swear, back in the tent, I just wanted you so badly. . . . "

Sam breathed out, relieved to be back on safer ground. He kissed Dean's neck quickly, flicking his tongue. The realization that Dean had told him he loved him struck him like a thunderclap giving way to blue skies. Like peace. Dean loved him. The world was what he needed it to be.

"We'll have lots of time alone," Sam promised as he stroked the soft veins on the back of Dean's hand. "It's just, you know how important Jack is to me, and they were so excited for us. I just didn't want to let them down."

"I know, honey. It's kind of the best and the most frustrating part of who you are. But tonight, Sam," he asked very seriously, "what would *you* have wanted to do if you weren't worried about Jack's feelings? Can you even separate what you want from what everyone else wants you to do?" As he parked the car, Dean leaned in and kissed Sam, hard and intensely, pushing his tongue, for just a second, into Sam's mouth. "Be a little selfish, OK? It's allowed."

Sam wanted to tell Dean that selfishness didn't work. But the taste of Dean was strong, and the flood of Dean's attention was too powerful to resist. They could talk about life and living it later. For now, he'd take all he could have of tonight.

"I love you too, Dean," he said quietly.

A thin line of cold broke the sanctity of the heated car, racing down Sam's neck and raising goose bumps on his skin. He traced the running veins on the back of Dean's hands, laced their fingers together for warmth. "I really, really do."

THIRTEEN

LAUREL TOOK a long, cool drink—yellow lemonade in a thick blue glass—and tried to swallow down the careening exuberance of life six months ago. She needed a little bit of last summer to get her through the phone call she was about to make. She closed her eyes to dial.

"Emily? It's Laurel. What's up?" She made her voice direct and no-nonsense; she had no strength to carry Emily's determined chitchat today.

"You got my message, right?" Emily started. "Laurel, Mom got lost today." A tumbling crash came through the phone, and Laurel had a flashing image of bright, primary-color toys in a pile with Emily's girls. Emily had redone her kitchen in a beautiful, impractical tile that had proven irresistible to socks on tiny feet. Laurel smiled as she heard her older sister shout "Katie! Ina! Ellie! Calm down! Now set the table for lunch," through fingers that covered the phone. She imagined her three suddenly serious nieces marching around the table, balancing plates and clutching silverware in their hands. The image distracted her, and for a single, peaceful moment she was in the kitchen setting the table with the three little girls.

"Lost?" Laurel righted herself. "How lost? Where lost? Emily, what do you mean?"

The restaurant's accounting program was pulsing insistently with the news that she needed to borrow money again, but she looked away and forced optimism into her throat with another gulp of lemonade. Mom would be fine. She was going home tomorrow, and again for the holidays, she was shutting Terra for Christmas weekend. There was nothing more for her to do.

"She got lost on her way to church, Laurel. She's driven that route ten thousand times."

Laurel felt the weight of a heavy seat belt settle across her five-year-old chest. It was true that their mother had been driving to the same stone church, only ten minutes and four turns from their front door, for over thirty years. Laurel knew those green and leafy roads by heart, remembered climbing in the sprawling cherry tree in the church's playground. Her mother knew that church and their neighborhood like the freckles on her own, or her daughter's, hands. For her to have lost the way was so sad.

"Laurel?"

She was cradling her drink above her chest, and her nose had dipped into its cup. The chalky lemon scent flashed her back to the bright endless summers in that leafy churchyard, in her own backyard, always with her mother as constant and affirming as the sun. When she swallowed again, the optimism was gone. It was as if she was being torn inside, as if her flesh and blood were wet dough being folded and stretched too thin.

"So, what then?" She asked, pushing the words through a thick mist of memories. She held her breath for a second, not wanting to ask what came next. "What do you need me to do?"

———————

SO WHEN Dean called from the studio, explaining in his typical, conspiratorial shorthand that he had a secret request, Laurel was actually relieved. Dean had been invited to a New Year's Eve party in Georgetown, he explained, by some "dear, dear friends," and wanted to take Sam. He hoped Laurel and Sam's long-standing dinner and fireworks tradition could be amended "just this once." Laurel had agreed, surprisingly glad to have an excuse to drop the routine for a while. She needed the income anyway, and a last-minute request for a private party, received just a week before, was too great an opportunity to pass up.

Something in Dean's voice affected Laurel as well. It was clear—as he explained that things felt a little bit strange going into the holidays and that he wanted to do something truly special for Sam—that Dean was deeply and confusingly in love. She wanted love too, despite how impossible everything felt these days, and couldn't bear it when Dean told her that Sam seemed to be listening to a soundtrack he couldn't quite hear.

And he sounded so grateful when she agreed. He wanted, he promised, to show Sam how special things were for them right now and how special their lives together could be. One of the party's hosts was also a scientist, a professor at American University, and Dean was hoping to give Sam a glimpse into a few more potentially satisfying options for his career and life. He loved how grounded Sam was, he explained, loved the simple focus on each day, the strong, working man's body that shoveling and carrying had shaped in Sam's flesh, but he could also see that Sam was stifled at the Zoo and in his life.

Laurel stopped him here, refusing to be drawn in. She felt a bit like she was being "sold" on something, that Dean was pitching her for approval of some unspecified, grander plan.

"I'll help you manage New Year's," she confirmed, "and I think you are completely sweet. But I won't talk about Sam behind his back. He'll figure things out."

Dean apologized, and somehow they agreed that Sam and Dean would be at Terra for a midnight toast and that Laurel would be the one to "officially" change the plans.

"Great, Laurel," Dean finished. "That's perfect. This way Sam won't have to choose."

FOURTEEN

FROM THE vantage of a creamy leather banquette in a high-end Cuban restaurant downtown, Sam was trying to make his family life make sense. He carefully reexplained the many quirks of personality and history to Dean, disclosed long-standing tensions and ties, and felt terribly disloyal but even happier to have this new refuge. Smooth, syncopated music surrounded them, and they were sheltered by artificial palms. Things had felt nearly perfect for weeks.

"So it's not that they're crazy, crazy," Sam clarified, punctured by a pang of guilt. The smells of butter and grilling fish ghosted in sheets around the room. Dean still hadn't met his family, and his excuses, like Sam's strange reluctance to introduce them, dug at him like a rusty spoon. Dean wouldn't come for Christmas, had his own stern family in Michigan to attend to, and Sam was trying to keep everything light. He wanted to enjoy the freedom of putting himself first, *was* loving being lost in Dean, but he still needed to protect his family a little bit. Calling them crazy wasn't fair. They just sometimes needed him to help steer an even course. He altered his approach.

"But you know how holidays are never perfect?"

Dean shrugged.

"At least, they're only perfect in teensy moments?" Sam thought of his mother's adoring expression at the concert they had taken her to a few years ago, or the time Jamie, eleven and newly bored by everything, actually jumped up and down over a new silver mountain bike. "You know, like the smell of cinnamon rolls when you walk in the door?" Sam offered, watching Dean's mouth for a smile.

"Or driving around in the car and looking at the neighbors' Christmas lights?"

"Yeah! Exactly. Anyway, we always had a hard time with Christmas since my dad died, but we *always* did Christmas at our house—my mom's house—until two years ago, when Karen and David bought their big house in Bethesda." Sam paused as Dean nodded for the waiter to pour him more wine. "So now there's all these weird tensions between Mom and Karen about who does what and who's"—he gave the next phrase finger-parenthesized quotes—"the keeper of the holiday flame or something." Sam paused to admire the appetizers, thank the waiter, and feel the warmth rising off his soup.

"Yummy." Dean looked expectantly at the food.

"So anyway," Sam resumed, waiting for Dean to look up at him again, "my sister makes this big deal about how in her house they celebrate this sort of quasi-Hanukkah now and how Christmas morning will really just be about me and Mom—my mom, of course, hits the roof about traditions, and they've both been trying to get me to take sides for weeks—and . . . "

Dean's fork rang onto the china. "Hanukkah? I didn't know you were Jewish." He took an anticipatory sip of wine.

"I'm not," Sam laughed. "I know, a typical mid-Atlantic melting pot. I'm not Jewish, but David—Karen's husband—is, and my mom was raised Jewish and wasn't really actively anything until she met my dad, so it's—" he paused again, taking a mouthful of soup, trying to swallow a strange annoyance at having to explain his father's death. He didn't like dwelling on it; it was enough to remember his father throwing him, over and over again, into the sparkling blue water of the pool. Happy as the memories were, they still hurt. Sam tried to push them away.

"I'm just so WASPy, you know?" Dean asked, twirling his fork.

"Anyway, Mom is really . . . well, she doesn't even think of herself as Jewish anymore. We never did anything Jewish growing up. Christmas tree. Christmas decorations. Christmas dinner. Like your family, the whole driving around to look at decorations thing." He looked to Dean for approval. "My mom says the Jewish stuff reminds her too much of the past. I think she doesn't want to have to deal with how it makes her feel."

In truth, Sam's mother had never fully explained to her children why she pushed her Judaism so far into her unspoken past. They had never seen any evidence of it, other than in blurry pictures of a thin, tightly smiling woman who looked vaguely like their mom and the tarnished menorah that stayed in a box in the attic with some old crystal that rarely came out. It was as if she had simply erased her past with repetitive motions: washing and folding it into a never-ending pile of clothes, punching out its flavor with endless slices of toast, rinsing it out with the gray she dyed out of her hair. He wondered about Dean's family, the way he never spoke about it. Sam knew enough to realize that they hadn't ever fully accepted that Dean was gay. Sam looked into his soup again, pushing around the heavy, sweet chunks of lobster, saving them until the end.

"So, Karen has really gone off the deep end now that she has this house. Even though they mostly actually celebrate on Christmas morning, the whole place is white and blue with lights and a huge menorah and that salty smell of latkes cooking?" Dean's face went blank, so Sam moved on. "I mean, it's like when she had Jamie—who still hasn't decided about Roosevelt, by the way—she thought she'd lose everything she wanted for herself, and now, instead, she's got everything—perfect husband, perfect house, perfect religion. Perfect life." He took another bite.

"So . . ." Dean followed up, "then it would be all right if I came to 'perfect' Christmas at 'perfect' Karen's after all?" He dropped the question like a treat to a dog.

Sam froze, and a flush of panic rose along his neck where excitement should have been. He imagined himself smiling but pushed another piece of lobster into his mouth just in case. He *was* smiling. It felt good, even though a part of him wanted to be annoyed. Weeks before, Sam had invited Dean to spend Christmas with him. He had mentioned it as an aside, assuming that Dean would be working Christmas morning, so when Dean had declined for *family* reasons rather than work, disappointment and relief had colored his mood through the whole exchange. Now that

Dean suddenly wanted to come to Christmas, the idea was thrilling. It terrified him too.

"Really?"

Would they all get along? What if Dean changed his mind again? Sam couldn't know. He needed to know. But he knew he wanted Dean there.

"Dean! That's great!" He was holding his knife and fork upright, like bookends to his plate. "What happened? You said your mother would never let you miss a year in Gross Pointe."

A sour look passed over Dean's face at the mention of his mother, but he recovered quickly. "I got a great slot doing a special 'year in review' program all day on Christmas Eve and can't make it home for Christmas morning, so it doesn't make any sense to go." Sam knew not to push for more; Dean was from an old Michigan family with protocols and expectations extending back hundreds of years, so his decision not to go home might mean something more. Despite Dean's claims that his family accepted him for who he was and that all was well at the McAllister house, the few vestiges of homophobia he nurtured seemed to come directly from his mother's need for everything to appear just so. When Dean's mother had been in town a few weeks ago for a meeting of a charity's board, Sam had conspicuously *not* been invited to meet her.

He wanted to press Dean for more information, but the dinner was so nice, the light so warm, and Dean's desire for happiness so strong that Sam decided to sit back and accept the happy news. Maybe Laurel was right, and he ignored things too easily. But he was certain that happiness couldn't possibly be a bad goal. Sam wanted to puzzle on the question more, but Dean was there, and his presence pushed all the other questions away.

"I do have to work that afternoon," Dean continued. "But I thought that, maybe, I could drive you out to your sister's on Christmas morning," he leaned in farther with a conspiratorial smile, "after I've had you for Christmas all by myself." He took Sam's hand, and the warmth shot through his body. Sam was suddenly very aware of the fabric of his pants and the texture of the table's cloth drapes. Dean was smiling now, looking like a tiny predator that has killed something and brought it freshly, proudly, home.

———————

LATE ON Christmas Eve, when Dean crawled into bed after midnight, Sam pretended to be asleep. The sheets were so warm, and the gust of air when Dean lifted the sheets felt so cold. Sam waited for Dean to spoon into him, to feel Dean's kiss on his neck. But for a minute he only heard Dean lying there, rubbing his hands together, warming them, before he reached over, sliding his warmed hands around Sam's chest, and breathing "I love you" into his ear.

———————

THEY WOKE early, with thin clear light sliding through the shades, rising from sleep quietly, and kissing with the warmth of morning between them. For once, Dean didn't jump out of bed to brush his teeth. "Merry Christmas." His long fingers stroked Sam's cheek. "I love you." Sam managed to whisper "I love you" in return.

Too quickly, however, Sam's anxiety returned. Dean idled in the car while Sam ran into his apartment and awkwardly gathered a tray of powdered sugar brownies and three shopping bags full of artfully wrapped gifts, carefully pointing out which ones Sam had bought for Dean to present as his own. Dean scoffed, but also thanked Sam. He twisted his keys on their ring and pointed at the two bouquets in the back seat. "So there's something for Jamie, then? Good. I know they'll like the flowers, but I didn't have time to get them anything more personal on my own."

The Christmas sky hung flat and white above them, looking like an empty tablecloth stretched taut above his street. The silence in the car, like the skies above, was tight with swollen air, and, as soon as they'd cleared the lights of Dupont Circle, Sam exploded with a breathless, apologetic list of warnings and instructions about what Dean should expect for the day. Dean didn't interrupt the river of explanations until Sam directed him onto Karen's street and pointed out her house at the head of the block. He pulled over half a block away.

"Dean, there's plenty of parking in front of her house." Sam was pointing to her front driveway, not looking at Dean, showing him the obvious space to park. When he turned to look at Dean, Dean started speaking very slowly, looking Sam directly in the eye. His hands were massaging the steering wheel, holding on as if for life.

"Sam, I need to ask you something," he began, the seriousness of his voice freezing Sam to his seat. Icicles frosted the windows of the cars parked on either side. "I need you to understand that this is hard for me too." When he paused, Sam could see his Adam's apple working quickly, as if hundreds of words were fighting a battle in his throat and the majority were dying there before he let them out. "You know that I still have some problems with putting the whole 'gay' and 'family' things together, and today, I'm going to need you to . . . to not ask so much of me."

But you're the one who said you wanted to come, Sam thought. He picked with determination at the leather of his seat, hoping to leave a welt.

"Sam, are you listening to me?" Dean went on. "This is going to be hard enough for me as it is."

Despite wanting to know just why Dean had brought this up now, on Karen's street, with nothing but the dead end of her house in front of them, Sam could feel how nervous Dean was and knew his own nervousness had contributed to the uncomfortable mood. He decided it was easier to agree.

"You're right, honey. I just want today to be perfect for everyone, and I want them to like you, and for you to like them," he added in a hurry. "So I was, I guess, just trying to—"

"Control the situation?" Dean pushed.

Sam didn't know how to respond, but his whole family was waiting thirty feet away, so he decided to ignore it instead.

"Yeah, I guess so." Sam's jaw felt tight, as if he had been biting down on tin. "Come on, they'll be waiting for us. Just relax, you can play video games with Jamie or talk current events with David. Or do nothing. They're nice people; the gifts I had you get them are perfect." He regretted the choice of words. "It'll be fun." Sam reached over and kissed Dean and was surprised by how urgently Dean kissed him back. It was as if this moment in the car was some kind of lifeboat in a storm. "You'll be fine," Sam repeated as they pulled slowly into Karen's driveway. And, attempting to absorb all of Dean's fear, he made a promise to himself that, even if he had to sustain the whole celebration through sheer force of will, he would make it so.

Outside the car, the air was cold enough to sting the hair inside Sam's nose, and the grass of the lawn made silvery crunches under their feet. A woven wooden reindeer stood welcome by the door, and a lush berry wreath added to the rustic look. The reindeer wore a blue ribbon with silver bells, and the wreath had blue and white lights. Apparently, where religious devotion was concerned, decorating necessities were an acceptable exemption.

Dean whistled, "Martha Stewart lives!"

A bird feeder hung by the front window, and two cardinals fought over bountiful seeds. Sam knew that Karen loved having the birds around the house. The window over her sink had three ornamental feeders filled at all times. Oddly relieved by the thought, he stepped back so that Dean could ring the bell, and they were overtaken by a confusion of welcomes, color, and noise. Karen hugged them both with strong arms, David called out a rough welcome from the living room couch, and Sam's mother edged forward, out of place in her red-and-green sweater, uncomfortable at not being the host. Sam loved his mom: her short, curly hair, the roundness of her cheeks, her shining eyes. It was like walking into daylight after hours in the dark; everything glowed with an intensity of happiness and joy. Dean stood in the door, still partly in the frozen outside, with an unblinking smile on his face. Sam reached out and tugged him inside.

They moved as a group from the stone-tiled foyer into Karen's soaring living room, filled with overstuffed leather furniture and adorned with both family photos (of Sam's small family and David's larger, happily unruly one) and abstract landscapes in soft, natural tones. The artist, a friend of Karen's from her office, had painted them specifically for the house. A massive river-stone fireplace anchored the room. And their mother's tarnished silver menorah sat centered on the mantle. Its renewed place of honor seemed fitting after the years it had spent in a closet while they grew up. He kissed Karen quickly, whispering into her ear that the menorah looked "right."

"Mom says it's vestigial," Karen whispered back, flashing a false grin at their mother who was walking, with her arms folded around Jamie's chest, out of the kitchen. "I swear, she's been picking at me all morning— you know she practically insisted on sleeping over last night so we could all wake up together, then changed her mind at the last minute—and since she's been here, since 8 a.m. mind you, she's been making constant, constructive," Karen hooked her fingers into quotes, "comments about how everything I've done is 'nice,' or 'fine.' But definitely wrong." Their mother passed back into the kitchen, running a soft hand along Sam's cheek as she went.

Embarrassed, Sam rubbed his sister's shoulders and ran his fingers through her hair. "I know, sweetie. But, remember, this is hard on her. She's out of her element, still. And don't worry, I talked to her last night, and I'm going over there tomorrow morning for breakfast while Dean's at work." He turned her to face him. "We're going to just have cinnamon rolls and coffee and pretend that everything's the way it's always been."

Karen gave him a withering look.

"No, it's fine. I'm actually looking forward to it. Besides, you'll be at David's parents, Dean has to be at the mall at something like 5 a.m., and—"

"Right. Sam to the rescue once again. Thank you." She kissed his cheek and walked into the kitchen, leaving Sam to seek out Dean. Naturally, he was doing a wonderful job, having offered dueling flower arrangements to Sam's mother and sister, made a joke about "missing the game" to David, and tossed the Sam-provided "belated Hanukkah" present immediately to Jamie at his new perch on the couch. Sam held back, watching his family examine Dean like a school of fish circling and testing an unfamiliar morsel that might or might not be food. Luckily, Dean wasn't famous enough to make people nervous. Sam had already learned that Dean only had the don't-I-know-you kind of fame, rather than the kind that made crowds press around you on the street. He took a seat next to Jamie, who had already torn open the new video game Dean had thrown him, and with an arm around his nephew, watched his boyfriend make his way.

Sam spent most of the afternoon leaning against the kitchen island's marble countertop, watching Karen wipe up after people and surveying the bounty of their world. A whole turkey's worth of assorted cold cuts, six or seven cheeses, and various rolls and breads from the local deli dominated the offerings, surrounded by plates of green cut vegetables, potato pancakes, noodle kugel, and the tower of Sam's brownies that received more regular, return attention than the rest of the items combined. The food pilgrimage brought everyone to Sam's side at least once, and he felt a warm sweetness rise inside him as his family catalogued Dean for him like a visitor from a foreign tribe.

"God, he's handsome," Karen offered, weighing two carrots against a brownie in her hands. "A little slick," she added, knocking her shoulder against Sam. He could feel how soft her black sweater was, knew it probably cost more than any piece of clothing he owned. "But you know me; you know I like things to look good." She sighed through her smile, popping the carrots into her mouth and pushing the brownie at Sam. He could see something working itself out in his sister.

Sam started to respond but was interrupted by Jamie sliding across the tiled floor in his socks. Karen collared him and extricated two of the four brownies he had grabbed from his hands. "And I'm sure this one will come around too," she added, pulling him in for a hug.

"Dean's cool, Uncle Sam," Jamie offered up from where his head nested in the crook of his mother's arm. "I've beaten him at Tetris five times, and he still wants to play." Karen released him with a swat, and he ran back to the living room and the couch where Dean remained.

She watched her son with what looked like a painful kind of love. Sam leaned forward until he could catch Dean's eye.

"He's got you hooked, doesn't he?"

"Of course. I mean, yeah, I love him. And he's into me too, which I love." He poked her in the ribs. "I mean, it's still new, but he's just so, so . . ."

Sam stopped, suddenly worried that the only words he could summon were *handsome, interesting,* and *smart.* He looked at Karen for a moment, trying to come up with the right thing to say, despite a terrifying blank space where the words to describe his happiness should have been. He drummed his fingers on the countertop, as, unbidden like a red fish swimming in a black sea, came the words *hungry, selfish, arrogant,* and *mean.* He stuttered out, "We're good."

"Really?" Karen asked, leaning forward and popping a brownie into her mouth like a guilty child and never taking her eyes off of Sam's. "You're rubbing that bald thumb of yours again, you know." She nodded at his hand, which he guiltily stilled. "Always an . . . interesting sign." She grabbed another brownie and muttered something about it not being time for New Year's resolutions yet. "So . . . you're . . . good." She raised an eyebrow, caught him with a smile.

"Yes, *good,*" he repeated, pinching her shoulder to distract her. Knowing the game, he asked for a tour of the master bathroom she'd just had redone.

FIFTEEN

TWENTY-FOUR LITTLE girls shuffled and skipped in a ragged line across the stage on Christmas Eve in Pennsylvania, the spotlights on their open faces and white tights the only brightness in the dark room. The auditorium's stage looked dark and waxy under their feet. Two of Laurel's nieces were there, six and four, their blonde, staticky hair swinging with the enthusiasm of their voices. They were like sugary cookie cutouts, the little girls in their matching red dresses, white tights, and shiny black shoes. Laurel was amazed at how many of them were blonde, remembered just how white her life had been growing up. She thought of Don, the surprisingly handsome fruit purveyor she had agreed to have dinner with after the holidays, and of the quiet rented-movies and single-partridge dinner she could have cooked at home. Laurel felt the weight of Emily's eyes as they sat together in the third row. She had missed the last two concerts because of the restaurant. Her eyes misted up, and the girls blurred.

Laurel grabbed her mother's hand and squeezed as the girls finished *Silent Night*, their falsetto tones fading quickly away. The song's seriousness turned the girls' bodies to stone, little red bells on white pegs, motionless except for gaping mouths and moving necks. They looked like goldfish on linoleum, gasping for air.

"They look like baby birds," she whispered into her mother's ear. She wanted a smile from her mother and added, "Look at their little mouths move." Her mother nodded in response without looking at her, and the pearls at her ears and throat caught what little light there was in the room, highlighting the straight carriage of her neck. Laurel touched her own string of pearls. "Hungry little birds," her mother responded a moment later, singing quietly to herself, as if Laurel weren't even there.

After the concert and back in her mother's house, jumpy from the many sweets of the day, Laurel's mind would not rest. She was vibrating with excitement and confusion. She thought of the monuments lit for the holidays, how Molly's parents would be doing in her apartment while she was away, how Sam and Dean were doing, or Miguel. She wondered how soon she could go home. She tried to keep her mother awake for a while, offering to make tea and toast, begging a last game of Hearts.

Her mother began repeating "bedtime, bedtime" as she walked up the stairs, and Laurel realized that, with this visit, her mother's bedtime was earlier than her own. Her stomach was sick with it. She turned on her mother's bedside lamp, laid open the blankets, helped her mother unbutton her blouse, and turned her eyes while she changed. Her mother was thankful, awkwardly so, and the purity of her appreciation embarrassed Laurel. Confusion at the state of things, and the exhaustion of travel and sitting in a hot gymnasium attacked her all at once, pummeling her face until she could barely hold open her eyes. If only someone else were here, she thought, I could run out and see a midnight movie and get out of here, just for a while.

Instead, she headed downstairs to the kitchen, shaking her head for clarity and telling herself she was being foolish. She realized she'd only been home a day, that her mother was mostly fine tonight, just the slightest bit confused. God, she realized heavily, this is just a sliver of what's to come. Through the windows she could see a cold blue night outside. Crossing the open floor, she stepped silently up to the sliding door and leaned her forehead on the cold glass. She wanted to put her tongue to it, imagined it would taste sweet.

Turning back, she ran her hands along the heavy counters and reached up to touch the hanging pots, remembering the feel and weight of each one, of learning to cook there with her father. A different kitchen, before her father's grand gift of a total remodeling on her parents' twenty-fifth anniversary. The smaller kitchen where she would sit with legs dangling from a bar stool and watch her father dance while he cooked. He would move slowly and calmly, likening his cooking to the chemistry he taught at the university. As Laurel grew taller and became a chef herself, the scene reversed, and—she could see it now—her father would sit heavily in his chair with an untouched glass of wine, watch her cook, and listen to her theories on culinary alchemy. She remembered him laughing and joking with Sam.

Static shocked off a heavy pot, and she realized how cold her fingers were. With a sudden burst of speed she began opening cupboards and cabinets, peering into the light of the refrigerator to check the availability of butter and eggs and milk. Pulling heavy canisters of sugar and flour onto the counter and ringing them with constellations of butter and eggs, she began to combine ingredients furiously, pausing only to reach out an arm and turn the oven on to bake. She needed the heaving warmth of cooking, the baking oven, the mixing ingredients, the heat of the warming muscles in her arms and hands. Like a reverse corkscrew, the steady motions of her twisting wrists unclenched the knots in her shoulders and neck. A quick check of the lazy Susan revealed an unopened bag of semisweet chocolate chips, and her course was set. She added salt and brown sugar, cracked the eggs into the shifting mass, and mixed.

After dolloping the cookie dough onto the slick metal sheet, she opened the warm, orange oven and slid the cookies inside. She felt her exhaustion return. She was standing in her mother's kitchen at one in the morning with an hour of baking yet to go. Looking through the tiny window into the clicking oven, she wished for a moment that she could just climb inside.

———

TWO HARRIED but uneventful days later, it was already time to go home.

Low mounds of snow shone like individual lamps on her mother's lawn. Christmas's wild, tearing energy was over, and the family was packed up and going home until the next occasion, or crisis, rallied them all together again. Laurel and her mother stood in the arched, wooden doorway, waving as Emily's tarnished green Volvo wagon backed slowly out of the driveway. Watching her sister's car (laden with children and husband, toys, extra clothes, and a worn, almost abandoned car seat for Ellie), Laurel could almost hear the "beep, beep, beep" of one of Terra's delivery trucks negotiating the alley downtown. It made her glad that Christmas was over and that she herself was going home.

Before getting in the car, Emily had grabbed Laurel and demanded that her little sister call her immediately upon getting on the road. "Call me the minute you're out of her sight," she instructed. "I want to know what you think." She had squeezed Laurel's arm at this, significantly, and looked deeply into Laurel's eyes. Laurel knew that tactic; she knew Emily didn't really want her thoughts. She knew that Emily and Charlotte had been talking without her, and she suspected that they had decided that she was the sister most likely to give up her whole life and move back here and take care of Mom. Knew that they saw her as the sister with the least to give up.

Laurel realized that she was having the whole debate in her head, spitting the thoughts out angrily, as if they were the bitter roots of some medicine she knew that, despite significantly doubting the cure, she was forcing herself to eat. A biting wind tossed through the trees, and her light sweater was useless against the cold. The air and her lips were dry.

Inside—she had to shut the door firmly against the wind—she could hear her mother moving around in the bedroom upstairs. Laurel dipped into the hall bathroom for some lotion before heading upstairs to grab her things. They were planning a "ladies lunch" downtown before Laurel left, and if they were going to eat before meeting her mother's ride home, they needed to get out of the house. As she walked up the stairs, hips moving from side to side, she felt her own hands moving against each other. They were smooth and greased with the lotion and smelled like her mother. She stopped briefly on the stairwell and watched herself rub the lotion into the backs of her hands, in between the fingers. She pulled extra lotion from the valley of her thumb. They could be her mother's hands, she realized; they weren't so different after all.

"Honey? Is that you? Are you coming up?" her mother called, breaking Laurel's mid-step reverie. After three days together, it was as if the specter of Alzheimer's had been pushed back beyond the waterline, and they were safe, temporarily, on a dune of dry sand. Laurel knew it would shift and flow now, knew the disease's relentless, windy power would obliterate any attempt by the family or doctors, or her mother, to halt its shifting advance. But for that brief holiday window, it felt as if her mother wasn't disappearing at all. Like she was still Mommy, who could fix any problem, kiss away any pain.

"Laurel—are you OK? Do you need any help?" Her mother was leaning her head into the stairwell, looking down on her stalled daughter from a haloed height. Laurel felt her eyes well up with water and let her eyelashes hold the tears.

"Yeah, Mom, some help would be great."

SIXTEEN

JACK AND Millie's house was a faded bungalow a few blocks from the busy 16th Street corridor just inside the Maryland line. Settled into its neighborhood of immigrants and working poor, their small, formerly blue one-story looked weathered from years in a gentle sun. It was hunkered down now in its bare brown lawn against the cold, but a festive, plastic Santa stood waving from the front step. Sam had offered to bring over a belated Christmas dinner since Millie was under doctor's orders to stay in bed, and Dean had long since left to host a "Christmas Moviegoers" special from the sprawling Potomac Mills mall. He felt an uncomfortable pride driving up in Dean's car.

Laurel had talked Sam through gourmet versions of turkey, stuffing, and sweet potatoes, and he had purchased a honey-baked ham the day before. When he had called her in a panic the night before, she laughed at his squeamishness in stuffing the bird and asked if he was this much of a wimp when assisting the vets at the Zoo. "Besides, Sam," she offered, clearly relishing the opportunity to make him squirm, "as a gay man, shouldn't this sort of thing be old hat by now?" Knowing she would forgive him, he had taken that moment to firmly hang up the phone. Staring into the turkey's gaping cavity, he had pushed and squeezed himself through what he found to be a very uncomfortable act.

The concrete walk to their door was skimmed with patches of ice, and Sam followed its narrow path across the front lawn precariously, laden with bags of food. He rang the bell with a holly wreath welcome mat under his feet.

Millie answered the door. She had been thin and wrinkled as long as Sam had known her, but seeing her that morning was still a shock. She was like a newborn stork made of wrinkled pink skin and long, poorly fitted bones. Two heavy-faced cats peered up from behind her ankles, where her green stretch pants tucked into tan orthopedic shoes, and her tiny face was capped with golden blonde curls that had to be a wig. Sam stood very still in her sight and tried to smile. Millie shamed him with an unwavering grin and a hug that proved she still had strength in her arms. She smelled sweet, from perfume, and embalmed—Sam didn't know exactly why—and a powder clouded off her when they hugged.

Inside, the air was warm and still; although the surfaces were spotless, a thin veil of dust hung suspended in shafts of light throughout the front room. The wood paneling and retroactively modern furniture gave it the feel of a dollhouse from the 1970s or a display of "future living" Sam had watched rotate before him at Disney World as a kid. Jack pulled Sam out of Millie's hug and clapped him on the shoulder, shouting "Merry Christmas" and waving a short glass of whiskey in his hand, the Christmas tree lights reflected in the amber glass. Jack had a second glass already poured, and he handed it to Sam, watching while Sam took a first drink. Coughing out a "thank you" while Millie led them all to the small kitchen table, Sam set down the bags and trays of food and excused himself to get the small turkey out of the car.

The cold outside their door stung Sam's eyes, and his breath frosted the air. In his hurry to pull the turkey from the car, Sam noticed a few drops of brown grease fall onto the leather seat. A flash of panic hit him in the chest—Dean's car!—but he refused to let it stick. Sam approached the grease as he would a skittish animal; he focused on maintaining his breath and moving slowly. Gently, carefully, he wiped the brown drips off the seat with his finger. After a moment, he caught himself saying aloud—to the car or to himself he wasn't sure—that everything was going to be all right. He tasted the salty grease on his finger and focused on how much Jack and Millie would enjoy their dinner. He refused to notice the bare, pale rings the drops had left behind.

Jack and Millie had already prepared the table when Sam returned, and they were warming the stuffing in the oven. The windows were beginning to bloom with fog. Millie was using a shining aluminum walker to move around the kitchen, punctuating the carols on the radio with tiny, rubbery squeaks. The rounded feet of her walker created a vague, artful distortion of scuffed gray half-moons on the floor. Sam busied himself pulling foil off the turkey, watching Jack and Millie move. Her arms where they poked from her thin red blouse were tiny, and they had a bluish color despite the kitchen's almost stifling warmth. Through the clothes her body looked like a skeleton made of straw. Jack moved solidly around her, doing nothing productive in the world except making sure his Millie was all right.

When they were seated, Millie immediately began asking for updates since the Winter Ball last month. She asked thoughtful, pointed questions about Dean and Sam's family, his hopes and dreams and daily business. Slowly, she began to tell him more about her own life: her sickness, how much she worried about Jack, their daughter Melissa's new job. Jack nodded his assent when he agreed with her, warned her with his eyes when she was pushing Sam too much, and ate his way through half the turkey himself. Millie was the family cook, and they were clearly eating to her diminished diet, not Jack's. Sam found himself leaning farther and farther over the table toward Millie, fascinated by her deep green eyes and the quick patterns of her mind. She assembled her comments as if she were designing a quilt, seemingly unrelated but all building to a thoughtful, meaningful whole. Sam had to check himself, as he often did, to really listen to her speak, rather than sit back, behind a wide, protective railing, and observe.

The table was sprawled with the unglamorous tubs and tins of their dinner, out of which rose chunky mounds of savory, heavy food. Plastic-wrap angels caught the light where they floated, trapped by their own humble legs, above the steaming mass. Long spoons stood at half-mast. At some point, while Jack polished off mashed potatoes, then sweet potatoes, and then the last of the green beans, Sam lost track of eating dinner as he and Millie talked. It was like she was radiating something through her thin, wrinkled skin, and Sam was sitting in her tiny linoleum kitchen, soaking up her light.

"Did you know that I lost my father when I was a teenager too?" she asked Sam quietly.

He leaned back in his squishy blue chair and said, "I wasn't quite ten."

She smiled again, reaching across the table for Sam's hand. Her face loomed toward him, suddenly blocking whatever light it might earlier have produced. Up close, Sam could see a tightness to her face, from the cancer, he guessed, and realized that he was having trouble breathing himself. Dad, he thought, and felt something inside him collapse. He wanted to lean into Millie and sob. It was always worse at Christmas time, he reasoned. Normally, Sam tried to let the feeling of his father's death lie low.

She rescued him with an uptick in her voice and the brightening of her face into a smile. "And that I almost became a nun?"

Sam looked to Jack, expecting to see him laughing his constant laugh, but he was sitting very quietly with his elbows on the table and a turkey leg in one hand. One thick hand moved below the table, and Sam could see he was nervously rubbing his leg. A single drop of gravy marred the clean expanse of his blue dress shirt. Millie noticed the stain as well and stepped carefully to the sink to wet a paper towel.

"A nun?" Sam repeated, parroting her unintentionally by raising his voice and cocking his head to one side. "No, I didn't know that." He smiled through an image of a high nun's wimple balanced precariously atop her curly wig. "Did you...?" Sam started again, then trailed off, realizing that he had no idea what follow-up question to ask.

Millie was leaning over Jack and dabbing at the stain. "I swear, sometimes . . . " she murmured quietly, looking down at Jack's wide chest. Briskly rubbing at a growing wet spot that had replaced the gravy spot, Millie leaned over and kissed Jack on the top of his head.

"That's right, Sam. A nun. Jack hates this story," she continued, sliding her eyes toward her husband, Sam knew, of almost forty years. "My father died when I was fourteen," she said, and visibly sank as if the air in those words had been all that kept her afloat. Sam nodded, very still, not sure he even wanted to hear this and rehearsing strategies to avoid telling her his father's story in return. Jack began collecting their plates, serving trays, and tins and carried a high, messy pile to the sink. He lumbered to the refrigerator and peered into the freezer's mist.

"Millie," Sam began, trying to force understanding, acceptance, and commiseration into her name. He began telling her not to strain herself when Jack returned to the table, loaded down. He pushed bowls overflowing with pie and ice cream in front of each of them, and stopped across from Sam, looking him directly in the eye.

"Just shut up and let Millie talk," he smiled. "She can be stubborn like a mother elephant, and she's easily twice as strong." He put his arm around her with pride, then went back to his seat and began spooning the already softening ice cream into his mouth. A chocolate brown installation began to assemble on his chin.

Millie responded by rolling her eyes and making a kissing noise in Jack's direction. Then, serious, she leaned forward on the table and waved Sam around to take the seat next to hers. He felt the speckled, shiny cushion give below his weight, felt Millie take his hand in hers again. It felt like soft, scented paper. Like an old monkey's hand. As a little boy, Sam had a favorite grandma whom he remembered only for the wet centers of her kisses and the wrapped candies in little dishes throughout her house. She was Sam's father's mother and died about a year before Sam's father had. He leaned toward Millie, realizing that he hadn't thought of his grandmother in years.

Her voice took him to an inner-city Catholic church, pale wafers drying out her tongue, a crush on a tall, black-haired priest. She talked about the confused fear and uncertainty of war. He watched and listened to Millie as Jack finished his ice cream and began slowly moving around her expanding shell of stillness, balling up wrappings and moving dishes and silverware to their tiny kitchen's sink. Briefly distracted from Millie's account of her long talks with a pretty nun, Sam watched Jack walk carefully with one hand gently pressing the silverware to a plate to keep it from making any noise. He watched Jack lean down to shush the cats with greasy bits of meat, then, catching Sam's eyes, lick his own fingers with a smile. His eyes were small and fanned with happiness.

It was as if that tiny kitchen itself were the world; the swishing dishwasher an ocean, the cats smacking through their food every hungry beast. A window crowded with spider plants and lacy white curtains was the sky and the earth, and Millie, Jack, and Sam were the only people in the world. And, as Sam slowly, quietly shared the story of his life, he realized that this tiny world, this red-tiled kitchen, this final triangle of Millie, Jack, and Sam could be enough.

"I think I understand you a little bit, Sam," Millie concluded, her voice shaking gently on the last words. "When I almost became a nun, before Jack here, I think I needed something to prove to me that there was something *greater* out there that could explain all the pain I saw in the world, all my own confusion. As if I needed to know there was something more." Jack began chuckling softly at this, and when she looked at his smile she blushed enough that it showed through her heavily made-up cheek. "It wasn't until I met Jack and had Melissa that I understood plain old living life was good enough."

And he thanked her, something new and unexpected choking his voice.

It was a dark blue evening when they discovered themselves leaning back, full and with stomachs aching from food and laughter, and Sam insisted he had to go. Dean would be happy from his day at work and waiting for a night with Sam and a ride home. Even as he pulled away from their grasping hands, he regretted it. Resented having to walk alone down the dark, icy path. Resented sliding alone into Dean's cold car and the thought of having to explain the tiny gravy stains. Sam felt silly for those thoughts; he would be picking Dean up soon enough, and the car would warm with his energy. It felt somehow less than what he was leaving, though, and he was tired of the confusion, tired of feeling stuck. The Zoo or a steaming jungle? Continued peacekeeping, or letting his family fend for itself? Sam knew it wasn't as simple as comfort versus risk, but it did feel like important questions were swirling with the tiny white whorls the car's movement raised. Still, he discovered, letting the car's heat warm him as he drove away from the small house resting on its snowy lawn, Sam didn't need to figure it all out just then. All he had to do, all he wanted, was to nest right there at Jack and Millie's for the night—odd smell, cheap furniture, limited horizons, and all.

ESCAPES

2001

THE DENVER ZOO. Two Asian elephants are being bathed by their keepers in a public area, when a large blue plastic water drum suddenly falls and frightens them. The larger of the elephants, weighing 7,600 pounds, steps over a low railing around the bathing area and heads down a path into the Zoo.

Over the course of the next three hours, she knocks over a stroller holding a baby girl, who hits her head in the fall. The elephant's trainer is cut and bruised while trying to calm her, and a woman suffers an asthma attack while running out of the elephant's way. No one is seriously hurt, and the elephant never moves more quickly than a casual walk.

Eventually, the elephant is brought to her knees after being shot with sedative-filled guns by veterinary staff. She is led back to her enclosure and locked into her night quarters to recover from the sedatives and trauma of the day. A smaller elephant, named Amigo, never leaves the bathing area. A brief outcry suggests that the elephant should be kept on a chain from now on, to ensure that nothing like this ever happens again. That demand is defeated. The elephant's name is Hope.

1995

THIRTEEN BUFF-COLORED, ground-dwelling Patas monkeys escape from their grassy enclosure at the San Francisco Zoo.

After two days, twelve of the thirteen are captured and begin readjusting to their captivity well. One female remains missing for an additional three days. Ultimately, she finds her way back to the Patas enclosure, climbs the concrete balustrade from the visitors' side, and rejoins her family inside.

1992

HURRICANE ANDREW, heading for the south Florida coast, is predicted to be the worst storm in almost a century. The animal-care staff at the Dolphin Research Center don't know what effect the storm will have on the dolphins, whose enclosures are shallow lagoons built into the northern beach of Grassy Key. They make a plan to take the animals into a deeper section of the Atlantic where Andrew can pass over without harm.

The day before the storm, nine dolphins are led to the designated drop point by staff tossing herring into the water in their boat's wake. At the drop site, the staff repeatedly signal to the dolphins to "stay," dump three full buckets of herring into the water, and start the twenty-minute journey back to shore.

Andrew hits, destroying thousands of homes and businesses and causing millions of dollars in damage. Many animals, trapped at other zoos and aquariums around the state, suffer injuries and delayed feedings due to the storm. When DRC staff return, they are greeted by what is described as a joyous, if stern, family of friends, playful and hungry, and simply awaiting their return. All nine dolphins remained at the designated site and all swim directly back to their cages, tight against the shore.

1981

BETHESDA, MARYLAND. Sam Metcalfe, unhappy at having to mow the lawn when he wanted to see the new *Star Wars* movie with a friend, and unhappy with the fact that his mother won't move his family back to Philadelphia, packs a backpack with Pop-Tarts, Coke, and $27 he had been saving to open his own bank account. Along with his dog, Buffett, he leaves the house on a Saturday morning, swearing out behind him to where his mother sits at the kitchen table that he is running away and never coming home.

When he returns three hours later, she reaches for him, the picture of forgiveness, and—once he is in her arms—shakes him with a ferocity that terrifies him. "You never run away like that, do you hear me?" She cries onto him, squeezing him tightly, punching his back and shoulders without any strength.

She takes him to work with her for a full week, a combination of punishment and fear at letting him out of her sight. Within three days, his mother has begun laughing with him again and made a family legend out of his running away. She calls him her little hobo. They buy more Pop-Tarts, more Coke, an expensive new saltwater fish. He is unaccountably happy to be home.

SEVENTEEN

THE NEW YEAR'S EVE party was held on Q Street in Georgetown. Jeff and Wes were, Dean explained, a "professor and an architect with adopted twins from Guatemala," and Jeff, apparently, had taken a sabbatical to stay in Guatemala and protect their right to bring their babies home. Not a bad place to come home to, Sam thought as they pulled up. The house, he recognized with a mixture of jealousy and excitement, was one of the houses—read: mansions—he always pointed out as one of the places he'd someday like to live in.

At the garlanded front door, confronted with their hosts' strong handshakes and white grins, Sam felt like he was being introduced to movie stars. He'd never gotten used to "A-list" gays, and after an hour of regularly interrupted chatter, Sam decided he didn't need to. The kids and the dog, he was disappointed to hear, had been sent to Wes's parents for the night. For a moment, Sam wished he had been too.

Jeff and Wes had tented and heated their brick-walled backyard and decorated the house with ivory candles and pale golden lights. Everything might have been from an antique store, but Dean whispered to Sam that Wes was from old money and that he'd inherited the house and everything in it from an aunt. Apparently, they were planning a more modern redesign in the spring. Silver and gold ornaments glittered everywhere, overflowing from bowls and vases on tables and end tables, mantels, and chairs. The striking Gina was holding court on the landing, surrounded by a raucous clutch of Dean's friends. Sam met a few nice people and managed to enjoy himself, but he felt like he was more of a curiosity to these people than something of real interest or lasting value. He felt picked up, glanced over, and placed back gently, but consistently, on the shelf. Within an hour, he found himself surreptitiously checking his watch.

At dinner, he was seated with a couple from the Smithsonian. It felt good. Clearly someone, probably Dean, had given the seating arrangements some thought. The husband, across from Sam, was a thin, older man with a deeply creased shirt and oddly uniform black hair. He catalogued specimens in the Smithsonian's tightly packed, behind-the-scenes, taxonomic storage warehouse. His wife, at Sam's side, was thin enough to look unhealthy and wore a sleek black dress that made her body look young and her arms look old. She wore heavy, dark jewelry in defiant chunks around her neck. She was an ethnobotanist who worked in sub-Saharan Africa. Sam nicknamed them "the monkey king" and "the giraffe."

He wanted to like them, and he was genuinely intrigued. This couple, carefully seated near him by their hosts, was his best shot. He'd never understood Washington, D.C.'s, particular brand of ambition and was sure he'd have more in common with scientists than with the real estate agents, legislative directors, and marketing executives that edged his vision like a too-bright light.

"You're scientists?" he began, leaning toward them, glad to share their light. Dean winked at him from a few spots down and turned to the gallery owner at his side. The couple—Claude and Maris—laughed and they passed a vibrant three minutes of relayed titles and histories before the conversation died away. Apparently, Sam's "Zookeeper" wasn't valid enough to hold their attention for long. As they cut into their filets and baby potatoes, the couple turned inward, chatting to one another over their silverware. Sam felt tired and disappointing. He felt ungrateful. Dean had hopped over to another table to kiss more cheeks and shake more hands.

What kind of scientist am I, he suddenly, desperately, wanted to know. Brazil's green treetops and animal calls flashed through his mind, and he felt suddenly small. He was too tangled in the branches of his own life happily, unhappily, he wasn't sure. With a sinking sensation, he suspected that he'd never figure it out.

Dinner was over, the scientists had politely excused themselves to the living room, and Sam was left standing. Sadly, Dean had been encircled by the hosts and some other guests, and it was difficult to do more than catch his eye. He seemed unbearably far away. Sam tried starting a few conversations, but his questions seemed uninteresting, and his jokes were falling flat. As his jokes became more bitter, the laughs he received were more regular, but they left him feeling angry and misunderstood. He knew he was being ungrateful and unhelpful and forced himself to widen his eyes and offer more interesting anecdotes, nodding or shaking his head whenever it seemed the appropriate thing to do. Briefly, Dean's friend Gina helped. She was witty and inclusive and let Sam seem interesting while helping him find connections with people who had seemed uninteresting moments before. She was brilliant and enveloping, but she was constantly working the room, and her magic didn't extend.

He realized he was focusing unfairly on negatives. Dean was too busy for him, the older women had all had work done, and when Gina hugged him, he could feel how quickly she released his back. Underneath his smiles and laughter, he was wishing like a schoolboy to be out of there, to be at Terra, to be home. By eleven, Sam had stopped attempting to fit in and had gradually receded to making sure he waved gamely at Dean from whatever social-looking perch he could find. He found that anyone would let him stand near them with a glass of wine and listen. Most groups even opened up enough to let him seem, however incompletely, a part. Sam realized that he wasn't even trying anymore.

Uncomfortable, anxious, and a little bit drunk, Sam pulled Dean out of a conversation with a group of three handsome laughing men. He walked Dean into the quiet and dim tented yard and, knowing Dean wouldn't want to leave, gave him an overly warm hug and a kiss. Dean was giddy with popularity; he wanted Sam's opinion on everything and everyone there. "And, how'd you like those two doctors we seated you with?" he asked, emphasizing the word with pride. Kissing Sam again before he could answer, Dean asked if they weren't the most interesting group of people Sam had ever met.

"I . . . sure," Sam managed to reply. "Listen, I know you're having fun, but do you think we could head out soon?" He was holding onto Dean's arm and punctuated the question with a shrugged smile and another kiss. He hated being so appeasing but realized it was all he knew how to do. "Laurel said everyone was gathering at 11:45." Dean smiled and asked for five minutes to say good-bye. They were both a little giddy; they kissed again. Warm and soft, each kiss felt like a tiny, mutual promise that there was nothing awkward going on. That they were happy together and would survive this and every night.

"Listen, why don't you come back in with me?" Dean suggested. "I promise I'll hold your hand the whole time!" They both laughed, but Sam explained that he was going to stay outside for another minute and enjoy the cooler air. "I thought I heard a cardinal," he offered, pushing Dean toward the door, "I'll see you in *ten*." He felt generous offering Dean the extension, wanted them both to feel better and to make obvious what a good sport he knew he could be. He was sure Dean would know to be back in five.

It got cold, and then it got colder, and twenty minutes later Sam was still standing outside. The red-orange glow of the heat lamps was reflected by the frustration creeping under his skin; he could feel sweat dampening the collar of the expensive shirt Dean "helped" him choose for the party. After seven slow minutes Sam had sighed and smiled as he imagined Dean trying to disengage himself from some conversation about stocks or the network or an art gallery where a woman was standing, for three days, without food or water or the ability to leave her spot. He checked inside after fifteen minutes, walking through the crowds of sloshing people and drinks, giving every group a second look to make sure that Dean wasn't surrounded, as he often was, by a small crowd. Gina hadn't seen him in an hour. After Sam had made two passes through the living and dining rooms and poked his head into the bright, spacious kitchen, he walked up a steep flight of stairs and didn't find him along the upstairs hallway or through any of the open doors. A moment of irrational fear kept him from knocking on any closed door on the upper hall: Bedrooms, Sam thought, and flinched at the thought. He retreated to the patio in case Dean was looking for him there. Under the orange lights, Sam got angrier and angrier, generating his own heat.

When Dean did walk outside at 11:47, he was still laughing over his shoulder at some conversation Sam couldn't see. Dean's silhouette was outlined against the bright doorway, and his features were entirely blacked out by the light. When he saw Sam, he apologized easily and with laughter, explaining that he had run into an unexpected old friend and couldn't get by without saying hello. Sam refused to be jealous of an invisible conversation, but he also refused to act as if Dean's making him wait, when they'd agreed to leave for Laurel's twenty minutes ago, was acceptable. It was new for him, he knew, this *not* automatically saying everything would be OK. Deciding he liked being mad, he pushed Dean's coat into his hands and then pushed past him toward the yard's side entrance and the street.

"Sam! What's gotten into you?" Dean followed and then faltered, looking at his watch. "Oh shit, honey," he said, leaping forward and grabbing Sam's elbow from behind, pulling it from where Sam had folded it like a broken wing against his chest. "I'm sorry." He turned Sam into him and tried to connect their eyes, stroking his arm nervously. "I just lost track of the time. I'm sorry. Really." He chucked Sam on the chin for forgiveness. Sam felt himself dissolving into Dean's apology, then realized that Dean was fully aware of the effect his sweetened motions would have, *then* thought of Laurel rushing to prepare a toast for him and their friends despite managing a paying party, and *then* he let the anger flare. It warmed him against the cold night, allowed him to deny Dean's warmth and explanation. Sam knew about losing himself, his anger, *who he was*, to the sweet obliteration of making everything all right. He felt as if he had always been flattened by the weight of other people's appreciation, attention, kisses, and hugs. Desperately he clutched at his anger, determined to keep it from slipping away.

"Whatever, Dean. Thanks for the apology, but it really doesn't mean anything right now, does it? Everyone's going to be standing around wondering where we are, delaying their New Year's Eve." They both looked to their watches to confirm—and Dean made another apology with his eyes. "And I'm just so frustrated. I mean, we totally agreed we'd leave in time to join them. I came to this awful party and talked to your awful friends . . . " Sam felt like he was caught with his hand in the cookie jar. A plunging nausea swept over him, but he rode it to a crest like a roller coaster when he was a kid. He was telling Dean what he really thought. He had opened the lid of Pandora's box. "And all because we had a deal that we'd split the night between our lives. And then you just didn't care, did you?" He knew he was too animated now, that his words were moving too fast for him to catch them as they flew, but he didn't want to stop. "You know how important these traditions are to me. But you just didn't give it a thought."

Sam felt strong and unhappy at once. Dean looked stricken, pale in the cold light of the street. His shoes scuffed the formerly adorable cobblestone street.

"But, Sam, you said you were having fun. I asked you less than an hour ago. And I'm sorry, all right? There's no great conspiracy here. I just lost track of the time!" His voice had risen, and he tamed it again. "And anyway, you seemed fine. You said you were fine!" He paused for a moment. "Well, at least Gina said you were a complete hit."

Sam snorted. "Please. Gina would say that about a cookie made of sardines and chocolate chips. Come on, Dean," he sniped, "you know you *never* lose track of the time." In the cold air, Sam felt himself softening; he watched breath cloud from Dean's lips. "I mean, I tried—I *try* to be good for your friends, Dean, you know that. I'm in my best suit when I don't want to be, wearing your fancy shirt when I don't want to be, trying to ask your friends about their meetings on the Hill or the latest bar." He realized he was pleading, raising his hands up and then dropping them, then raising them again. "I try to do good for you. I do," he finished, trailing off. "I just don't think it matters. Those Smithsonian people were so rude. They treated me like I work at a pet store." He knew he was coloring the situation unfairly, but he also knew, fully and unexpectedly, exactly how he actually felt. "Or maybe I was the rude one. I don't know. I just didn't fit here. I never will. And it's obvious that none of them really care." He felt empty, scoured. The cold of the night had penetrated him and moved deep inside.

"Sammy . . ." Dean kissed Sam's forehead and left his lips there for a long while.

"Look," Sam offered, giving Dean's hand a little shake. "Can I borrow your cell phone? We've already missed midnight, and I don't feel much like going to Laurel's anymore. I'm sorry I got so pissed off, but maybe we could just go home and get some sleep." Dean nodded, and they managed to hold hands for the short walk to the valet. Dean didn't comment on Sam's short, shouted conversation over the phone. "She's good?" he asked, tentatively, and they rode home quietly, holding cold hands, the sound of the heater running like cotton in their ears. At home, at Sam's, they kissed a bare but tender good night, and their backs bowed away from each other like the curves of a violin. The air that flowed in the space between them was cold.

"LAUREL?" SAM whispered into the phone, knowing, as he hunched out of his sheets on the first ring, that it had to be her. The clock read 4 a.m. in blinking green light, and he felt his nipples tighten in the dark, cool air. The house smelt vaguely of cinnamon and his boyfriend's breath. Quickly he looked at—and away from—Dean, loving him so deeply he felt a pressure in his chest, remembering the pain of their fight. He remembered lying in bed, not touching, his nose cold in the winter night. He didn't remember falling asleep.

Sam stepped silently out of bed, cradling the phone against his ear and pushing the sheets into a gentle swell against Dean's back. A moment of annoyance flashed at how easily Dean slept through the phone, through anything, how remote and unshakable he was. A brush of his hand against Dean's hair, soft in the light from the city night outside, restored him to tenderness and love. The fight hadn't really been so bad, he knew. And didn't fighting, and making up, somehow confirm they were in love?

"Laurel? It's you, right? I'm so sorry we missed the party. Things were . . . " he rubbed his face, not knowing what, exactly, "things were" after all. "What's up?"

"Of course it's me, silly. Who else wakes you up at all hours of the night?" He could hear the false cheer in her voice, heard her palming the phone from hand to hand. "I'm wired and can't sleep, and the party was *such* a hit—I thought maybe I'd bring over some breakfast treats in the morning. Leftovers," she assured him. "They're frangipanes so they need to be eaten quickly. I thought we could hang out." Sam stood, confused, in the light of the open refrigerator door. She sounded almost manic. He had a desire for milk.

"I'm just, I was thinking . . . " she paused, and he could see her standing in the cold night air. He didn't say a word. Laurel wasn't one to dwell on her confusion, and it was better, Sam knew, just to let her speak.

"So, should I bring over some junk food in the morning? Can we convince Dean to not diet for one day? Hey!" She stopped herself. "You sounded upset tonight when you called. Is everything OK?"

Sam had two options, he realized, listening to Laurel and easing himself down onto the couch with the luminescent glass of milk held above him. He could chatter with Laurel about her party and his party— Dean's party—and laugh away any discomfort either of them might be feeling. Sam was tempted; it would be so nice to make fun of the monkey king and his wife or hear Laurel mock the rich ladies who'd (inevitably) have wanted to set her up on a date, and just relax into the familiar, safe space of their friendship. Or he could ask her what was really going on. It would be tricky—Laurel never wanted to talk seriously during her late-night calls—but he heard something in her voice that made him push.

"Laurel?" He started slowly, resisting the urge to put off until tomorrow what he wanted to say tonight. "Do you ever feel, just, trapped? With your mom and the restaurant and everything? Just kind of . . . by life?" He felt audacious and brave sitting cold in his boxers in the light from outside. He felt like the questions were coming from outside as well as in. The sound of two women walking and talking quavered quietly outside. "Do you ever just wish you could just get totally far away?"

"What?"

Clearly this wasn't the direction she'd expected Sam to go.

He felt a little guilty, leavened by a tiny puff of pride.

"Sam, I'm fine. I just wanted to touch base. Is something going on with you?" He regretted raising the question. Laurel was standing outside her struggling restaurant, locking up alone, wired, at 4 a.m.

"Are you unhappy about Dean again?" She asked, sounding distracted.

He knew her well enough; she was digging through her purse for cigarettes.

"Me and Dean? No, we're, we're fine. Christmas was really good, you know. And tonight . . . " He wanted to tell her not to smoke. "No, tonight was hard, but it's a blip, I think. It wasn't fun, but we really talked it through. Besides," he paused for effect, "what would the holidays be without a little drama, right?" Sam knew that would make her laugh, knew he was bargaining away a deeper conversation, and knew, with some annoyance, that he wanted, as much as she did, to just love one another and say good night. "I just wanted to make sure you're doing OK," he continued after hearing her laugh over the phone. "I know Christmas is always hard for you, and with your Mom's health and everything, and then having to rush back . . . " Through the silence he could hear the whole big, dark emptiness of the night. "I, just . . . making everything work, you know? Sometimes, it can all feel like too much." He felt his voice shake, knew Laurel would hear it too. "Hey, I thought you were quitting this year?"

"Shut up!" she laughed. "I still can."

They were safe; he knew it. And Sam wasn't just worried about her. He was confused about his own life, and her changing life, and how it could possibly all fit into the comfortable world he had constructed. How Laurel's Medusa-head of responsibility would leave room for their perfect friendship. How Sam could build Jack and weakening Millie a safe place to rest. How he could make sure Jamie grew up brave and strong and happier than his sister managed to be. How Dean would fit into his family and make everything work right. He also knew, deep down, how despite looking perfectly fine on the surface, everyone in his family still nursed and hid terrible, shattering cracks.

"Honey, listen." Laurel swept in. "I'm fine. Really. Things are a little hard right now, yes, but my mom is fine, my family is fine, Terra will be fine." He heard the telltale, hollow inhale. "*You'll* be fine," she added, stressing and repeating the words. "Just go back to bed with that big hunky boyfriend of yours and think of the yummies I'm bringing you tomorrow. Pretend you're a monkey happy in your own little nest."

"Howler," he corrected her.

"There *are* other animals, you know."

"Thanks."

After a moment, she finished with a quick "I love you, you know."

"Go to bed," he whispered. "I love you too."

Sam did as he was told, climbing into bed and conscientiously warming under the covers, then fitting himself against Dean's smooth, beautiful back. He ran his hands from Dean's shoulder to his hips, feeling like an antelope exploring miles of virgin, moonlit grass. They would be all right, Sam knew. Me and Dean, Laurel—we're all going to be fine.

A sleepy rumble came from under the covers and Dean's honey-dark hair. "Sweetie?" Dean's voice was all Sam needed to hear. The blue light out the window wasn't from a street lamp, he realized. It was moonlight. He leaned over and kissed his boyfriend deeply, one eye open to the first soft and gentle flurries of winter snow.

BUT THE next morning, Sam retreated to his Zoo.

It was one of his many unspoken traditions, the long emptiness of New Year's Day, and as he stood on the great slope below Lion Island, shuffling his heavy boots to shake out the cold, Sam breathed a word of thanks. That he could walk half the Zoo's length without seeing another human being, without ever feeling alone. Bronze sculptures dotted the grounds with animal life. Evergreens marched alongside railings and against buildings, guarding entrances and unexpected paths. The planted firs and spruce brightened the Zoo in a way that the faded red, and yellow, and blue summer signs did not. Cardinals were like leftover Christmas ornaments, brightening the trees' harsh branches, red against green.

The wetlands exhibit, a wide expanse between sloping hills, froze in its perpetual rot, with stands of stiff grass puncturing black, iced-over ponds. Ice formed tight sheets on the black puddles that dotted depressed pathways, on the buckets of water left outside, and on the many small ponds and pools that punctuated the grounds. Sam waved to the few, die-hard regulars who wandered about in shivering clumps. It was a hardy time, Sam thought, slapping his thick gloves together to motivate his blood.

The distractions of popcorn and ice-cream kiosks were quieted; no stuffed pandas or monkeys cajoled from membership desks. Winter at the Zoo quieted the animals too. Only a few species of bears and birds and wolves, from Canada and farther north, thrived. Sam sought them out for a quick hello on his way from lions to monkeys, pausing to watch the shaggy bisons' frosty puffs of breath.

Sam and the other keepers, always a solitary group, went about their duties mostly in silence, waving to each other rather than wasting even one white cloud of breath. Short-sleeved uniforms had been taken home and put aside to make room for long underwear, heavy jackets, and thick, unbending gloves. The Zoo's winter uniforms were the same green as in the summer, as if in defiance of the cold black-and-white world outside. He remembered the blizzard of 1987, everything layered in white, when the keepers moved into the animal houses for days, feeding and working with their animals throughout the isolating storms. Sam had done that more than once. It had been some of the greatest experiences—sleeping near his animals—of his career.

On the paths and in the buildings there were no children asking questions, no public presentations to be made while leaning against the low railings fronting the sea lions, or bison, or orangutan cage. There was time to wonder and to think, time for administrators and veterinarians, for construction crews and schematics, and planning for the year to come.

EIGHTEEN

"ANOTHER FIGHT with Dean?" Jack asked over the steaming mug he was padding from hand to hand. He was leaning on his elbows at his desk, clutching the warm mug, dripping a cold puddle onto the concrete floor. His office was stuffed with the comforting smells of sweat and breath and animals and coffee, and the less certain flavor of rum.

"What do you mean, *another* fight?" Sam asked. "That's not fair. You know New Year's was our first fight, and it wasn't even that bad. At least we didn't go to bed mad," Sam added a little proudly, then hoped his sleeping arrangements weren't more detail than Jack wanted to hear. He breathed on his fingers to bring them back to life.

"Course you didn't," Jack chuckled and looked back into his cup.

Sam stamped his feet to shake off the wet. He was behind schedule after a late night researching Alzheimer's disease and Dr. Anderson's project in Brazil, and a morning shower that wasted twenty minutes waiting for the water to heat up. In a fit on New Year's Day he had sent a follow-up letter suggesting he was very interested in the project, and it was true. He did want the research opportunity and the validation of it all, and he sincerely wanted to want the move itself, but he kept finding himself looking for flaws in the plan. It felt like life was too crowded for his occasional, lush green dreams.

That morning Sam had left messages for Karen and his mother, pulled his howler proposal back to the top of its pile, and then spent twenty minutes reading an article suggesting that Dr. Anderson was a rogue, an unreliable scientist, a quack. He relished the news. Things with Dean, besides the dull sliver of ice left unwarmed since New Year's, were good, and Sam desperately wanted to keep them that way. Since Christmas, Laurel had been paling with guilt about her mother, and Jamie, despite having basically acknowledged he would go to Roosevelt, was barely speaking to his mom. Sam felt needed in D.C. Indispensable. The thought of those responsibilities chafed him, and they kept him very warm.

"I said things are fine. Can we just leave it at that for now?" Guilt over Brazil scratched at Sam, and like hunger, the guilt fed itself and grew. He hadn't asked Jack about Millie in days. "How is she?" He offered, apologetically. "I'm sorry. I just keep . . . forgetting. Christmas was so nice. Do you have any news?"

Jack dismissed Sam's entreaties with a wave of his hand and started to pour a second cup from his Thermos. "Don't shit with me," he started, pointing at Sam, but suddenly stopped and poured what was in Sam's mug back into the industrial sink. Before rinsing out Sam's mug, he ran his finger along the edge and licked it. "Heh. Anyway. Maybe you're right. Now's probably not the time to talk." The smell of liquor popped open Sam's eyes.

"It's not that anything is wrong, really," Sam mumbled to fill the sparking air. He was clutching his arm against his chest and shifting from foot to foot. "We did have a fight on New Year's Eve, but I told you that. Things are fine, they're good. Even with how busy he is, we're getting really close. Anyway . . . " Sam moved to Jack's desk and unrolled a page of photos of a new interpretive wall they were planning to install. He wanted to push the focus back to work. Jack stared at the dark, glossy photos as they shined on his desk. He didn't comment on either the photos or what Sam had just said.

"Hey," Sam found himself talking again, wanted to clamp his lips together and just shut up, "did I tell you he's taking me to Hawaii in March?" He tried to put all the brightness of imagined Hawaiian skies into the words. He loved that Dean had dreamed up the vacation, except for the fact that it was a "gay" resort and that Dean hadn't involved Sam in designing the vacation, petty as that made him feel. He also had only two months to work out and not eat in order to bear taking his shirt off in front of all the other men. It was always hard for Sam where Dean was concerned. Dean with the flawless, muscular body and complete comfort in his own skin. Sam knew that Dean found him sexy and attractive, knew that his height and big arms balanced out the extra pounds at his waist. But he still hated the thought of all those staring men; equally, he hated the thoughts that surfaced every few weeks of Dean working out and showering during those mid-afternoon, waiters-and-escorts hours at the gym.

A few of Dean's friends from L.A., including the shirtless men from last summer, were meeting them there, and Sam imagined himself a new animal, once again, being introduced to an established group. It had always been that way. The odd one out, standing alone at the bar or the party or the pool, wishing the popular kids would see him for what he wanted to be.

———

ON VALENTINE'S Day, Dean treated Sam to dinner on the harbor in Anapolis, a meal that left them both so heavy and full that the hopeful effervescence of champagne and loving words was bulldozed by straining stomachs and exhaustion. They climbed into Sam's bed at midnight, laughing at their predicament, only slightly disappointed that they wouldn't consummate their first Valentine's together with sex. Dean promised Sam that there was absolutely nothing wrong; he was simply far too full to move.

The next morning, when the phone rang at 5 a.m., Sam wanted to ignore it. Even after two rings, he wasn't awake enough to believe that the ugly ringing that was grinding into his temples was real. He tried to sleep through it, but the phone's angry jangle pushed in.

Grumbles emerged from where Dean's head disappeared under his pillow. "Answer the phone," he managed, lying on his stomach, completely covered by the faded yellow sheets.

Sam reached an arm out from under the sheets and comforter and pulled the receiver to his ear. He thought about his voice for a moment. "Hello?"

"Sam? It's Jack, kid. How are you?" His voice was thick but almost giddy, and Sam had a sudden image of Jack in pale, baby blue pajamas, sitting like a little boy on the edge of his bed. It took him a minute to focus before responding.

"Jack? Jack?" He rubbed his face to get the blood circulating.

"It is, Sammy. It's Millie. I'm afraid she's passed." His voice had lost its giddiness and was strangely smooth and calm.

Jack's voice and his oddly formal phrasing—"she's passed"—sounded wistful to Sam, as if maybe this was all a joke with a punch line that he hadn't yet figured out. Sam sat up in bed, feeling the unreasonably cold air of February hit his chest and shoulders. He realized that Jack probably sounded so calm because he was drunk. He dropped an arm onto the mass of warmth that was Dean, wanted to cry with relief when a tuneless tune rose from the pillow over his lover's head. He cradled the phone between his shoulder and chin and slid a hand under the blankets to rub the small of Dean's back. His thumb ached. He needed something solid so he wouldn't disappear.

"Oh my God. Jack, I'm so sorry," he exhaled, not knowing what else to say. He started tapping Dean's back in a distracted dance, some small, disengaged part of him hoping that Dean would wake up and help him know what to say.

"Are you all right? Is there anything I can do to help?"

Still burrowed and hidden by the blankets, Dean rolled toward Sam and cradled his waist in his warm arms. His breath misted Sam's back like a moist tropical wind. The Reptile House. The heat of the Amazon in winter. An anchor in warm Caribbean sand. Jack explained that his daughter was flying in from Tennessee that morning and that he would stay at the hospital with Millie until she arrived. "I just wanted to know if you'd take over for me today, kiddo," he laughed nervously. "I know it's your day off and all, and you were excited to see your guy—"

Sam cut him off. "Jack. Of course I'll go in. Don't think about that at all. Don't worry about anything. I'm already up. I'll call Gwen. I'll take care of everything." Sam pushed off the covers, carefully disengaging Dean's hand. "I'm getting up now so I can come by the hospital before the Zoo. I'm bringing you breakfast." He wondered if he had eggs in the fridge, wondered how he would keep them warm on the ride to the hospital. His mind was on Tupperware and towels. Jack's mumbled good-bye sounded as if a deep well was flooding his throat.

Dean shifted and began kissing Sam's back and hips as he hung up the phone. "Jack OK?" he asked, shifting around so that his face was in Sam's lap. "Anything I can do?" He grinned and raised an eyebrow, breathing heavily between Sam's legs. "Just that," Sam responded, pushing Dean's head gently into his crotch, wishing Dean wasn't there, wishing he could just get in the shower by himself. He needs me too, Sam reminded himself, rising unplanned to meet Dean's warm mouth, and slowly forgetting that having sex right then wasn't exactly what he wanted to do.

MILLIE'S FUNERAL was tiny and spare. As she had requested, the only flowers were those left over from the Sunday service, and their lack made the white-washed room look even smaller. Any donations were to be directed to the local Catholic church. People wore black if they had it, or navy blue. It looked like a nun's funeral, Sam guessed, and the thought made him glad. The plan was for just a few people to meet at the church, with an afternoon of visits and hot food later at their house. Besides the priest, the only attendees were Jack and their daughter, a sister of Millie's whom Sam hadn't known existed but who lived less than twenty miles away, four ladies from Millie's (previously unknown) book club, one or two older keepers, and a few younger friends, like Sam.

Jack had offered Sam the opportunity to bring Dean, and, even though they weren't touching, Sam could feel Dean's presence moving across the thin air between them, lending him strength. The solidity of Dean let Sam do what Sam did best: instead of listening to the words about Millie, he focused on all the things he could do to ease things for Jack. He mentally arranged schedules to cover Jack's work at Lion

Island, coordinated cooked meals from the keepers that he would leave, surreptitiously, on Jack's battered desk. Visits he would make to Jack's house on the weekend. Ways he could make everything better for his friend.

Dean's arm brushed against him, and he felt, terribly, briefly, the power of their first touches; the electricity of their simply touching arms. Sam felt a brick fall out, a chink in the wall of himself, the hard, dark cage that sheltered him and protected him from all the pain in the world. Millie was gone, and the world was emptier. The brick of her assurances fell out, and Sam felt bathed in a new, cold, white light.

NINETEEN

THE STREETS of Georgetown were wide and silent in the echo after the storm, and the tires of Sam and Jamie's bikes whirred against the wet, black street, sending up cool sprays against their legs. A wild, almost tropical thunderstorm had trampled across the city that morning, and the air felt alive and active on his skin. He carefully followed the snail trails made by Jamie's bike along the wet, leaf-matted road. Everything was dampness and color—wet streets writhing with rainbow swirls of awakened oil, the green and yellow of new leaves clinging onto trees or clumped against curbs, pear and cherry trees raising delicate fists of petals that blinked and paled in the light. Sam couldn't help but worry about all the new flowers—crocuses, cherry blossoms, daffodils; it seemed like they always pushed themselves out of the earth too soon, and a late frost could still kill them, making a mockery of spring. Alternating rivers of wind—warm and cool—streamed across Sam's face.

They were "calling tomorrow," a game invented by Karen in the months when her main diversions were drives to the gynecologist, then doctor, then hospital, then home. When she was pregnant with Jamie, hiding from her college friends, and looking out her mother's car windows with envy at everything that moved. In "calling tomorrow," each player attempted to claim the best things—houses, cars, office buildings, careers—first, and in doing so, claim the best possible future. Back then, Sam had hated the game, had played with a sullen complicity despite feeling that Karen had called *his* tomorrow, his future, away. Naturally, Karen had always won. When Jamie was born, Sam's resentments had evaporated in the face of Jamie's wide blue eyes and wet laughter. Now,

Sam was happy to let his nephew win the game. He had his own life, and anyway, calling tomorrow wasn't something Sam really liked to do.

Their tastes were very different. Sam pointed out tidy, neatly trimmed old houses with deep porches, imagining them as places where a very different, very easy kind of life took place. He could envision whole rainy afternoons spent on the porch while gray-uniformed maids brought sandwiches and tea on rectangular, blue-flecked trays in the time it took to pass one house by. It was strange, looking at those houses. Sam's whole life, he realized, had been about creating comfort—for himself and for his family and friends—and yet, he still imagined, when he imagined it, *true* comfort as something for other people, in other houses, with other lives.

Returning from his imaginary visit to the deep wicker couch on his imagined, shady porch, Sam would tap Jamie and jerk his chin at a soft colonial with simple, shuttered windows marching across its front. Jamie always countered with plans to buy the stark, modern houses that stuck like angry origami from among the classic houses that still held sway. "When I'm playing for DC United," he would explain, as if any future he claimed was an inevitable conclusion, "I'll have two houses, one here and one at the beach." Sam would laugh and occasionally want to throttle him with the fact that life doesn't always turn out the way you plan.

Looking up from the winding tire paths on the street, Sam began pedaling hard, surging forward and making Jamie scramble to catch up. He wanted Jamie to know how hard it was to get your dreams. He needed Jamie to understand that work was required, that wrong paths were taken, that life could surprise you, and not always in good ways. Jamie, oblivious to anything but the wind in his face, rode hard and passed his uncle quickly, shouting an echoing "Yes!" into the trees. From his secured position at the front, Jamie began pointing out the staccato bursts of modern houses that marked the hills above Rock Creek Park. With their jutting angles and windows, they looked built of fire in the afternoon sun. Sam, pedaling hard and tired of listening, braked to a hard stop.

"And just how are you planning to pay for all these houses?" he needled. "Are you going to Roosevelt or not?" Sam wanted to slap himself, but it also felt oddly good. It was exactly the sort of thing Jamie's mother would say to him—exactly the sort of thing a cool uncle *wouldn't*, but Sam didn't care. Jamie needed to go to Roosevelt. Needed to grab for his dreams and run.

He didn't read the insight in reverse. He didn't feel trapped himself, most days, except sometimes when it caught up with him from behind. Besides, it was Jamie's future he was worried about. It was just the bike ride that made him sweat and breathe through his nose. Jamie didn't respond. "Jamie? Roosevelt?"

His nephew's face broke into component parts like a folding paper game. He rode in silent circles until Sam raised his feet and began pedaling again. They turned downhill, sloping into Rock Creek Park, riding easily between hillsides crowded with misty green trees. Sam saw a cloud of blackbirds billow across the sky, flicking north and out of sight like a sheet in a washerwoman's hands. He couldn't identify the species and lost himself in wondering where their migration took them for the summer, imagined a flat, cool, lake-riddled northern land. Jamie pulled up, yanking Sam back from his sudden travel with the birds across the sky.

"Yeah, I'm going to Roosevelt." His shoulders, which normally hunched to his ears when he rode, had slumped awfully low. He seemed to be brachiating across the handlebars, unsure of himself, constantly shifting his grip. "And I'm even mostly happy about it—they have a really good science program, you know." Sam knew. There were still days when he wished he could have gone there himself. "And I *would* like to be a marine biologist if I don't make it pro."

Sam watched the little muscles shift under the yellow soccer jersey on Jamie's back. The idea that Jamie would be a scientist tasted like a bright red lollipop on Sam's tongue. He wanted to be thirteen again, or nine. Jamie continued, "Or an engineer."

"Or an engineer," Sam repeated quietly, smiling so Jamie wouldn't see.

"And, anyway, Jessica is going there, so at least I'll know someone."
The name Jessica was new to Sam. "And—"

Sam watched Jamie chew his lip. "And?"

"But, please, Uncle Sam, don't tell Mom!" Jamie looked at Sam with
such intense unhappiness that Sam wanted to agree, to affirm, to accept
whatever Jamie needed. Jamie began speaking quickly, like the words
were a scratching sore throat he wanted to expel. "She's just . . . she's
so mean and is always telling me what to do and how I have to act, and
she's so . . . I don't know, embarrassing. It's like, Roosevelt isn't even
for me or something. Like it's all for her."

It was true. Jamie was Karen's calling tomorrow, her proof that
everything did, and would, turn out all right in the end.

"I just don't want her to win again. She always wins, Uncle Sam. She
never lets me or Dad plan anything. She's so mean, and—" Sam cut him
off with a look. These conversations were a balancing act; Sam was the
only adult to whom Jamie felt comfortable complaining about his mom,
and he knew that Jamie's trust was an honor he'd do almost anything to
keep. Still, it was a bladed gift; Sam knew how easy it was to be caught
between what *felt* best and what was actually the right thing to do. He
adjusted his gears so that he could work less hard pedaling to keep up
with Jamie.

"What do you mean, don't tell her you're going? Why not? There's
a lot she has to do, right? Books to get you, plans for that prefreshman
trip . . . ?" A combination of feelings pushed around inside Sam, as if
they were being mixed and stirred by his pumping legs. "It's already
March."

Sam started to tell Jamie that he wasn't being fair and that he needed
to tell his mom right away but stopped himself, biting his tongue. He
realized that he was actually proud of Jamie. Proud that, at thirteen, he
was so easily resisting the expected, denying the easy path, refusing to
placate for the sake of day-to-day comfort, demanding that his desires
and rights, however shortsighted, be heard. Sam wished, again, that
he'd become a field biologist or a wildlife vet. He wished he could be
so brave with Dean.

He reached out and patted Jamie on the back. They coasted toward a grassy field above the river and parked their bikes against a rough, wooden table.

"Jamie."

They sat.

"Look. Your mom just wants what's best for you, OK? You're just mad because she's asking you to do things in a way that makes you mad. You know how important these things are to her." He took Jamie's chin in his hand. "You haven't had to deal with some of the hard things your mom has gone through." Jamie tried to look away. "Listen. You want to go to Roosevelt, right?" Sam hated asking again, but he needed to confirm. There was a delicate assessment preparing itself inside Sam. He didn't want to be another reason for Jamie to do what he might not want to do. He wanted to tell Jamie to put himself first, to do what he felt was right.

"Yeah." Jamie looked defeated.

"Well, then, it's pretty simple, ain't it?" Sam asked, punching Jamie's not-so-small shoulder, as he hoped a big brother would. "Tell her when you're ready, but," Sam knew he was overdoing it, trying to juggle and catch every ball in the air, "if you need a little time for yourself, that's all right too."

Jamie smiled from below his cap, and Sam stood and grabbed his bike.

"Just be respectful, OK? Even if it doesn't seem like it sometimes, she's a person too." He climbed on while Jamie was still sitting and prepared to push away.

"Now," he stretched out the word, playful and happy with the outcome and enjoying what was about to come next, "why don't we go get some ice cream before the movie? If you beat me," he called over his shoulder as he pushed off, pedaling fast to make Jamie scramble for his bike, "I'll buy you anything you want!" He pedaled hard, hearing a "Yeeehah!" close behind.

Two nights later he was on the phone with his sister when, with an uncharacteristic throb of emotion, she thanked him for whatever it was he had done.

Mother, Daughter, Son

James Metcalfe, Anne's husband and Sam and Karen's father, simply doesn't come home for dinner one Friday night. Anne makes his favorite dinner of broiled chicken and mashed potatoes. She imagines him in his brown tie and short-sleeved dress shirt, driving the back roads toward home. At 5:30, Sam scrambles up to the counter, measuring milk and butter and pouring the potato flakes from their bright red box. Anne lets him dab his finger into the melting butter and taste the salt; the blue kitchen is bright with the high-voiced, cartwheeling narrative of his day. Karen stomps downstairs to join them at the last moment, just in time for dinner. Her daughter's lip shows just the hint of the pout that will reconfigure her face for years.

When James doesn't walk in as she pulls the chicken from the oven, she ignores the buzzing flashes of danger in her brain. She tells herself it is a normal reaction to the blast of the oven's heat on her face. She makes the kids sit for dinner: "Philadelphia traffic can be so bad." They eat at the round, white kitchen table, watching as his food settles into itself, cooling and congealing, the orange carrots wrinkling like soaked fingers on the plate. Anne keeps the kids busy with established rhythms of talk about their classes and friends, keeps moving her own food in slow circles. Sam asks if he can bring home the class snake for the summer. Karen rushes to finish, anxious to get to her favorite show.

Anne feels a jabbing pressure behind her right eye. Jim is never late. He doesn't have that kind of job. He is usually out of the office in time to beat the worst of the traffic. He lives for his family—she presses her fingertips to her eyes—even if he doesn't announce it very often or very well. He is just there, safe like the brightly lit circle of the cast-iron street lamp on their neatly clipped, suburban lawn.

Six o'clock, maybe 6:15, and he will walk in the front door. Maybe a few minutes later if he stops to talk about the heat with a neighbor or to quickly spray the brown, crackling lawn with a hose. He loves his yard, takes a farmer's—or a father's—joy in watching it grow. He can stand frowning for hours over plants that don't take and patches of lawn that remain a stubborn, starchy, yellow-brown. She thinks, for a second, that maybe he'd warned her he would be home late, but she dismisses the thought. He will swing open the screen door any second, letting it slam behind him with an unthinking enthusiasm that used to be sweet, and walk purposefully to the kitchen to find them all. He is easier with the lawn than with his wife; Anne is never fully ready for his kiss.

For the past few years, James' kisses have caught Anne half on the mouth as he threw one heavy arm around her shoulders, one hand feeling blindly for Sammy or Karen's head (when they were little) or their shoulder or side (as they grew.) Theirs is no great love story, and she knows it. Their kisses take place mostly in the kitchen, or in hotel rooms on vacation, quietly so the kids in the next room won't hear.

Anne keeps looking toward the front of the house from her seat, hearing in every child's voice or metal slamming of a car door her husband, their father, coming home to have dinner with his family. She strains her neck so as to keep one eye on the big wooden clock.

After dinner, while Sam and Karen stand together at the sink washing and drying the dishes, Anne takes the phone onto the back porch and slides the thick glass door closed on the cord. The day is still so hot. Sam knocks on the window to get her attention, making wild, smushed faces against the glass. Jim's secretary doesn't answer, even though she listens through five or six hollow rings. She's probably already gone home. Back in the kitchen, after perfunctorily checking the kids' job with the dishes and making Sam re-dry a few plates, she sends him to join Karen in the den for a half hour of TV. Karen has made the point, one white-socked foot stamping the tiled floor, of demonstrating that her whole weekend's homework is already done.

Where is that man?

Sam calls out a pealing request for ice cream, which, distracted, Anne tells him to get for himself.

She walks up the stairs, one step above the next, one foot rising after the other, and both hands on the banister that runs along the wall. She is going up to the bedroom to watch the news, to confirm that it is just bad traffic, that there is an accident between Jim's office and home, that there is a power outage downtown due to the thunderstorm that had blown through Philadelphia like a slamming bruise earlier that afternoon. He is only half an hour late. Jim, she promises herself, is sitting in his car fuming, fumbling with the radio, perfectly, normally, late.

The phone rings, a shout in her ear, and Anne kicks one toe into the green-carpeted top step. She shouts "I'll get it!" from the top of the stairs. For Anne, things get very muddy here. The patterns of the wallpaper unresolve themselves; the colors blur. She walks heavily to their bedroom, still holding onto the banister above the stairs, and sits fully on the bed, both feet on the floor, before picking up on the third ring.

"Hello?" She feels stuffed with paper towels.

"Annie? It's Louise." Jim's secretary. Anne loses her ability to breathe. "Annie, oh God, Jim was in an accident. I don't know why they called us here first, Annie, they just called here, and I got the phone, and . . . It's just been such a day. I know they'll call you, but . . . Oh, God. I'm so sorry, but he's gone." The phone is cold in her hand like a winter bone.

Her first thought: I shouldn't have hoped for traffic.

And then no thoughts at all. The voice on the phone keeps tumbling and squeaking in her ear, some words about "family" and "take the kids" and "file a report," but Anne doesn't understand. Her heart and stomach and chest have already exploded in that second without breath. She feels scorched, razed like a demolition site, and then stormed upon, wet, rotting, and dead. She feels all of it. None of it. Both.

And then, air. The impossible onslaught of breath, of having to breathe, of even being able to breathe, starts to leap back out of her as a wail, and she jams her hand, hard, into her mouth. The next morning her upper lip will be swollen and she will never remember why. The skin on her knuckles, she will notice in the shower that night, is bitten raw. But in that moment she moves, blindly and using her hands to pull herself along the hall, downstairs to make her children a bowl of popcorn—shoving the tinfoil pan across the coils of the stove until it explodes—and calls Polly across the street. Only then, only after she has told them, and shushed them, and sent them to the neighbor's for the night, only when they are gone, out of the house, and she is alone, does Anne Metcalfe's mind fill with the thousands of birds that have been wheeling white inside her skull, their sharp wings slapping the inside of her eyes. She sits on their bed and punches herself in the stomach until she loses the ability to cry.

It saves her; her children do not see her cry until weeks later, and then only when they catch her off guard. Sammy seems fine on the surface. He sits with his hamsters struggling in his arms, poring over his books and favorite shows on TV. Karen's is the wet, red-faced grief that overwhelms Anne. She chokes herself on Karen's tears for days, stuffing her daughter's misery down her throat to block her own. It is a month before she lets herself cry with her daughter. Their crying together foreshadows the fighting that will overtake them within a year.

Always Anne swallows the moans and louder mournings so that Karen and Sam won't hear. I have to be strong for them, she tells herself, late at night, when all she wants is to die or disappear. She bites her tongue repeatedly. I have to show them we'll be OK.

Through the lawyer's meetings, the lunch at Jim's office, the funeral, and shepherding

Karen and Sam back to school, Anne fails to understand one thing: The road Jim was driving on when he was hit by the truck wasn't on his normal route home. She doesn't know why he was there. It doesn't make any sense. And it is over a month before the calls—insisting that they pick up their new puppy—break through her confusion and explain why he'd been on that road, that afternoon. They pick up the puppy, and she hates it, resentful and guilty, since she knows how badly James wanted it for the family and since her porcelain Sam is instantly, blindingly, in love. The puppy is a white puffball with black eyes, and she wants to throttle it, to make its pink tongue loll. She hates herself for the feelings. The puppy is their last gift from Jim.

Eleven months later, when Anne is offered a job outside Washington, D.C., it feels like a chance to try and start anew. The Metcalfe family of three moves to Maryland within a year. They purchase a smaller house on an easier lot, in a neighborhood with lots of teenagers (for Karen) and a few adolescent kids (for Sam). And Anne tries hard to keep her children aloft, tries to accept when they seem so tired of life, tries to keep her own gaping pain at bay.

TWENTY

FLUSTERED FROM an angry call with a city health inspector who was somehow blaming *her* for a garbage spill in the alley behind the restaurant, Laurel ran into the marble lobby of the museum twenty minutes late. Sam had suggested Julie Taymor's Lion King exhibit as a consolation prize since there were no movies that particular week that either of them had wanted to see. He had reasoned that he could have his animals and museum, and she could have her theater and film. They would have crab cake sandwiches afterward as a treat.

"She arrives!" He crowed. "And guess what?" he offered, telegraphing his forgiveness of her half-hour-late arrival, "They have movies *incorporated* into the exhibit! It's the best of both worlds, I swear!" She laughed and pulled him into a long hug.

He pulled back to look at her. "Tell me how you are, really," he began.

She'd missed him; with everything else, it had been weeks since they'd had any real time together. It was like the circumstances of their lives were conspiring to pull them apart.

"And don't give me what you want me to hear. I know this stuff with your mom must be so awful." She let him drag her onto the elevator and out into the exhibit's bright, musical entryway. "How is she?" He kept up. "I feel so guilty about it all, I swear. I mean, I sent her a card at Christmas and tried calling once or twice a few weeks back, but—"

And in that very second, as if the lights had flashed on and off inside her, Laurel decided to move home. It wasn't a conscious decision, wasn't something she even knew, truly, she had been considering. The decision entered her like a butterfly made of light, toured through her insides, and cleaned all the thick red cords of confusion away. The idea that she would give up everything to care for her mother exulted briefly inside her, pulling all the weight from the back of her neck and shoulders and wrapping it gently around her arms and chest. It was a new weight, soft and relaxing, like a cool blanket on a warm day. She took a long breath and felt her shoulders and neck loosen, unclenched and free.

"I'm OK," she gave him a quick, shy smile. "Actually, I'm almost good." They stepped into a darkened room filled with large, framed shapes that should have been rustling. From the corner of her eye they looked like animals reduced to the frames of wooden boats. "But I have to warn you, I think I may need to go home and take care of her for a while."

"Go home?" Sam looked stricken. "You mean, go home more regularly, right? To check in and make sure she's OK?" Sam was framed by the shaggy multicolored shape of a baboon-priest. He looked tiny against its thousand fingers of color. "But the restaurant's been doing so well."

Laurel realized, after the bright blindness of her epiphany, how much loss her new decision would entail. She pulled back from the finality of her decision. It was too soon, and to probe it, to watch its effect on others, would be like prodding a bruise. It might scare her away from letting it take shape and heal.

She laughed and pulled Sam away from his hairy backdrop. "Of course, just to check in on her," she lied into the face of her best friend. She tried to ignore the unimagined future that was assembling itself, like the set of a play, before her eyes. She realized, with a little sadness, that it wasn't realistic to give up Terra, to give up her own life, and that she probably wouldn't go. "Of course I wouldn't go for good."

A WEEK later, Laurel was full of doubts. It had been a week since she silently decided to move home, a week since Sam's stricken face halted her, a week for the seeded doubts to sprout. In a conspiracy of second chances, everything about the restaurant was suddenly going well: reservations were up for the next few weeks, and they even had some for a month or two ahead; Mathilde's work papers had come through; Molly's mother had booked a *very* expensive fourth birthday party for Mae-Lin; and, just that morning, she had received a call about another review, calling Terra the perfect location for an intimate dinner and highlighting Laurel's dedication to organic, locally grown food

The restaurant glowed as well. Miguel had brought extra candles for every table and placed them around centerpieces of artfully arranged palm fronds. An extra-rich contingent of friends filled the heavy central table with laughter and shouts for wine. It was like her world could sense that she wanted to disappear and had colluded—her friends, success, a cool night—to give her the most beautiful collection of reasons to stay.

She hid her confusion well. Laurel moved fluidly, like a swimmer, checking in with her cooks, touching a back here, giving a bubbling brown sauce a stir and hitting it with shakes of nutmeg, cardamom, chili paste, and salt. Then back out into the dining room to thank the local commissioner for finally repairing the street. She should be happy, she thought. She almost was. But there was also this smooth, constant weight pulling her down.

Pushing through the swinging door into her kitchen, her mind blurred and faded to the memory of a summer at Avalon years ago.

Emily and Charlotte's heads bob around her like seals, just their heads above the choppy, deep blue water. Emily, the pale one, wears a tight rubbery helmet with flowers molded into the form, protecting her scalp, covering her white-red hair. The waves are glistening, reflecting blinding flashes of sunlight that highlight the girls' shocking peals of laughter. Charlotte swims truncated laps on her own. Mother and Father are at the shore, Mom shading her eyes with her hands, a dark blankness where her eyes and nose should be, one hand on the dark ruffled hip of her swimsuit. Her father is wading into the water, his calves and knees a darker color than the rest of him, stained by the sea.

Laurel is ducking her head in and out of the water, delirious with the taste of salt and sunshine. They have finished their lunch of potato chips, soda, and cheese sandwiches on the beach and have been promised taffy later this afternoon. Laurel's two front teeth, not yet fixed by braces, jut from her laughing, open mouth. Boats bob in the waves beyond her reach. She has never been so happy.

Mom was perfect then, Laurel realized, back in her kitchen, leaning near the photo of her father on the wall. She managed everything so smoothly that it didn't appear to have been orchestrated at all. Her father had brought home money and love and huge impossible theories for their heads. It wasn't until years later that she learned how her mother's family money enabled their trips to the shore. That there were cracks in her perfect family smoothed over with ironed cloth napkins and perfect, summertime tea.

Her mother's image filled her. Her mother then and now, as a young woman in fuzzy gray pictures, swimming alongside Laurel's younger self, just underwater and banded with white-yellow and blue-green. Her eyes playful, like a porpoise, then filling with water as her smile fades and she begins to sink deeper under the surface, sinking like a weight is pulling from below, her arms hanging above her toward her daughter. Dead weight around Laurel's neck.

Laurel shook herself, shuddering back into activity, noticing the confused faces of her cooking crew. She stepped into the kitchen and, shooing someone, leaned briefly on the clean, brushed-metal plane of the prep table. Thank God we're serving pulled chicken, she thought, grabbing a warm bird from its pan and ripping into the fibrous white meat; I have thirty-seven dinners to serve.

Tearing into the chicken, Laurel could feel her decision reasserting itself. She knew, without wanting to know, what she was going to do. Handfuls of shredded chicken arranged themselves on plates. But she couldn't, could she? Really leave? Laurel looked out upon her table of friends, on the soft, giving light of their presence. She rinsed strings of chicken off her hands and walked back through the kitchen toward her office, trying to look focused, determined to cover the fog she was in. She missed her father so much.

In her tiny office-closet, surrounded by spreadsheets and stacked napkins and a misplaced plastic tub of local goat cheese, she picked up the heavy telephone.

"Emily? Em? I know it's late. Sorry." She refused to take a deep breath. "I'm coming home. To Pennsylvania. I'm going to take care of Mom."

TWENTY-ONE

TWENTY-SIX CHILDREN, bright in their red, yellow, and green raincoats, bounced in their places near the entrance to the Zoo. Sam was leading his neighbor Nick's third-grade class on a tour, and their multicolored slickers were sugar-speckled with drops of rain. Despite the adorable fidgeting of the kids, the pervasive, wet chill perfectly matched Sam's mood. He should have been excited, packing for his trip to Hawaii with Dean, but the vacation had been sacrificed to another "real chance" in New York. Someone named Ariel, whom, Dean mentioned casually, he had been talking with for months, had a new round of network meetings for him to attend. "We'll go to Hawaii another time, soon," Dean promised, rubbing Sam's shoulders with both hands. "You never seemed totally into the trip," he continued, pressing the meat of one palm into Sam's back as his other hand pulled Sam tighter into him. "You didn't really want to go anyway, right?"

It had been very clear that, despite Sam's offer and although Dean assured him he wished it was otherwise, Sam wasn't needed in New York. Dean *had* invited him to join him for the weekend, but wanting to help out Jack and, secretly, wanting to punish Dean, Sam had declined.

Dean was already gone, having finished taping the morning news and flying up for a series of meetings that Friday afternoon. Sam had pushed him out the door that morning while Dean struggled for another, apologetic kiss. Rain in his boots, Sam wanted to kick himself for being so stupidly agreeable about it all in the vain hope that, through some miracle of new priorities, Dean would come home from New York happier to be in D.C. Maybe even missing me, Sam thought. There had been no mention, this time, of whether Sam might consider a move to New York as well.

And Sam still couldn't see New York as anything other than the stifling gray canyons of buildings, the dirty neon signs, the trash that blew like grit on every street. He knew there was more to it than that— great restaurants to share with Dean and show off to Laurel, museums and universities where he could try for another degree. But Sam couldn't see himself there, even when he tried. He also couldn't imagine—assuming Dean would even ask him—saying no. The shimmering possibility of the Bronx Zoo was like an oasis that Sam could almost breathe in, and he even thought he could be satisfied, probably briefly, at the small, rich-moms-and-strollers Central Park Zoo. Sam didn't even know if he *would* go to New York with Dean, but for the first time, he was convinced he wasn't going to be asked.

His jaw ached from pretending to smile.

Now, Dean was gone until Sunday, and Sam, suddenly, had seven days off from work and nothing to do. Jamie's spring break wasn't for another two weeks, and Laurel—with Terra's sudden success and her constant trips to Pennsylvania—was dissolving from his life like sugar into water. Maybe there wasn't so much to give up, he thought, maybe he could go to New York with Dean. He would talk to him when he got back, Sam resolved; he would bring it up even if he was scared. Sam's world, hemmed by a half circle of third graders, seemed unexpectedly small.

As the children, guided and hushed by Nick and their parents, settled into a quiet, attentive group, Sam resolved to call Dr. Anderson the next morning and just go to Brazil once and for all. Dean would barely notice, he told himself, watching rain pool off a stand of green eucalyptus leaves and the brim of his shiny hood.

"How many teeth does an alligator have?"

The question caught him off guard, and Nick saved Sam by taking his arm through his jacket and introducing, in alphabetical order, his students. "Guys, this is the Zookeeper, Mr. Metcalfe. He'll answer your question in a moment, Dakota. Remember, everyone gets one special question, but we're going to take our turns. Mr. Metcalfe is going to give us our tour today, and I want you to listen to him very carefully." The kids' upturned faces were both scrunched against the rain and wide-eyed as they watched Nick speak. "This whole day is a privilege for you, and I want you to show how appreciative you are." Sam wanted to laugh as Nick told the students how lucky they were to be standing outside under cold, insistent drifts of rain. Instead, he gave Nick a responsible, appreciative smile, and began explaining the rules for the tour. The parent-chaperones stood, like weary guideposts, all around.

"Because of the weather, you guys are going to get some special treats: first, we're going to the Elephant House where, if you're all good, you'll get to feed a giraffe." Cheers and a few whimpers bubbled together. "Then we'll go to the Reptile and Small Mammal Houses"—silence greeted that comment—"where the monkeys are!" "The monkeys" got cheers, and Sam was glad to have learned showmanship from Jack. "And finally, we'll go to Lion Island, where my friend Jack will show you how he takes care of the lions and tigers!" His last remark got more than half of the kids focused and excited, while their parents hovered over them, looking into the sky and frowning at the rain.

As he walked the children through the drizzling Zoo, Sam realized how rote his presentation had become. "The giraffe," he intoned as fearful eight-year-olds reached forward leafy branches and jerked them back at the looming swing of a giraffe's overwhelming head, "has a prehensile tongue that can reach twelve inches long." The rich, pungent smell of the elephant house had elicited squeals and wrinkled noses from the kids, but when he'd shuffled them to the giraffes, they'd fallen neatly in line. He would step in behind a nervous little blonde girl, scooting onto one knee, and cup her elbows and guide them upward to meet the giraffe's round, liquid eyes and grasping tongue. "Do you know what 'prehensile' means?" He would hug a nervous boy with dark eyes. Sam used to love giving tours more than anything—he had always felt like an ambassador for the Zoo. He still loved it, but today, he just felt tired.

It was Jack who saved the day. Jack whose wife had died, Jack who drank in the evenings and mornings and dozed off sometimes in the middle of the day. Jack, the Tiger Man whom Sam had been afraid might not handle things well, put on a show that widened twenty-six children's eyes and made their parents stand straighter and grasp their own children's shoulders with shared glee. Sam watched the parents' faces work as Jack spoke, watched their mouths struggle between smirk and smile and "oohs" of appreciation. Jack left every person there feeling like he had been talking directly and meaningfully to them. Every adult took materials on the Save the Tiger Fund as well.

Sam walked his charges slowly back uphill through the steady drizzle to the top of the Zoo. Nick, in a barn jacket, faded tie, and baseball cap, thanked him repeatedly between rounds of calls and gentle cuffs as he herded his kids, like a sheepdog, to the bus. Sam envied Jack so much that day; Nick too, he realized. Envied the simple, pure satisfaction of loving a job and doing it well. Sam had lost that joy, he realized, in disillusion, in distraction, in a distrust that he could direct his own fate at the Zoo. His poor howlers. Watching Jack, watching Nick and the children, Sam saw something in them all—a peacefulness, an innocence that he almost couldn't understand. He resolved to figure out why.

Later that afternoon, at the close of a contentious meeting in which he had negotiated a later move date for the golden lion tamarins to their summer free range, gotten a verbal commitment to move his howlers to a larger enclosure in proximity to the cotton tops, and spoken, in Jack's place, on behalf of acquiring a new African lioness, Sam realized that he and Dean had not had sex in a month and eleven days.

TWENTY-TWO

THE ZOO filled with babies, and it was as if the animals were almost wild again, as if their truest natures and instincts shone from their nests and warrens amid the green and budding leaves. The boa constrictor's lethargy gave way, briefly to energized hissing; the Asian elephants surprised their keepers with brash trumpeting; smaller mammals ripped wildly through the paths of well-worn exhibits; the African crowned crane stalked his enclosure, eyes as fierce as a hunter again. Sam rushed to work early and lingered late, watching his howlers, spiders, and golden lion tamarins rocket to life, sitting with Jack as the cats toured their tiered enclosures, smelling the revitalized smells. It was as if the world had woken up and remembered something long forgotten.

Sam's mother called him at work. It wasn't easy for Sam to take the call—it was never easy for any Zookeeper to take calls while moving constantly, up and down the hills and through the back corridors of the Zoo. There were no phones in the heavy concrete strings behind the cages and no Zoo could afford outfitting every keeper with a cell phone; Sam had resisted getting his own cell phone for years. He got the word from the Zoo dispatch operator—who doubled as the hoofstock curator's assistant—over the too-public scrolling radio system. "Sam, your mom's calling for you," she chirped into the walkie-talkie system for everyone to hear. Sam was using the phone at Woody's desk while she entered data into her computer, studiously pretending to ignore everything he said.

"Sam? It's Mom. How are you?" He heard her tapping a pen against the mouthpiece of the phone. "How are the monkeys?" she asked, already distracted by the time she asked the second question, clearly still focused on whatever project was in front of her at her desk.

"The monkeys are fine, Mom." Work wasn't a good time for either of them to talk. "I'm actually kind of busy. What's up?"

"Nothing," she responded after a moment's hesitation. Something in her voice caught a string in Sam's chest. "I just wanted to see how you are." Her voice entered him and pulled the string tight. Mom, he thought, with love. He could tell she wasn't tearing through folders anymore.

"Well," he warmed, "there is this one cool thing I've been wanting to tell you." He felt her resume looking over her contracts, felt his own, smooth-papered relief. "You know the tamarins we let free-range in the Great Ape House?" A pen tap of assent. "Well, we've just gotten approval to participate in a similar program for our Buffy-headed marmosets, and I've got this one pregnant female who I'm so excited about. She's never bred before and is totally new to the gene pool. There's a lot to figure out. And, her offspring have already been approved by the SSP, so—"

"SSP?"

"Species Survival Plan. They get to say which animals breed and which don't. You know that, Mom. It's to protect the gene pool. We do it for the tamarins, the howlers, all the animals now. Anyway, if she has a baby, we'll be able to send it out for breeding and I'll have the ammunition to really get a release program started." He rushed on—the pregnancy and the potential to institute a new captive-release program for the Zoo had distracted Sam effectively for nearly a month. He had caught himself, more than once, sketching teeming jungle enclosures for an overgrown, south-facing slope at the Zoo. He also knew that his mother loved her children's successes, and so he overcompensated by raving about his work.

"You're giving her baby away?" His mother asked in a concerned, distant voice, then called out "five minutes" to someone in her office. Sam heard her cup her hand over the phone.

"Really. Sometimes . . ." She trailed off. Her voice had switched from concerned to accusatory, and it raised Sam's hackles. Occasionally Sam's mother would decide that Zoos were cruel places that jailed animals and tore mothers from babies, husbands from wives. She and Sam had haggled over those questions for hours when he was in college, sitting up late at night while he fed and burped Jamie, and she, towel ready on her shoulder for her turn, read over reports from field organizers in California and the South. She had once likened the Zoo system to slavery and the circus, and the ugly silence—as if they were both walking on shredded feet—that followed had led to Sam's brief, one-semester move into the dorms half an hour down the road.

He braced himself. He was worried about Dean and Jack and the marmoset's difficult pregnancy, and he didn't have the time or energy to debate the relative good and evil of his work at the Zoo. He'd certainly never been invited to question the value of his mother's work, or anything his mother did. Sam's job, he had always known, was to counsel, to console, to agree. He took a deep breath, preparing to cut the conversation short, when she sighed.

"It just makes me think of Grandma, somehow," she breathed, her voice higher than normal. She wasn't angry. He'd read her wrong. "You know how she used to get, those last few years, when we would drive by her old synagogue in Detroit?" Sam nodded into the phone. He could remember the long, empty drives up gray Telegraph Road, the endless Thanksgiving stream of closed fast-food restaurants, closed party shops, closed car radio stores. His grandmother would shake her head angrily as they passed the old synagogue, low and brown in its flat parking lot, saying over and over again how she'd never felt at home there, how she didn't miss the old community at all.

Sam started to say something about missing Grandma or missing Dad, when his mother went on: "We just all seem to give things up so easily nowadays. It's nice that Karen keeps a menorah, isn't it? It's like your monkey's daughter—things just get so easily lost."

"Mom . . . "

"Listen," she continued, all the wistfulness gone from her voice, and Sam was relieved to hear that she had shifted her attention again.

"Sam, I was thinking that, since we haven't decided on anything for Mother's Day yet, we should try and plan something busy, so we won't have to watch Jamie and Karen fight all day long." She paused, waiting for his reaction, then continued. "Maybe dinner at Laurel's? Or a movie out here?" He wondered if there was some other agenda hidden somewhere.

"Well, Terra might not work. Laurel's been spending a lot of time with her mom lately."

"Of course. I need to call her." He could hear her making a note. "And would you like to invite Dean?" Silence. Sam hadn't mentioned Dean in a few weeks and needed a moment to decide how to answer. He could see his mother, sitting in her office at the shabby edge of downtown, surrounded by cabinets and plants, wondering if she might have asked too much. She was expert at this, applying her incredibly sensitive trigger finger to familial emotional situations and retreating so instantly and apologetically that the only option was to assure her that everything would be all right.

Sam wanted to get to the Zoo's hospital and his own, expectant mother, so he gave her the most basic version of what she wanted to hear.

"Dean's fine. I'll ask him to come." He left out the fact that, just as likely, Dean would again be out of town.

"And, yes, I'll talk to Jamie again, though I don't know what good it'll do. I know he wants to go to Roosevelt, but please don't tell Karen I said that. I think he needs to know he can make the decision for himself." Sam could hear his mother's relief, and a whispered "two minutes" through clenched fingers and teeth, through the phone.

"And Dean?" She persisted.

"Mom." Sam breathed out through his nose. "You know I can't just chat while I'm at work." He rubbed his forehead while she waited for him to go on. "Dean is fine, Mom. We're both just busy right now. He's got his new schedule and everything." Sam tried to resist sounding tired but knew his own resignation was crawling across the phone to his mother. He ran through their conversation in his mind, trying to make sure that he'd said enough to put her mind at ease. "I'll call Karen and get Mother's Day all set up." He worried that she had sensed the disillusionment in his voice.

Her voice came through an ocean of tinny air. "Honey? That's great to hear. Thank you. And that Dean *was* so nice. Don't be too quick to let him go."

———————

THE ZOO'S Buffy-headed marmosets were ideal animals for exhibition—active in the daytime, energetic and small, with bright fluffy bursts of tan hair around their heads, striped tails, and active, inquisitive minds. Like all his tamarins, they were a treat both for visitors to the Zoo and the keepers who cared for them. He had to admit it—compared with the antic smaller monkeys, his howlers might not actually be the most exciting of animals, and his mind flew to images of an enclosure with both howlers and marmosets living in the same space. Mickey, the pregnant female, would blend well with other species, he knew.

Mickey had been a special favorite of Sam's from the moment they had first introduced her into the group. She was small for her species and initially timid but fierce.

For the first few weeks, Mickey kept largely to herself, staying near the edges of the enclosure and retreating to an unused nest box at night, but she was slowly intermingling with the group. Sam liked what he saw of her behavior and what he called, despite knowing he wasn't supposed to assign human traits to animals, her plucky charm. As a rule, animal introductions are always monitored very closely, and Sam, having coordinated the interior free-range program for the tamarins, had been asked to supervise Mickey's observation. He jumped at the task. Despite exhaustive studies on animal behavior for every species, Sam never trusted the books entirely; with animals, you never knew what to expect.

Unaware of Sam's prompting and the approval of her species survival plan, Mickey had bred immediately with an immature male (who was also new to the captive gene pool) soon after her introduction to the group. Toward the end of her gestation period, Sam had pulled her from the marmosets' group enclosure and begun weighing her every day. She hadn't gained as much weight as called for and, as she approached her due date, had oddly glassy eyes. Sam found himself checking his watch incessantly, going in earlier and staying later, so he could sit near her nest box and keep her close. Dean was busy and distracted, and the excuse of nights at the Zoo arranged itself neatly, without Sam's even knowing it was there. The Zoo regained its firm hold on Sam's heart: Jack, despite the stiffness he'd exhibited since Millie had died, clapped for Sam and offered himself up as a surrogate grampa for Mickey's child.

Leaning back in a plastic chair in the small corridor that held Mickey's cage, Sam dozed off with a book in his lap. It was 5 a.m. and he had been sitting by her, munching through a bag of Laurel's cranberry scones, for more than two hours. The warm darkness and sweet crumbs lulled him to sleep, and when he started awake, minutes later, he was unnerved by Mickey's heavy breathing and the tiny gasps that had permeated his dreams.

She had her baby the same day. She had a terrible time of it, and her keepers, by extension, were exhausted too. Sam, Gwen, and the veterinarian had crowded the small window into Mickey's nest box for almost two hours, watching her hunch and moan and claw at the straw before, regretfully, sedating her and pulling her out of her tiny patch of straw. Sam cradled her in his palm for one too-short second before placing her in the thickly padded crate for the short drive to the hospital. He could feel her tiny heart beating faster than he could bear.

Once at the infirmary, the vet was able to induce labor, and she had her baby immediately. Every step was taken to minimize the impact of the unnatural circumstances of the birth, and the actual moment, when it came, was incredibly rich. Without cleaning the baby or touching it more than absolutely necessary, the vet confirmed it was breathing and took a quick, squeal-inducing blood sample. Sam was able to replace the mother and newborn in the nest box before Mickey woke up. The infant, dark and still slick, burrowed into Mickey's underside. Sam's own sweat felt sacred and well earned.

He and Gwen hugged. They had seen a lot of births at the Zoo, but each and every one was completely magical. His sweating hands shook long after he had replaced Mickey and her baby in their nest. Flushed with energy and exhaustion, he ran to the keeper's office and the phone.

"Dean!" he called out, louder than intended. "I have the most amazing story to tell you!"

"Sam? What's up, hon?"

Sam could hear something in Dean's voice, like he was holding his mouth very still and far away from the phone. A cold pool began to spread through his stomach and chest.

"Dean? Are you eating something? I thought we had dinner plans tonight." Sam hated that such a stupid, useless question was the first thing he said, hated that he couldn't rush into Dean with all the pent-up energy and love he was feeling, that he was always jumping to unhappy conclusions, that he couldn't be excited and enthusiastic for one minute without fearing that Dean's reaction would smack into him like a choking wave. He realized in that second of confusion how terrified he was. Gwen, who had been hovering like a sister behind him, slowly backed away. He waved her out the door with what he hoped was a respectable smile. Desperate to hold the power of Mickey's birth like a shining shield, he tried to keep his voice light.

"Oh, shit," Dean sighed, trying to speak without chewing again. Sam was right; Dean had forgotten their dinner and was already eating. His story felt absurdly, unreasonably, lost.

Dean apologized through the food stuffed into his mouth. "I forgot, honey. It's just that I got word on the most amazing story, and I lost track of time. See," he started, revving into enthusiasm as Sam's continued to die. Sam listened with as much interest as he could, his own heat dissipating into the street. When Dean, seven minutes later (by Sam's watch), interrupted himself to ask what Sam's news was, Sam told him it could wait. He even assumed a fascinated expression on his face as if Dean could see him through the phone.

TWENTY-THREE

SAM ROUNDED the corner to his apartment, his face dappled in leafy-green light, feeling fresh and strong from the gym. He was ready to reverse the effects of weeks of cold rain and too much food; he felt buoyant, spring-loaded, ready for whatever might come. He felt like he looked better than he had in a long time.

Sam needed to feel better. It was the first full weekend he and Dean would have together in over a month, and it was going to be a good weekend for a change, a *perfect* weekend, even if he had to make it so. They had two whole days together, and the impossibly blue skies seemed to promise that everything would be all right. The ground exhaled its loamy smell.

As a cool breeze pushed Sam toward the front stoop, he saw Dean waiting on the steps, cast in gold by the morning light, standing with their bikes balanced precariously under his hands. He almost choked on his happiness. Dean was vibrating with enthusiasm and welcome, and Sam's constant, vague fear of New York was momentarily banished. It was April; it was springtime. A few small, white clouds studded the sky.

"We're going bike riding!" Dean shouted when he saw Sam walking toward him. Two guys from the third floor, one's hand resting on the other's broad neck, looked indulgently behind them as they stepped through the lobby door.

"We are?" Sam asked, hopping up the two steps of the stoop to take his bike from Dean. They kissed, and Sam patted his boyfriend on the butt. He felt, through blue shorts and black Lycra, Dean's firm flesh.

It was hot to the touch. Distracting. He left his hand on Dean's ass as images of stripping him and biting into him strobed across his mind. He imagined the pale fur on a peach. "Half an hour?" he asked, squeezing and trying to send mental messages of sex. Dean vigorously wagged his head, stubborn as a dog shaking his own leash for a walk. "Now."

Sam was disappointed, a thirsty bird hopping just out of reach of water, but decided that Dean's enthusiasm would have to be enough.

"OK, OK!" He laughed, hands surrendering in the air. "Just let me put my bag inside. Do we need water or anything?" Dean presented two full bottles and a fanny pack for Sam to wear. He was giddy in his silence.

Through the lobby door as he stepped inside, Sam heard Dean call: "I got the weekday anchor job! My weekends are free from now on!"

Sam saw a great stretch of lazy Sundays amass before him, warm light through the window, their feet touching on the couch.

"Morning anchor! We have to celebrate! New York can't be too far off now!"

Sam tripped on the first step.

They rode south across Dupont Circle and down P Street, two animals held in quarantine together, sniffing and testing the air and cautiously exploring their newly expanded home. Sam was lost for that portion of the ride, the easy back and forth of their bikes, even though— perhaps because—it was disjointed. They were held to a gentle pace, cruising a few hundred feet and stopping to pause and observe the city around them. They crossed the P Street Bridge toward Georgetown and dipped into the swath of green grass and yellow daffodils that heralded Rock Creek Park.

Their speed increased as runners, walkers, and other bikers fought to keep pace with the oceanic swell of traffic that rushed forward at their side. Sam had to peddle harder as Dean forged into the currents of the path, his back always just ahead like a dolphin breaking the waves. Sam wondered what happened to all that rush and noise of cars and buses and movement; the roadside banks funneled it up and away, but he couldn't imagine it all simply evaporating into the sky.

The ride was more intense than Sam wanted, and his legs were already sore from the gym, but he bit his tongue, not wanting to ruin Dean's mood. They had regular off-ramps and stop signs, and at each one Sam pulled up beside Dean and ran a hand down his back, and they talked for a moment before pushing off again.

"How far do you want to go, you think?" Sam asked, looking at Dean from the side of his eyes as he took a long drink of water. He'd have to be careful, he thought, not to run out.

"Dunno." Dean was in a simple, playful mood. "Alexandria, at least? Maybe Mount Vernon? What do you think?" The traffic blocking their progress ceased, and Dean was off before Sam could respond.

Sam had a last reprieve. There, before the Kennedy Center's rectangular overhang cloaked the path with shade, where the bike trail first curved out to run along the river, they stopped, leaning their bikes between their legs and wrapping their arms around each other. They did nothing more than breathe in the warming air, the sunshine, the rowers on the water. We look good together, Sam thought, rich with pride.

Suddenly, he was aware of a rapidly cooling spot on his shoulders where Dean's arm had just been. He pushed off, following Dean toward the bridge. Dean was pedaling fast—adjusting his seat, lowering his shoulders, clenching his elbows and triceps and leaning in over the handlebars. Sam could no longer see his head, just a glossy black hump where his helmet cleared his shoulders. That and that glossy black butt. Sam wasn't used to this voyeuristic back view of Dean, and for a moment he just enjoyed the broad "V" of his back and the mechanical pumping of his legs. Sam loved Dean's calves, thought of them sometimes as drumsticks he wanted to eat. Relished the feeling of Dean's legs against his chest. He pulled in close behind his boyfriend and enjoyed the sight.

His view began changing, though it was imperceptible as long as Sam didn't look away. When his focus shifted to the river, or to a helicopter searing the sky above him, Sam's view of Dean, upon looking forward again, seemed suddenly, significantly, changed. Dean was diminished. Dean was farther away. Sam played the game with himself, as if conducting a lab exercise where he had to identify the element of change that causes a chemical reaction. Testing, he looked away again, and tried to identify the point of play in a volleyball game across the street. He found himself focusing on a tall, tan man with dark, clipped hair and a shiny bald spot that was winking in the sun. Probably a marine, Sam thought, and looked again. He managed to keep his eyes away from Dean for almost a minute, testing, testing, testing. When he looked back, Dean was gone.

When he found him, a hundred feet ahead and hidden by a crowd of heavy, midwestern tourists, Dean was already on the upslope to the broad, granite bridge, passing the powerful winged horses that guarded the exit from D.C. Sam stared up at the ripe, stone sculptures, loving the richness of animal sentinels (horses, lions, eagles, men) that guarded every bridge and circle they rode past. Accelerating, he caught Dean at the top of the great flight of steps where presidents used to arrive in Washington by boat. Where Sam was still, always, hit by the grand sweep of the river—dazzling sun on water, black roadway, white stone. He thought of the crowded history of his city and loved it. He caught the back of Dean's shirt just as they reached the full, clean span of the bridge.

"Hey!" It sounded sharper than he had intended. In all those separated minutes, Dean had probably never even looked back.

Dean looked up from his riding—a man reduced to the determined, fierce line of rider and bike—and broke his concentration with a smile that knocked Sam's anger away.

"Hey, honey. Isn't this amazing? I love the sun! And wasn't that group of old people a hoot? It took everything I had not to stop and do a human interest story on them. Bible Belt Betties, or something!" Sam laughed along. "You better get moving though, sweetie," he patted Sam's ass. "I can't wait to really open up and ride." With that, Dean's face rejoined the arrow of his body, and he surged ahead again.

Crossing the river felt like leaving something behind—even as Dean was leaving Sam behind—and penetrating some kind of invisible barrier. Even though it didn't look that way, D.C. was a peninsula, hemmed in by rivers or poverty on all three sides, and for a moment Sam almost caught a thought about his own boundaries, his own difficult places to pass. Dean coursed off the bridge like a river in a sudden storm and shot onto the riverside trail.

The Virginia side of the bike path was folded into a wide green park enriched by stands of evergreens, magnolia, and low, dark holly, and edged by either the river or small patches of richly reeking marsh. Dean kept disappearing around high banks of deep green grass. Even across the river from D.C., the path was still crowded with bikers, meandering social groups, walkers and joggers, the occasional coordinated group. Sprawling families dotted the grass, endless picnics with unmoving, boulderlike grandmothers and brightly draped mothers chasing gorgeous, dark-eyed kids. Sam rode easily, in love with the path, telling himself that just being out in nature with Dean was enough.

He loved the variety—old and young, fat, thin, white, Latino, black. Fishermen and their sons, mothers guiding small hands on the strings of kites. There were Canada geese and hundreds of ducks with bobbing lines of fuzzy babies and sternly quacking moms. An oriole, jet-black with brilliant orange patches on its shoulders, flashed past. Sam caught himself wishing he was riding alone, stopping whenever he wanted to sit and watch the world go by.

When he looked for Dean again, it took a minute to find him, and Sam realized he was probably half a mile ahead.

"Dean!" Sam yelled. "Dean!"

This time, Sam didn't disguise his anger at all and refused to kill himself to catch him. He rode, fast but comfortably, and looked around at the freshly blooming trees. He focused on the long, classical stretch of the glassy Potomac, the monuments and memorials standing tall and hazy across the river, and refused to let Dean's hurry ruin his view. He kept his own pace, making Dean ease off his pedals, apply the brakes to his bike, and balance, waiting for Sam to catch up.

"Jesus, Dean, when did you decide we were having a race? I thought this was a bike *ride*." He tried to weave in a laugh with the last part, nervous at his own anger and the incredulous look on Dean's face.

"What? We are having a bike *ride*, thank you." Dean muttered. "I just want to actually get some exercise too—isn't that what a bike ride is about?" He was breathing hard, and a rivulet of sweat was making its way down the crease of his temple toward his cheek. It looked salty. Despite himself, Sam wished he could lean in to lick it off.

"Actually, I thought it was about spending the day together, which isn't so easy when you're riding twenty feet ahead of me all the time." He felt audacious and stomach-churning scared. Dean's eyes had gotten sharp, and the irises were very small. Sam could feel the barbed energy Dean was giving off.

"I just want to ride, OK?" Dean began, apologetic and curt at once. "And I don't want to fight. Can we . . . " He took a deep breath and assembled his face. "How about if we go fast until we reach Alexandria, and then we can ride back at whatever speed you want?" Dean was trying to please Sam with this compromise—it was perfectly reasonable, smart, and helpful—but, irrationally, it infuriated Sam. He knew that it wasn't entirely this bike ride that was making him so mad, but the furious beetle-clicking inside his head obscured rational thought. He checked himself, leaned over his handlebars, and gave Dean a quick, ringing kiss.

"Sounds very fair. Sorry I yelled. Ride on."

Having agreed to a fast ride, Sam knew he shouldn't have been so upset when Dean shot away, his back tire leaving a riverine scar in the pebbled soil. Sam watched it slowly fill with brown water, leaning his shadow over the ground like a cloud and watching as white particles pushed above the waterline to create a tiny, perfect beach. It was like watching natural succession: a lake becomes a pond becomes a field. Dean had to call back from ahead to pull him out of the reverie.

"Sam? You with me?" he asked, trying to make it sound like a joke. "I'm going to really just ride full out for a bit, I think," he called over his shoulder, looking away briefly as a man and a woman rode past. "I'll meet you at the bakery when you get there." Dean waved and turned away, kicking off. Sam pushed himself forward, already twenty feet behind. He rose onto his seat and started to ride, leaving his little landscape behind.

The first minutes of riding hard were the worst, but Sam tried to focus on his own knees pumping down and pulling back up, tried to enjoy the tightness in his shoulders and chest and the flying greens and blues that whizzed like a thousand cicadas on a summer night. He tried to remember moments of exultation when riding in the past, whizzing down hillsides to the beach or, as a kid, flying down neighborhood streets with friends.

It didn't work. That morning, all Sam had wanted was to be with Dean, and right then, Dean felt gone. Sam pushed through the next few miles, head low and legs feeling like they were filled with molasses instead of blood. It took another half hour to reach the bakery, and Dean was nowhere in sight.

Sam pulled his bike to a stop and rested one foot on the bakery's shady front step. Through the leaded, colonial window Sam watched the people lined up for chocolate croissants, bagels, and coffee. Dean wasn't inside. Sam unhooked his helmet and pulled it off, squinting against running sweat to look up the street. Noon. A breeze cooled his sweaty head. The street wasn't too crowded, and after a minute Sam heard the screech of tires and felt a hand on his neck.

"Sorry. Got here a while ago and figured I'd get in some more exercise before you showed up. What took you so long?" Dean was still bouncing, but the exuberance was tempered, and annoyance and interest mingled in his voice like two bumblebees in a wobbly dance. He shaded his eyes to look into the store. "Did you get something to eat?" He made a slow, wide circle in the street before berthing next to Sam again.

"No, just got here. I'm fine. Just not into racing, I guess. My legs don't feel great." Sam felt sullen and resentful, like the last kid picked for the team who tries desperately to pretend he doesn't care. "I did already do four miles on the treadmill this morning, you know."

"OK. Well." Dean thought for a moment. "I guess I hadn't realized you'd be tired. I'm sorry. But I'm feeling super pumped, and I really want to ride on a bit. If you want to have lunch, why don't you rest for a few minutes while I put in another couple of fast miles. Then I'll meet you and we can eat." Dean had taken a deep breath before offering this second compromise, and Sam knew by now to recognize the signs. Projected ease. False helpfulness. Looking earnestly at Sam, Dean was really just talking to the light.

"Just go for your ride," Sam offered in return, carefully extracting any spiteful sounds from his voice. "I'm not really that hungry anyway. I'll head back now, and you can ride out and catch me on the way back in. I just want to see the day." Clouds, heavy and gray like the ones in his head, were barreling past the buildings above him and beginning to dilute the sun. "I actually think I'll duck into the bookstore for a minute." Dean looked doubtful. "I promise I don't mind." Sam emphasized the word "promise" to let Dean off the hook and to block his inevitable, duty-bound, protest. Sam knew Dean really just wanted to ride, knew that he was holding him back that morning, and that he would stay with Sam, *walk all the way back if needed*, even though he would resent the slow pace the whole way. Sam loved him and felt sick at the thought.

Dean grinned like a puppy just unhooked from his leash. He bounded into Sam and away again, riding additional circles in the street before starting to ride away. Watching Dean glow in the cobbled light of the street made Sam love him so much. He thought of a poster from his sister's room, years ago, when they were teens. A soft-focus image of a unicorn under a rainbow. *If you love something, set it free.* God, how ridiculous we were, he thought, gazing up at that stupid poster and thinking it was the answer to love. It was a beautiful idea, Sam knew, but he also knew, from experience, that relationships were never that simple. He knew, from the Zoo, that sometimes when you love something and set it free, it runs away.

In the bakery, Sam bought a sandwich and a bottle of water and a brownie bigger than his fist. He ate it all sitting in the sun and rode slowly, lingeringly home. The arched height of the bridge into Georgetown seemed like too great of a span to push himself across, and he thought of the questions children always asked at Lion Island—"Why don't the lions just jump out?"—which Sam always answered, blindly, without thought: "They could get out if they really worked at it, but it's just high enough, just daunting enough, that they don't even bother to try."

Sam walked across the bridge. In Georgetown, he had two disappointing slices of pizza and a Coke in a dirty bagel shop with smudged, red-and-yellow seats. He spent half the ride looking over his shoulder behind him, but Dean never came into view.

———

THAT NIGHT, when Dean did get home, he had flowers in his hand. Sam was sitting, carefully arranged, on the couch. He wanted to look casual, handsome, self-sufficient, and welcoming all at the same time. He had watered all the plants and changed his "thrown-together" outfit twice. Dean swooped in for a fast, deep kiss and thanked Sam again for letting him ride. Nervously, they avoided each other's eyes. Dean took a shower, and when he emerged, Sam ran a hand across his chest.

"I thought we could go to Terra tonight," he suggested, beginning to rub Dean's shoulders but avoiding his eyes. "Laurel says Saturday nights are really starting to pop, and—"

"Terra isn't the only restaurant in D.C., you know," Dean sighed, and it didn't sound like an appreciative sigh for the impromptu massage. "I was thinking we could try that new—"

"What are you talking about, Dean? For God's sake, I know Terra isn't the only restaurant in town," Sam mimicked, mincing through the words. His anger was flaring again. It was becoming kind of a regular thing. "Can't I like what I like?" He realized he was still kneading Dean's shoulders, and stopped, but in removing his hands he saw the long line of Dean's back, and his anger fell. I like *you*, he wanted to say, but in that moment couldn't push out the words. "Terra is a great restaurant, you have to admit that. We met there." Sam wanted to punch himself for the last words. Why did it always sound like a whine?

"Yes, Sam, we met at Terra, and it is a genuinely wonderful place. You know I love it. But there are trattorias, and tavernas, and Ethiopian and sushi and that new dumpling place in Georgetown and about a hundred new, cool restaurants downtown too. Sometimes I think if you had your way, we'd never eat anywhere else." He stepped away from Sam and toward the bedroom. "I'm going to get changed. Please consider living for a moment without your desperate loyalty blinders on."

Dinner that night, at a sleek new Thai place in Dean's neighborhood, was fine.

TWENTY-FOUR

IT WAS cooler than usual, even for May, and Sam zipped his sweatshirt up to the neck, pulled the hood strings tight. Laurel had invited him to the restaurant for dinner, and when he arrived, twenty minutes early, the door was locked. He swung his arms listlessly as he looked up and down the street, waiting for her to arrive. Dean had called, thrilled from the success of his first morning as anchor, sounding as if their fight had never happened, and promising champagne the next night. A colorful new card store across the street looked inviting, and Sam thought of running in quickly to buy Dean a card, but he was nervous. He wasn't used to being *summoned* to Terra, and he didn't want to miss anything Laurel had to say.

Molly and Kara walked up, swinging Mae-Lin between them. They hugged him and asked where Miguel was, realizing all together that Laurel had orchestrated *something*, and wondering, with nervous laughter, what special occasion she had cooked up. Looking into Terra through the large glass windows, Mae-Lin, in her pink cap and puffy coat, reported to no one in particular that it was dark and empty. Around them in the cool night, a few people walked by, and the branches of the trees waved tenuously in the breeze. They waited together, Sam holding Kara's hand, Molly's hands on Kara's shoulders and Mae-Lin huddled at their knees.

Laurel arrived with plastic bags straining her hands and bending her arms. She pulled up at the little crowd and handed everyone a bag. Sam was amazed at how powerful the lack of a hug and kiss felt in that moment. He and the girls shared appraising looks over Laurel's back as she leaned down to unlock the door. Laurel had put on a lot of weight in the past months, standing around the fading restaurant and worrying about her mother with a batter-covered spoon in hand. Sam was worried. Laurel had always been disarmingly, nonchalantly skinny. She never dieted, she always ate whatever was served, she was constantly baking elaborate, buttery desserts, and she never worked out beyond whatever physical toll running her restaurant took. She was so tall, and everyone just muttered "metabolism" as she pushed a pumpkin cheesecake onto the table and took herself a heaping slice. Sam sometimes hated her for that, and he knew Molly did too.

But in the past few months her arms had become heavier and the swells of her hips and breasts had become more pronounced; watching her lean into the glass-centered door, Sam wondered if everything was really all right. Laurel had been staying home a lot, giving Miguel the restaurant's reins a few nights a week, and talking to her mother every day. She told Sam that she was seeing every new movie that came out. He and Molly had become twice-a-day talkers, dissecting any and every signal Laurel sent.

Laurel seemed to lean against her door forever, pushing keys against the lock and blowing her hair from her forehead in angry little bursts. When she got the door open, she barreled through. "I prepared everything at home so we can eat pretty quickly. I hope you all want soup." They followed behind her, into the empty room, quieting as if entering a cathedral. Quickly, they discarded their jackets, purses, and bottles of wine; Laurel had already regathered her bags and charged, headfirst, into the kitchen. Left behind, they turned on lights and listened to the clanging sound of metal spoons and mixing pots. Molly gave Mae-Lin a coloring book and box of crayons, which she bent her dark head to in deep concentration. Sam heard the hot *whoosh* of the gas burner on the stove.

Miguel entered with a shouted "Possums!" and his arms flung wide. He looked past them to Laurel in the kitchen. "Hey, girl," he called to her, over their heads, and headed straight back. He was nervous; the restaurant, in a way it would never be for Laurel's other friends, was his too. He straightened a picture on the wall as he walked through, and Sam wanted to touch his slim waist and tapered back. He was surprised with himself. He should be thinking of Dean right now—Dean who hadn't been invited to come along. He shook the feeling of Miguel's firm waist out of his hands.

"Listen," Miguel continued speaking to Laurel across the room, "I heard about a great new wine purveyor at lunch today, and—Laurel?"

She had disappeared into the huge, walk-in freezer, and her best friends, her regular home-away-from-home crew, felt suddenly lost.

"Laurel?" Miguel repeated, his voice sounded young. "Can I come by early tomorrow to talk over some ideas?" Everyone was looking to where her small hand emerged from the freezer. It waved, haphazardly, in Miguel's direction. It wasn't an answer, but it was a typical Laurel reaction, and they continued turning on lights and setting the table for dinner.

Gathering spoons from the tall pine hutch where Laurel had arranged silverware, plates, and menus in gleaming rows, Sam watched his friends go about their individual tasks. A sharp, rich smell was beginning to reach him from the kitchen. "It's just squash and some light herbs, guys; I hope that's OK," Laurel called out, though no one ever questioned her cooking. "I just wanted something summery and light." Sam felt confused tears welling in his throat. He pawed through a soft pile of napkins as if he were stroking the head of a child.

"Come on, sweetie," Miguel chided, knocking Sam softly on the arm. He had a full glass of wine in one hand and an open bottle in the other. Sam smiled down at himself. He was standing, head down with his arms crossed against his chest, the napkins fanning out like drooping leaves. "You look like a goddamn dead peacock. Now get the silverware on the table. Laurel says she wants us to sit down." They sat, descending like flowers slotted each into its established place in a vase. Mae-Lin settled between her parents and began pushing orange goldfish crackers around her plate. Miguel, humming, refilled everyone's wine. Laurel walked over slowly with dark mitts over her hands and placed the huge steaming bowl on the table, sitting heavily at her seat at the table's end.

"Guys," she began, then stopped to rub her eyes and forehead with her hands. "Guys, shit. I don't know what to say." She tried again, stopping everyone's helpful muttering and rearranging. Sam watched as Molly's hands dropped to her daughter's shoulders and Miguel's came carefully to rest on the table's edge. Kara's hands remained above her plate, spoon suspended, as if preparing for the food that should be arriving in front of her to eat. Sam couldn't feel his hands, his difficult thumb, and didn't want to risk looking down. It was as if they were young birds, watching their mother's beating shadow block the streaming light, awaiting whatever morsels were to come.

"I'm closing the restaurant," Laurel announced. She took a deep breath against the silence. "And I'm moving home to Pennsylvania to be with Mom." Her voice broke on the word "home." Laurel gathered herself with a shrug of her shoulders and raised her face with an expression of determined openness and hope. He couldn't tell if she felt better for having told them, or if she was just trying to appear cheerful in spite of her news. Later, she told Sam that saying the words out loud that night had made her feel lighter than she had in months. As if, in closing one door, she had opened one to somewhere new.

That night, however, she avoided her friends' eyes and rushed on. "It's just the right thing to do, you know. Terra is so much work, and my mom really needs me, and Charlotte's in California, and Emily has the kids, and it just, I don't know, seems like, well . . . " She trailed off. Her hands reached out across the table toward Kara and Sam, climbing blindly toward them. Changing course, she took a gigantic ladle in one hand and the deep, comforting bowl of soup in the other. No one spoke as they began passing their own small bowls down the table toward her. "It's OK, guys. I promise. I actually want to go."

Everyone began talking at once, the crystallized air shattering under the weight of their shocked response.

"You're not serious, are you?" Sam half-shouted, half-laughed, and Laurel stopped ladling the soup. "You're moving to Pennsylvania? When are you leaving? Where will you live?" Sam asked, laughter and a scream fighting in his throat. The others were silent. Of them all, Sam clearly relied on Laurel the most. He was the one who always arrived early on Tuesdays for dinner, the one who stayed late, hanging around for dropped touches as Laurel passed by, rather than going home. Even Miguel, his livelihood in question, had more self-control.

Sam and Laurel stared at each other like old lovers surprised to run into each other across a foreign square. "What about the restaurant? Terra's been doing so well," he suggested, grasping at possibilities to keep his Laurel right here. "You can't go. I mean, where will you live?" He repeated, then repeated it again.

"Sam, she'll be . . . Laurel, you'll get an apartment, right? You'll get a chef job somewhere?" Kara stepped in, pragmatic and helpful, hoping to move the conversation forward and away from Sam's bald need. She stroked Mae-Lin's dark hair. "We'll all miss you, but you'll be back here all the time. Right?" She took an aggressively nonchalant sip of her stew.

And Laurel, weary but appreciative, said, "Yes." She tasted her soup as well, hiking her eyes to get her friends eating as well. "I'll be back a lot, and no, I'm not going to rent an apartment. You all know about my mom, and she's not getting better—she's not going to get better." She forced it out, and Sam could hear from her tone that it was the first time she'd ever said the words. It was a night of endings, he thought. Of firsts.

"I'm kind of thinking of it as a new start." She ladled more soup into everyone's bowls, called on Miguel to break apart a warm loaf of bread. "This is my chance to be with her and thank her for all she's done for me and to take care of her for a change." Her voice didn't waver. "She deserves that. I want that. I do. I just . . . do." Her voice broke, and her eyes welled with tears. They spilled over, marking isolated circles on her cheeks.

"Hey," Miguel offered, and Sam watched him swallow so deeply that his chest heaved. "It was a good dream. You had a good run. And now you're going off to do something else good, right? You want to be with your mom now, don't you? And we . . . you . . . you can always open another restaurant down the road." He raised his glass and broke into a wide smile. Candles reflected warmly on his face. "Let's make a toast," he announced, teeth white in the flickering light. "To next steps, big journeys, and who-the-fuck knows where your dreams may take you!" They all raised their glasses, which made hollow, ringing chimes in the air.

After dinner, Sam walked up behind Laurel and wrapped his arms around her waist, joining her in looking toward the front window, gazing at nothing at all. She had a dishtowel in her hands, one she had gripped throughout the night, and was constantly wiping first one hand, then the other. Sam put his hands on the towel, stopping the motion. He noticed its small flowered pattern as Laurel glanced with a smile at his face. In that moment, he loved more than anything that he could give comfort to his friend. "I'll miss you," he told her. "Terribly."

"I know." She reached up to stroke his cheek with a wet hand, then returned it to the pearls around her neck. "But it's going to be good for you too."

Sam stood there, rocking with his arms around his best friend, and couldn't begin to imagine what he'd do when she was gone.

TWENTY-FIVE

MILLIE HAD once told Jack that God is in the morning, and Jack had, in turn, told Sam. Sam knew it too—God spent his mornings at the Zoo. It was barely 6 a.m., and the mists that rose from Rock Creek's green valley were still clinging to the buildings and trees. The air was cool, but an enveloping humidity warmed it comfortably. Sam's skin steamed after his run. Scattered birdcalls flew like blue jewels through the air, and Sam kept his head up to catch the runnels of scent that marked the Zoo. The grass was wet with dew and beginning to sparkle in the growing light. His tennis shoes and socks were wet from the grass and his run.

Sam had just been to see the Zoo's new Mexican wolves, after Benny had promised Sam that, if he visited their enclosure early enough in the morning, they were active and interested and would engage. The public never saw them, she said, because they were too shy. The wolves—Sam had gotten up at 3:15 a.m. with Dean and jogged to the Zoo as soon as dawn began to lighten the sky—had rough, spiky manes and fur the color of desert rock. They were smaller than Sam had expected, even after the presentations that preceded their introduction to the Zoo. The wolves' SSP mandated breeding for return to the wild; it was another point of which Sam could be proud. He had also been happy to wake up with Dean for once, even though Dean didn't come to see the wolves. Since Dean's promotion, Sam had gotten very used to waking up alone.

When Sam had approached their enclosure and heard their high howling—almost like a coyote's yip—he had hurried to the wrought-iron fence that kept the public from the animal's space. Benny had been right:

both wolves were alert, their nostrils dilating at Sam's scent, and for ten minutes he ran, giddily, up and down the length of their enclosure, as the wolves, intrigued or aroused somehow, followed him. It was a rare, unusual thrill. Sam had been in a bad mood for far too long; the wolves' gift reminded him of just how much he had to be thankful for. He was red and panting when he reached the keeper's quarters and bright-eyed when he walked, anticipating coffee and a long talk with Jack, back down the hill.

He hurried up the wet lawn and fumbled for the heavy set of keys. The cold metal sobered him. Jack had been falling further and further behind in his work and was obviously drinking more, and Sam felt increasingly duty-bound to help him. Sometimes, the tangle of his obligations made Sam feel like he couldn't breathe. But Jack deserved help and support, so Sam swept up behind him and covered for him as the old Tiger Man licked his wounds after losing Millie. "His sweetest girl," he'd always called her. Sam thought of his disappearing Dean. A quick pain stabbed through his wrist as he turned the keys in the lock.

The smell of whiskey in Jack's small office was like a punch in the nose. Sam's eyes began to water as he stepped into the room. Jack had been coming to work with liquor on his breath pretty regularly for weeks, but the smell had never been this strong. Sam assumed Jack stashed the bottles away, possibly in his locker, before anyone came in. That he gargled with Listerine before smiling his watery smile each morning for the world.

The smell and the overall disarray were overwhelming. There were two bottles of Jack Daniels on the desk and a third spilled sideways on the chair. The bright little lunchbox that Millie had always filled for him sat in the center of the desk, open and empty; its white metal mouth yawned wide. Around the lunchbox were piles of Jack's signature black notebooks, telling the stories of Jack's cats, of the years he had spent in the old Lion House and then this warm little room. Photographs, too. The books and pictures were scattered on the table, pushed around what looked like a space for Jack's head and arms to sleep there overnight.

Sam knew that Jack slept at the Zoo occasionally; there were enough half-eaten sandwiches and hardened red spatters of soup in the microwave to prove that someone had been eating there at least a few nights a week. Jack never mentioned Millie's death, never failed to ask about Sam's own ridiculous problems, and in light of it all, Sam's own small need to talk about Millie had seemed selfish and unfair. Sam didn't bring it up anymore, and Jack, typically, just joked one day over a strained, lip-licking smile that he guessed he would have to start buying lunch from now on.

Leaning over the small table and its pool of brighter lamplight, Sam flipped through the pages of Jack's messy observations, smiling at the sweet notices he continued to include despite their anthropomorphism and lack of scientific sense. Picking up one large, heavy book, Sam noticed Jack's keys on the heavy linoleum top of the desk.

He's here, Sam thought, and froze. He didn't want Jack to know that he was coming in to cover things up. Where was he? Sam's heart sped up, and he started out of the office. To leave things like this, Sam knew, Jack must be in a horrible place. "Jack!" Bending and stooping to look under the desk, Sam was terrified he would find Jack curled up like a wounded dog. "Jack!" He walked out of the office into the central room, the well, ringed by the big cats' cages. The musty, fecal smell was a relief from the assault of spilled alcohol in the tiny room. Most of the cats were outside in the mixing light of night and morning. All the cages were empty except Sheba's. She was inside, as always, particularly since her daughter—and Borneo's—had died of a liver infection shortly after birth. Even knowing, as Sam did, that infant mortality was a regular part of a tiger's life, it seemed an awful tragedy. It still killed him that he couldn't explain it to her, though Jack, with Sam's self-conscious help, had tried.

Sheba was lying with her striped back toward Sam, her vertebrae jutting like knuckles through the bars of her cage. Her head and shoulders were moving steadily. "Jack?" Her movement was soothing, and Sam remembered Jack's sweet, genuine attempts to talk Sheba through the death of her child. Sam tried his name again, more quietly this time, thinking it would be just like him to break the rules again and enter

Sheba's cage to find some comfort. He wanted Jack to know he was on his side.

Sheba's heavy head was moving rhythmically, soothingly. It made Sam empathize with Jack; she was so loving, who wouldn't want to crawl in with her and rest? Tigers constantly groom themselves, and these days, Sheba was constantly licking and grooming. It was as if, since giving birth, and even in the absence of a child, she hadn't seemed willing to give up caring for something. More than once, Jack and Sam had watched silently as she gently licked and fondled her large blue rubber ball. Jack often petted Sheba as Sam, officially disapproving and heartbreakingly jealous, watched. Sam knew that he wasn't supposed to impose his own emotions on the animals, but it felt like, and Jack agreed, she was pining away from loss.

Most tigers, both in the wild and in captivity, are fiercely independent. Even in captivity, they are likely to try and bite off your hand as you toss them their meat. Sheba, however, had been raised, mostly by Jack, as a pet. Even fifteen years ago, orphaned animals were still often treated like cuddly toys, and Sheba had been raised on a mixture of milk, vitamins, and blood from a bottle in Jack's own hand for almost a year. Jack had once told Sam that he used to sneak her home to spend the night with him and Millie. Imprinted on humans as she was, mating her had always been a challenge, which was part of the reason the introduction with Borneo last summer had been such a success.

There was a puddle of something on the floor, and she was definitely licking something. "Jack?" Sam called again as he walked toward her cage. "Sheba?" Her front leg and paw were draped over something—large—in her cage. He didn't see the top of her blue ball. "Jack?"

Craning his neck to see around her, he prayed it was a bone she was gnawing on, or a length of knotty log. He walked up behind Sheba and reached out a hand to stroke her back, but she suddenly swung her huge head backward and let out a chilling growl before turning away from him again. Her black gums gripped yellowed, fierce teeth. She had Jack under her arm, a very dead Jack, a completely *unmauled* Jack, and she was licking his face over and over and over again. The skin of his cheek was red and raw from the loving ministrations of her sandpaper tongue. Sam froze. Sheba looked at him again, widening her endless, amber eyes, and turned away, going gracefully back to licking her child, her father, her friend. Sam stood there silently with them for a long time.

WITHIN DAYS, the Zoo's public relations director orchestrated a city-wide public period of mourning in honor of Jack's death, carefully saying only that he had "died in service to the animals he loved" and omitting any mention of the fact that he'd effectively drunk himself to death. Sam couldn't be too mad; Jack had been a hero and community character for years—the Tiger Man of Washington, D.C.—and many people genuinely wanted to say good-bye. It was confusing, too; Sam had always felt that by managing his relationships, truly fostering and maintaining a few, closely guarded, dear friends, he was getting more out of life than all those too-social people who smiled and laughed with everyone. Jack, though, unreserved and welcoming, seemed to have been really happy. More than that, he seemed to have been widely and truly loved.

Dean immediately volunteered to leave work early and join Sam at the funeral, and Sam felt himself almost cry. He hugged Dean close instead. The funeral would take place on a weekday morning, and Sam knew it meant Dean would have to run over after the news rather than stay at the station and work, or network, or do whatever it was he was always seeming, lately, to do. It relaxed something between them, briefly. Things had been stretched tight in the weeks since the bike ride, deceptively fragile like a piece of paper pulled taut. There was strength there, still, but the paper would, at the slightest additional pressure, rip. Knowing Dean would be by his side, Sam felt better than he had in weeks.

The morning of the funeral he slept in, alone in the warm bed, and woke up groggy. Gwen had offered to have another keeper, one who hadn't worked with Jack, take over Sam's string that morning, and made a newer keeper—lower on the totem pole—cover Lion Island as well. Hunched over his cereal and cold milk, Sam didn't know exactly what to expect. Jack hadn't seemed to have much family—Millie and his daughter were the only people Sam had ever heard him talk about—and he didn't have much money either. Standing under the shower, rubbing his neck, he smiled at the thought that Jack would probably have requested huge photos or paintings of his cats at the ceremony. He imagined, through hot steam that was like a movie version of a dream, a tacky hall filled with slow-moving, older mourners, photos of lions and tigers arranged on standing easels and artfully placed behind junglelike ferns. . . . A chuckle escaped his lips, and he realized that he sounded just like Jack. He turned off the tap and stepped out.

Dressed in a black suit and dark tie that Dean had laid out for him before he woke up, Sam arrived at the church earlier and colder than he'd expected. Spring's first, enthusiastic hold on the world had faltered, and a wet wintry mist filled the air. Probably just nerves, he told himself, hiking his collar higher on his neck. Sam ascended the broad stone steps of the church carefully, strangely worried that he might trip. His hand grabbed onto the wrought-iron railing just in case. Even before pulling open the huge wooden doors, he could hear the running murmur of the conversations inside.

It was a shock. The church was opulent and crowded. There must have been eighty people milling around, greeting each other over the backs of brown pews, talking in clumps, sitting alone. Sam recognized a group of volunteers from the Zoo, older women in black elastic-topped skirts with black stockings blending thick ankles into black orthopedic shoes. The Zoo's whole administrative team was there, at the front, sitting correctly and respectfully, except that Sam noticed Dr. Baskin checking his watch. Some inappropriately happy and talkative students who interned in the membership and concessions stands were piled into two pews near the back. Many others, many of whom Sam had never seen, were seated, or talking quietly, or pointing out others in the room.

He took a seat near the front, at the aisle along the outer wall of the church, and looked back over his shoulder regularly so he could silently hail Dean when he arrived. He knew he should sit with the bigwigs up front but didn't have the energy for showy mourning with professional peers. The pews filled in like water permeating shallows in the sand. It was getting late. The service was about to begin. Sam's shirt felt too tight, and he worried his collar with a finger. His neck felt prickly and runny with sweat. Minutes passed. Dean did not arrive. Sam was hot, and angry, and uncomfortable. Every time he craned his neck to look for Dean, the starch of his collar chafed.

Dressing that morning, Sam had felt handsome in that suit—had even, putting it on, looked forward to Dean's expression when he saw Sam all dressed up—but it felt wrong suddenly, too tight at the waist. His underwear was twisted and pulling on the skin of his thigh. He noticed Dr. Baskin checking his watch again and wanted to rip it off his arm. When Dean finally arrived, in the last hot seconds before the priest began to speak, he skipped sideways up the silent aisle and slid into his seat next to Sam. Sam kept his eyes on the priest, and, as a miser husbands coins, turned his cheek to Dean.

The priest with his shining pink head delivered a series of useless biblical clichés, balms so watered down for the masses that they meant nothing to Sam. Dean was not alone in reading his program instead. The program, Sam had to admit when Dean flapped it at him with a smile, was great. The front cover had a photocopied image of Jack hugging a lion, his face partially obscured by the ratty mane. It was everything the priest's overblown presentation was not. Blurry and black-and-white—the brochure was a folded piece of typing paper—it reminded everyone, reminded Sam, just what a special man Jack is, was, had been. He felt a pang of jealousy that he hadn't helped put it together. Wondered who had. As he held the folded paper, his fingers begin to shake.

Gwen, sitting at the front with the official Zoo team, looked back and winked. Sam didn't smile back at her and shifted to keep a shoulder turned just away from Dean. He was pulling into himself, he knew. Retreating into his own shell again, where he knew he would be sheltered and his back would be safe. The dark wood of the pews seemed to scratch at his jacket, though he could see it was actually smooth. Sam didn't know why he was so angry, so anxious, so desperate to jump out of his seat. He wanted everyone around him to just shut up. Everyone—Gwen, Dean, the priest—seemed to be personally bent on disappointing him and shutting him down. Dean reached over gently and took Sam's hand, but Sam, shaking his head, pulled away. The priest droned on, ending with an unexpectedly soft smile as he invited Jack's daughter to the podium to speak.

Melissa Kinsley had dark red hair and had been sitting between a shapeless woman and a thin man at the very front when Sam arrived. There were no children with her, and Sam remembered Jack, and Millie, admitting to their disappointment that she didn't have a child. Melissa stood resolutely when the priest called her name, and when she reached the lectern she turned and looked out at the congregation with a small smile.

She isn't much older than I am, he realized, and knew that it could easily have been him standing at the podium right now. His mother, who had offered to come to the funeral with him despite an announced "back-breaking load at work," could have been the one who had died.

If she did die, Sam thought, I'd be an orphan too.

He watched Jack's daughter closely for clues to what he would be like in that situation. Would Karen prop him up with an arm as she stood tall and unbending under the lights? Would he, as he had so long ago, have to pick *her* up from her puddle on the floor? God, what church would they even use?

Melissa seemed happy to see so many people, and she seemed so sad about her dad. Her eyes looked brave though; she was a girl who had played with tigers in her crib.

"Thank you," she said to her hands below the microphone, raised her brown eyes from whatever was in her hands, and began to speak. Her skin was dry, and she had papery yellow moons under her eyes. Her small mouth was rich with dark lipstick and twisted into awkward little smiles at unexpected moments. Sam was suddenly very sad he had never met her, hadn't been a better friend to Jack over the past few years, couldn't hold onto this woman and hug her, and make it all OK. The sense of having his arms around someone, the pull of his jacket sleeves, the starched folds against his waist, made him want someone's arms around him instead.

Sam felt the bricks loosen before he recognized what was happening. The wall that kept things down, things buried, was failing under the weight of his love for and sadness about Jack. The dam, the one that kept everything agreeable and workable, was bursting inside. Hot water welled in the brims of his eyes, and he felt a first tear splash on his cheek. Dean looked over at Sam and then up at Melissa, trying to pay proper attention but becoming visibly alarmed by what he saw. Sam never cried. It was almost his motto, and when Dean saw the crumbling face of his boyfriend just inches away, his eyes went wide. Sam thought Dean was going to take his hand again, but instead he just lifted his own hand like a leaf that, falling to earth, rises briefly on a gust of wind before grounding, and rested it back in his own lap. Sam felt another tear drop down.

"I want to thank everyone for coming and say that my Dad would've been so happy—*is* so happy—that all of you are here. You know my mom," she paused for a second when she realized her voice was shaking, "His wife," the tremble continued, echoing out through the black microphone and over everyone's heads. Sam saw her gain control in a visible clenching of the muscles of her cheeks and neck. "Mom passed away a few months ago. You know," her eyes darted around the room as if they were following a swift, leaping bird, "I loved, and I miss her, terribly, but she was really my dad's whole life. Of course, he loved me. He obviously," she generously inclined her head to the audience, "loved his friends and the Zoo and especially his cats." She bowed her head again, and Sam watched her lips move over themselves like ripples in a brook. "He just loved her so much, and I think, in a way, that he just needed to go on and be with her now."

Sam's eyes migrated to Dean's face, and for the first time that morning, he really looked at the man sitting next to him. A white sheen of sweat on his forehead caught the flickering light of a fake candle in a cast-iron sconce, and there were tiny blond hairs growing in patches on the crests of his cheeks. Dean would hate them, Sam knew, he would want them waxed or blasted off, but to Sam they were wonderful. The way Jack's bubble-red face and crooked teeth belonged to Millie, the way her involuntary shaking was all Jack's. Their world, so incredibly small, was so big in the way they looked at each other. Sam felt a weight come loose in his chest. He looked at Dean and smiled, and the dislodged weight rising in his throat pushed all the anger out of its way. It was a wild, rushing feeling, as powerful as the anger of moments before, and the two emotions mixed together like crosscurrents where a strong river meets the tide. Sam was rocked by it and wanted to grab onto Dean's hand for life as dearly as he wanted to throw Dean out into the river to drown.

Sam didn't know what he was doing then, but he knew what animals do. Cradle themselves in your palm or arms when they are babies, let you stroke them, touch them, look up at you with love, and then suddenly, without warning, screech and bite and claw you until you set them free or one of you is dead. A cornered monkey, a trapped tiger, *me*. He missed Jack. He loved Dean. And it all felt so fucking bad.

"Dad certainly did love his cats," Melissa said with a wet laugh, indicating the snarling, blown-up photos that did—as Sam had predicted—perch awkwardly on podiums around her. She laughed, and it released a fresh gust of air and relief from the crowd, "and I'm sure he's up there playing with them now." She gripped the sides of the podium the way Sam was gripping the curved end of the pew. "You know, when I was a little girl, he still got to bring the baby lions and tigers home for the night, and I'll always remember him telling me about those nights, just him and my mom and, as he would say, 'his little boys and girls' all curled up together and warm. The way he told it, we were always just snuggled up blissfully in blankets and fur."

Sam put his hand on Dean's knee.

Melissa stopped for a moment and looked up, blinking away tears as her eyes shone in the lights from above. "I hope he's somewhere warm and blissful, with my mom, and Rena, and King, and all his cats, drinking milk together and purring." Her words pulled Sam back from his private swirling tide pool and into the larger currents of the room. It was silent and shuffling, with everything directed toward Melissa's shaking hands and soft, nasal voice. Sam could feel the high, white vault of the ceiling yawning above him. "Thank you all for coming," she finished. "Dad, I'm sure, says 'Hi' too."

It was beautiful, and so true to Jack's spirit. Sam felt the dam burst.

He could see, for the first time, the great, black, howling pit, the unspeakable fissure that had been gaping beneath him his whole life. The death of his father. The deep, freezing well he skated blithely over everyday. The chasm, stitched together with the threads of soothing his mother's tears, his sister's fury, that he had tightened with a panicked strength every day of his life. Until today. Suddenly, the pit opened. And Sam, uncatchable, fell.

He was crying in a way that made it obvious to Dean, and to the people sitting nearby, that the big man with coarse, salty hair had no idea how to cry. Big tears were running down his face and catching in the corners of his mouth. It was like he had dunked his face into water—it was covered everywhere with wet. Every breath felt like he was being born, or giving birth, or cracking open inside and letting every sadness shoot out of his chest. The weight that had covered the pit was being expelled in choking chunks. Dean was looking at Sam, alarm and concern contorting his face. He had thrown one arm over Sam's shoulders, an arm that felt like a paper trenchcoat against torrential rain. Sam put his hands over his face to hide himself. His shoulders shook with the effort to stay silent and not embarrass anyone, embarrass Dean, embarrass himself. Dean was leaning over Sam, shushing him and comforting him, and keeping an eye up both to ward off and comfort their neighbors in the pew.

During an ebb in the flood of tears, Sam's mind locked on a single image—a small silver fish flopping wetly in his hand at the reservoir near their house. His dad had been an avid, if limited, fisherman, and he had taken Sam a few times for early morning fishing trips together. Sam had loved them, having his Daddy pull him out of bed and tug on his clothes. Waking slowly in the warm motion of the car, watching Dad pay for breakfast through the drive-in window.

Even the fishing had seemed fun—Sam loved the intricately painted and feathered hooks—though they never caught anything. He remembered their last trip. His father made them fish with worms, made Sam puncture the worm's smooth, striated flesh with the ugly hook. He'd said it was time for Sam to learn to fish for real. Sam hadn't wanted any of it. The sick lump in his throat had been growing since his father made him spear the weakly twisting worm, since fishing had stopped being the smell of his dad's canvas jacket and started being the cold stink of mud. When the fish came up, flopping and gasping, he had met his father's triumphant hooting by bursting into tears. After a minute they tossed it back, but Sam could tell he had done something horribly wrong. They didn't talk or stop for pizza like normal, and he watched a vein pulse in his father's neck all the way home.

Melissa stepped from behind the podium and quickly walked down from the platform, distracting Sam from the memory. He watched the priest thank everyone and offer directions to a reception in a restaurant at the Zoo. Suddenly, Sam realized that his father had died within weeks of that last fishing trip. They had been surly and strange around each other all that week, and, he realized with a freezing, white-lit crack in his chest, that he had been glad for one endless second that his father was dead, if only so he'd never have to go fishing again. Sam's tears doubled, and Dean, dumbfounded, stroked his back. He covered his face again and cried some more.

WHEN THEY were seated in Dean's car around the corner from the church, Dean let out a breath that sounded like the world had come to an end. He looked at Sam for a long time. Sam felt scoured inside as if by a cold wind. His face was crusty from crying, and Dean's stare was strangely terrifying, like the expression on a dog's face that might lick you but also might take a bite. Sam couldn't see what was inside Dean's eyes, could only tell that what was coming next was going to be bad.

Dean was sitting with his hands placed carefully on his legs, one resting flat above each knee. The car, which Sam had first sat in almost a year ago, still smelled new.

"I'm sorry I lost it in there," he began, rushing to turn the tension into laughter even as he realized that there was nothing to apologize for. "I don't know what came over me. Jack and I weren't even really that close." He bit the inside of his cheek to punish himself for the lie. He was sick of making things easy at all costs.

Dean smiled at this, lightly, like a feather brushing Sam's throat.

"I just, well, I just got so caught up in what he did with his life, how simple it was and yet how big. He just loved his cats and Millie and his life. I guess, with you too, I envy him that, you know?" Sam shrugged, a little helplessly, still waiting for the imagined guillotine to fall. A small voice was shrieking deep inside that he should stop giving in on everything, stop appearing helpless and apologetic, didn't need to make Dean comfortable with simple, useless asides. The voice felt liberating. It was also terrifying, since Sam's whole life was built around making people feel better, about putting other people first. If that wasn't how he was supposed to live, he still didn't know what else to do.

"There just ended up being all this Dad stuff, you know? My dad, stuff. I . . . "

Dean was pulling at his keys, and Sam couldn't help himself; his index finger brushed against the meat of his boyfriend's hand.

"Do you know how hard it is to find another species with opposable thumbs?" He tried to lace their fingers together, but Dean pulled his palm away.

Turning the ignition, he shook his head, hard. "You know, Sam, do you think we could try a *different* metaphor for once? We've been doing this for hours already. I really just don't have the energy for another 'animal metaphor' today." He squinted into the morning, flicked the windshields against the accumulating mist. "God, I hope it doesn't rain all day."

Sam let the word "dick" push itself out of his mouth, and they both watched it drop between them on the floor. Dean took a deep breath and put his hand over Sam's.

"Sam . . . shit. Honey," he started, slow and careful, "Of course you can cry like that. I just don't . . . Well, I just don't totally get it. You are so much better than Jack was, you can do so much more than he did. That quote from *Where the Wild Things Are?* It was sweet, but he wasn't a king—he was just a guy with no life who played with tigers. *You* could be the king of the wild things if you wanted, if you just pushed a little more at work . . . " Dean's eyes went far away then, and as he toyed with the fingers on Sam's hand, he began explaining, again, how he was moving toward his goals at work, how he was finally getting some real recognition in the industry, how people were starting to talk. He had ideas for Sam, Sam knew, a vision of what *should* come next. Sam knew that Dean loved him, and wanted him to be better, to be more. And he knew that he fed that desire in Dean, fed it with his complaints and unrealized plans. A thousand bees interrupted the thought, swarming inside Sam's ears. He threw Dean's hand away.

"Are you serious?" Sam wanted to spit on him. "Dean, we're at a funeral for God's sake, not some career counseling session. My friend just *died*, OK? *God!* I swear, sometimes I don't know you at all. Or I don't want to, maybe. I don't know." He took a breath that pulled up all the shattered anger from before. "Everything can't all be sunshine and positive thinking all the time. I know I'm not always properly forward-thinking for your taste, but I just lost a goddamn friend, OK? I'm not ready to bulldoze his memory on the highway of my—no, on the highway of *your* vision of my—career. God, Dean. God."

Dean looked shocked. He cradled his hand as if it had been burned. The sleek gray interior of the car seemed suddenly dead, and the thrumming engine humped along, underscoring their silence. Sam's throat felt hot and raw. They sat silently in the car for what felt like forever, until all the other cars had left the parking lot and a small gray rain shower had passed.

Sam was crying again, in a tiny way, the way he had sometimes cried before the huge rush of the funeral. It wasn't even enough to wet his cheeks. He was watching Dean, who sat ice silent, except for one huge loud breath every few minutes that heaved his chest up and crinkled the skin under his chin. Sam found himself watching the green lights of the clock on the dashboard and counting along with the seconds. *Eleven forty-eight and nineteen seconds, eleven forty-eight and twenty seconds, eleven forty-eight and twenty-one . . .*

Dean turned off the ignition again and turned partially toward Sam. Spot-shadows from the rain mottled his face. "I don't understand what's going on with you, Sam. It's like, suddenly, you don't want us to be anything, or do anything, or think about anything at all anymore. It's like you want us to actually *be* the couch you love to sit on. I just . . . I feel like we're pillows now, not people, you know? I'm sorry. I just . . . I love you. I just . . . " and he trailed off again, and they sat in silence while he stroked the silver car keys on their chain.

"I should really get to the reception," was Sam's only response. He felt emptied out inside. "Can you just give me a ride over? I don't think I need you to come." Sam said it quietly, spitefully, since he knew Dean would be hurt, and also that he would be relieved at the excuse not to attend. It still felt ugly to say the words, and some of the bright light of crying tightened back up inside. "I just want to go be with Jack." Dean looked as if he was starting to say something, but then his mouth folded in on itself and down into his chin, and he turned the keys of the ignition, and looked finally away from Sam, pulling the car into reverse.

THAT AFTERNOON at the Zoo, Sam spent a long, grateful minute with his howlers, passing pale slices of cantaloupe through the bars to where they perched, quietly together, on a ledge.

TWENTY-SIX

THE LAST night of Terra coincided with the end of spring; it was a fond memory of that heady green rush and an inheld breath against the pulsing heat to come. The night was cooler than it had been in weeks, and inside, all was light and magic, shadowed by light and magic's inevitable end. Laurel's emotions tumbled inside her chest; she had to push the image of her empty, dusty restaurant from her mind. Forcibly, she overlay it with the images actually in front of her: Miguel moving like a dancer in elliptical sweeps through the front as favorite guests bickered over the menu—a fixed menu she had designed to clean out the last food in her walk-in freezer and shelves. Her beloved center table, her homage to her dad, was full with friends, sitting quietly, pushing around their food. Sam in particular was quiet, but he was gamely smiling, and working to keep everyone's evening bright. Dean, next to him, was making half the table laugh.

As the night faded, as Terra faded into everyone's immediate past, Laurel pushed everyone out, one by one, until she was left alone in her warm dark room. It was a cocoon, she realized. It was the place where she had evolved most completely into who she was today, and now she was leaving it, not for the skies and beauty, but for another burrowing. It felt like a reversal she was enduring, despite deeply wanting her mother to be well. Despite somehow wanting to go back home and take care.

She switched off the lights one by one, moving slowly away from the front windows and her view of the empty street outside. She passed through the wreck of her dining room, running a hand along the back of a chair, straightening a picture on the wall. At the entrance to her kitchen, she removed the photo of her father that had guarded her and guided her since he died. She cradled it to her chest with one hand, while the other ran itself along the heavy metal prep table, along the oven's familiar, cool face. She flipped off the lights, one by one, rested her hands on the small THANK YOU sign she couldn't yet bear to put out. Stepping outside the narrow back door, she was surprised to find warm air rather than cool. Summer's here, she thought. She would come back for her things tomorrow, she decided, and lit a nostalgic cigarette against the night.

TWENTY-SEVEN

THEY WERE out shopping together for Jamie's gift in the high, bright, air-conditioned warehouse of a Target in Virginia, and Sam had been peppering Dean with questions—What did Dean think Jamie might like? Would Dean definitely be able to do Provincetown in August? Did he want to go in with Sam on Jamie's gift?—while Dean maneuvered the cart. Sam noticed that while three of the wheels rolled smoothly on the flecked, white floor, one wheel kept wobbling, lolling and rebounding and trying to pull the cart off course. Dean didn't acknowledge the errant wheel and kept their movements through the aisles clean. The muscles of Dean's hands and forearms were tightly clenched.

In Sam's mind, things had been changing ever since that bike ride in the spring. Everything had seemed so possible that morning and so darkened, headed for nightfall, by the end of the day. Dean spent more and more time in New York, taking meetings and exploring possibilities, he explained. He spent three or four evenings a week with his local agent or at the station working. Even their nights at home felt disjointed, with Sam calling out ideas and questions from the kitchen or couch, while Dean worked at the small table by the window where he could set up his laptop and watch the street life outside.

Sam did want to share in all of Dean's excitement, but it was harder all the time. Images of Brazil's green trees and flying birds assaulted him more and more often, and he flinched from them, focusing instead on the mutual possibilities that would take place between them as a couple, the ones Dean never seemed ready to talk about. Sam's own work—his new ideas for a multispecies exhibit, the untested, improbable possibility of housing smaller primates in the same exhibit as the cats—seemed very far away.

The only time they had sex these days was when Dean would counterweigh Sam's fears about the future with the heat of his lips or the pull of their bodies onto the couch. It had become an unhealthy sport, Sam knew, trading his fears for the reassurance of Dean's wet mouth and strong hands.

"Dean? Jamie's graduation is coming up really soon, and Karen needs to know if you need a seat. I've asked you a couple of times already, and I know your schedule is tight, but do you think you can make it?" He took a deep breath. "Or . . . is there something going on?" He managed to direct the question at a precarious display of purple and green cleaning supplies just behind Dean's head. He didn't want to see the reaction in Dean's eyes.

Dean stopped the cart and turned to look at Sam and said he didn't feel comfortable going to Jamie's graduation. It all felt like too much. He needed to be a little more careful now that he was becoming a more public figure; he needed to pull back.

"From me?" Sam asked, as every shelf around them tumbled in a heap onto his head. "You need to pull back from me?" He asked it again, hoping he had misunderstood, that Dean wasn't saying he wanted to go away from Sam. He rationalized, desperately, that this was just Dean's careerism talking, that somehow, instead of a need to leave Sam, it was just a practical need to keep his sexuality unknown. "Openly closeted," Dean had called it, and Sam was willing, suddenly, to accept that openly closeted was OK. That being closeted was a *good* thing, if it would make Dean stay where he was. Sam wasn't a fool; he knew things had been hard lately, but he also liked the shape of his life with a boyfriend. With Dean. He needed that supporting structure. He wasn't ready to throw in the towel just yet.

Dean leaned against a stacked tower of Sprite, taking Sam's hand and giving it a gentle shake. "No, not from you, Sam. Just . . . I just need to be slightly less obvious for a while, just while I'm figuring out my next move. New York is different, you know . . ."

Sam tuned him out. He could visualize, from repeated discussions over dinners, and drives, and in bed, Dean's vision of a huge, warmly technological set, the team of assistants who would do the legwork on his reporting, prep his stories, style his hair. He also recognized, for the first time, his own thoughtless reliance on the idea of Brazil. He might not have seriously looked at his own work in months, but the glittering hope of Brazil kept him feeling, somehow, safe. It was amazing how well they knew each other, Sam thought, as he waited for the compromise that by now he knew would come.

"Hey," Dean delivered, cuffing Sam lightly on the back of the neck, "why don't you ask Karen if they'd want me to give a speech. It would let me be there with you and Jamie, and I'd get some good community service brownie points too." He presented it with such a proud, problem-solved look that Sam thought it couldn't possibly be anything at all but the best idea in the world. He loved that look in Dean's eyes, wanted pictures of Dean as a little boy.

"Karen would love it," Sam confirmed. He decided that it was enough, decided that he would love it too.

DEAN STOPPED by unexpectedly a few days before the graduation. He stood, pacing, in the middle of the room. Sam sat on the couch, one hand toying with a brown pillow's fraying zipper.

"Sam."

I'll have to fix this, Sam thought as Dean began to speak. He toyed idly with the loosened string. "Sam. The network job came through. They're willing to buy out my contract here. I've got my shot in New York, honey. I've got to take it."

Sam listened, but it was as if Dean's words, and the very letters of the words, were separating themselves as they left Dean's mouth and batting against Sam's forehead rather than penetrating his brain. He wanted to push them away like flies. Trap them in a cage so his own thoughts would have the chance to resolve themselves among all the sharp, black words buzzing around his head.

He started to his feet with congratulations, and Dean smiled back, but shrugged in a way that felt as if he was gently pushing Sam back down onto the couch. "That's great," Sam continued anyway, and reached one arm across the coffee table to touch Dean's leg.

"Thanks, honey. I'm really excited about it too. But right now I am so tired, I've got to go home and get some sleep." When Sam offered to go along, Dean looked scared, but Sam kept talking anyway, jumping up to pull a bottle of champagne out of the fridge. "I can't drink tonight, honey," Dean frowned, but Sam popped the cork anyway, and they toasted to Dean's new job. It felt surreal, like Sam was forcing frivolity into the room despite all the air having been let out. He gave Dean a fizzing kiss and announced he would grab a few things for the night.

As Sam was collecting his uniform for the next day, Dean relented and offered to stay the night rather than have Sam pack everything up and go to Dean's. His champagne sat, flat and untouched, on the counter. Sam felt like the girl who takes her brother to homecoming, but he told himself it was really his first choice. He buzzed around the kitchen wiping down the counters and front of the fridge, asking questions and patting Dean's arms and back. Despite Sam's nervous entreaties, Dean wouldn't say much about what the job meant. Sam volleyed questions as they circled each other warily in the small kitchen—when will it start, what kind of show did you get, who will you work for, when will you leave?

Dean refused to answer anything, claiming exhaustion and saying that the specifics were still being worked out. He told Sam he needed a shower and walked out of the room, pulling off his tie. "Want me to join you?" Sam tentatively asked Dean's back, but Dean just shook his head and pulled the door shut behind him. "I'm fine."

When he heard the rush of water that meant Dean was in the shower, Sam went back into the living room, attempting to put things in order for the night. The remote went into its basket, the magazines in a neat pile. Back in the kitchen he put their flutes in the dishwasher, the spent champagne in the fridge. His hands shook as he slapped off the living room lights. Passing the bathroom door he faltered, as if the wood had buckled beneath his feet. Something inside him shifted. He rapped lightly on the door and went in.

Dean was stepping out of the shower with a faded green towel around his waist. He glanced up to see Sam and quickly corrected the annoyance on his face.

"Hey there," he said into the mirror, watching Sam from the corner of his eye. "What's up?"

"What's going on, Dean? Really. This job and everything. You've been so quiet lately, it's like you aren't even here." Sam was terrified. "What's going on with you?"

"Nothing," Dean sighed through his nose, grabbing his toothbrush. Purple. Sam had bought it for him after they'd been dating for a month.

"Dean." Sam stood in the doorway, feeling the steam push against his face, and refused to move. He had Dean cornered and suddenly, he realized, wasn't going to let this go. He had to know. "Dean, talk to me. Tell me what's going on. We can work on this, can't we?" He felt desperation creep into his voice, felt as if his arms were reaching up imploringly toward Dean even though, physically, he kept them clutched tight across his chest. "It isn't just the job, right? Is it just the job? You've been so distant."

Dean spat toothpaste into the sink and turned to him. His body was beautiful. Wet hair pushed back in a messy tangle, water that clung to his chest and the ladder of his abs and ribs. It was like the floor was disappearing beneath him again, and Sam braced himself against the door.

"Look, Sam, you're right." Dean's eyes went flat and wet. "It is the job, and it isn't. It's everything. I just . . . Give me a minute." He leaned against the counter, replaced the toothbrush in its cup. "I just think it would be best if I went to New York alone."

" . . . Okay . . . "

"And, that, well, that you *not* come with me, you know. That we give it some room, and . . . "

"It?" Sam asked. Knowing and not wanting to know and pushing back anyway.

"It. Us. You know what I mean." Dean pushed his hair back from his forehead, tightened the towel around his waist, and draped a second towel over his shoulders. Sam could barely see him through all this new information. He came toward Sam, and Sam opened like a flower for the hug, the assurance, the erasure he thought was coming his way. Instead, Dean waited for Sam to move out of his way. "Sam . . . come on, can't we just get some sleep?"

"No," Sam pushed the words out. "No, Dean!" He felt like a kettle venting or a sewer spewing foul air. "Stay here. Talk to me. Tell me what you mean. We can't just go to bed again, you know? I can't do it. What is happening here?"

Dean stepped back into the bathroom, his head down, his hands pulling on the ends of the towel around his neck. He looked at his bare feet. They were still red from the shower, Sam noticed, and he wanted to kiss them and hold them in his hands.

"It's just, I guess . . . Sam." Dean reached up and cupped Sam's cheek. "I think it has to be over. It does. This just isn't what I want. I love you. I'm sorry."

He stood entirely still then, a statue of a man resigned to his fate. It was as if he was waiting for judgment in the form of a kick. A few trails of water snaked down his legs.

"Sam?"

But Sam didn't answer him. Couldn't answer him in that moment. Everything in Sam was fighting to keep himself from crying, struggling to keep the pain down. It felt like a rising tide inside him, a geyser that could explode out of him and drown them both. He shook his head instead, fighting the crumple of his face. Refusing to move.

Dean came to him then, pushing himself inside Sam's crossed arms and grabbing Sam into a slow, stilled hug. His body felt so good and solid and warm. His skin was like that tropical ocean. It hit Sam like a sledgehammer blow.

"I love you, Sam. It's just . . . everything, though. I think I just don't love you enough."

Tears gusted out of Sam then, as if his breath had become liquid and he was emptying his insides. They stood like that for a few minutes, Sam crying into Dean's wet, slowly cooling hair, Dean stroking Sam's back and whispering "I'm sorry" over and over again. Finally, with a long breath, Sam pushed Dean away.

Wiping his eyes, he looked at Dean through the wet screen of his tears and loved him more than anything he could bear. He stepped back so that they were in the hall, on wood flooring again, out of the steam.

"You should go," he told Dean, who reacted by reaching out to him again and trying to pull Sam into another hug. "No. You're right. You have to go."

"But you don't want this," Dean whimpered, shaking his head in a strange, sudden denial. "I can't do this to you. We can work on this. Let's talk about—"

"No, Dean. You can't. . . . I can't. . . . " Sam stopped himself. "You were right. You don't love me enough, not with everything else in your life. And I . . . I think I love you too much, maybe. Or need? For my own good. It's like . . . I don't know." He turned away and went into the bedroom, and Dean followed. "It's like trying's not enough anymore, or something. I can't *just* be about you if you aren't even a little bit more about me." He felt Dean's hand on his back and started crying again.

Dean's clothes were tossed across the bed, and Sam sat to one side while Dean gathered them up, slowing pulling on one leg and then the other, gradually putting his arms through the sleeves, undressing himself in reverse. Watching Dean dress, Sam realized how little he had to collect before leaving, how Dean would not leave even the slightest trace. Sam stood and began organizing the bedroom as Dean slipped into his shoes and stood there, waiting. Silently, Sam walked to the door as Dean followed. For a few minutes, they stood in a hug.

"I'm sorry," Dean breathed into Sam's ear as he left.

And Sam cried. And cried. Sprawled on the couch, keening like a woman, a high-pitched venting that matched the slick of tears that ran down his face. He pushed his hands into his cheeks and eye sockets. He wandered his small apartment, touching things and staring at pictures. A photograph of Dean, laughing in a charcoal gray hat and red scarf in the snow. It felt to Sam like dying. Like he was pushing out all the air that kept him alive. Panicked, Sam dialed Laurel's number and listened to it ring but didn't leave a message and didn't try her cell phone. It was after midnight. He was alone; his whole sticky spider's web of connections was useless. He stared out into the street and night, resting his head on the warm glass. I am alone, he repeated and repeated. There was no one else to call.

A while later, Sam went to bed, more tired than he'd ever been. On his bedside table, the information from Dr. Anderson shone underneath his headphones and a pile of change, but he left it untouched. He tossed his clothes in the direction of the hamper and dropped into bed.

When he woke up, his face riddled with red dents, curled on his side and clutching the comforter in his arms, Dean was still gone. It was 3:15 in the morning, and his alarm, set for Dean's early morning call, was blasting the news. Dean's station. His first dose of each day, Sam thought, and now Sam's first taste of the morning's news.

TWENTY-EIGHT

THE HEAT of summer's first ugly morning lay like wet cloth over Sam's mouth. He surveyed the crowded bleachers of Jamie's middle school graduation in search of some kind of joy, but it was simply too hot. The shifting, wilted crowd was using anything available—commemorative booklets, newspapers, T-shirts and hats—as ineffective protection against the sun. There should have been enthusiasm in the greetings between fathers who only saw each other at football games and older siblings who knew each other from high school; there should have been a breeze to lift collars and cool sweat. Instead, bright metal bleachers burned elbows and the backs of knees and reflected the white glare into people's eyes. White light glinted off people's glasses, the uncovered lines of the football field, the printed pamphlets describing the activities of the day.

Sam felt crowded in his seat, and sweat ran in uncomfortable rivers down his sides. He was surrounded by family but still alone, the hot glare of the day blocking everything. The heat made him feel thick and unhealthy, but he tried to cool himself with happiness for Jamie and pride in his smart little boy.

He could just make out the back of Jamie's head on the field below where he and a few friends had made illegible, tape-written slogans on their mortarboard caps. Jamie's was supposed to read "Outta Here!" which suggested he was much cooler than Sam had ever been. Jamie had called Sam the night before to tell him what to look for. "Mom doesn't know, so don't tell her, OK?" They had shared a laugh, the first Sam had enjoyed in days. He tried to determine who Jamie was talking to, if he looked too uncomfortable in his shiny green gown. He recognized

Jamie's friend Saj but couldn't read his cap. The top of Sam's chair was burning a hole in his back.

Dean was there too, Sam knew, but the thought was like food that wouldn't go down. He sniffed himself surreptitiously, testing his own smell. Everyone was uncomfortable, fanning themselves, craning their necks for family, or plucking their clothes away from their skin with slippery fingers. Sam imagined Dean, pressed and golden in the cool blue shade of the stage's drapery, conferring and laughing with the principal. He probably had a cold bottle of water in his hand.

At least he had his family with him, and Laurel, their arms touching despite the heat. Karen had come early to reserve seats so they were in the middle of the first row of bleachers above the football field. David pointed out that they were on the twenty-yard line, which he explained was appropriate since Jamie was finally going for the touchdown. Laurel and Sam smiled first at David, blankly, then at one another with childish grins.

The eighth-graders had marched in to triumphant, piped-in music and were assembled on the green grass of the field. Sam's mother was on his left, and Karen and her husband had the seats closest to the aisle. Two other families, friends of Karen's from the PTA, blocked them in. Sam tried to focus as the kids walked, sauntered, or skulked across the stage, but it was so damn hot. He could see the unflattering outlines of Laurel's and his mother's breasts and felt his own hips sticking to his clothes. Sam assumed that Dean, hidden behind the blue curtain, would have a flawless outline despite the heat. He missed him. He sipped his warmed-over water and looked at the program in his hands. He was furious and terribly sad.

Sam couldn't believe what a coward Dean had turned out to be after all. They had barely spoken since the breakup, and he hadn't called Dean once, refusing to be weak anymore. He had called Laurel, and Laurel again, and Laurel again, sobbing with the newfound freedom of sobbing, into the phone and into her ear. He had picked himself up quickly, gone to work, and forced a brave face both out to the world and in on himself. It was only that morning, in the hot sun, when he was supposed to be so happy, that Sam realized he was utterly drowning in despair.

Laurel and Karen each grabbed one of Sam's hands as Jamie emerged from the long line of gowns and strutted across the stage. He was comfortable with himself in a way Sam had never been, and accepted his diploma with a jaunty smile and half turn to the crowd. Sam felt like a weather map was scrolling across his body, showing the meeting of warm and cold fronts in the air, the red and blue arrows and the storm that explodes out of the mix. He resented the fact that weather maps would always remind him of Dean, and a metallic tang sat heavily at the back of his tongue. He began to cry silently, hot tears still cooler than the air splashing off his cheek. There was too much joy and too much pain. Dean was gone. Jamie was growing up. Everything kept changing all around him, as hard as he tried to keep it safe, and unchanging, and the same.

Jamie rejoined the sea of green caps, and the students were all seated. The audience rose through the heat into a wild confetti of cheering and applause for the graduates, and then Dean walked out from behind the partition to give his speech. Sam's family and friends were smiling through their happy tears and clapping as if Sam was not right among them, drowning in cold sticky mud. He imagined himself to be perfectly, painfully still, but when he looked down he saw his own hands clapping as well.

"Congratulations!"

Sam heard Dean's voice with his stomach rather than with his ears. Heard Dean call out to the students and the crowd as if he were a king addressing his warriors after a bloody and victorious fight. He paused while the high-voiced students cheered and a wave of polite applause scattered the air above the stands. Sam blinked rapidly, against the light, and to hold down whatever was rising in his throat.

"First, I want to thank you all for having me here today," he continued, as another small bird-flight of applause followed. Someone shouted "Thank YOU!" from behind Sam's head, and he resisted the urge to turn and scowl.

"My name is Dean McAllister," he began, "and as Channel 8's local news reporter and morning anchor, it is so important to me," looking beneficently over the shiny green sheet of students at his feet, "to be a *part* of this community. Your community, the Eisenhower Middle School's class of 2004!" Laurel nudged Sam and he joined her, and the rest of the crowd, in applauding once again.

"Now, I want to talk to you all today as someone whom some people might call a success," he went on, his cadence shifting as he moved into his speech. There was no discernable stutter, nothing anyone else in the audience would see, but Sam relished the falter in Dean's rhythm. What looked like a casual brush of his hair to everyone else in the audience was undoubtedly Dean's nervous hands moving into action. The intensity of his stare was really an attempt to resist sweat-stung blinks against the sun's glare. He moved the papers of his speech around on the podium. Sam whispered in Karen's ear that apparently even "Mr. Perfect" had broken a sweat.

Resentfully, Sam admitted that Dean's speech was good. Inspiring. Tough. Hopeful. When he surveyed the crowd, Sam was convinced Dean was looking at him.

"So," he held up a finger, "don't forget to decide whether you want to take French or advanced biology, and whether you will try out for cheerleading, the football team, student government, or band. I don't care what you choose, but you do have to *choose something.*" His voice was booming. "*Do the work*: figure out what teams and groups and classes you'll enjoy and go after them with the bravery and gumption you showed in getting yourself to this point today. But also," his finger went up into the air again, and Sam wanted to grab it and twist it and maybe bite it off and spit it onto the grassy ground, "start to think about this: Do you want to be on a track toward college, or art school, or the army, or a job? Start to think about where you want to go to college, what kind of job you might want to have someday. Who you want to be."

Don't let your sisters get pregnant either, Sam thought, and dug a knuckle into his thigh.

Dean went on to congratulate and lecture them all some more.

"Thank you," he continued. "Now, I want to keep this short due to the weather," he pulled at his collar and rolled his eyes, "so I'll finish with the words of a great man. As Henry David Thoreau once said, 'If one advances confidently in the direction of his dreams, he will meet with a success unexpected in common hours.'"

"Now, guys," Dean leaned heavily on the lectern and shook his head at the sea of green caps and bright faces, "Thoreau was telling you something here. He was telling you to get off your couches and stop watching TV. He was telling you to take risks, be brave, to make decisions that might seem hard but will take you where you want to go. He was telling you to go for it!" He raised his hands again, calling forth more applause, then lowered them together. Sam had a moment of gratefulness that Dean was so obviously full of cheese.

As he finished, Dean was silent for a moment, perfectly orchestrated, Sam thought, to impress upon everyone the deep meaning of what he had just said. "Thank you very much." He nodded and waved in response to the applause, shook the principal's hand firmly, and with an offhand salute, left the stage.

"God, fuck him," Sam whispered to Laurel as they stood, balancing awkwardly, among the jostling crowd. "At least he kept it short. I'm surprised he didn't have them studying elocution and signing up for the A/V club as well." He leaned his head toward her, keeping their overheated bodies separate.

"I liked it, Sam," his sister injected, leaning in. "I think it can't hurt these kids to start to think about the future a little bit. Now that Jamie's decided to go to Roosevelt, his chances of going to a top college are up 100 percent."

When Sam didn't respond, she softened and took his hand. "I know it's hard for you, seeing him up there," she reached out and touched his sweating forearm, "but it was nice for the kids, and for me." She squeezed his wrist. "It was kind of a big deal. I really appreciate it, and I'm sorry you're hurting. Really. But you are going to be OK, I promise. We're grown-ups. Part of what that means is that we get over things, right? And we need to focus on Jamie for today." She kissed his hand and dropped it, and when she let go her fingers left a wet mark on his wrist.

TWENTY-NINE

LAUREL SLOUCHED, chin to chest in the passenger seat of her mother's ancient Volvo wagon, plucking at her sweaty T-shirt with fingers and thumb. She had been too overwhelmed by the reality of the move to drive, had made Sam take a wandering route out of D.C., wanted to look at everything one last time. Her eyes reflected the high, sandstone buildings and trees with tired green leaves. Sam was silent as they maneuvered through the late-morning traffic on Connecticut Avenue, around the Beltway's clogged artery, and north toward the farms and open spaces of rural Maryland and the Delaware line.

"Everything's so dusty," she said.

"Everything" seemed to be pushing Laurel deeper and deeper into her seat.

They were approaching the Pennsylvania line when she told Sam how much she was looking forward to the fall.

"It would be great if we were just taking the day to play," he agreed, looking over at her strong nose and dropped chin. She was still tucked into herself against the necessary air conditioning and direction of their drive. "We could get lunch somewhere cute, buy apple pies and useless antiques, and then go back to Terra for dinner with every—" He glanced at her, guilty and sad, and she rubbed his strong arm. "I know I shouldn't say it, but I really wish you weren't going away."

Laurel shrugged. "Me too." She was worried about him; he hadn't mentioned Dean in days.

They drove for another hour, occasionally commenting on the scenery or bickering over the music on the radio. As they passed the white-dirt and particleboard skeleton of a new subdivision, they lamented the sprawl that was turning what they remembered as farmland into endless suburbs and malls. Laurel wondered which organic farms might be struggling forward; twice, Sam mentioned his dad. When they reached Laurel's neighborhood of light-dappled streets, sloped curbs, and thick, grassy lawns, it was a relief for them both. Suburb, yes, but old and shady and green. He slowed the car, and they drove slowly, almost reverently, looking at the landscape of their youth.

Too quickly, they pulled into the wide curved driveway of Laurel's mother's house. The car clicked and cooled on the cracked pavement of the driveway as Sam and Laurel breathed in the wide, ivy-choked shingles, the stone fronting, the deep green trim. Six windows marched neatly across the front of the house; a small, round window peeked from above the porticoed front door. Laurel took his hand and whispered "be warned."

They stood like that until her mother surprised them by jerking open the door.

"Were you planning on coming inside?" she asked, standing above them on the doorstep in jeans and a wrinkled pink shirt, with a barn jacket cinched at her waist. She was wearing loafers without socks, and her feet looked very small. She seemed fine, burnishing Laurel's cheeks with kisses, then pausing to look over Sam.

"And who's your nice friend?"

Laurel quickly put a hand on Sam's shoulder when he dropped back, bracing him and protecting them all. "Mom. Mom. Don't be silly. You know Sam, Mom. This is Sam."

They retreated to the car and gathered the untidy, insufficient boxes and bags that constituted Laurel's life. The cardboard scratched the insides of her arms and under her chin. The smell made her want to sneeze. At least it was cooler, west and north of Washington, and the old chestnuts and willow trees provided plenty of shade. They carried everything into the house, through the wide front door, and up a narrow flight of steps. Behind her, Laurel heard her mother call back to Sam as if she'd expected—and recognized—him all along.

"Watch out, Sam—these steps are worn entirely smooth from Laurel's behind." Sam smacked Laurel's butt when he put his boxes down.

In her old bedroom, which was so small, the sudden presence of the heavy boxes, of three fully grown adults' size and energy conspired to push her tiny dresser and desk deeper into their shadows against the wall. Her posters still hung on the walls, horses coexisting with peace signs. There used to be a poster, she remembered, of a shirtless man wearing only a blue Speedo, submerged in a pool, that Sam had bought for her sixteenth birthday. She was the first person he'd told that he was gay.

As Laurel walked around the room touching and remembering, Sam dropped back, and Laurel's mother sighed occasionally as she continuously stroked her hand up and down on the wall where a light switch might have been.

———

SCARED, DEPRESSED, and oddly exhilarated, Laurel went straight to the windows to push the drapes aside. Pale sunlight shouldered its way into the room and made dust-dancing columns in the air. The green leaves outside bounced in friendly waves driven by the wind, and Laurel started talking about growing up in the room, how her dreams had always been outside it, but how it had always, somehow, seemed so safe. With a curious note of recognition, she waved her hand vaguely at the tree outside her window. She had a vague recollection of thinking of that tree as her only friend.

Her mother walked over and slipped a hand into the cup of Laurel's hand. They both laughed quietly when, as he backed toward the door, Sam bumped into a low table with the back of his knee and gave a small shout. Laurel came quickly over and then stopped cold, staring at the table Sam had just hit.

"Oh, my God!" She breathed through a forest of fingers that had flown to her mouth in a failed attempt to cover a smile. Her mother was beaming at her, eyes shining with a confusing mixture of motherly pride and the sheer, unthinking brilliance of a mirror. She looked like herself, but superimposed over that image Laurel could see her as a very old woman and as someone very young. On the table was an Easy Bake Oven made of pink plastic, with flower stickers covering its sides. Like everything in the room, it was impossibly small. Laurel leaned over the gentle little oven, flipping a tiny yellow switch. "This is the oven, you see? This little bulb," she explained softly, "still works."

"I replaced it for you a few weeks ago when you said you were coming home," her mother explained, speaking with the nervous enthusiasm of a child presenting a gift that her mother has made her buy. She was holding her own hands, rubbing them over themselves ceaselessly, since Laurel's had been given over to the pink-and-yellow vision from her youth. "I pulled it out of the attic," she sounded almost apologetic, "and wiped it off for you. Do you like it? I don't think it's the kind of thing you'd like anymore, but I remember how much you loved it. Do you still like it?" She looked slightly nervous. "Do you want me to put it away?"

Laurel stared hard at her mother, the woman who'd sternly corrected their grammar even when they'd all moved out and started their own lives, who'd taken the dogs on long, firm-striding walks before anyone else was up, who'd pushed Laurel out of the house to the cinderblock dorms of a far-away college when she was still only seventeen.

"Mom . . ."

Laurel turned from her crouch in front of the Easy Bake Oven and walked quickly to her mother, enfolding her in a huge hug. The two women were the same height, for today, and they stood tall together, like two giraffes twining necks, or two saplings with slim trunks growing together against the wind. Laurel stroked her mother's hair and whispered something into her ear, while Sam tiptoed silently from the room.

She found him in the kitchen a few minutes later, flipping through the paper, trying to look engrossed. She leaned against the counter and waited.

"Your mom?" He asked, holding a corner of the paper up with one hand.

"She's OK. I think this has all been a little much for her, though. I think she's tired. She went to her room to freshen up." Laurel enunciated "freshen up" with wide eyes and then pushed off from the wall and began walking around the kitchen. "God, I love this kitchen. Remember when my dad gave my mom the renovation for their anniversary?" She ran her hand over the table. "This table's the only thing they kept. You know this kitchen is where I really learned to cook. Remember how I used to hate cooking?" She wrinkled her nose at how ridiculous a thought it was. "It was only during college, that summer Mom was sick, and after college that I fell in love with it."

She was opening and closing drawers as she talked, not looking at Sam or any one thing in particular, silently taking inventory. Three boxes of kitchen supplies were being shipped from D.C., three terribly small boxes of her favorite bowls and cutting boards, her marble mortar and pestle, her knives and whisks and spoons. She took a glass down from an upper cupboard and smiled into it. "This kitchen . . . Mom just kind of let me have it when I started learning to cook. And once I was in culinary school, poof!" Laurel waved her hands as if a small explosion had gone off in front of her, "She just turned it over to me. I think she liked watching me go for my dream."

"Of course she did." Sam got up and crossed to her. "Now, don't go getting all maudlin. One, I've got to get to the train station. Two," he raised his fingers in front of her face, "you've got that big family dinner at Emily's tonight, and I *know* you want to cook up something fabulous. And three," he looked at his fingers. "Hell, I don't know. Go get the car ready. I'm gonna say good-bye to your Mom."

Father and Son

The tan station wagon squats in the parking lot against the heat. It faces a low ridge of newly planted evergreens; behind it loom the concrete, glass-fronted buildings of a suburban industrial park. The buildings range across the car's rearview mirror like an army barracks in the desert, and the tall black lettering of the sign over the door stares down. James is leaving early, which is something he does not like to do. Not, he supposes, that he really has any choice at all.

James Metcalfe is a computer programmer; he writes, analyzes, and deconstructs lines of numbers that become codes that become actual things. He loves his work—string enough letters and numbers together, and he has created something real. A tinkerer, Anne had called him once, when he'd pulled off the back of the television set to show Sam and Karen how it worked.

He removes his hands from the wheel to wipe them on the cloth seat; it is definitely too damn hot. Looking back at his office again, he realizes that the meeting that replaced lunch had thrown everything into question. All the order of his world is suddenly gone. Their top client has pulled out, and James' new project, his job, the whole company's future, may fall apart. As a consolation prize, since it is Friday, the boss has given them all the afternoon off.

All around him, the edges of the parking lot shimmer in the heat. He slowly reverses the car and executes a wide corkscrew turn in the empty lot—the steering wheel slides under his palms. He has put off driving away because it feels uncomfortable and final, but he knows he has no choice. He has to go home and tell Anne. As he pulls onto the road, he imagines Anne seated on the wide expanse of the front seat next to him, of sandwiching Karen, in her short dresses, between them when she was still a little girl. Once they'd had Sam, the competition had become too intense, and both kids had been relegated, semi-permanently, to the back. A still-hot breeze pushes his sleeve above his shoulder and reminds him of driving with his family. His thoughts disappear into their drive, last summer, when they took the kids to Disney World.

The first morning of the trip is surprisingly cool, and they set out with freshly scrubbed faces and enthusiastic yelps. Anne has packed a healthy lunch of tuna fish sandwiches and carrot sticks that, by father-kids collusion, is ignored in favor of a midmorning breakfast at a fast-food restaurant off the highway. His nose tingles with the memory of the sanitary wipes that Annie pulls from her purse, without fail, after every meal. For a few hours, they tell stories and laugh at billboards and sing songs, snacking on juice and pretzels. For a few more hours, despite increasing heat throughout the car and whining from the backseat, they are lifted by the adventure of the day. By the time they hit South Carolina (after a frustrating series of stops during which everyone manages to pee a few times while Sam, too anxious in the crowded, sour-smelling roadside restrooms, cries and refuses to go), the thick, awfully sweet smell of lowland swamps perfectly matches their mood. Eventually, Anne convinces the owner of a small convenience store ten minutes off the highway to let them use the bathroom of their home. They stay that night in a budget hotel and eat at the attached restaurant. Air conditioning and showers help, particularly Anne, and they wake up refreshed in the morning. James loves the shifting sighs of Karen and Sam sleeping in the same room.

But the day does not go well. Despite Karen's fast-flying puberty—her determination to be treated like an adult and the confusing push and pull of her new moods—she has reverted to "big sister" quickly in the car, and she and Sam fight in the backseat, poking at each other with giggles that grow into a grating series of pinching and shouts. James is relieved, at first, that Karen is even acknowledging her little brother; there had been a short-lived battle of wills when she claimed that, if her best friend Rebecca wasn't allowed to come, she would rather just stay home. The kids' backseat warfare escalates until Karen shoves Sam sideways into the hot, metal door. James turns off the radio. Anne climbs into the backseat between them. The vinyl seats are slick with their sweat.

But James is content despite the heat and frustrations. He had mapped their route weeks in advance, planned their hotel stay, and arranged to reach Orlando by the second afternoon, allowing the kids to play in the hotel pool before driving to Disney for the evening parade. He walks his family up to those gates with Sam on his shoulders and Karen holding one hand. Anne, beaming, looks over them to the castle in the sky, and her smile confirms what he has known for years. This is the greatest thing he can do. The greatest thing they can do. The smiles on their faces threaten to crack James' chest in two.

As he pays their entrance fees—he had taken the kids to the bank earlier in the week and let them watch as the teller counted out over a thousand dollars in crisp green one-hundred-dollar bills—and they enter the vast park, all the bright shapes and colors appear to be bleached white from the heat, heat like the air outside the window of his car as he drives away from the office afraid for his job. But it had been different that day, he knows, and everything the bright sun shone down on in Florida had been neat, and orderly, and clean. His wallet in his pocket, his keys on their loop on his belt. Anne, Karen, and Sam at his side.

They have cheeseburgers again that night, tucking into the meal with relish and glassy eyes after their day. Sam leans into his dinner, one leg kicking gently against James' shin and Karen—against her own, adolescent instincts—wilts onto her mother's shoulder as she eats, her hair looking wet against Anne's arm. Anne is wearing a pink, sleeveless shirt, and James notices that her arms have grown thicker since they met: she has put on weight, but he decides that he loves her more this way. Her arms are nicely flushed from the heat of the day, and an almost clear stream of pink grease runs down her chin. He wipes it off with the crook of his finger; their eyes meet and they share a tired smile. When Anne produces a candle and places it into his slice of chocolate cake, nodding to Sam and Karen so that they can all sing "Happy Birthday" to their Dad, he wishes, for a moment, that they had gotten the kids a separate room. Luckily, both kids collapse into deep sleep immediately upon returning to the hotel, and James and Anne manage a long series of sweet, quiet kisses before they fall asleep as well.

The next morning, Karen wakes up early; she was noisy and unsettled throughout the night. Her face looks puffy and pale, and she has a dull, mistrustful expression on her face. She arrows unsteadily to the bathroom, where James hears water running constantly for a few minutes as Anne swats Sam out of bed and opens the doors to the balcony so he can take his toys out and play. A hot breeze pushes into the air-conditioned room.

When Karen emerges, she holds an arm across her stomach and asks in a small voice if "Mommy" can come to the bathroom with her. James, as he increasingly does with his daughter, feels slightly left out. He goes to the balcony to feel the heat and check in on Sam. A few minutes later, Anne taps on the balcony's glass door and mouths the word "period" through the glass. She is unaccountably beautiful in her long, pink nightgown; tears sparkle in her light green eyes. Sliding the door just far enough to poke out her head, she says, "I think we're going to have a girls' day, today." As she pulls back inside, disappearing into the darker, cooler hotel room like a lily receding underwater, she pats James, firmly, on the butt.

"So, sport," he turns to his son who stands looking up at him with two action figures held at odd angles in his hands, "it looks like it's just us guys today. Let's get going," he adds, cradling Sam's head to his hip. He is so glad that his son is still small. "I think there's a dolphin feeding at ten."

Dolphins, James knows, is the magic word. Sam slams into his Daddy, rocking James' legs and holding fast to his waist, and the two men of the family head through the hotel room, pulling on flip-flops and souvenir visors and calling good-bye to the women through the steaming bathroom door.

Sea World is bright and, if possible, even more furiously scrubbed clean than Disney. James pulls Sam past a gift shop, its high windows beckoning with towers of stuffed gray dolphins, green turtles, purple-blue jellyfish, and black-and-white whales, and hurries to the dolphin show. They are early enough to claim seats—low, metal bleachers—within feet of the pool. A young employee warns them that, sitting so close, they will definitely get wet. James asks Sam if he wants to move farther back, but Sam's enthusiasm pulls them both nearer to the sparkling pool's edge. They do get wet: waves of clear, blue water sheet down over them after each dolphin's jump. Sam screams happily, throwing his hands over his head each time, as if welcoming the oncoming wave. After the show, James asks permission to linger at the edge of the pool. An indulgent female employee, middle-aged, with long, bleached hair and a roll of stomach over her pleated shorts, lets them stay. James sits next to his son, one arm on his shoulders to keep him from leaning too close, and watches as Sam watches the smooth, gray animals glide past.

One of the dolphins—though he has trouble admitting it—seems to be focusing on James. He thinks it is one of the older dolphins, who the trainer explained had been at Sea World for almost ten years. The dolphin, his rounded nose—"rostrum, Dad," Sam corrects—and liquid black eyes breaking the surface, circles past them a few times before coming to rest at the nearest edge of the pool. James is so spellbound by the rocking, light-struck water and dolphin's presence that he completely misses Sam's intaken breath. He loses track. He sits in the shaded pavilion, looking directly at the dolphin's huge eyes and smiling baseball bat of a mouth, and feels himself pulled into something—out of himself—that he can't describe. He is aware, from the buzzing in his brain, that he is afraid, in fact, of trying to describe it too closely. Afraid that naming what he is experiencing will make it, somehow, unreal. Like trying to make solid boxes out of refracted colors in the air. He is simply there with the dolphin, communicating with him, removed from land and acceptable behavior, rocking in an ocean of their own.

He wants to close his eyes and drift.

"Daddy?" Sam's small fingers, still cool and wet with saltwater, pull James back to the world. He looks down, eyes slowly refocusing on his tousled and wide-eyed son. Daddy. Karen never called him that anymore, and Sam, watching his sister at all times for clues, rarely did either. "Daddy?" Sam repeats the question. "Do you like the dolphins? How long can we stay?"

James feels a terrifying rush of love. As he pulls Sam toward him and begins to answer his questions, the heavy woman steps back into the arena and explains, gently but firmly, that they will have to move on. "It's awful hard to tear yourself away from them, I know. And Kibby, well, he'll grab your attention like that for hours. He's a pretty special guy." She tells them that they are welcome to get in line for the next show.

"I do like dolphins, Sammy, very much," he assures his son, wondering if Kibby ever feels trapped in his smooth, round pool. Does he ever wish for the ocean, he wonders, pulling Sam up onto his hip. Or does he enjoy the life he has here, surrounded by well-wishers, blue water, and yellow sun? "Let's go to the gift shop and get you one to take home."

Sammy chooses an overstuffed, plush dolphin as long as his arm and carries it with swooping motions throughout the park. He makes splashing sound effects with his mouth. When he isn't flying his new dolphin, he clutches the stuffed animal to his chest. They spend a long morning wandering the exhibits, see an orca show (though not, as Sam points out, the real Shamu), and have pearl divers, in bathing suits and tight flowered caps, dive for pearls for Karen and Anne. James is surprised at how much he enjoys Sea World, the saltwater smell and sanitized grit. At the end of the day, only duty, hunger, and Sam's small hand draw him home.

———

But there won't be a vacation this summer, James knows, as the day's bad news reasserts itself in his head. He doesn't know how he will explain the situation either; he hasn't told Anne how much his company had been counting on the new contract. As a result, she, and the kids, believe everything to be fine. Dammit. He'd even been talking about a new car, about putting a pool in the backyard.

He punches the steering wheel with the side of his fist, determined to figure out how to save the day. Luckily, he has a secret weapon, already planned, that is going to guarantee a warm reception at home. James turns onto an old rural route in the direction away from *home, drives for a few minutes, and then turns again. A weathered gray fence, nailed and lashed together but fallen into disuse, runs alongside the road. He loves driving outside town, and it had only been that past weekend when, driving Anne to their favorite fruit and vegetable stand, he had seen the sign: "Puppies for Sale." They had laughed, together, at how much Sam wanted a puppy, and then he had dropped her on the gravel driveway of the highway that abutted a worn fence and musty-smelling, light-striped barn. Anne had warned him, "No puppies. Just be back in half an hour."*

He remembers the warm, dark laundry room filled with the shuffling sound and sweet smell of puppies and smiles. *It is a good idea.* He'd been repeating that fact over and over since he'd called, on a whim, and arranged to buy one of the puppies for Sam. It will be his birthday in a week, and, in addition to the bike he and Anne have already hidden in a neighbor's garage, he is going to surprise his son—his whole family—with a dog. A little fuzzball to ease the news. He is sure he can convince the farmer to give him one of the puppies today. James' eyes rest on the recently mowed fields on either side of him, the wide, green fields that he is trying to replicate with his own lawn. He loves the area he is driving through—pre-suburban—consisting primarily of expansive, underutilized farms.

He lets his arm surf the wind outside the window. He will present the puppy at dinner and then later tell Anne the news about work. *She'll be fine,* he tells himself. *She's the strongest woman I know.* Hell, it was why he'd married her, he had joked many times. *A woman who always, instinctively, knew what to do, and wasn't afraid to say it out loud.* He will tell her, and then they will tell Sammy and Karen together. He nods once, firmly. *That's the way.* Anne is the strength where the kids are concerned.

Things are changing so fast it makes his head spin; Karen's shirts are suddenly, disconcertingly tight, and Sammy is shifting like a Florida chameleon, changing colors and moods so fast James can't keep track. He wants a simpler equation. *A puppy,* he hopes, *will help restore equilibrium for a while.*

Karen is all right. Even with her sullen adolescence flaring, Karen is still, with James at least, his good little girl. He knows that Anne is having more trouble on that front. But James' challenge is Sam. *Especially since the fishing trip,* he admits, as he turns off the highway onto a rural shortcut that leads to the puppy farm. *Should've known better,* he thinks, and checks his watch, noticing how tan his arm looks against the black band. It reminds him of Florida again, and his regular weekends with the kids at the neighborhood pool.

Maybe that's what prompted the puppy idea, he thinks. *It wasn't that long ago, now.* And he had been pretty short with Sam on the way back from the lake. A fly shoots through the window and smacks into his cheek.

The hit stings, and its lopsided buzzing through the car annoys him. His son is so confusing, so strangely self-sufficient. Almost unnaturally so, he considers, and then pushes the thought away. He reaches behind him to roll down the back window in an attempt to make the fly disappear. He doesn't want to think of Sam as unusual, or unreadable, but, he guesses, that's what his son is. And how could he be anything else? *I'm no talker,* he knows, *and Anne's so*—he suddenly remembers watching his wife as she stands in the kitchen, calling Sam in from a pile of dirt where Karen is directing him to build a castle. *No wonder he's quiet,* thinks James.

The cardboard "Puppies for Sale" sign shimmers into view on the scraggly green side of the road.

THIRTY

THREE WEEKS after Jamie's graduation, Sam spent the night throwing up and shaking with sweat, not knowing if it was food poisoning, depression, or the flu. His sheets were twisted and damp, it was 2 a.m., and he was alone. He wanted to cry because he couldn't fall asleep. Sam had made a muddied attempt to approach the problem scientifically, counting on his fingers the possible causes of being sick. He identified missing Dean, eating a pint of ice cream with chocolate-covered pretzels, or working (for the past two days) with a howler female that had been producing diarrhea and a runny green discharge from her eyes. His thoughts disappeared as, in a rush, he sat up and ran to the disheveled bathroom and attempted to expel whatever it was that was going so wrong inside. A sheen of something sticky edged the sink. He should have known better, he told himself, than to think he'd get over Dean so quickly. He'd never been good at handling radical changes to his world.

The phone woke him the next morning. He was generating a dull heat himself, and the sweltering summer morning pushed past his windows and air-conditioned defense. He licked his cracked lips with a fat, dry tongue. Laurel was on the phone, and her voice was like the green tea with honey that sat cold in a blue mug by Sam's bed. He wanted her to come to his house and take care of him, so that he'd never have to face the world again. She asked him how he was.

"Fine," he began, then remembered who it was. "Actually, Laurel, I feel like shit. I think I have the flu." He coughed a little bit then, for sympathy.

"Oh honey, I'm so sorry." Her voice was like rain; it made him wish that this flu had brought chills instead of fever. "I hate that I'm not there for you anymore. Is there anything I can do to help?" She added a laugh at the end, recognizing the futility of her offer. Sam didn't know how to be best friends with someone so far away. He wanted Laurel to bring over movies and hold an ice-water-soaked towel to his forehead, not just tell him she was sorry over the phone. He wanted, he realized, Dean.

"No, I'm fine, but thanks. How's your mom?" Sam drained the last of his tea. He could feel his voice strengthening. It felt empowering to have something to do. Laurel began to talk about her mother, but she was distracted, talking as if she expected to be interrupted at any point.

"She's fine, I guess. No, really. She seems fine, which makes this all the weirder. She's out in the garden right now, just like every morning of my life, but this morning, when she *made me* breakfast, she asked where my babies were. Just like that."

Sam hooted with surprise and rolled back onto his pillows, looking up at his ceiling as if it were the sky. His head was horribly thick, and he could feel unhealthy movement below his stomach, but talking to Laurel helped. It was like a cold compress on his forehead, like gulping huge drafts of cool air. Sam heard Laurel's fingers slide over the phone and imagined her looking over her shoulder nervously, as she had in college when Sam made her call a friend to get them pot, and she didn't want her mother to walk in and overhear. "I feel like I could just start telling her, every time she walks into the room, that my husband and kids have just left. She'd always be just a little disappointed but expectant. At least she'd think I was married." She paused. "No Mom, little Bobby and Judy aren't here right now; Darren's taken them to the Zoo!" They both burst out laughing. She sounded like a fat girl sneaking cookies, and the thought of food made Sam want to retch.

"Oh, God, Sam, I'm sorry," Laurel said, cutting herself off. "I'm awful. *You* sound awful. How are you doing? Can't someone in your building bring you soup or something? What about Kara? Or Molly? Or that nice neighbor guy? God, you haven't called Dean, have you?"

"No, Laurel," Sam answered with a bite. Frustration and nausea fought in his stomach. "I haven't run into Dean, and I haven't called Dean, and I'm fine. I think it's equal parts flu, exhaustion, and sadness. You know that with Jack gone, I've been practically running half the Zoo." Wanting Laurel to know that he didn't need to be taken care of, Sam refused her offer to call Kara and arrange a care package. "I was just about to walk over to the pharmacy anyway," he promised. "I can get anything I need while I'm out." Through the phone, he could hear a famous chef attacking food on the TV.

The street was worse than his dirty house. Everything seemed coated in a smudged film—the men walking their dogs had frowns on their faces, and the dogs themselves looked scraggly and tired. Clouds of mosquitoes hovered over stagnant sidewalk ponds, and flies circled in lazy loops. Despite the trapped feeling that had driven him up and out his door, Sam wished he hadn't left the house after all. He was a miserable hunch of sweatpants, flip-flops, and a long-sleeved T-shirt and baseball cap as he walked slowly down 17th Street, a huffing old man focusing all his energy on getting to the grocery store one block away.

He wiped his nose on the cuff of his shirt, leaving a snail's translucent trail. His eyes had grit in the corners, and his teeth felt fuzzy against his tongue. His head was so heavy he felt like he was walking in a tunnel, creeping in the dark, when in actuality the bright sunshine was pressing its demanding hands on his shoulders and back. He yanked off his baseball cap and stuck its bill into the elastic of his sweats. His hair was matted and wet with sweat. It felt wet and cool, and he pushed it around on his head.

The lines at the grocery store, even viewed through the windows, made Sam quail. He couldn't face them, he realized, and plowed his head down into the impossible, blocks-long task of the walk to the drugstore. Determined to avoid the faces on the crowded sidewalks of the main business drag, Sam stayed on the west side of the street and passed an old black man and woman, almost gray in the heat, sitting on their blue apartment's wide front stoop. On that side of the street there was a small stretch with a furniture store, a psychic, a sweet little card store, and one restaurant that tried, against the odds, to be slightly upscale.

It was where Miguel and Sam had wanted Terra to be, but Laurel had thought a more mixed neighborhood might be a better fit. The thought of Terra defeated Sam. He was tired and ugly, and the drugstore seemed miles away.

Through the restaurant's cast-iron railing, Sam looked up and saw, perched on the front patio under a shady green umbrella, Dean. In a crisp yellow shirt and dark green tie. Laughing at a table with two people whose faces Sam couldn't see. A glass of icy water sparkling in his hand.

Staring down at the unruly cracks mapping the sidewalk, Sam stumbled a half step before righting himself. He barely avoided some calcified dog shit and a dark, wet puddle that was ringed with unhealthy-looking foam. His heart thudding with embarrassment, Sam righted himself and looked up into the restaurant's lunchtime crowd. And caught Dean's eye. They both froze, and at the moment that Sam raised his hand and tried to smile, Dean's eyes dropped to his plate. After a stunned second, Sam stomped on. Fuck him, he told the hot sidewalk. The bastard didn't even wave.

The sliding doors of the drugstore split wide to admit Sam, and he wanted to collapse on the cold, nubby, blue floor. He wanted to run away—from Dean, from the heat of the day, from himself. At the pharmacist's counter, his reflection assaulted him from a maliciously placed mirror, and the urge to run grew. Sweat wet the brim of his hat as he passed by the aspirin he had come for. He felt a nauseated flush when he didn't get the Imodium A.D. Sam checked his glands again and then, weak and humiliated, lurched out of the store and walked directly downtown.

He had accomplished nothing, and it was almost too much. A dam wanted to burst in his chest, and he felt himself start to cry. He rubbed his face furiously to break the welling tide. I finally learn to cry, he muttered, and now I can't fucking stop. He realized how ridiculous he was being, and raised his eyes toward the tall, glass buildings of downtown. He knew where he was going, even if it hadn't been clear before. At the corner of 18th and K, he turned into an airline ticketing office and walked up to a small blonde woman behind the counter. "I need a ticket to Brazil," he told her, and, refusing to listen to the price she quoted, pulled out a credit card to pay.

———————

AS HE peered out from the plane's protective darkness, Sam shielded his eyes against the sharpness of the landing strip's light. Hot air slapped his face, and, carefully, he tested the uncertain steps of the plane. The rutted, red mud edges of the runway made it seem scratched out of the jungle by the claws of giant, scavenging birds. The trees that enclosed the tiny airport were a rustling green wall, and Sam imagined he could hear the sounds of thousands of animals living wild, natural lives all around. Just being there, stepping out of the tiny dark plane and into the heat and thickness of Brazil, Sam felt as if all the constrictions of his life were falling away. The trees writhed. He wondered how far from the river they were.

He could sense a change in himself already: a juvenile bull elephant pushed out of his gray circle of pachyderm mothers and grandmothers and aunts; the thin-maned young lion, striking out from his tawny, one-mind pride. He felt a part of it all. In most animal communities, there is a social structure wherein every member contributes somehow to the greater good of the whole. Female lions hunt in packs and provide food for the whole pride. In wolf communities, the alpha female bears young, and every other female contributes to raising them. Orangutans, the most solitary of the apes, keep their rare and precious young with them for years, raising them almost like humans do, until they are ready to go off on their own.

Another hint of wind, filled with rich, decaying smells, blew past Sam's nostrils as he stepped onto the baked, cracked ground. He stretched his arms over his head, flexed his shoulders. He felt like he was becoming a silverback gorilla, claiming his own leafy territory, about to establish his own place in the world.

It was the trip, he decided, eleven days away from his life, and the possibility of actually moving somewhere entirely new. It felt invigorating just to be *away*. In the hugely social extended families of most gorilla species, there is an alpha male, a silverback who has fought his way to a position of power and holds all the rights to first food, first females, the best spot to make his bed. Around him is a shifting constellation of females ranking from alpha (the silverback's first wife) to outcast—tolerated apes haunting the fringe of the community, begging for scraps, and suffering regular cuffs and attacks from the leaders. Finally, there are the young, cared for by the whole community, and ranging in age from infant to young adult. There are no young adult males. In species after species, the young males are cast out.

Sam scented the air, using his hand as a visor to scan the breaks in the jungle for anyone. The pilot had trotted across the runway and disappeared into a small building at the edge of the field. Young males get chased away, with whatever violence is necessary to push them into the world on their own. It's about proving genetic strength, the right to carry on their genetic line. Young males, from apes to elephants, are pushed from their communities and made to find their own way.

Sam laughed nervously. He was in the jungle, ready for adventure, and there was no one around to guide the way. Typically untypical of me, he thought. I'm gay; my life would have followed the ape model exactly. But his dad had died, he reasoned, and short-circuited the natural order of things. Sam had become this miniature man of the house. Had his family been composed of apes or elephants, Sam decided, his father's void would have been filled almost immediately. They would have gained another male leader/parent/father, or their little family would have been subsumed into another tribe, with another leader, and been cared for and protected by his strength. His mom, though, had been too strong for that. And then, when Sam had been ready to leave, Jamie had been born.

He ticked off the facts. Gay. No father. Surrogate father-uncle at seventeen. Pretty removed from the natural order after all.

It felt like a massive, beautiful web, with Sam moving around the intricate pathways and thoroughfares in a careful dance with his mother and Karen and Jamie and Laurel, with Jack and everyone at the Zoo. Even Dean. Sam had created an endless, silver-light landscape where he and all the people he loved could walk smoothly and with ease. And yet, he shrugged his pack higher on his shoulder, the web seemed to have gone sticky. It had become something of a trap. He grabbed his second bag from the belly of the plane. This might be the place to start over, he considered, looking around him again. No other option, really. He headed toward the small building, thinking, I'll just have to make my own way.

"Dr. Metcalfe! Dr. Metcalfe!" The words rang out like blue lightning. *Dr. Metcalfe*. Sam grinned and waved. No matter that it was technically incorrect; it sounded wonderful. A muscular older woman with slick, dark hair appeared from behind the building, her low-slung breasts stretching the material of her black Cesar Chavez T-shirt. Her arms were thrust forward as if she was ready to pull him into a smothering hug.

"It's not 'Doctor,'" Sam started, but she shook her head furiously, her stubby fingers in his face. "Now, Dr. Metcalfe, none of that," she said, making Sam feel like a third-grader in a favorite teacher's room. "I read the article you sent Dr. Anderson, and if you don't deserve to be called 'Doctor,' then I don't know who does." They were jockeying for Sam's bags as she said this, leaning across one another and dripping sweat onto each other's arms. "My name's Eleanor, and I've been here volunteering for two months. Another month and a half last year as well. We're just glad to have you," she chuckled, rolling her finger in a loopy spiral at her temple. "Any new face would be a treat out there. Now, give me those bags." She stopped moving and just held the handle of Sam's pack until he gave in and relinquished his hold.

"Thanks, Eleanor." It felt good to have someone to talk to, to thank. The flights had been long. Sam followed her toward a faded orange Jeep and relaxed into the moment. *Dr. Metcalfe*. It was like silver fire. It felt amazingly, distractingly good.

Eleanor loaded them into the Jeep, talking constantly about her volunteer work with the research project, about her late husband's boring ideas of vacation and how rich she felt being able to help real scientists do their work, how she had already lost ten pounds on the diet of rice and beans "and stomach troubles, you'll see" up at the camp. Sam mentioned his own sick stomach of weeks before, and she laughed him off with a wave.

"We're an hour from the nearest real river—don't drink from it though, or anything that hasn't been sanitized—you took all your pills, right?—and all our water sits in huge drums for days. By the end of our week's rations, we're lucky if the whole camp isn't dead!" She plucked at her T-shirt, lifting it off her chest and blowing down into her collar. "You don't know diarrhea, my boy," she patted his hand, briskly, "until you've had it here."

They drove out of the sledgehammer sun and into a filtered green tunnel of trees. The leaves and vines and flowers were like cousins he had never met, and Sam's skin came alive to match the vibrant life of the jungle. He could feel animals everywhere; it smelled like an uncleaned cage. Bugs whizzed by like memories, and a branch sprung wild above them, released from the weight of some animal disturbed by the passage of the Jeep. His pores widened and welcomed all the new sensations. He was a scientist recording his world, a scientist traveling a winding path through the jungle to where the real, the free, the *wild* animals lived. Ideas for Zoo exhibits hit him, but, like the whizzing bugs, he pushed them away. He was absorbing—he needed to *just* absorb—the endless scurrying, climbing, flying, rushing, snuffling, grasping movements of the sharp leaves and dark earth below.

"Anyway," Eleanor continued, turning onto a cooler path furrowed between the towering roots of trees, "we really hope you'll decide to come down here long-term like Dr. Anderson said. He's been hinting that some new blood could really do wonders for the place."

Cool breezes rushed past his face, making him feel mobile, unencumbered, free. A thrill of cold fear ran through him. He couldn't imagine ever going home.

At Sam's request, Eleanor drove him past a few of the hollow metal towers that he would climb into the canopy in the coming days. They were incongruous-looking, heavy and linear, built of unbending red metal like something from a downtown construction site. And yet, looking up into them as they ascended alongside ancient trees and dangling ropes of vine, they fit in as well. Sam couldn't wait to climb them, and he hoped he wouldn't fall.

Sitting in the open Jeep with his head hinged backward over the black seat, Sam looked up into the trees as Eleanor promised him "later," and took him to a small collection of corrugated metal buildings around a semi-cleared central yard that comprised the camp. She stopped and dropped his bags in front of the shack that would be his quarters for his stay.

"But, I won't even be here for two weeks," he apologized when he realized that they had cleared out three local men who had been assisting the project for months. Eleanor shushed him again, giving him a warning look, and he decided to accept her mothering. He had a moment of imagining she was his mother, and that this would be his new home. She told him to put his things away and that Dr. Anderson would be by soon. His small bag was empty in three minutes, and he went out onto the tiny porch to wait. The hair on his legs, freed from the pants he had worn for travel, revived in the air. He breathed deep; it smelled sweet, like rotting fruit. He clutched his notepad and camera against his chest, warding off fear and uselessness as the cluttered emptiness of the research station rustled by. A lean, beautifully mottled dog sniffed its way down the center of the leaf-strewn, dirt-brown yard.

Dr. Anderson hurried up a few minutes later, playfully swatting the dog out of sight. He swung onto Sam's small porch as if he owned it, which, as Sam would soon discover, he effectively did. "Sam!" he bellowed directly into Sam's face, one arm pitched around the post that held up the tin roof. Dr. Anderson was short and wiry. Like a monkey, Sam thought, before insisting to himself that he stop referring to everyone he met in those terms. He was short and wiry, Sam repeated, and weathered from years in the sun at the tops of very tall trees. He was also younger than Sam expected. Maybe forty, if years working in the sun hadn't prematurely aged him. "You getting settled in all right?" he asked, dropping to sit next to Sam.

"I am," Sam offered eagerly, looking closely at his savior's face. "Dr. Anderson, this is such a great opportunity. Thank you so much. You know, I don't want to cause any trouble, but I'd really love to get up in the trees."

"Don't worry about that, Sam," he offered, clapping a hand to Sam's knee. It was hot enough that his hand slid off. "First, call me Jam. Everyone does, and don't ask because I can't tell you why. Then we'll get you some dinner and introduce you around. You don't have much time here, so I'd like you to meet everyone. Then we can talk monkeys until you drop." He surveyed the compound. "I think you'll be impressed with what we've done. I was glad to get your email last week, and I'm glad you finally decided to see it for yourself. I think you might do very well in the jungle with us for a while." He pushed himself up and led Sam across the small research station, pointing out the office-shack; the gravity-showers-shack; the open dining area; and his own, well-appointed metal shack. Half the broad, rough tables were under a waxy-looking tarp strung between a cluster of trees. As Sam took his seat at the quietly buzzing dinner table, he felt echoes of the night he met Dean edging their dark shadows in on him. It was the first time he'd thought of Dean since he landed. He pushed the creeping sadness away and willed the swirl of faces and information to distract him instead.

Dr. Anderson shook him awake at 3 o'clock the next morning, well before light had begun to inch through the cracks between the ceilings, the walls, and the floor. "We've got a rare morning without rain, Sam." His face was bristly with brown and silver growth. "Let's not waste it!"

Massaging his face back into shape, Sam laced his boots and followed Jam to the truck where a small pack had been prepared. He wondered why he wasn't missing Dean more. As he stepped into the Jeep, he realized that he'd never really given Dean his full weight. Never given it to anyone. Never trusted that anyone's strength would be enough.

Jam pointed off to the right as he gunned the motor against the slight coolness of the morning. Twists of mist were dancing lazily along the ground. He indicated a wall of trees indistinguishable from any other direction.

"We're going over there today. Sector 34-B. Yesterday's team saw some signs that a family of howlers was moving back into the area. There are also some goldens out there, some of them reintroduced by your buddies, in that territory, so it might get interesting. You think that'll get your juices flowing?" He laughed and tore out of the camp, sticks and mud flying everywhere.

Climbing into the canopy was not fun. Despite his regular complaints to the contrary, Sam had thought of himself as—belly aside—mostly in pretty good shape. His work at the Zoo, after all, required plenty of physical activity. Climbing into the canopy was different. Reaching the canopy station required navigating a series of stairs, anchored platforms, and ladders, and in two cases necessitated Sam pulling himself up onto platforms with his own strength. His shirt was completely soaked through halfway up, and he began to pull it off. "Wouldn't do that if I were you, unless you put bug spray *everywhere*," Dr. Anderson said, wowing his eyes for emphasis. Sam dropped so that he was leaning on his knees and watched the sweat drip off his nose. "You're doing fine. And don't worry, once you're down here, you'll drop that extra weight in two weeks." He clearly meant it as an enticement. If Sam had had the energy, he would've told "Jam" to fuck off.

They climbed the last, creaking distance, and everything made sudden, perfect sense in Sam's world. Clarity entered him like cool air. They were standing on an orange metal platform above a cloudscape of green trees. He could see flocks of birds settling together like floating white flowers, thrusting branches that broke the treetops and grew flowers and vines Sam had never seen. The sky was clear and almost white and endless, and only at the most distant point of his vision could Sam see any smoke or signs of humanity to interrupt his view.

SAM DID lose eight pounds that week, through a quick combination of humidity, exercise, and Eleanor's promised diarrhea. He spent a good portion of the expedition waving concerned researchers away from whatever clump of bushes he was awkwardly squatting in. Despite the cramps and constant hunger, he felt better in Brazil than he had in months. Leaner. He felt very clean. The continuous sweat drained him of heavy pizza and ice cream, and made a mockery of the lethargy of his bout with the flu. He had been stuck and swollen, swimming in molasses for the last three months, if not the last twenty years. He found himself watching his body move with pride, sweat slicking his forearms and back as he climbed into the trees, sweat sticking his shorts to his legs as he ran behind any available bush. He found himself laughing about it, actually, relishing the discomfort. He felt like a snake sloughing off old, restrictive skin.

They did see a few groups of tamarins, through the distorting eyes of binoculars, moving across their research site on his third day out, and to Sam it felt like beautiful music was sweeping through his soul. Their simple, chattering ease in the trees, the way they moved in hopping patterns among each other, among the branches, always staying a safe distance from the smelly, human-pink obstructions in their way. Sam missed the Zoo, in those moments. He missed the tamarins he had set loose in their planter islands, their forest islands among the curved paths of the Zoo. Missed passing raisins and carrots into their tiny hands. He decided that, if he stayed at the Zoo, he would get more involved with the captive-release program, and no one would get in his way.

There were more birds than he had ever truly imagined, crowned by the gorgeous macaws and a red-tailed black cockatoo who presided over their camp breakfast one morning for almost an hour. On a day trip toward the coast, Sam had even glimpsed, briefly and barely, a pair of Buffy-headed marmosets—he thought warmly of Mickey—across a small ravine. The simple math of seeing so many different kinds of animals, intermingling, affected him deeply. His focus on the howlers had become myopia. His focus on the invisible lines of force that, he had always believed, needed his undivided attention to keep his family and friends safe. Sam needed to let go of simple equations. He needed to expand his view. He realized that he wanted to do more. Something big, something multispecies, and huge, and expansive, and immersive.

He wanted to do something; he was sure of it. If only he had a clearer idea of what it should be.

Days later, on his last day up in the trees, Sam had his first intimate contact with a wild howler monkey. He spotted the heavy black tail first, and tracked the animal's body until he found the face emerging from a clump of rotting fruit. It was actually the first monkey that Sam had seen so breathtakingly close, his earlier sightings consisting mostly of noting droppings and scratch marks that suggested animals had been nearby. Even the tamarins had never been close enough to touch. This specimen was moving slowly, plucking dainty selections from the fruit of a large, flowering tree. He was beautiful, and Sam, watching him from less than 4 feet away, could hardly breathe. He was *graceful* here, artfully moving among his endless, ropy world of trees and branches and fruit to eat. He had a 100-foot vertical world and miles in either direction to go.

"That's X-22," said Jam, "we can almost always find him there. That's the one constant with this work, Sam. You can always narrow them down to their nest, their final territory, their home." Sam kept the binoculars to his eyes until Jam noticed the silence and climbed on ahead to the ground.

As Sam climbed down the high, metal tower for the last time, he felt like an animal released from a cage. He realized that, as fulfilling as this work in the jungle was, he missed his own howlers and the ease with which he found them. It was a trade-off, he decided: jungle versus Zoo, like every choice in life. Zoo animals don't have to forage for their own food, but they live in cages. They are utterly dependent on human kindness and human moods. But they are safe, and they are the same as the howler in the tree above me, Sam thought, living in the jungle, eating and grooming at his nest. This tiny patch of jungle is the howler's nest box, Sam decided. And then he was ready to go home.

THIRTY-ONE

LAUREL SAT close to the window, staring out. Through the dark, wood-squared panes of glass, trees and bushes twisted in an unusually strong, late summer wind, making Laurel feel as if she was tilting, as if the whole house was a storm-tossed ship. Her mother was declining badly, and the worst part was Laurel's utter inability to prepare.

She woke up each morning not knowing whether her mother would be puttering happily in the garden or perched on her bed crying, having forgotten how to put on her shoes. They could have long conversations about when Laurel and her sisters were young, or about their favorite novels, or eternities of dinner without a word spoken, when all her mother wanted to do—her mother who had taught her to read in her own warm lap—was watch the blinking lights of game shows on TV.

Laurel held her breath for Thursday afternoons, which Emily had, with grandiose generosity, agreed would be her afternoon to take care of Mom. Walking her mother to Emily's door and making the gentle, awkward exchange, Laurel had to hold herself down to keep from running to the car. The grass would shine greener, the sky would break open with blue, and she would turn up the radio and peel off like the teenager she desperately needed to be. In those afternoons, Laurel returned to her church, the one boon she had discovered in moving to the suburbs, the multiplex. That great, wide-winged building hulking at the back of a new outdoor shopping center. The cool-at-any-time-of-year interior, with its vaulted ceilings, geometric carpeting, and cheery sculptures of happy concessions glowing above it all. Laurel took huge, gulping breaths in the theater, bought herself more soda and popcorn and candy than she had ever allowed herself before. She would see two movies in a day or see a movie and drive into Philly to try a new restaurant for dinner, sitting with a book and talking, lame and misunderstood and needy, to the waiters and host. She ignored her own errands. They felt useless. There was no time or need.

Sitting in the family room that had become her father's office and that she had now converted into a vestigial office of her own, Laurel noticed that she was marking her mother's appointments in black ink, her own in blue. "Dammit," she breathed, her eyes suddenly sore. It had been her system at Terra for keeping personal and business-related appointments distinct. She jammed her pen back in the mug with the others and scuffled all the pens to mix them up. Black pens and blue pens. She had adopted her mother as her job.

The smell of coffee followed the awkward burbling of the machine, and she fought a wave of panic as the smell popped in her nose. Her mother would be waking up any second; she had to take her mother to the doctor's office in half an hour; and she still needed to wake her up and help her get dressed before they could leave. The trees swayed in awkward circles as Laurel straightened her hair. Some mornings, her mother woke before Laurel did, had a healthy breakfast made, and was already kneeling on her green foam pad in the garden when Laurel walked, stiff-legged, across the kitchen's wide tile floor. Some days, her mother was like a little girl, vacantly disagreeable, and the whole day evolved into a battle of Laurel's wits and cajoling will against the rock-hard pronouncements of a child. Emily, three excuses bouncing blonde in her kitchen, was very little help.

With gentle fingers, she removed all the pens—black and blue and red and green—from their jar and arranged them neatly next to her day planner, stroking them a few times as if they needed reassurance of their place. Mom could very well be fine today, she repeated to herself, looking over the clean and orderly calendar. She would bring up the coffee. Today could be a total breeze.

But when she reached the door to her mother's room, Laurel already knew. The weight of the coming years, hoped-for years, desperately wanted and dreaded years, crashed down on her as she saw her mother, silent and confused in her bed. Light from the windows shone through her mother's hair, making it look like spun sugar, too thin. She wasn't even seventy. Laurel was suffocated by the close, laundry-smelling future as she helped her mother choose an outfit, guided her arms through her sleeves, and buttoned her pink blouse. Her mother chatted amiably throughout the process, pointing to her coffee mug when she wanted another sip. At least she wasn't in a bad mood.

They moved slowly downstairs as Laurel waited for her mother's fog to resolve itself. Waited for her mother to come out from under the clouds. Instead, the clouds above their great oak tree seemed to collude with Laurel's mother and obscure everything. By the time they reached the car, Laurel felt as lost as her mother seemed to be.

"Where are we going?" she asked. "Where's Emily? I don't know why you won't let me drive. Why don't you let me drive?" It was constant and unrelenting. "Whose car is this?"

Laurel chewed her upper lip and answered them all.

At the doctor's office, Laurel watched as her mother docilely accepted the thermometer proffered by the nurse. Watched her mother's eyes dart like a rabbit's, watched them water over at the pinch of a needle. Laurel felt confused, the natural roles reversed, as she looked into her own mother's eyes and reassured her that the hurt wouldn't be too bad. She almost had to leave the room when she felt tears welling in her own eyes and a hot tightness in her chest, but a cry from her mother stopped her mid-turn. Her hand was outstretched to Laurel, making the paper-thin gown expose the wrinkled lines of her shoulder. Laurel met her pleading eyes and held them, walking over and taking her mother's hand. She tried to think of reassuring things to say.

"Why are they doing this to me?" her mother snapped.

After a devastating talk with the doctor that consisted of phrases like "not looking good," "much faster than anticipated," and "consider a private nurse," Laurel rushed her mother into the car to take them away from there. Laurel's family had been going to that doctor for years. He had given her a lollipop when a dog bit her arm and magically produced plastic spider-rings from her ears. Now he said, "Prepare." Laurel felt abandoned: she was driving fast through a spitting rain, hurrying to a phone meeting with her lawyer to finalize the death of Terra, yanking out the last remaining straws and strings from the nest that had been her life. Out of nowhere, her mother started tugging at Laurel's sleeve and pointing at the golden arches of a fast-food restaurant on the two-lane highway that led toward home.

"No, Mom. We don't have time right now, and you don't like fast food." It had been a firm rule of their lives as girls growing up, and one that had become both a family legend and a source of family pride.

"French fries! I want french fries!" her mother demanded, as Laurel, speaking calmly while driving, repeated herself. "No, Mom. I've got a great salad ready to go at home. You love salad, Mom, right? I bought you avocado, remember? You love avocado."

Growing up, Laurel, Emily, and Charlotte had all begged and connived for chances to participate in the family outings of friends in the small hope that a McDonald's or Burger King would be included in the plan. By high school, they called their mother a food snob to her face. Their mother, forever healthy, confident, and maddeningly calm, knew the unhealthy banalities of fast-food cooking and claimed she could smell the grease on them when they came home.

"French fries french fries french—" Her mother's voice was high and insistent, spiraling to a pitch that cut through Laurel's ears. Turning too fiercely with a finger to her mouth to shush her mother, she almost ran a light. The car screeched to a halt, quieting her mother's chanting and shocking Laurel with its rough stop.

"Goddammit, Mom!" Laurel hissed, turning and grabbing her mother's chin to force her to look Laurel in the eyes. She had never touched her mother that way before; as the daughter, she had always been the one being touched. "Listen to me!" she shouted over her mother's small mumbling sounds. "Dammit, Mom, I made us a great lunch. I *hate* this! And *you* hate fast food!" At an angry honk from the low, red car behind them, Laurel grabbed the wheel again and pulled into the next parking lot, furiously swinging the car into the closest space. "Listen to me," she shouted at her mother's tiny face, "Listen to me, dammit!" She was yelling, grabbing her mother's arms and pulling her roughly around. She was going to make her listen if she had to beat them both.

But her mother wasn't there. It was a two-year-old trapped under the advance of a crushing uncle, or a nine-year-old watching his parents scream and fight. That rabbit, from the hospital, in the headlights of a crushing train. Laurel's mother was staring back at her with wide, unblinking eyes, crying quietly, mumbling "french fries" under her breath.

"Oh, my God," Laurel whispered, "Oh, my God." She pulled her mother into the birdlike bones of her chest and stroked her hair.

After a moment during which Laurel took a number of deep, deep breaths, she turned to her mother again. "You want french fries?" she asked, and a spark of joy reignited inside her at the sight of her mother's wide, innocent smile. "Let's go get french fries." The offer made Laurel laugh, and it made her mother start to clap and sing. Laurel ordered them french fries and cheeseburgers while her mother looked at the bright, clean surfaces like a tourist in Times Square. They made obscene pools of ketchup and lifted salty, red-ended lollipops to their mouths. Their *mmms* and *ooohs* should have been embarrassing, but Laurel didn't care. She was happy and light again. Her mother was as happy as she had ever seen her. She might not be the mother Laurel remembered, but she was happy, and it made the blue balloon of Laurel's heart swell and almost explode with joy. They sat in the uncomfortable plastic seats for an hour.

The next morning, Laurel took the blue pen and wrote in "McDonald's" for lunch twice a week.

THIRTY-TWO

DUST MOTES danced in the air of Sam's apartment, catching lazy shafts of light. The window shades were half drawn, and a spread of new mail and magazines brightened the couch. It was half-light, late afternoon, and Sam had to resist the urge to take a nap. The rippled spaces between the floor's wooden planks narrowed toward a horizon at the living room wall, and the fringed edge of the carpet looked like summer grass peeking out from under a picnic blanket. Mingling, ever-present smells of lemon floor cleaner, candle wax, and his neighbors' cooking lifted toward Sam. He let his bag fall to the floor, enjoying the solidity of the sound.

It was home, but Sam wanted to go out. Staying home meant ice cream and bad habits, and there was no longer a Terra to tempt him with the "altruistic" purchase of butter-drenched berry pie. Since his return from Brazil, Sam had a renewed pleasure in his life, and in the possibilities of his life, in D.C. Laurel's absence, Dean's disappearance to New York, and Mom, Karen, and Jamie's two-week vacation with David's family at the beach, however, only made it obvious how narrow Sam's focus had become.

And yet, he was tired of the old, familiar-sounding complaint: Dean was gone, Laurel was gone, Sam was alone. It was old news, it was tired news, and Sam wanted something new. He opened the windows to the street and straightened a picture against the wall. So I never bothered—or managed—to make many friends beyond my safe little group. So now that group has changed. Move on.

After a last-minute, unsuccessful call to Molly and Kara, Sam realized that what he *actually* wanted was to go out and get laid. He called Miguel, who would notice and comment on the weight Sam had lost in Brazil. He called Miguel, hoping it was his night off, wanting someone to lead him through the things a single gay man should be doing on a Saturday night. Miguel wasn't home. Clea's, his new restaurant, was a hit in Laurel's old space. It was full and lively every night. The new owners had dressed the rough space up with purple velvet swags and candles with tiny beads hanging from their shades. They had created cozy groupings of dimly lit tables, low couches, and chairs, and eliminated all but the simplest of food. Even Sam could see that it was an amazing transformation; he still missed the period of mourning that never was.

Sam had been back from Brazil for a week, and a renewed energy permeated everything he did. He had a wild-armed enthusiasm he hadn't felt in months. He was physically exhausted: the backs of his arms and legs tired and aching, his lower back tight, and his shoulders pulled toward each other as if by massive, calcified rubber bands. The strain felt good, though; it felt good to have worked so hard.

And people were noticing; he had seen Gwen and Dr. Baskin walking by him twice in the past few days with odd, encouraging smiles. He had proposed two new free-range projects for the tamarins and marmosets and was talking with the Education Department about a new Great Cats program he had in mind. He had completely rearranged the howler exhibit in the past three days, luring them into their nest boxes and moving every perch to a new location, removing six large dead branches, and adding almost 100 feet of heavy, corded rope. The enclosure was now looped with a serpentine highway of thick, tan cord and small platforms. In the morning, the howlers would emerge into a whole new universe of adventure. He knew they wouldn't do too much with it—they were howlers, after all—but he needed them to know it was there. He was also researching the possibility of adding native birds, lizards, and plants to their exhibit, trying to replicate a little of Brazil in D.C.

Sam wasn't scheduled the next day, but he was planning to work anyway, sneak in early and hide their favorite snacks—carrots, raisins, chopped potatoes, apples, and pears—in all the new nooks and crannies of the cage. He would paint some high corners with honey. Give them a reason to explore. He did wish Jamie was in town to tag along, but it wouldn't slow his momentum either way. On Monday, he was pitching his redesign of the tamarin exhibits as well.

He grabbed a bottle of water and paged through the mail on the counter. It needed dusting, but he was willing, for the night, to let it go.

Pulling off his green workshirt, Sam walked to the bedroom where he kicked off his heavy work pants as well. He pulled on a pair of running shorts, sat on the tan comforter to lace up his shoes, and leaned back onto the bed with his arms thrown back and his hands playing with the air on the other side of the bed. Do I really want to run? he asked the ceiling, noticing a warbly spot in the corner that might mean his neighbor's toilet was leaking again. That confirmed it. He needed to get out of the house. Sam curled upward and all the way down to his feet, tightened his shoelaces, and jogged for the door.

Half an hour later, Sam's body was permeated with oxygen and a powerful rush of blood. His whole face radiated heat. The run had flooded his brain with ideas. He didn't have to stay in D.C., as much as he loved it. He could still go to Brazil, find a new joy in distant, unreachable animals living free. He could enter veterinary school or work for a conservation group; he could ask for a permanent transfer to Lion Island. Jack came into his mind then, and Millie. He realized he should add to his list: I could meet someone new. He could join the gay running group that met in Rock Creek Park, train for a marathon, really get in shape. He could take a vacation somewhere with lots of sun, take Laurel away for a weekend, be happy without Dean or any other man. The thought that he *could* just drop everything and take the job in Brazil surfaced again, and he stopped walking to let himself hear.

Could I really do it? he wondered, with the beginning of a delicious confusion roiling in his chest. My family; my life. Briefly, he imagined how much easier it would be to have a geography, a landscape all his own.

A man turned back and smiled at Sam as he walked across the bridge toward home. It was enough. He could do anything he needed to do.

At home, Sam ignored the answering machine and caller ID, and poured himself a blessedly cold glass of water. He stood in the refrigerator's light for a minute, one hand on the door, one holding the glass to his lips, and drank until his stomach, throat, and mouth were full. Despite himself, after kicking off his shoes, Sam did check the phone. No messages, still. There you have it. He felt himself deflate. Felt his hips and stomach clinging to his wetly cooling shirt. Sam walked into the bathroom and turned on the shower. He shucked his clothes and kicked them into a damp pile under the sink.

Standing under the hot water, Sam let all the sweat and dirt and stink disappear. He relished the flood of water on his shoulders and back and wished, for a moment, that his body was made of pale soap, and that the water would just slowly and gently wash him completely away.

He was tired of it: of being fine and happy and OK but not complete. He was tired of waiting around, looking for the answer he thought was always due, just due, to appear. Dean, Jeremy who'd talked him into this apartment—all the boyfriends, all the way back. The idea of college, the idea of Brazil. The first year or two at the Zoo. Here's the answer; now it will all make sense. Standing under the hot water, Sam didn't know what, exactly, he was supposed to do. He was single again, again. Jamie was doing fine; his mother and sister had their lives. Jack was gone and with him the compact distraction of being too busy at the Zoo. He stood in the shower, not knowing which way to turn, knowing he would have to make a decision, any decision, when he got out. It was just that he didn't know how.

But he wasn't genuinely tired, and he missed the powerful feeling of his run, so Sam went out alone. He stalked the electric smells, lights, and laughter of 17th Street with a grim determination. He would meet someone, he would distract himself, he would make bad decisions worthy of the conflicted—horny, angry, depressed, elated—mood he was in. Sam didn't see all this as he walked down 17th Street, looking up eagerly to catch any handsome man's eye. He was just walking toward the bright restaurant lights.

He walked into a bar. Facing the crowded runway of men in baseball caps and tight shirts, Sam felt lost. The men in their rarified groupings always seemed so exclusively *exclusive* to Sam. For a moment, he felt frozen and unable to move. This was not his world. He hadn't been to a bar without Dean or Laurel's insistence in years. Looking at that disinterested gauntlet, Sam felt something shift in his chest, like an iceberg groaningly giving way to the sea.

I'm doing this, he told himself. Taking a deep, smoke-shocked breath that made him cough, Sam put on his best, uncaring game face and waded into the crowd. He recognized a few friendly faces from the gym, the dry cleaners, even Terra. Each smile was like a shot of adrenaline. His face relaxed into a smile. Sam kept moving, pulled by unfamiliar tides, until he found an empty spot along the wall by the back door. He hadn't admitted to himself—not fully, not yet—what exactly he was there to do. He waited in line to order a beer, then breasted the crowd to reclaim his perch against the wall. The beer felt cold in his hand and like a mountain stream when it hit his throat. I could be an alcoholic if I had more energy, Sam thought, smiling an inward smile. He leaned back against the wall and watched.

Sam could spend hours at the Zoo watching the minutiae of a tiger's day—the number of paw licks, circuits around the enclosure, bowel movements, interest or lack of interest in certain foods. Pages of notes were devoted to the variations of familial grooming patterns in his tiny howler clan. He devoted himself to that cataloguing instinct again, hiding himself in his observations, standing at the back of the bar. He watched as men strutted, walked nervously, waved or avoided eyes, moved through the crowd with confidence or aggression, or let the crowd push them around in its wake. He noted handsome men with bright white smiles whipping from friend to friend to friend, watched a group of tall, beautiful young boys walk the runway of the crowd, averting their eyes from their admirers with disdain.

He classified everybody. "Insecure" or "Needs to relax" or "Bottom" or "Can't find his pack." The group of young males thoughtlessly claimed their territory—bright tight clothes being pulled off in a protective circle on the dance floor—and formed a circle around each other as if they were musk oxen on the Arctic tundra, heads down and horns out, denying access to any less desirable players in the mating game. Sam also classified the ones he was attracted to himself. The handsome ones in groups of friends, the silverbacks and alpha males of the gay bar scene. When they walked by, Sam would watch them from his sheltered cove along the wall, pull a deep sip from his beer, and, if he caught their eye, look quickly away with what he told himself was a rueful smile. He was husbanding his resources, he told himself.

But maybe his observations were really just so much distancing. Maybe it was time for him to switch approaches; to experiment with being predator instead of prey.

Sam was on his third beer when the man caught his eye. He raised his beer in the man's direction, making a safe greeting from across the bar and receiving an affirmative nod in return. The man was handsome, and Sam so out of his element, that he found himself looking nervously away. Busying himself with his beer bottle, Sam worried the wrapper into oblivion. When he had stripped the bottle of all but a few clinging, paper dregs, Sam looked up to see the man standing inches from him, smiling a wolfish smile. The guy was taller than Sam and had dark, wavy hair, cut short. His face was a little fleshy, like a married father from New Jersey, but he had a strong, solid chest that made Sam want to lean against him and rest.

Not tonight, Sam told himself. This isn't about collapsing or backing down. Tonight is just fun, just selfish. Tonight is about getting laid. Thankfully, the guy looked absolutely nothing like Dean.

The man continued to smile as he took another sip from his beer, and Sam, defiant, made the first move.

"Hey," he said, raising his beer in greeting.

"Hey, you."

I remember this, he thought. And the banality made him fierce.

Not much more was said that night. Sam grinned and nodded toward the door and let the man follow him out. They went to Sam's apartment and, barely speaking, grappled to the hallway floor in a heated, clumsy clinch. By the time Sam had pulled himself up to lock the bolt behind them and was leading the man to his room, he was tired of it and wished it was over. As the man pulled off Sam's shirt and bent down to lick his tightening nipple, Sam wished he could simply go to sleep. He struggled to unbuckle the man's belt and thought it wasn't worth the work. When Sam finally came, it was eye-popping, lung-choking, ecstatic. But when they finished Sam felt empty and relieved, and pushed the man unceremoniously out the door.

———

THE NEXT morning, Sam pulled the sheets, blankets, and pillows off the bed and tossed them into the hamper, where they spilled over onto the floor. In the vestigial "office," he pulled a tattered navy Paddington coat off its hangar and tossed it on the floor, gleefully adding unworn shoes, dress shirts, and a fraternity sweatshirt (inherited from a boyfriend of Laurel's on whom Sam had had a devastating crush) onto the pile. Old skin. He would donate it to charity later. He had emptied and half-cleaned the kitchen cabinets. The fresh smell of foaming cleanser popped in the bathroom, where another cleaning project was half done. A landslide of magazines decorated the living room floor. He laughed amid the ruin. Maybe a little devastation was needed to give birth to something new.

He moved back into the office, noticing how far from white the walls had become. He would repaint the room, clear out the storage, open it up. A desk, a few, active files, something else. He grabbed at the beginnings of a plan but decided to let it go.

Under the desk, where his legs would have gone had he ever actually used it, were boxes of photographs from the past few years. Another project—photo albums—that had been put aside for too long. He scooted the boxes out from their cave, sneezing a few times at the roils of dust, and, removing the top of the first box, sat on the cluttered floor.

The first photograph: two dusky, blue geese standing on their short legs, one honking furiously, with wings bent back into an aggressive fold, the other fading behind. A blurry hand pulled away from the angry beak, dropping a yellow spray of corn. Sam had loved those geese. Nelly and Magda. Both female, they had chosen each other as goslings and nested together for their entire lives at the Zoo.

He raised his head to the ceiling, laughing back tears. Sam knew full well that very few species of animals mate for life. It did not encourage natural selection or the distribution of the gene pool. It was not the natural way animals work. "Still," he said aloud, rubbing his eyes, and looked at the picture again. Humans are always denying that model, and are told, will tell you, feel all the way to the pit of their souls that being half of a couple is the greatest and most important way to live their lives. Sam felt that way, despite himself. Missed Dean even though he was starting to know it was for the best that he was gone. He decided he would paint the room blue.

Sam had been working with "nonmonogamous" animals for over ten years. He knew that they did love each other, even if he was required to note it in his study as "extended affectionate displays." He saw Karen and her family. He had faith that it sometimes came true.

Sam smiled at the photo, incredulous at its effect. It was his hand, in the photo, one of his early days at the Zoo when Jack had introduced him to the geese as a way of saying everything would turn out all right.

Or not.

One day a few years back, Nelly had gotten suddenly, terribly ill. Her internal organs, without reason, seemed to be shutting down. Within days she went from a fierce, honking presence defending a small corner of the aviary to an unbearably light, weak-breathing, cooling mound of feathers and hollow bone. She died within twenty-four hours. Her keepers buried her with genuine sadness in a small grove below the eagle's aerie and moved on with the business of running a Zoo. Sam, Jack, and a number of other keepers attended the funeral. Magda, her partner, sat at their nest for days, refusing to eat and furiously hissing and honking and jabbing her snakelike neck at anyone who came near.

It went on for days after Nelly's death. Eventually, Magda had to be sedated and put on an IV. She would have died of mourning. Sam had volunteered to take a shift watching her, nestled uncomfortably on her makeshift nest, as her gorgeous neck curved downward and the tip of her black and orange beak slowly, slowly traced circles in the ground. At any sound she would raise her head slowly, eyes wide, and let issue from her mouth a thin, desperate bleating sound. She never took solid food again, and died within weeks. Sam felt like Magda that morning, sitting in his own disheveled nest, surrounded by the mess of his life.

But *this* mess was good. Sam would get up again and move on. Last night, disappointing as it was, had been a good start. It's really over, he told himself, rolling the words around his mouth. Dean, this lethargy, that whole stuck chapter of my life. He tried to take heart, telling himself that Dean wouldn't come back, and trying to extinguish the tiny point of foolish hope that said he might come back soon. Sam hadn't even been given the chance to decide if Dean was his true "mate." Dean had just disappeared on him, without any real explanation, simply fading away. A helpful anger kindled. Screw it, he told himself. This isn't all about Dean. And *I'm* not an old lesbian goose.

Pushing himself into movement, Sam made easy, comfortable circles around his apartment, organizing the various piles and making a plan for the rest of the day. He worked for hours without stopping, filling massive black trash bags with items for charity, for the Zoo, for the trash. He reorganized the cabinet underneath the bathroom sink; a layer of gray scum came off the tub. The office was an office again, though he didn't know what work he wanted to do. He cleared the living room furniture away from the wall. He pulled his grandmother's tarnished menorah from a newspaper-packed box and put it on the mantel in a spot bright with afternoon light.

Finally, he dragged the last of the bags out to the curb. Nick, surrounded by his own gardener's pile of weeds and bags and dirt, joked that spring cleaning seemed to have come awful late.

Afterward, after dark, Sam collapsed on the couch. His senses popped with the smell of cleaning and open space. The last vestiges of Jeremy, of Dean, were stored neatly in with the boxes of photographs, and Nelly and Magda held a position of honor in a frame beside his bed. Sitting still for the first time in hours, he realized that his face was tight with the salty remnants of tears. He decided *not* to jump up and wash his face, decided that he'd reached a point where crying must be good. A buzzer sounded, and Sam moved to the hallway to finish the last of the laundry before bed. Before the past few months, he knew, the abyss that crying opened had seemed too starkly, overwhelmingly big. Somehow, over the last few months, that had changed. Sam rested in his emptied apartment with tears still marking his face, realizing that he'd learned to look into the abyss and not fall.

THIRTY-THREE

"LOOK! IT'S the monument!" Jamie called out, tugging Sam out of an easy reverie of sunlight and gently falling leaves. *James*, Sam reminded himself. With the start of his new school, Jamie suddenly wanted to be called James. Sam looked up at the monument, almost yellow in the thin sunlight, piercing the perfect blue of the fall sky.

Sam and Jamie were crossing 15th Street toward Dupont Circle, their unzipped coats flapping behind them in an early fall wind. They moved slowly, like old-fashioned milk farmers, carrying heavy pails of paint in their hands. Jamie—James—had been telling Sam all about his new school, about the tryouts for soccer and a party where the girl he liked had had a friend tell his friend that she liked him, and how they had danced three times.

"Did ya kiss her, James?" Sam sang the question directly into Jamie's face, enunciating the new name into multiple syllables, letting Jamie hear his uncle try it out. Jamie's face bloomed red, like Sam's own, into a shy smile. He is so brave, Sam thought, going to a new school, making new friends, meeting a new girl. His pleasure was punctured, however. Like biting into a crisp apple with a rotten spot.

Am I jealous, he wondered? At how easily his bravery seems to come? Sam shook his head and refused to accept the reaction. If Jamie's bravery scares me, then I should learn from it. Stay or go, he thought, as he switched a can of paint from one hand to the other, move on or stand still. Sam was suddenly angry at his own indecision for not wanting to go to Brazil, for wishing, occasionally and against his will, that Dean would come back, for not pushing harder at the Zoo.

"Hey, Sam," Jamie responded, ignoring Sam's question about the girl. Another new one, Sam thought: "Sam" instead of "Uncle Sam." He liked it, even if it made him a little nostalgic for little Jamie swinging on his arm. "What did Mom tell you about my wanting to be called James?"

"Just that it was important to you," Sam replied, keeping his eyes on the monument, not wanting the conversation to go anywhere other than where Jamie needed it to be. "I told her I liked it. You know, she and Grandma used to call me Sammy. It's cool." Jamie smiled at his uncle and ran ahead to race a yellow light.

It was worth everything, that moment, with red-tinged leaves edging out the green and an almost grown nephew looking to his uncle for advice. Sam realized, with a crisp blue clarity, that he didn't want to go away after all. That Brazil, the research, and Dr. Anderson *were* a dream come true, but they were the dream come true of a different man, a different Sam. Brazil's sweaty green heat and dense opportunities were the fantasy of a younger Sam, the one who couldn't see the magic in walking with a nephew or in redecorating an apartment he'd lived in for ten years. It was the dream of Sam, sitting with his chin in his hand in a vertebrate Zoology classroom, wishing, more than anything, that he could be as exciting as the *National Geographic* magazines he had hoarded as a kid.

He called after Jamie and offered to race him back, ducking from the sudden downpour that swept in on heavy clouds and chill air. Sam ran into his apartment behind Jamie, laughing and wet; in the two blocks it had taken to get home, they were both drenched.

They were shaking themselves out when the phone rang, and Sam pulled off his jacket to answer the phone. He pulled his shirt off with it, the fabric clinging to his back. Grayish water collected on the tops of the paint cans, in dotted pools on the newspaper covering the floor. Jamie had gone directly into the bathroom, and Sam heard the rush of water from the shower. Karen said that Jamie was always in the shower these days, and Sam hated to think what that meant for his shower floor. He had taken to hanging a bottle of disinfectant on the caddy that carried soap and shampoo.

"Sam?"

Dean.

It was like a frozen stake to the heart, a gorgeous, iridescent shard of ice. Sam's skin prickled into goose bumps and he struggled to pull his shirt back on. Through the thin blue fabric, breathing deeply of his own smell, Sam asked, "Dean?"

"Hi. Yeah. It's me. How are you?"

"Jamie's here. I mean, I'm fine. How are you?" Sam was surprised to find the icicle inside of him glowing red, its sharp edges sparking with blue flame. He was angry at Dean for calling. Impatient. The day had been so simply nice: a Saturday with Jamie, all his messy scribblings and note taking about the Zoo. It had felt, without feeling anything overtly, full of hope. Dean didn't have the right to do this. He couldn't just suddenly be there now that Sam was doing fine.

"I'm fine. I'm . . . Sam, I miss you. I think I . . . " Fear froze the icicle again. Sam couldn't bear to hear, couldn't wait to hear whatever it was Dean was about to say. He checked to be sure Jamie was still in the bathroom. Hot steam curled out from around the partly closed bathroom door. Sam waited silently, dreading and praying what would come next; the newspapers covering the floor crunched and slipped under his feet. He had pulled a towel from the closet and was drying his head and neck.

"I love you." Sam's stomach churned, an explosion of red and yellow and blue. "I want to see you. Will you come to New York?" Dean stammered out, and Sam could hear the strain in Dean's voice. He sank onto the couch, clutching the towel against the nape of his neck and blotting it against his hair. The noise from the shower drummed loudly, and he remembered Jamie. Shit. He stood up briefly and pulled the bathroom door firmly shut.

"What? You want me back? What?! Dean, it's been *months*."

"I know. I just . . . I don't know. I didn't say that," Dean specified, and Sam dropped the towel to the floor. "I just miss you. Things here in New York are . . . great, I'm really happy, but I want to share all this with you. I still love you, Sam. Will you come? You could be free the weekend after next, right? It's your quiet time, right? At the Zoo?" His voice quieted. "It was quiet this time last year." They had taken a weekend and gone into Virginia to browse antique stores and buy pumpkins. Sam felt his chest break open and tears announce themselves in his eyes. "I want to fly you up."

And Sam forgot the "not enough" of three months before. Because he still loved Dean, and because all of his new-forming happiness threatened to wash away under the tide of that single possibility, he agreed. Sam loved when Dean wasn't scripted, when he faltered over words like everyone else. Rationally, he decided, he wasn't willing to accept Dean again, but in his heart he couldn't imagine saying no. They talked for a few more minutes, tentatively deciding that Sam would call Dean the next day to make a plan. When they hung up, Sam sat on the couch looking at the phone like a map he couldn't read. The receiver fit neatly into its cradle. When Jamie came out of the shower, Sam announced that their painting plans were cancelled for the afternoon. They rushed to an afternoon matinee so that Sam could sit in the darkness and think.

———————

LAUREL TOLD Sam she was coming into town for business; she needed to sign some final legal papers and relinquish her apartment for good. Sam knew she was lying but didn't care.

"I'm not a fool," he told her, "but whatever it takes to get you here." It was the night before Sam's trip to New York.

They drove out to Bethesda, and Sam watched Jamie's swim meet with Laurel at his side. He acted like a giddy teenager in the warmth and pungent smell of chlorine. He played the fool happily, glad to make her smile.

After the match, they offered to take Jamie for pizza and ice cream, but Jamie opted to go with his friends instead. Sam emptied like a balloon, and Laurel spent the next hour comforting him through the inevitable fact of Jamie's growing up. They had gourmet pizzas and a full bottle of dark, rich red wine. Despite his nervous stomach, he tried to eat.

Spiking fresh, wilted spinach and crispy onions on her fork, Laurel looked at Sam for a long moment. "You know, this has been a funny year for us both. It's almost like we've led opposite, parallel lives. Like the two curves of a parentheses or something."

Sam took a bite of pizza. "How so?"

"Well, a year ago, right when you met Dean," she made a face to indicate that that topic wasn't closed, "I had everything I wanted in life. The restaurant. Andy, or so I thought. And then with my mom, I ended up giving it all up for something I never even wanted." She shrugged. "And ended up *getting* something totally unexpected, and totally, unexpectedly wonderful in return." Sam leaned across the table to squeeze her elbow.

"Wonderful?"

"I know, you're right. Wonderful is probably too much. But I *am* doing better than I ever imagined—living at home and taking care of my mom—so I'm not *un*happy. I like being with her, helping her out. And some of Mom's rich neighbors want me to be their personal chef, so . . . I guess we never know."

For the first time since Laurel had told him she was moving home, Sam believed that Laurel was going to be all right. That *he* was going to be all right as well. Something inside himself let go.

"And you," she continued, pointing at him with her fork, "you sort of had everything too, but . . . but it was all wrong for you somehow. It was almost like you'd arranged it all so well that you couldn't see how it was strangling you. Forget the men in your life. I don't think you'd been happy for a while." She looked into Sam's eyes.

"I'm fine, honey. You're right. Go on." No more fear, he'd decided. He could take whatever she needed to say.

"OK. Well. So there you were, maintaining everything. You, me, us, everything, and then you started to lose things. Lose control?" She offered the question up carefully, pausing for Sam's reaction. He waved her on with his wine.

"You lost Jack, and you lost weight."

Sam burst out laughing, and Laurel smiled.

"And came out somewhere, also unexpected, that I think is going to be really, really good." She took another sip of the purple wine; it was clear that she had been thinking this idea through. "It's like, we both had to lose or give up how we *thought* we were supposed to make our worlds work, and in doing that, we both get to find out how we'll really get to be happy. I don't know." She picked at something in her teeth. "Am I totally full of shit?"

"Yup," he grinned, full of life and possibility and ideas.

When they stepped outside in the cool air, the street was quiet, and the stores and restaurants spilled yellow light. Laurel looked good, Sam thought. Her long coat swung like birds flying around her legs. They bought ice cream cones and fell into a revolving walk around the fountain in Dupont Circle. Cascading water mottled the light and freshened the city's noise. Walking, Sam let the fears and excitement of his visit to Dean bubble outward and talked for a few revolutions about the mingling of hope and unease.

"I know it's crazy and everything," he assured her. "The call, this weekend, all of it. But I think that, first, before all this other stuff, or as a part of it, I need to figure me and Dean—*us*—out once and for all. I think I'm way better equipped to handle it all now. I'll make my own choices this time. For me. I promise you that." Laurel walked quietly next to him, and they ate their ice cream in peace.

"Anyway," she interrupted the silence again, "I do have one more thing to say. I want you to be careful in New York. Dean, and this visit, may seem like a perfect solution, but, like we were saying earlier, perfect doesn't really work. Not-perfect, I think, is a much better way to go."

Leaning back against her car, she took Sam's hands in hers.

"Just be careful, honey. Dean isn't—well, no—he *is* exactly what we thought he was. He's 'perfect.'" She dropped Sam's hands and made the symbols for quotes with her fingers. "Perfect like rigid. And uncompromising. And, Sam, he just wasn't nice enough to you, and that kind of perfection isn't. . . ."

"Shut up," he told her as sweetly as he could. "I'm fine. Now, you have a safe trip back. You sure you can't stay tonight?"

She shook her head and kissed him on the cheek.

"It's barely a two-hour drive," she assured him, before climbing into her car. He stood for a while in the cooling evening as Dupont Circle, untethered, rushed by.

THIRTY-FOUR

AND THEN he went to New York, a three-ring circus dancing in his head. He would be at Penn Station in New York in less than three hours, and Dean would meet him just outside the train. Sam nestled his chin into the comforting wool of his turtleneck sweater. It helped him imagine the skin of Dean's cheek. Helped him imagine the strength of Dean's arms. "What am I doing?" he wondered aloud, needing to open and steel himself all at once. Sam leaned back and spread his paper and coffee on the plastic tray hinged over his seat. He would simply read the paper. His forehead against the train's window was cold.

It hadn't been easy for Sam to take Sunday off, especially with a series of strategic planning meetings coming up that he had, oddly, been invited to join. To his own surprise, however, Sam had simply announced that he was taking the weekend, and Gwen had meekly agreed. It was Brazil, Sam was sure. Anderson had sent a letter to the director making it clear that Sam was wanted on the project there. Since that letter, Sam had even made some headway about getting his howler research project going at the Zoo, though, he had to admit, he was less and less focused on the howlers and more excited about his glowing plans for a multispecies rainforest on the last undeveloped slope of the Zoo. Gwen and Director Baskin were encouraging, hinting that they had "plans" for Sam with the new budget allocations in January. A cool runnel of air on his forehead made him feel like he was on a plane. Images of Brazil, New York, and D.C. fought with wobbly swords in his brain.

It was strange. All these options in front of him, this *sense* of options, just when things in D.C. felt almost right, somehow, for the first time in a long time. The first time in years, he considered, watching out the window as two boys played in the pebbled ditch below the tracks. Casting his thoughts back like a shadow, Sam couldn't remember a single day when he'd felt truly and totally at ease.

But lately, since Jack and Millie had died and Laurel had left, even with being dumped by Dean, everything seemed to be coming together. As if, by letting go of the tightly held strings, the weave was finally falling into place. Mom had actually met a man. Karen was pregnant, finally, after years of trying with David, and Jamie loved his new school. Sam congratulated himself on helping to broker that deal between them and then realized that what he had truly managed to do was to *let them take care of themselves*. It felt like a big deal, that revelation: they could all take care of themselves, leaving Sam room to do the same for himself. He was demanding more at the Zoo, had run with the gay running group a few times, was connecting with a few of the other keepers, was actually making some new friends. The morning after Dean's call, he and Jamie had painted the living room red.

The train jolted, and Sam's forehead bonked against the window. At Sam's insistence, Dean had promised he wouldn't make too many plans, and Sam was looking forward to hours on Dean's couch, just reading and maybe touching feet. He loved Dean's feet, the softness edged with calluses, how, unlike Sam's, they always seemed warm. For the first time in months, Sam's thumb ached, and he worried it with his other hand; he pushed away the misgivings that threatened to creep into his mood.

Sam had also proposed a trip to the Bronx Zoo's newly renovated gorilla exhibit, and offered, if Dean had work to do, to make the trip by himself. Dean hadn't really responded to Sam's suggestions, just said something about wanting to eat Sam up. He thought again of cuddling on Dean's couch and realized he couldn't imagine it. It wouldn't be in the living room Sam knew and loved, but in some new room, in a new apartment, in a new city, with a possibly all-new Dean. It was a scary thought, and Sam was suddenly too agitated to read. He tried to lean back and watch the world go by.

When the train pulled into Penn Station just before noon, Sam didn't know what to expect. He grabbed and lost the handle of his bag at least two times while waiting for his turn to exit the train. He was scared: Would they go right back to Dean's apartment and have sex? Would they eat lunch first, at some new place Dean wanted to show off, then hit a museum, and then go home? Would it be horrible? Would Sam be on the next train to D.C.? His merry-go-round thoughts gradually fell below the increasing tide of excitement and dread at the imminence of seeing Dean. He wanted to swing off the luggage racks like the gorilla in the old ads, bounding from one end of the car to the other, pulling hats off people's heads and staring into everyone's eyes.

"Look at me! I'm in love! I'm terrified! Look at me," Sam would shout, turning all his nervous energy into action. Instead, Sam checked for his sunglasses, made sure his wallet and keys were safely in the pockets of his new coat, and rearranged his sweaty grip so that his bags would be easy to hold when Dean swept him into his arms.

Sam edged his way forward, then accelerated through the crowds once he had stepped off the train. He pushed to the front of the escalator and into the bright white tiles of Penn Station. Dean was there, standing like a Greek statue with a fall of white lilies hanging from his right hand. His long gray coat fell like a rainstorm from his shoulders, and Sam wanted to drink every drop. Seeing Dean was like Sam's expectation of New York—he was flooded with light, dizzied by the sights and sound, battered by the intensity, almost erased. Something in the station smelled wrong.

For a moment, Sam stood blinkingly still. Then Dean smiled, and Sam walked into his arms. Sam grabbed Dean in a huge hug, scooping his arms inside Dean's jacket and lifting him almost off his feet. He felt Dean's chin on his neck and the wide back under his shirt, and he almost choked with excitement. He wanted to cry, from happiness and fear. He didn't know whether it was victory or defeat but didn't care.

"So, how is it?" Sam wanted to know. He had a thousand questions but was exhausted and relieved just to have Dean in his arms. All the questions, all the thoughts and fears and hopes and ideas, were stuck in a logjam in Sam's throat. To free them would have taken more energy than he had. Sam didn't know what he'd been holding on to, but it felt so wonderful to just let go. He wouldn't think about it, about anything. He would just be. Dean's eyes were happy and bright, and he brushed his shoulder against Sam's thigh as he leaned down to take his bags. Sam felt a thrill of excitement shoot through him at the touch. "Can we, can we . . . "

Dean laughed, clutching Sam's bag. "I'm good, I'm great. It's so good to see you." He gave Sam a fast, hard kiss. It was disappointing. Sam followed Dean out into New York.

Dean's building had a sleek, tall lobby with a daze of blue curtains and metallic panels on the walls. It looked like a hotel. The elevators hushed them to a dizzying height, and Sam followed Dean, one hand holding his, the other patting, stroking, grabbing his back and shoulder and butt. Sam fell on Dean as he was opening the door, and they stumbled backward into the room. He didn't take the time to look around; he didn't care what Dean's apartment looked like. He didn't want to think about anything at all. All he wanted was to devour Dean again, for the first time after sad, dry months. The wet of the inside of Dean's lips was like a waterfall. All he could feel were Dean's lips, all he could see were Dean's eyes, all he could hear was Dean's heartbeat, all he could taste was Dean's fat tongue. Sam's whole world became Dean's hard chest, his long, smooth waist, the fit of his cheek against Sam's palm. The warmth their bodies generated when they touched. For the next hour, fireworks candescing inside, Sam didn't think anything at all.

He came to, and came to himself, when Dean strolled to the shower and Sam went to the windows to gulp some fresh air. They wouldn't open, and Sam felt a claustrophobia grabbing at this throat. He stood naked in Dean's small, spare living room, looking out at New York through tall windows while Dean showered away the sweat from their sex. Sam thought of Dean's wet body and was surprised to feel relief that he had a moment alone. He let his body rest against the window, sure they were high enough that no one could see him, but not taking the energy to care.

But the windows wouldn't open, and Sam needed to breathe. He ran his hands over the glass, feeling for the third time the decorative, useless windowsill. He heard the shower cut off, heard the door open, heard Dean moving in the room behind him, felt the warm damp air from the bathroom penetrate the room's artificial chill. He jerked at the window ledge a few times, staring out at the great gray walls of buildings across from him, knowing the windows wouldn't open, but wanting to feel his shoulders move. A lone bird's reflection flicked by.

"Hi," Dean stepped up into the cool of Sam's back, warm from the shower, their skin tacking against each other like clean cloth. Sam pressed closer against the window, and Dean, misreading the movement, moved with him, his breath rifling the hair on Sam's neck. "You're not getting out of here so easily," he laughed. "None of the windows on these really tall buildings open up this high." Sam kept his eyes and body to the window. "The air conditioning is working fine, you know. And I had Merchant's deliver us a gourmet lunch, so you aren't getting out of here for a while."

Dean snaked his arms around Sam's chest, and Sam felt himself shift toward Dean again.

"It's so great to have you here," he continued, his chin on Sam's shoulder, his fingers brushing Sam's nipples and the hair on his chest. Sam felt himself faltering, again, felt himself believing that Dean knew what was best and that the best thing to do was just to follow along.

Dean finished his sentence. "In my world."

Your world, Sam thought, and stayed where he was, with his hands against the cool window, until Dean moved away. Sam listened as his ex-boyfriend moved around the apartment, dressing and tidying the sheets until the food came.

———

DURING THEIR lunch of grilled salmon salad and towering, ice-frosted bottles of water, Dean's cell phone rang. Apologetic, he took the call, and with sad eyes explained that he simply "had to" rush into the studio "just for ten minutes, just for an hour at the most." He kissed Sam repeatedly, apologizing for not having an extra set of keys, and tore out the door. Sam, in the silence after Dean's departure, laughed out loud. He wasn't staying inside Dean's apartment for a whole afternoon. He didn't need keys; he'd head out and take his chances on the street. Sweeping up his wallet, he realized with a dumbstruck clarity that he wasn't surprised by Dean's actions, and even more interestingly, he wasn't annoyed. Instead, he rode the smooth elevator to the lobby, pushed out into the dirty-newspaper, hot-dog-water smell of the city, and followed his nose and sense of direction toward downtown. He had a hot dog from a vendor and, at the waterfront, took cooler, deeper breaths of air. After an hour or two of walking, without a follow-up call from Dean, Sam recognized how glad he was for the chance to explore the city on his own. Dean would call him when he was ready, and Sam would meet him when his walk was done.

AFTER A glittery, boring night in Tribeca, Sam pulled Dean out of bed so that they could be at the Bronx Zoo early, before the day heated up, before the crowds arrived and the animals retreated to the quietest hiding places their enclosures allowed. He insisted on taking the subway, still claiming—both to himself and to Dean—that this was an exploratory visit. That he might be taking the subway to work there one day soon. Dean muttered and grumbled at the dank smell of the subway and the scummy sheen on the seats, but whenever his eye caught Sam's, he was clearly trying to appear game.

At the tall, embroidered Victorian iron gates, Sam took a deep breath, grateful to be surrounded by the crisp smell of river and trees. Dean played his fingers along Sam's shoulders. "Here we go, babe, your Zoo." He glanced at his watch, and Sam realized that what he actually wanted was silence. He wanted this adventure on his own. He really didn't care what Dean was about to say.

"I didn't realize it would take so long to get up here. I have a conference call at four, so I think I'm going to call a car service to get us back." He flipped open his phone, and Sam walked ahead into the Zoo.

While Dean cradled his tiny phone, Sam collected a brightly colored map, realizing that they could take a long loop through the Zoo, past the Himalayas, the World of Darkness, and African Plains before getting to the Congo Gorilla Forest, the multispecies, immersive exhibit he specifically wanted to see. The map alone filled him with excitement. Unfolding it felt like unfolding the possibilities of a better way to live his life. Sam began walking forward, taking deep, restorative breaths of the rich, piney-sweet smell of mulch, animal scents, and crisp fall air. Dean spoke into his phone behind him. Seeing a blue-clad keeper behind a screen of trees near the baboons, Sam was momentarily disappointed that he hadn't planned any meetings in advance. But, overwhelmingly, he felt alive, thrilled to be walking around a new Zoo, and somewhat guilty for wishing Dean wasn't around. He couldn't believe he'd never come here before. Dean held up one finger—"hold on"—while he finished arranging for his car.

At the African Plains, Sam leaned forward over the railing and let the sun hit his forehead.

"Those are pretty," Dean pointed out onto the mini-savannah at a trio of black-and-white antelopes with long, elegantly curved horns.

"Gemsbok." Sam answered. "Ibex. Ostrich," he continued, nodding his head at other animals, at the tall, awkward birds farther out on the enclosure's grassy sward.

"Pretty day," Dean commented to the air.

Sam realized then that as much as Dean relied on the surface of things, as much as Dean viewed the world as a series of obvious, necessary steps, Sam hid from reality as well. He hadn't pushed for his own needs in their relationship, or with his family, or at the Zoo. Only in the past few months had he even taken the time to really look around him and ask himself what he wanted. He was culpable too. He'd spent so much time determined to keep his head buried underground.

He turned his attention to the map, needing a moment to catch the thoughts turning in his head. It felt, he realized, as if something was settling inside him, as if some new, calmer reality was easing in. Sam could work at this Zoo, or his own Zoo, or any other. He might not work at a Zoo at all. He might marry Dean, or leave him, or struggle together for a few more years. What Sam realized, quietly and without fanfare, was that neither Dean, nor his family, nor a job was the answer to anything—there wasn't any kind of golden key. Sam would be fine on his own, whatever came. He had new possibilities, new approaches, *a new self* he wanted to explore. Sam couldn't help remembering another walk, in another Zoo, almost a year ago. How desperately he'd wanted Dean's approval. How little he needed it now.

"God, there's just so much here," he said, "so much I could learn, so much money to try new things, so much space to grow." He was talking to himself more than to Dean. "I mean, just the Congo Forest is over six acres, and the Conservation Society is constantly sending staff out into the field."

"See how all these animals are mixing together, like they would in the wild?" He jutted his chin out toward the mini-savannah again, and Dean nodded. "I want to do that. I could work here," he went on, "with a full troop of my own, mixing with other species, and so much space to . . . " Sam trailed off, staring at the sky beyond the African Plains, beyond the railing with Dean, beyond the Zoo.

They were silent for a while.

"You know, Sam," Dean murmured, shaking his head, "it's a really nice idea. It is," he continued, "but it's just that I've heard it so many times before." Sam's head jerked toward Dean, but Dean looked resolutely out at the exhibit, pushing on. "I'd really hoped that, coming up here, you'd have seen something *besides* another Zoo. Do you know how happy you sounded when you talked about Brazil? I still don't see why you're not doing it." Sam waited; Dean breathed. "And there's museums, and conservation groups. There is so much in the world, but it's like I can't make you see it. I want so much from life, but it feels like you're stuck on mediocre again." Dean said it, those words, in the most unthinking, unrehearsed tone Sam had ever heard him use. It was like listening to Dean's internal, secret spirit spoken aloud.

"But I love working at the Zoo." It was a statement, not a question.

A declaration from somewhere deep inside. The croak of a maribou stork reverberated in the air.

Dean sighed, snaking his arm around Sam's shoulders and leaning in to kiss Sam's temple, to make everything all right with the press of his lips against Sam's skin. "You know I just want what's best for—"

And just as easily, just as unconsciously, Sam stepped away. From Dean's damning, comforting hold. From his strong arms and square fingernails and the hair at the small of his back. From his brilliance and arrogance and ignorance. From his belief, in the end, that Sam, being who he was, would never be good enough. It was like that—so simple, so . . . untangled. As if, after everything—after *everything*—there wasn't even any decision to be made. Sam didn't need Dean's definitions anymore. He didn't need anyone's. He knew who he was, and he would choose for himself whatever territory he wanted in the world.

Sam stepped away. He left Dean's outstretched hand dangling and shook his head at Dean's confused, disbelieving eyes. "I'm sorry," he said. "I love you. It's just that I deserve more."

"But—" Dean stammered. "I ordered the car."

Sam leaned in for a quick hug, saying, "It's OK, I'll get my stuff later. We'll figure it out later. For now, I'd rather walk." He apologized again and then simply turned and walked away.

FIVE MINUTES later, he was standing at the entrance to the Congo Gorilla Forest, breathing in the wet heat of their simulated African jungle, barely believing what he'd just done. Grateful for the overwhelming presence of tall trees and animal scents and sounds, he passed through the high wooden wall, committed to moving forward, careful to listen for the cuckoos and tambourine doves. Sam focused on breathing. He had just left Dean irrevocably behind. Animal smells and flashes of black-and-white colobus monkeys shot through the air. He was in the jungle; he was breathing for what felt like the first time.

Maybe I will move to Brazil, after all, Sam wondered, and the question felt surprisingly open. It felt easy; it felt unencumbered. There was no danger; the act of questioning itself felt surprisingly free. Or maybe I'll create something totally new for the Zoo, a living jungle right in Washington, D.C. The idea that Dean could have reported on the exhibit opened a fissure of pain, but its ragged edges faded quickly. It was his choice; it was Sam who had walked away.

Sam moved into the exhibit, past artfully disguised enclosures for native fish and frogs, and caught a shadowed glimpse of an okapi, making a mental note to consider one of the rare zebra-giraffes for his own Zoo. He felt a rush of love for this Zoo, for his Zoo, for Zoos when they do things well. If he wanted it, he could be the Zoo's new Tiger Man. Maybe he'd create an exhibit with tigers and monkeys and lizards and amphibians and birds. This forest held Wolf's monkeys, DeBrazza's monkeys, red river hogs. He realized that he was scribbling furiously in his notebook, not even stopping to make sure his notes were clear.

Finally, Sam rounded a turn in the path and came across the gorillas. He gave himself one last moment to think of Dean. He was gone; Sam was looking forward. He would take this experience, this Congo Forest, for himself.

Initially, Sam could only see seven or eight of the Zoo's twenty-three gorillas, but they were clearly making good use of their large space. A plaque explained that the gorillas were encouraged to live in relatively normal social groups and that there were currently at least five juveniles in the group. Sam was happy to see that the exhibit seemed to be working. He'd wanted to visit these gorillas for years.

He stood in the rounded glass tunnel, deep inside the exhibit, and watched two females sitting back on their hips, pulling up long blades of grass and wetting them between their lips. A group of youngsters, ranging from toddlers to young adults, gamboled and play-fought over the grassy slopes, downed tree limbs, and fake termite mounds. He thought of Jamie and Karen and Laurel and Mom. A silverback sat regal on a rock, watching Sam watching him, watching his extended family gathered around. They had acres of land in their enclosure, and yet, Sam saw, they stayed together as closely as they could. The silverback turned to look at Sam, complacently chewing a twisted stick but alert to every sound. Seeing the gorillas was bittersweet. Despite the acreage and grass, the sunshine and hidden treats and trees, the gorillas, ultimately, were trapped in a cage. *For their own good*, he knew, but still, they could never leave.

And he finally understood: I've made my nest box too small. I'm like one of these animals, he thought, looking into the old ape's eyes. But worse. They have no choice in the matter, but I've trapped myself in this life even though it hasn't made me happy. I convinced myself it was all I could ever need. Dad dying, Karen and Jamie, every good excuse. My family really did need me, and it has been—it still was—a good life. He had spent his life doing what was good, and doing good had almost been enough. Sam thought of the brief escape of Brazil, of Dean again and the false, unconscious belief he'd always held that in keeping everyone happy, in finding the right husband, he would have the key to freedom. Something came clear to Sam in that moment: Brazil wasn't the answer, a man wasn't a cure, a specific item of difference at the Zoo wouldn't change his life. I am the cure, he realized, that afternoon in another city's Zoo, and any happiness I claim, any freedom, will have to come from within.

He put a hand to the cool glass and watched as one of the toddlers tentatively approached the great, graying ape and climbed onto his lap, settling in to rest. He smiled, thinking of the sudden clarity of his actions, of the power of simply making decisions at all. I'm ready, thought Sam. I'm ready to find my door.

And with that, Sam was ready to go home. He wanted to see Mickey and her growing baby, and Sheba, pregnant again with hers. He wanted to watch Jamie kick his way through high school. To find a man to love, or spend some time on his own. He would throw out his long-suffering howler plans and try something completely new.

Sam gave his naked thumb a reassuring tug. He stood at the window of an artificial jungle in New York for a long time, reaching up to rest his hand on its own reflection in the cool glass, his feet in cleverly molded imprints of a gorilla's feet, finally feeling at home.

ACKNOWLEDGMENTS

THANKS TO the whole MacLennan-Young-Schottenfels-Darnell-Antonson Nearest-and-Dearest crew. I wouldn't be who I am, and *The Zookeeper* wouldn't be who *he* is, without you.

To Kermit Moyer, Carolyn Parkhurst, Richard McCarn, and Andrew Holleran for seeing not only what it was but what it could be; E. J. Levy, Denise Orenstein, and Rick Reiken for shepherding various chunks and flows; the Fine Arts Work Center (Hunter and Melanie) for their gentle push; and Holly J. Moore for allowing me to discover *one* artist's way.

There are too many wonderful friends to recount, so I will thank the readers in, I hope, chronological order. Kerri, Erik, Jeff and Tim, and Britt. Karen Oosterhouse. Catherine, Delia, and Chris, who read that first, awful outburst, and my whole American University community of peers. To Tom Avila in particular—you are the most generous cheeseburger-and-fries writing partner in the world.

Thanks to Angela Brown (for seeing the novel's heart), to Richard Fumosa (for being as nit-picky as I am), and Joe Pittman (for helping it regain its shape).

To the San Francisco and National Zoos, thanks for letting me muddle you both for my own purposes.

Finally, thank you to Byron, Jim, Bob, and Brad. And I know this novel is, in some important ways, about my father. I love you.